D0260947

303200165 7

Alexandra Connor was born in Lancashire and educated in Yorkshire. She has had a variety of careers, including photographic model, cinema manager, and personal assistant to a world-famous heart surgeon. Yet it was only after being stalked and assaulted in London that she found her real forte — during her convalescence, she discovered an ability to paint, and a further relapse resulted in the writing of her first novel. Although traumatic, Alexandra believes that the assault changed her, and gave her a life she could never have imagined before. She still has strong connections to Lancashire today; and as well as being a highly popular novelist, she is a presenter on television and BBC radio.

You can discover more about the author at www.alexandra-connor.co.uk

THE WELL OF DREAMS

To outsiders, David and Virginia Hall are a golden couple, living expensively with exquisite taste and glamorous friends. But in reality they are perfectly imperfect — living a lie of false love. When Isabel is born, David pours all his love into her; she looks set to inherit not only wealth and comfort, but her parents' talents as well. Then tragedy strikes: Isabel's life is shattered and her future threatened, and she finds herself the reluctant inheritor of her parents' complex and bitter past. As she slowly unravels the truth and seeks the love so cruelly denied her, her ambitions and dreams are foiled time and time again, and she is drawn inexorably in her parents' footsteps . . .

Books by Alexandra Connor
Published by Ulverscroft:

THE MOON IS MY WITNESS
MIDNIGHT'S SMILING
THE SIXPENNY WINNER
THE FACE IN THE LOCKET
THE TURN OF THE TIDE
THE TAILOR'S WIFE
THE LYDGATE WIDOW
THE WATCHMAN'S DAUGHTER
THE SOLDIER'S WOMAN
THE WITCH MARK
MASK OF FORTUNE
PRIVATE VIEW

ALEXANDRA CONNOR

THE WELL OF DREAMS

Complete and Unabridged

CHARNWOOD
Leicester

First published in Great Britain in 1992

First Charnwood Edition
published 2016

The moral right of the author has been asserted

A catalogue record for this book is available
from the British Library.

ISBN 978–1–4448–3030–9

Published by
F. A. Thorpe (Publishing)
Anstey, Leicestershire

Set by Words & Graphics Ltd.
Anstey, Leicestershire
Printed and bound in Great Britain by
T. J. International Ltd., Padstow, Cornwall

This book is printed on acid-free paper

For G.

Prologue

There is a house two miles west of South Stainley. Stone-built on three floors, like many a Yorkshire house, it is faded but still impressive, the central portion of the building bowing outward and busy with windows. Under a glowering winter sky at times the roof seems the colour of treacle, the chimneys all straining to outdo each other as they stretch their long necks into the cold air. Yet in summer the house is altered; no smoke curls from the unused chimneys and the curtains are often drawn to keep the sun off the piano, although the garden is less tended and a few keen weeds creep up from under the stone flags.

There are some who thought it a mansion when it was first built; but now its grandness seems to have eroded slightly, or perhaps it has merely snuggled into its background like an old cat ready for sleep.

Much time has passed here. Much money also. This house holds more secrets than usual, and more magic has occurred within its walls.

Some of it touched everyone who lived here, and although some rejected the magic, others recognised it and wore it like a talisman. For luck, and for life. And those who did were changed by it, and knew that something extraordinary was in them. Isabel knew it too: as a child she soon understood and made friends with the spirit of The Ridings. She believed herself born lucky, and looked on the world smiling.

No one told her that life can kill dreams, and so when defeat faced her she fought back; and kept fighting. Not just for herself, but for her child, her lover, and her hopes. For all of them, Isabel Hall fought hard and believed she would triumph.

The magic was in her — how could she fail?

PART ONE

1

The Ridings
South Stainley, Yorkshire

'Hold your palms out flat,' David Hall said patiently, laying a small painted panel in Isabel's outstretched hands.

Her eyes widened as she looked at her father. 'Is it worth a *lot* of money?'

Laughing, he sat down next to her on the settee as she gingerly laid the painting on her lap and looked at it, awestruck. The figure of St Michael glanced back to her, the colours vibrant.

'It's not the value, my darling,' her father said gently, 'it's the *beauty* of the painting which matters.' His forefinger pointed to a detail as he explained, his hand moving over the panel and casting a faint shadow.

Isabel heard very little of what he said, she was too contented to take in the words. The room her father called his den was warm, a fire blazing out from the grate, the bloodhound pup Ivor snuffling in his sleep, his legs jerking slightly as he dreamed. Isabel treasured this time spent with her father, when her mother was away and the house was hushed and safe. His hand moved again, and she noticed the faint smell of pipe smoke on his jacket, the leather button on his sleeve dulled with use.

Knowing she watched him, he smiled and she

smiled back, her little hands warm under the heavy panel.

'The man who painted this picture was called Ouwater.' He paused. 'Can you say that, little one?'

Isabel repeated the name dutifully and he nodded, pleased. 'Very good.' Then carefully he took the painting from her and laid it on his desk, his attention drifting to a typed piece of paper as his daughter shifted her position and glanced into the flames.

As she was only seven years old, her feet did not reach the floor when she leaned back, and that irritated her and made her feel like a baby. Too many times she had seen her parents' elegant friends sit in the drawing room, the women's legs long in fine stockings, the savage arc of their stilettoed shoes forcing their feet into strange shapes.

Not that her mother wore stilettos. She could have done, her legs were as slim as anyone else's, but she said she couldn't balance on them and instead wore plain courts with reliable heels. Isabel shifted in her seat again, the flames hissing briefly with smoke.

' . . . don't you think so, sweetheart?'

She glanced over her shoulder, startled. 'What did you say, Daddy?'

He laid down the paper on the desk and moved across the room, leaning against the back of the settee and looking down at his daughter. 'You were daydreaming,' he said, without reproach.

His voice was indulgent, a slow, dark voice

which was unlike any other. Isabel studied her father carefully, her glance taking in the sandy, greying hair, the tortoiseshell glasses and the familiar features. No, she thought sombrely, you aren't handsome, but you have the most beautiful voice in the world.

'When's Mummy coming home?' she asked suddenly.

Her father's eyes flickered for an instant. 'Do you miss her?'

'No!' Isabel said quickly. Too quickly. 'I was just thinking . . . wondering where she was.'

'She's in Rome,' her father replied evenly, glancing over to the desk. 'I was just looking at her itinerary, in fact. She's going on to Turin tomorrow and she'll be back on Wednesday.' He smiled at his daughter and immediately sat down next to her on the sofa, putting his arm around her as she laid her head on his shoulder. Affection offered and accepted gratefully, he thought, taking off his glasses and rubbing his eyes as he settled into his seat.

Isabel had been born when he was fifty-one and Virginia forty. The news of her pregnancy had been unexpected and faintly embarrassing, his wife reacting with studied practicality, and imparting the news to him with forced cheerfulness, like an introduction to one of her less popular lectures.

'Obviously I won't be giving up my career, David, I think we're agreed that it would be folly.' Were they agreed? He wasn't sure, but *she* was, so there was little more to be said. 'I think it would be best when I travel if Eleanor looked after it . . . ' The word 'it' hung solemnly between them. 'Well, he or she, whatever it is . . . your sister is very good with children.'

Very good with children, David thought, realising that she could as easily have said, Very good with pastry, her tone had been so detached. A *child*, he had wanted to shout, half silly with pleasure. *Our* child.

The years rolled back as he remembered Isabel's birth; his first sight of the small red-haired baby, painfully silent after a long labour. She's dead, he had thought helplessly, his disappointment and sense of loss suddenly turning to determination as he looked down at the little body and willed his daughter to survive.

'Oh God, live, baby, live,' he had said repeatedly to the silent child. 'Cry, baby. Please cry.'

Finally she did, gulping in air and taking her first breath to join the world. Why? he wondered afterwards. Because he had wanted her so much? Or because she was destined to be special? Who knew for certain?

She had been a little baby, smaller than most, too small to live, the doctor had said, but David knew he was wrong. His daughter was small, but her heart was always great and fierce. All heart. *Cry baby, please cry* . . . But after that first wail of anguish as she burst into life, Isabel was a quiet baby, ready to smile, ready to respond to affection. Faces bent towards her pram were met with smiles of pleasure, hugs eagerly exchanged.

David Hall glanced down at his daughter, her eyes closed as she dozed, her head hardly making an imprint against his shoulder. Her red baby hair had been replaced by sepia brown, interspersed with paler streaks which glowed in the firelight like tortoiseshell. He stared at her sleeping face, the straight line of her nose giving her a classical look — too classical for a child. She had inherited that fine, well-bred look from her mother.

Yet there was another quality in Isabel, David thought. Apart from the refinement of her features there was a spontaneity — the way she shrugged her shoulders, or threw back her head to laugh. Yes, there was in his daughter some warmth of spirit not present in his wife, and that pleased him. He had been aware of it as soon as she was born, and it had awakened something in him; some memory of a primitive life force or magic which had bonded the two of them immediately.

The feeling had been so intense that while Virginia slept after the birth, he had opened the curtains in the room and let the moonlight flood in. Then carefully he had carried his newly born daughter over to the window. There he had lifted her high to let the moonlight pour over her, and softly uttered an ancient African blessing.

'Dear Lord, let her have the heart of a hunter.'

★ ★ ★

David and Virginia Hall were an esoteric couple: she had earned world respect as a lecturer in Hellenic Art; he was a renowned authority in early Netherlandish painting. Their golden intellects perfectly matched, they lived expensively with exquisite taste and glamorous friends; perfectly in tune, except that they were moved by different music, different pictures, different books, different emotions — so that in the end they were perfectly imperfect.

In all other ways, David's life was charmed. Money he had in excess, mostly inherited and wisely invested, giving him the freedom to indulge his passion for art — which was what had brought him and Virginia together in the first place when they had been two mature people, both gifted and lonely. The ideal match — or so it had seemed. But the years had passed and the marriage had staggered on, David adjusting to his disappointment and consoling himself with the fact that he had The Ridings — the family home which he had loved since childhood. Sexuality was repressed, Virginia not frigid, but uninterested, David too embarrassed to admit failure and look elsewhere. Caresses had all the affection of a forced handshake, although his admiration of her was genuine, as was her admiration of him. Two clever people; too clever by half.

Then suddenly and unexpectedly Isabel was born. David stretched his legs out, Ivor sleeping soundly in front of the fire, the steady ticking of the grandfather clock taking the day away. Tomorrow I will write that article, he thought, tomorrow I'll do it. Isabel stirred in her sleep, then smiled and drifted back to her dreams. What are you thinking of? her father wondered. Where do you go to, my darling? And who goes with you? I hope it's me, he wished suddenly, desperately, leaning his head against hers. Dear God, I hope sometimes it's me.

2

Virginia came home the following morning to find Ivor lying in the hall asleep, and the drawing room curtains wide open to let sunlight fall straight across the piano. With a quick stab of irritation she pulled the drapes and the drawing room dropped into shadow, a bee humming crossly against the velvet. Footsteps behind her made her turn as her sister-in-law walked into the room.

Eleanor has put on weight, Virginia noticed, feeling guilty for having such an uncharitable thought. She was too critical, she knew that, but having a sharp eye was invaluable in her work and alerted her to other subtle nuances that others would miss. She tried repeatedly to turn a blind eye to people's faults, but since childhood she had had an inbuilt sense of perfection, and only David Hall had lived up to her expectations; not physically, but mentally — he was possessed of a keen brain which functioned with precision. To Virginia, a good brain was the most powerful aphrodisiac of all.

Eleanor Hall knew it, just as she recognised her sister-in-law was in a mood. There would be no histrionics, just a low-toned, perfectly reasoned, complaint.

'Eleanor, I know I sound like a bore, but please see that the curtains are drawn in here. The sunlight spoils the veneer on the piano.'

'I'm sorry,' her sister-in-law replied, one hand extended towards Ivor as he ambled over to her. 'I forgot. It's been so dull lately, no one was expecting sun — '

'You see, it's so difficult to repair the damage after the event,' Virginia continued, glancing round for other signs of domestic mutiny. Finding none, she turned her thoughts elsewhere. 'How is everyone?'

At last, Eleanor thought, at last she's finally remembered her husband and child. 'David's out with Isabel. They've gone into Skipton. They thought you would be back later.'

The news was received with equanimity, Virginia smiling and moving towards the door. 'I'll just have a bath and freshen up,' she said simply, her familiar air of unease already obvious.

She wants to be gone, Eleanor thought, even though she's just come home she is longing to be packing and going somewhere. To talk, to keep her clever audiences enthralled, not to be here in this quiet house with all its empty corridors and silent gardens. She doesn't see the beauty of the light changing and coming through the window at the top of the stairs, or smell the logs burning in the grate or even catch the faint trace of David's cigar. There is nothing for her here, Eleanor thought, because only the dead have any meaning for her. Perfectly preserved, perfectly formed Hellenic statues that remain immaculate and do not live to disappoint her — or leave the curtains open to let the sun fall on the piano.

Isabel came in soon after, borne high on her father's shoulders and dipping her head as they walked in through the front door.

'Duck — ' he shouted.

' — or grouse!' she shouted back, in their usual ritual.

David stopped immediately when he saw the gloves on the hall table and the well worn copy of the *Burlington Magazine* lying beside them. He turned to Eleanor as he lowered his daughter to the ground.

'Is Virginia home already?'

She nodded.

Standing between them, Isabel glanced up at her aunt and felt suddenly awkward. Eleanor's stout figure was erect, even a little stiff, she thought, her thick brown hair brushed back from her face, her bare hands planted on each hip defiantly as though there was trouble. Maybe there was, Isabel thought. Her mother was home, and that usually meant trouble. Not arguments, just unease, and restrictions. No port after dinner for her father, no long phone conversations for Eleanor, and no chases around the stableyard with Ivor for her — just perfect behaviour, in perfect order.

She was too young fully to understand, but she resented the stifling atmosphere immediately and her frustration made her petulant. 'Why does she have to come home! I hate it when she's home!'

David Hall looked at his daughter in amazement. 'Go to your room, Isabel. I won't have you talking about your mother like that.'

Her mouth opened to protest, then her eyes filled and as her father looked away she ran up

12

the stairs two at a time, sobbing.

An hour passed, footsteps moving towards her door, pausing, then moving on. Not her father's steps though, or even Eleanor's, this was the steadier footfall of her mother. She could picture her outside the door, tall and sparely fleshed, her expensive discreet clothes falling in an elegant line from fine shoulders. Not like Eleanor, whose jumpers strained over a full bosom and whose hips swelled good-naturedly under her Jaeger skirts.

The footsteps returned minutes later. Isabel held her breath, watching as the door opened slowly, her mother's figure silhouetted against the hall light.

'Are you reading?' she asked simply. 'Because if you are, you should have the light on. Otherwise you'll strain your eyes.'

Isabel remained defiantly mute. All she knew was that this woman had made her father angry with her and that hurt.

'I thought we could have a little talk,' Virginia continued uncertainly. She had no desire to be cruel, but felt hurt by her daughter's attitude. Other people's children ran to them when they had been away — but not Isabel. In fact, unless she was very much mistaken, her daughter wanted her gone.

The realisation made her momentarily cruel. 'I had a present for you, but since you've been such a naughty girl, I think I'll give it to someone else.' The words had no effect, which angered Virginia further. Really, she thought, to be at the mercy of a child's tantrum. Coldly, she struck out. 'Your father told me to tell you that although we were all going out tomorrow, you've been so difficult that you can stay at home . . . He told me to tell you.'

The words rattled in the air between them. Anything her mother said or thought could not hurt Isabel, but to disappoint her father and make him so cross that he didn't want to see her . . . She swallowed, her eyes burning with tears. They *always* went out on Sundays, they always had, either with her mother or without her, but he had never left his daughter at home. *Never.* Childish despair almost overwhelmed Isabel — maybe he didn't love her any more. Maybe he would never talk to her again.

Virginia had little comprehension of what was going on in her daughter's mind, she was simply gratified to find that Isabel was momentarily cowed and with a final fierce glance, she silently closed the door.

The dining room was warm, the stained oak panelled walls and ceiling forming a dark box around the diners. A subdued Virginia sat at one end of the table, David facing her with Eleanor on his right, a selection of dishes materialising and disappearing effortlessly as the meal progressed. A dark portrait of Mary Tudor hung behind Virginia's chair, and to David the painted figure seemed more real than the woman seated before it, for Virginia was peculiarly ephemeral in her beige dress, her fair hair and fine-boned face melting without colour into each other.

Only her eyes were alive and brilliant with intelligence as they turned to her husband. 'You

14

mustn't worry, dear. Isabel will be fine soon.' The clear eyes flicked to Eleanor. 'Just one of these childish ailments.'

'I think I'll pop up and have a word after dinner,' Eleanor said, some instinct prompting her. She had not fully accepted Virginia's story, although it was possible that Isabel was running a temperature and didn't feel like going out tomorrow. It was possible, even if she did look forward to her Sunday outings all week. Eleanor peeled an orange thoughtfully — children changed, grew out of things. She knew that. But still . . . her thoughts wandered. It had been unlike Isabel to show such a display of temper, she was usually so cheerful.

David Hall read his sister's thoughts. 'I should go up to see her — '

'I don't think so, dear,' Virginia interrupted immediately. 'Better not to fuss her at the moment. Leave her to me.'

He was torn between wanting to see his child and letting his wife look after her. Perhaps he *should* step back a little . . . The thought winded him but he steadied himself rapidly. Soon Virginia would be off again and things would go back to normal, it was only right to encourage any maternal feelings while she was home.

'Well, give her my love, and tell her to sleep well.'

Virginia nodded, satisfied.

She had always known that Isabel was closer to her father than to her. It was her fault, she decided, trying to suppress her innate jealousy; she had been away too much and her daughter

15

was spoiled. Children had to be controlled and disciplined, she knew that. After all, it was better for the child in the long run.

Refusing her dinner, Isabel sat in her bedroom upstairs and looked out of the window. Tears had given way to rage, and as she glanced out she imagined her mother's car in the driveway pulling away. Going. Leaving . . . But she knew she wasn't going anywhere tonight, or tomorrow. She was staying, spoiling everything. Her father didn't love her any more and didn't want to see her, she thought helplessly, pressing the palms of her hands against the windowpanes, the cold chilling her.

Her mind wandered as she thought of their usual Sunday outings. Trips to Skipton, chocolate bought at Whittakers, then the drive to Harrogate, the long run up Montepelier Parade to Betty's for tea. At other times they walked across the fields, bundled up in warm clothes in the winter, their faces burning with the cold wind blowing over the moors. They had seen a pheasant once, walking only yards from them, his plumage bright against the snow, his call cracking the cold air as he spotted them and flew off. Isabel had laughed in delight and her father had pinched her cheek, his hand clumsy in gloves.

Sometimes when her mother was at home she came with them, but then they went out to dine formally, visiting The Box Tree to see people and be seen, the food not important, the contacts invaluable. Isabel knew that her father was not as happy in these surroundings; his friends, mostly

16

men, came to The Ridings and played snooker with him, or drank whisky in the den, escaping London to relax; they were not on display like her mother's acquaintances. Her friends were brilliant but distant, asking to see Virginia's child almost as though she was another exhibit to be stared at and considered.

And always, after they had completed their scrutiny, a baffled Isabel was ushered out by Eleanor and given a treat in the kitchen.

'They never talk to me,' Isabel said, bewilderment obvious in her voice as she drank the hot chocolate her aunt had made for her.

'That's just because they have a lot on their mind, sweetheart,' Eleanor said tactfully. 'They're very clever people.'

Isabel considered the information. 'Well, I don't want to be clever,' she said finally. 'I don't want to be like them.'

Laughing, Eleanor refilled her cup. 'But you are clever, pet. You've a good brain, and some day you'll be glad of it. Believe me.'

The memory of that conversation was fresh in Isabel's mind as she pressed against the window, the glass growing warm under her hands. Maybe she would never see her father again, she thought, suddenly frightened of her mother's power. Maybe he would go away as Virginia did, and forget her, staying in foreign countries for weeks at a time . . . her child's mind panicked, her security for one instant so threatened that unhappiness clawed at her and made her reckless. In that second she howled, and having formed a desperate plan, banged her hands against the glass, the force of her blows shattering the panes and sending her little hands, cut and bleeding, into the chilling air.

3

The blood dried on the broken glass and along the windowledge as David Hall sat up all night with his daughter after the doctor left. The broken window of Isabel's room was boarded up, a makeshift bed made up in a spare room, a fire built up in the grate. He sat with her bandaged hands in his and stroked her face and called her his pet name, 'Knuckles', after the time she had accidentally struck him when she was in her pram. She dozed, woke suddenly, saw her father and clung to him.

'What happened?' he asked, his voice low.

The bedroom was not decorated for a child, the bed was large and the wallpaper dark green. It was a guest room for a man, filled with substantial Edwardian furniture and a trouser press. But the firelight made it cosy and the extra blankets on the bed felt comforting and heavy on Isabel's legs.

'Oh, Daddy, I'm sorry.'

He hushed her. 'Sssh. You've nothing to be sorry for, Knuckles.'

She smiled at the nickname, her eyes closing. Outside, a clock chimed suddenly in the hallway, the noise invading the room as her mother walked in.

'Dr Hunter said you will be fine,' she said, addressing her words to her daughter, her eyes unfathomable.

'Good, good,' David said absently, turning

back to Isabel. 'But what happened?'

Immediately Isabel glanced at her mother. For an instant she wavered, knowing that she could damn her for ever in her father's eyes if she chose to; and yet there was something in Virginia's expression which made her hesitate.

'She fell against the window . . . she slipped closing it. Didn't you, dear?'

Isabel continued to look at her mother. She could tell the truth and know that her father would side with her, but at what cost? He was here with her now, he had forgiven her, so why strike out at her mother unnecessarily? To hurt her, as she hurt you, a voice said softly.

'I didn't slip closing the window . . . ' Isabel said quietly, glancing away from her mother's tight face as she continued. 'I was upset . . . ' She turned to her father, binding him to her with the words: 'Mother didn't want me to come out with you tomorrow.'

Virginia drew in her breath, knowing at that moment that her daughter had declared war on her. Rigid with anger, David turned to face his wife and out of the corner of her eye Isabel watched her mother, a cold shiver going through her like a chilling premonition. She had challenged her mother for her father's love, and had temporarily won. Virginia was not going to forgive her for that; or forget.

★   ★   ★

Yet the premonition seemed a false one as the years passed and life continued in the same way it always had. Isabel attended the local school where she was soon recognised as one of the brightest pupils, her tuition extended at home by her father. But if Isabel relished his ideas of education, Eleanor had her reservations.

'You push that girl too hard,' she said firmly. 'Why can't you just go out for the day and enjoy yourselves without having to make an issue out of it?'

'Only so much can be taught by books,' he said. 'Practical knowledge is more important. Isabel has a good brain, she needs constant stimulation.'

'And gimmicks?' Eleanor asked, picking up the expensive camera David had bought for his daughter's use. 'She's only ten, David. What makes you think she can use a camera?'

He took it from her quickly. 'I taught her,' he replied. 'And if I encourage her to take photographs of places and objects she'll remember them better and start keeping albums.'

Eleanor shrugged, unconvinced. 'Cameras, albums, painting lessons.' She stopped short. 'That reminds me, Stanton Feller rang, he asked if you were around tomorrow because he's up in Yorkshire for the weekend.'

David smiled with real pleasure. 'That's marvellous! I haven't seen Stanton for months.'

'Well, you can't be lucky all the time,' Eleanor said drily, flicking the lid down on the picnic box.

David scrutinised his sister's face. It had always been obvious that Virginia loathed Stanton, but he wasn't sure just what Eleanor felt about the artist. 'You don't like him, do you?'

Her brown eyes were calm. 'I don't trust him, David. That's all.'

'But he's a great man, and a great talent — '

She interrupted him, throwing her hands up. 'Your glowing opinion of him could never live up to his own. He's a braggart.'

David glanced away and began to tie the leather straps on the basket. 'He has immense talent, Eleanor, and that marks a man out — '

'That theory doesn't hold water and you know it. You have a fine brain, but you're not a bighead. You're ten times smarter than Stanton Feller will ever be — '

' — it's not the same. Oh yes, I can appreciate works of art and write about them, but he *makes* them. He's a painter, someone who creates things, beautiful things, out of his imagination. That makes him special.'

'That makes him insufferable,' Eleanor countered brusquely.

Stanton Feller was indifferent to Eleanor's opinion, and walked into the The Ridings the following day with the air of a man who refused to be impressed. He had always behaved this way, wanting to be a man of property himself and yet unable to control his reckless spending long enough to invest in anything worthwhile. Instead he preferred to waste the portrait fees he earned, and spend what was left on presents for his two mistresses who lived at opposite ends of London.

'Stanton,' David said, crossing the hall and clasping his friend's hand affectionately. 'How good to see you.'

'I don't doubt it,' Stanton replied, pushing a small framed sketch in David's hands. 'Here, I've a pressie for you.'

Moved by the gesture, David took the picture and studied the woman's head admiringly, the deft charcoal lines and the deep shadowing as much Stanton's trademark as the triangle with the entwined S/F in the bottom corner.

'It's a marvel. You get better all the time, Stanton.'

He shrugged, his heavy face deliberately nonchalant. 'Just some tart from Hackney I picked up. She stayed with me for a week and then left — just like that.' He paused, as though astounded. 'Some muse, buggering off like that.'

'Maybe she was more amused than a muse,' Eleanor said cheerfully.

Stanton turned to her. 'You should sit for me, you know. You have just the hips to fill a six-foot canvas.'

'And you have the mouth,' she replied deftly, walking off into the kitchen.

The two men talked all afternoon, David wise enough to know that there was a reason for the visit and patient enough to wait until his friend confided in him. But the truth was slow in coming and instead he was treated to an insight into the life of a fashionable painter, the machinations of dealers, and the intricacies of Stanton's love life. All of which he had heard before; and tolerated as no one else did. He knew that Stanton's personality came from books, that everything he had read as a boy about roistering artists had fixed an image in his mind of what a painter should be; and that image he had adopted and lived. Immensely original in his work, Stanton Feller was a stereotype in his life.

David found the paradox intriguing but as he listened to Stanton's familiar rantings, he found himself wondering if all the bravura and bluster covered a melancholic nature or just simple immaturity. He should have known the answer; they had been friends for many years; but the painter was one of the few who escaped David's complete understanding. All he knew was that Stanton had a quality which was worthwhile. What that ephemeral quality was he wasn't sure, but he loved the shadow *and* the man.

'She's married!' the artist said, rubbing his forehead with his left hand. 'And I got involved with her, can you believe it?'

David smiled, and took another sip of his whisky.

'I've been so pissed off with work, I thought I'd drop everything and travel. You know, get a look at another country.' Stanton paused, watching David's expression. 'You think I'm a jerk, don't you?'

'Not always,' he replied, smiling.

'I think I am,' Stanton said quietly. 'I keep thinking I should settle down with someone properly.'

'You couldn't, you still believe all those old stories about artists and their muses. You couldn't settle with one woman.'

'I might be happier.'

David frowned. 'You might — until another

24

woman came along that you fancied.'

Stanton recognised the truth in the words and, discomforted, changed his tack. 'So what keeps you tied to Virginia?' he asked suddenly.

David raised his eyebrows, his melodious voice even. 'I'm not tied. We don't see enough of each other to get bored.'

'That's a hell of an answer!' Stanton replied, going for the kill. 'Do you love her?'

Before David could answer, the door opened and both men turned as Isabel walked in. She had grown quickly, her composure remarkable for her years, although it had been steadily nurtured by her father. Many times he had taken her to Private Views in London, visiting the Bond Street and Cork Street galleries, where she was introduced to the dealers and the critics, forcing her to mature rapidly, his pride the only encouragement she needed. There was plenty of time for her to be a child when they were alone at The Ridings; but out in the world she presented a different picture.

The child looked at Stanton Feller now.

'Hello, is this our lovely Isabel? How you've changed in a few months,' he said, walking towards her and lifting her chin with his hand. 'You're going to be quite handsome. Even lovelier than your mother and she has formidable bones.'

Isabel smiled, polite as ever, seeing her father watch her out of the corner of her eye. 'Hello, Mr Feller. How are you?'

Stanton laughed and let go of her, leaning back and folding his arms. 'My God, she's a little Virginia, isn't she?' he asked, turning to David.

'She has good manners,' he replied, defending his daughter against the slur of primness. 'I think she's a good mix of both of us.'

Stanton laughed. 'She a frigging masterpiece,' he said, and then grimaced and bowed to Isabel. 'Forgive my language, my lady, but I am only a commoner, here to swear his allegiance to serve you all his days.'

She laughed, just as he meant her to.

Laughter was a sound frequently heard at The Ridings, laughter amongst friends and between father and daughter; mutual affection growing as Virginia spent more time abroad. Encouraged by David Hall, Isabel started to keep a cuttings book, sticking reviews of her mother's lectures in it together with photographs of the clever Virginia Hall. She was fiercely proud of her mother and respected her from a distance without ever once forgetting the damage she had tried to inflict. As for Virginia, she kept to the periphery of her daughter's life, like a skater unwilling to try the thinner ice and risk drowning.

But when Isabel reached thirteen, Virginia returned from an American trip and confronted her husband.

'I've been thinking. Isabel has to go to school, David. She has a good brain and it needs training.'

'She's doing well here,' he said defensively, the thought of losing his daughter too huge to bear. 'She's top of her class — '

'I know that, but just think what she could achieve if she had real teaching. If she went away to school, for instance.'

The threat stung him. No, not his child, not the little baby he had willed to live.

'No, I forbid it.'

Virginia's wide eyes narrowed. Things had gone too far. They were much too close, she thought, tying the belt on her dressing gown and glancing at her husband. Such a clever brain, but so easily led. The memory of the night that Isabel had pushed her hands through the window came back, as did the sight and the smell of blood — such a grand gesture for a seven-year-old.

'We should spend more time together,' she said uneasily, touching her husband's shoulder. Did she want sex? No, she was too composed for that. But if that was what it took — well then she was quite willing. 'Darling, it will be best for her.' She measured her tone carefully. 'You want the best for her, don't you?'

He nodded, too kind to shake off her hands.

'She's such a clever girl, and talented too. She could do anything.' Virginia swallowed and dropped to her knees like a supplicant. 'We have to think of her and not be selfish.'

David tried to lift her, but she resisted and together they fell back on the carpet. For an instant an image of Stanton came into his mind and David nearly laughed, but embarrassment took over quickly. 'Virginia,' he said awkwardly as she kissed him, 'I don't think . . . '

She drowned out his protestations, seducing him with the same determination she used to educate her pupils. 'David, I need you,' she murmured, pulling off his clothes and sliding under his naked body as he moved on top of her.

The moonlight swung outside the dark curtains, a late owl hooting derisively from a nearby tree as they made love, David's mind mixing images of Stanton and the girl pictured in the drawing, his thoughts hardly settling on this new version of his wife, clambering naked to bed in front of him. Gradually they both settled to rest, Virginia feigning sleep as David rose at one in the morning and went to his den to smoke.

In the darkened room the smell of the prints seemed particularly strong, even under the scent of Cuban cigars, the rows of books peering down on him, the bust of Dante disapproving from the top row of the bookshelf. He settled back in a chair and looked out down the dark lawn of The Ridings as clouds scuttled across the moon and a quick fox bolted for cover. To part with Isael was too great a sacrifice to consider, and yet if it gave her the best chance in life wouldn't it be selfish not to let her go? His thoughts wandered back to Virginia, to her unfathomable eyes, and the excitement she had so unexpectedly aroused in him.

Dante seemed to follow him with his eyes as he stubbed out his cigar. Which was the right decision to make? To part with his daughter and find his wife again? Or to fight to keep Isabel with him and jeopardise her future chances? He leaned back in his seat and sighed. Knuckles, his little girl, the child of his middle years. So smart for her age, so kind, so loving . . . The moon rose higher. Higher and higher he watched it go. How high could Isabel go? What *couldn't* she achieve? She was his, born in his magical house, and capable of anything.

The decision made, David Hall hung his head, and the moon turned away behind a sudden cloud.

4

Oakdean
Brighton

The sea was black, the high tide dark under a
solemn sky as David Hall drove his daughter
up to the entrance of the school. Above their
heads, seagulls wheeled and called out into the
disturbed air, the smell of ozone coming up from
the pebbled beach. Isabel shivered and sat rigidly
in the front seat, her father turning off the
ignition and staring straight ahead.

'You'll like it here, darling. Really you will.'

She didn't look at him and remained immobile.

'Just give it a try, it's one of the best schools in
England,' he continued, taking off his glasses and
polishing them on his handkerchief. 'I'll write.
So will your mother.'

Isabel glanced over to him with her mother's
eyes. The expression was disbelieving and
hostile. 'Why?' she said simply.

'Because we'll want to keep in touch,' he
explained, realising suddenly what she meant.
'You need the finest education possible. You have
a wonderful brain and a splendid life ahead,
Isabel. Please, sweetheart, believe me, I don't
want you to go, but it is the best thing.'

Her eyes filled and she glanced away. 'I don't
want to go,' she said, the composure in her voice
cracking, suddenly very much the child again.

'Oh, Daddy, don't leave me.'

He took her hand and looked at her carefully, choosing his words. 'You know how much I love you, don't you?'

She nodded, unable to answer.

'And you know that I would only do what was best for you?'

Again she nodded.

'Then believe me when I say that this *is* the right thing to do.'

Isabel glanced at him helplessly.

'Remember that whenever you're lonely I'll be thinking of you. Just close your eyes and you'll see Ivor, all muddy and smelly from his walk . . . ' Isabel laughed, thinking of the bloodhound ' . . . and then think of The Ridings and that bust of Dante, and the piano, and how we have to — '

'*Keep the curtains drawn in there*,' they said in unison and laughed.

The moment passed, the time clicking on with every tick of the car clock. Thoughtfully, David glanced at his daughter. 'Did I ever tell you that you have little green flames in your eyes?'

She blinked. 'What?'

'You have little green flames,' he said, 'and that's special.'

He turned down the sun visor on her side of the car and she looked closely into the mirror. He was right, amongst the hazel brown of her pupils were a few flecks of green. Smiling warmly, she turned back to him, knowing that he was playing a game with her to put off the moment of their parting.

'What do they mean, Daddy?'

He stroked her hair gently, his voice hardly above a whisper.

'They mean luck . . . they mean that you'll have four wishes granted in your life, Isabel. One for every little green flame.' She nodded without speaking, and laid her head on his shoulder. 'Just be careful what you wish for, darling. Be very careful.'

★   ★   ★

'*Move it now!*' she snapped, flinging open the door of the locker and facing Isabel squarely. A big girl with a broad face, already sniffing out the term's newcomers.

Isabel hesitated. Having hardly ever been away from home before she was unprepared for such treatment and felt a mixture of fear and anger. 'But — '

'*No buts!* I'm in charge here, and when I say do something, you do it!' the girl replied savagely, pulling Isabel's bag out of the locker and throwing it on the floor. 'That's for answering back, Hall.'

Isabel stared disbelievingly at the girl as she moved off and then slowly bent down to pick up her bag. Eleanor had spent hours stitching it and now it lay in a crumpled heap because some spiteful girl had thrown it there. Fury made her straighten up, her eyes fixed on the receding back as she took in her breath and began to follow her.

She hadn't gone four steps when someone

caught hold of her arm. 'Let her go,' the voice said, 'the fat cow will only make life difficult for you if you fight back.'

Isabel turned to answer but her adviser was already walking off, leaving her to find her own way back to the dormitory to unpack. Stiff with loneliness, she took out her clothes and hung them listlessly in the wardrobe, looking out for any sign of the fat girl, her mind churning with a mixture of homesickness and misery. Carefully she laid out her things in the drawers and then followed the example of the other girls and Blu-Tacked a couple of large photographs of her parents on the mirror.

Satisfied, she then sat down and remained sitting, not knowing what to do, or where to go.

'The homesickness passes,' someone said.

Isabel glanced up, recognising the voice she had heard earlier, but this time able to see its owner.

Anna Leonard walked into the dormitory eating a Turkish delight, a look of heavy-browed disapproval on her face. Her shoulder-length hair was thick with waves, her legs long and developed under the school skirt, and her foot as it edged Isabel's pillow off the bed was narrow and full of energy.

'Is this your first time away from home?'

Isabel nodded. 'Yes, the first.' Her eyes moved to the abandoned pillow. 'Why does everyone put everything on the floor here?'

Anna laughed loudly. 'What a prig you are! I was actually doing you a favour. We're only allowed one pillow per bed.' She glanced at

Isabel critically, wondering about her current expression of annoyance.

'Who was that girl in the locker room?'

'Fat Fiona,' Anna replied, extending her hand towards Isabel and smiling, 'and I'm Anna Leonard.'

'I'm Isabel Hall,' she responded politely.

'No one calls me Anna though,' the girl continued, swallowing the last of her Turkish Delight and throwing the wrapper into the wastepaper bin. 'I'm called Prossie.'

'Why?' Isabel asked, fascinated.

Prossie dug deep into her pocket and pulled out a crumpled postcard of Rossetti's painting of Proserpine. Isabel glanced at it, and then looked at Prossie with complete understanding. 'You're just like the model.'

She smiled, hugely satisfied. 'Jane Morris was Rossetti's muse for the painting of Proserpine. She was called Prossie for short,' she said wistfully, 'and he loved her, you know.' Isabel nodded, the story was familiar territory and oddly comforting. 'She was married to someone else, but slept with Rossetti anyway.'

Isabel blinked. 'Oh,' she said simply.

Scenting innocence, Prossie pressed her advantage. 'Has anyone — a man I mean — ever told you that you're beautiful?'

'Well . . . my father has.'

'Fathers don't count.'

'Mine does,' Isabel said stubbornly.

Prossie dismissed the interruption. 'The first man who said I was beautiful was an Italian . . .'

On instinct, Isabel doubted the truth of the

statement. 'He was tall and handsome and he had very white teeth.' She glanced over to Isabel. 'Smile.'

'*What!*'

'Go on, show me your teeth. It's a sign of breeding to have white teeth.'

Confident, Isabel bared her teeth and was rewarded by Prossie's reluctant approval. 'Oh, that's good, yours are almost as white as mine. Fat Fiona has teeth the colour of Edam cheese,' she said phlegmatically, pulling two more chocolate bars out of her pockets and passing one to Isabel. 'We have to do what she says because she's older than us. Anyway if you argue she makes you do extra duties, and she takes away the tuck rations.' Her teeth sank into the chocolate. 'She once made a new girl sit up all night in the toilet *in the dark*.' Prossie hooted with laughter and then frowned suddenly. 'If you like you could be a friend of mine. I've been here the longest of anyone. My parents dumped me when I was eight, then they separated . . . ' She glanced over to Isabel to see if the story was having the desired effect. 'I suppose your parents are blissfully happy?'

'I'm not sure,' Isabel said thoughtfully, biting into the chocolate bar and pulling her knees up on to the bed. She had never considered whether her parents were 'happy' — besides, how could she judge when they were hardly ever together?

'Well, are they miserable then?' Prossie asked hopefully.

Isabel considered the question carefully. She liked Prossie and was grateful to her, and was wise enough to give her the answer she wanted.

'Actually they're not happy at all.'

'Miserable?' Prossie asked eagerly.

'Oh yes,' Isabel replied ruefully. 'Very miserable indeed.'

The following Sunday Isabel wrote a letter home. Knowing that her mother was in New York, she opened her heart to her father on paper, surprised that she could articulate her feelings in words. Over the first week her homesickness had not passed, the hierarchy of the school confusing her, her own reluctance to be browbeaten making her unpopular with the likes of Fat Fiona. The teachers found her difficult too. Having been brought up in an environment where her questions were encouraged and always answered, Isabel found herself irritating the staff with her precociousness. Prossie often laughed behind her in the classroom, hissing for her to sit down.

'Let someone else answer, you idiot, and stop sucking up to the teachers.'

'What?' Isabel replied, baffled. 'What's that supposed to mean?'

Prossie raised her eyebrows. 'Don't look too clever or the girls will hate you and make life hard for you, and the teachers will think you're a stooge for them and besides, no one likes a swot.'

The lesson was a hard one to learn after a lifetime of David Hall's tutoring, but bit by bit Isabel learned and day after day she laid out her misery on paper and addressed it home to The Ridings.

Dearest Daddy,

I don't understand anyone here. I answer questions and they say I'm a swot, and if I don't the girls say I'm a stupid Northerner and mimic a Yorkshire accent — *which I don't have*. Only Prossie is kind here, the others are bullies.

Isabel paused, not wanting her father to think she was picked on. Besides, she could stand up for herself.

Not that anyone bullies me . . . but I miss you, Daddy, and Eleanor, and even old Ivor! It doesn't get so cold here though, but it gets windy and the seagulls come right over our heads when we play hockey . . . I think I want to come home, Daddy. I have tried to like it here, but I miss you and the teachers aren't *that* good honestly — not like you were. I could learn more at home, Daddy, and I promise I'd work really hard. Just let me come home. Please.

Lots of love,
Isabel

The reply came almost immediately, together with a photograph of Eleanor petting Ivor.

Dearest Knuckles,

You will never know how difficult a letter this is for me to write. I have read and reread your letters and hate to see how unhappy you are, but really, darling, I have to be fair and honest with you and tell you what I feel. We have always been honest with each other, haven't we? Well now I have to be truthful and say that you have to stay at school. You've got such a wonderful chance to do something with your life, my love, you have talent and ability and courage. You could achieve things that other people only dream of. So don't be reckless and let it all go. Be careful, be *wise*. Believe me, I know it's difficult, but it will pay off in the end. I have such pride in you, in your goodness and your talent, and I want you to get to the stars where you belong.

Remember I love you and remember the four wishes to be granted. Use them wisely, darling, too many people waste their dreams

Your loving father.

Isabel had been so immersed in her father's letter that she hadn't heard the footsteps and when the hand snatched the paper away from her she jumped up, startled. Fat Fiona stood in front of her, her face white with spite.

'You should be at games, Hall, not reading.'

'I have a cold, I was excused games — '

'You didn't come and tell me. I didn't excuse you,' she said, starting to read the letter. 'Is this from a boyfriend? Because if it is, we're not allowed letters from boys.' Her eyes alighted on the name at the head of the page. ''Dearest Knuckles,'' she read spitefully and began to laugh.

Isabel reached out to snatch the letter back but the girl continued to laugh and turned away, her broad back protecting her as her fat hands held on to the paper, her mean eyes gobbling up the private words.

'It's mine. Give it to me!' Isabel shouted and then, without thinking, struck the girl hard on her back. 'Give it to me! Give it to me!'

Maddened, Fiona tried to shake her off, then having the advantage of height and weight pushed Isabel away so roughly that she fell off balance against the wall, her legs splaying out as she slid downwards.

'You should learn to show some respect — ' Fiona said viciously, but the words were cut off as Isabel lashed out with her foot and kicked her hard on the shin. Howling with pain, the girl dropped the letter and limped out of the dormitory, casting a threatening glance behind her as she left.

Isabel immediately scrabbled towards the letter, clasped it and smoothed it out carefully on the floor, breathing heavily as she reread the words. They seemed to cheer her, to bolster her courage, and soon she found her fear evaporating and she smiled, thinking of how her father would laugh when she told him what had happened. Then suddenly from the doorway came the sound of a slow hand-clapping.

Isabel looked up to see Prossie standing there. 'I've just heard about the fight.' She raised her eyebrows. 'I have to admire your guts in taking her on, she could give you at least forty pounds.'

Isabel shrugged her shoulders. 'She was

laughing at my father's letter. I couldn't let her do that.'

'Oh no,' Prossie said drily, 'but I hope it was worth it, because you're in trouble now, Isabel. Real trouble. That girl is a bitch and she will make you pay.'

★ ★ ★

Over the weeks that followed, Isabel paid dearly. As a prefect given wide-ranging powers, Fiona concentrated all her efforts on making Isabel Hall miserable, and succeeded. Before breakfast it was custom for each boarder to make her bed, then afterwards to go on to lessons; but Isabel instead would be called back to the dormitory, her bedclothes scattered, Fiona waiting for her response.

'What on earth!' Isabel said angrily, then, recognising the aggressive look in the other girl's eye, modified her tone. 'What was wrong with it?'

'You didn't do the corners correctly,' Fiona replied. 'Here at Oakdean we like everything done right. You're not at home now.'

A quick wave of homesickness welled up in Isabel as she began to remake the bed with Fiona watching over her. She had almost finished when the prefect wrenched back the covers again, and stood, maliciously triumphant, goading Isabel to react.

And Isabel knew that was what she wanted; so she resisted and, gritting her teeth, began again just as the school bell started to ring. 'I have to go now, or I'll be late.'

'You're going nowhere until you've finished making your bed,' Fiona replied with relish. 'If you're late you'll just have to explain why to the teacher, won't you?'

'If I'm late I'll get detention — ' Isabel began, knowing suddenly that she had played right into the other girl's hands.

'Don't answer me back! If you get detention, it's your fault, isn't it?' Fiona's eyes peered spitefully into Isabel's face. 'You've got to learn to toe the line, Hall. You might have been the Queen Bee at your little hick school out in the sticks, but we do things differently here.'

Isabel arrived late for class and continued to be late for the next three days, each morning undergoing the sadism of Fiona's repeated bed-making ritual. On the second occasion she was given detention and forced to do extra home-work after supper, her solitary figure working until eight, Prossie waiting outside the classroom door as the teacher finally relieved her. On the third occasion she was given detention and denied access to her tuck box, then when she finally got hold of it at the weekend, half the contents had gone.

'That bitch has taken my food!' Isabel said helplessly, turning to Prossie who immediately handed her a Turkish Delight. 'I don't want *yours*, I want mine!' she snapped, regretting the words immediately as she slumped against the wall. 'I can't go on like this, Prossie. That girl hates me.'

'Yeah,' Prossie replied, 'and she'll go on hating you. So what are you going to do about it? You could write home and tell your father what's going on — '

'No! I couldn't do that. I don't want to worry him,' Isabel said emphatically. 'Maybe I could report it to the housemistress instead.'

Prossie raised her eyebrows. 'I don't want to depress you, Isabel, but I don't think Miss Fellows would be on your side.'

'Why?'

'Oh, because she's lazy and because she's only too pleased to let Fiona do all the work for her — and because Fiona happens to be her niece.'

Hopelessness welled up in Isabel, as did a sudden yearning to go home. She closed her eyes and swallowed back the threat of tears. Nothing had prepared her for this kind of treatment. It was light years away from what she had known. An image flitted into her mind — she was a little girl again, her father lifting her on to the top of the library steps in the den, then telling her to hold on. With a whoop of laughter he then pushed her along, the titles of the books blurring as she passed, her head thrown back with delight. Whoosh, went the steps. Whoosh, as they passed the rows of stiff-backed volumes. 'Whoosh!' her father cried, finally stopping to catch his breath, Isabel's face on a level with the Dante bust. It was always the same routine, the rush of noise and laughter, ending in front of the disapproving Italian poet.

'What is it?' Prossie asked, knowing that her friend was close to tears.

'I was thinking of home,' Isabel said brokenly. 'I want to go home . . . '

'*I've* said that a thousand times,' Prossie replied dramatically, 'but no one ever came for me. I was left here and forgotten — '

'Oh, shut up!' Isabel replied, rallying suddenly, her first wave of self-pity closely followed by her determination not to be beaten. 'You just put it on for effect — and I've got *real* problems. I have to get myself out of this mess.'

'It's your own fault,' Prossie responded with pique. 'I *told* you to leave Fiona alone, but you would annoy her — '

'She took my letter!'

'And you dented her shin,' Prossie countered. 'There is a pecking order here, Isabel, which you have to follow. Fiona is two years older than us, and she is a prefect, therefore you have to treat her with respect — '

'Why?' Isabel asked, genuinely mystified. 'She's not done anything to earn my respect.'

Prossie rolled her eyes. 'So what? It's the way it is.'

'Then it's stupid!' Isabel concluded, folding her arms. 'Daddy always taught me to stick up for myself.'

'Good advice,' Prossie responded neatly. 'Only Daddy isn't the one remaking his bed every morning and having his tuck stolen.' She pulled a face to lighten the atmosphere. 'Oh, Isabel, have a bit of common sense. Stop fighting the system and go along with it. Life's easier that way.'

'You mean give in.'

She shook her head. 'No, I don't. What I'm saying is that you are setting yourself up for a very hard time here, when it needn't be. The teachers think you're being difficult because you're always late for class, and Fiona will terrorise you as long as you keep challenging her.' She put her head on one side. 'I've learned how to survive here and now I've got it taped, but I've seen other girls made miserable, really miserable. Don't be a mug, make life easy on yourself. After all, it shouldn't be too difficult for you, you're one of the clever ones.'

'I don't want to be clever,' Isabel said dully. 'I want to be liked.'

But try as she might, she kept running into trouble. Fiona made her life harder, chores piled on repeatedly as Isabel refused to buckle or apologise; her ordeal suffered alone as she refused to tell her father or report the bullying to the school authorities. Day followed gruelling day, week after week. Prossie tried to make things easier for Isabel, but seeing that her friend's attitude only brought more grief down on her head, she conceded defeat and simply helped out with her extra duties, or waited with a chocolate bar in hand outside the detention room.

By the beginning of November Isabel had slid from the third position in the class to the middle. Her teachers could not understand her decline, and when they questioned her she was uncommunicative. Sullen and defensive she waited for the next cruelty from Fiona and missed The Ridings with all the passion of a bewildered thirteen-year-old. Then suddenly matters came to a head in the second week of November.

Having found a dead mouse in her music case,

Isabel sought Fiona out. 'I'm reporting you.'

The girl blinked. 'Mind what you say, Hall. Cheeking a prefect is very serious.'

Isabel stood up to her, a slight figure, several inches shorter than her opponent. 'I've had enough of you and I'm going to sort you out.'

Fiona's eyes were challenging, her brain slipping into overdrive. 'You're going to 'sort me out'! You're just some little Northern hick — '

Isabel's eyes blazed. 'Watch what you say!'

'No, *you* watch it! You might be Daddy's little pet at home, but no one gives a damn about you here. 'Dearest Knuckles,' ' she said spitefully.

'You bitch!' Isabel said, seeing the effect the word had and knowing then that she had fallen into the trap.

'It's very serious for a girl to swear,' Fiona said quietly, enjoying the pain she was about to inflict, 'and to swear at a prefect is very serious *indeed*.' She was almost glowing with delight, hating the attractive girl in front of her and relishing the power she had over her. 'Swearing always gets a stiff punishment.' She paused before delivering the body blow. 'Your exeat's cancelled.'

Isabel stared at her disbelievingly. For weeks she had looked forward to the Saturday exeat, her father travelling all the way down to Brighton to take her out. She knew that a whole day with him away from school would allow her time to forget her problems and enjoy herself . . . and now the chance was being taken away from her. The injustice winded her and, unable to respond, Isabel could only watch as the bulky figure of her tormentor walked away.

Throughout the next day, Isabel plotted how she could escape her punishment and get to see her father. Perhaps she should apologise to Fiona? Isabel dismissed the thought immediately. Never. Then what could she do? Prossie watched her sympathetically but could offer little advice. The punishment was the same for every girl, there was no way out of the situation. Or so she thought.

Isabel thought differently, and watched Fiona throughout the next few days like a hawk watches a rabbit. The older girl was at first amused and then became peculiarly unsettled as the day wore on and the scrutiny persisted. Anything she told Isabel to do, she did immediately, but with defiance burning in her eyes. Laundry was fetched without murmur, baths cleaned, hair-brushes washed, and even extra games completed silently, the boiling resentment coiled, waiting for a chance to strike.

It soon became apparent to the other girls too, and they began to take sides, admiration for Isabel Hall growing hourly. They began to see her as a heroine, watching as she took everything that Fiona could throw at her and remained stubbornly unbowed. Soon everyone was talking about the cancelled exeat and waiting, with uneasy curiosity, as the week wore on.

And Isabel waited too. She waited for her chance, only once thinking of using one of her wishes to send Fiona over the Brighton clifftop. No, she thought, this situation I can sort out for myself, the wishes I'll need for another time.

46

How she was going to get out of her predicament she didn't know, but instinct told her that the opportunity would present itself, and that all she had to do was keep her nerve and bide her time.

Wednesday ground past, and Thursday, and when Friday dawned Prossie suggested that Isabel should phone her father and tell him not to make the long trip down for nothing.

'He's going to have to stay overnight, so he'll be setting off this afternoon,' she said reasonably. 'Isabel, you have to tell him or he'll have a wasted journey.'

'I am going out on that exeat,' she said defiantly. '*I am going.*'

By two o'clock, Prossie was seriously considering phoning David Hall herself, but a curious confidence in Isabel stopped her and she too bided her time.

Having spent the day tracking Fiona's every movement, Isabel was just taking some dirty sheets down to the laundry when she saw her on the stairs talking to a junior. The new girl was little more than a child, very pale and very frightened as Fiona towered over her and told her to run up and down the stairs ten times as a 'punishment' for leaving her wet towels on the bathroom floor. Isabel listened, her own anger rising to boiling point as she watched the child being bullied, her sense of injustice heightened with every syllable Fiona uttered.

Then slowly an idea formed in her mind. She frowned, then began to smile, and then noiselessly crept up the remaining stairs and into her dormitory. Her hands shook with a mixture of excitement and anticipation as she found what she was looking for and made her way silently towards the junior common room. When all the other girls were at games she knew the room would be deserted, and crept in, hiding herself behind the far lockers. Then she waited, praying that Fiona would come; that her greed would force her there.

The place remained silent, the terrified new girl's footsteps ebbing and flowing as she ran up and down the back stairs, the faint cry of seagulls wailing plaintively outside the window as Isabel waited. Finally the door opened and Isabel ducked back against the wall quickly, seeing Fiona's reflection in the mirror, the fat girl glancing round furtively before continuing into the room. Come on, Isabel willed her, come on, you greedy bitch, I'm waiting for you . . . Fiona's eyes moved along the rows of lockers avidly, then flickered with pleasure as they lighted on the new girl's name. Silently her fat hands pulled the metal door open.

Isabel watched through the mirror, the sound of the child's footsteps still echoing outside as Fiona took down the girl's tuck box, pulled open the lid, and began to eat. Isabel waited a moment longer, her heart banging, then she triumphantly stepped forward, aimed the Polaroid camera at the startled girl, and took the shot. Blinded by the flash, Fiona could only blink, disorientated, as Isabel took a second shot and ran out of the room.

She kept running until she reached safety, then she put one of the photographs in an envelope and posted it to herself at The Ridings, and

48

tucked the other into her blazer pocket. The pictures had come out better than she had hoped — both showed Fiona in what was clearly the junior common room, stealing tuck from another girl's locker. She smiled in satisfaction and was still smiling when Prossie caught up with her.

'What the hell's so funny?'

'I'm going out on my exeat tomorrow,' Isabel replied.

'Oh, that's nice,' Prossie responded. 'Does Fiona know?'

'I'm just waiting to tell her actually,' Isabel replied, straightening up as the girl walked round the corner, her face impassive as she confronted her. 'Oh, Fiona, I just wanted to ask if you're still going to cancel my exeat tomorrow.'

The girl's eyes were suspicious. She hadn't seen who had taken the photographs, but she knew what they meant. Disgrace, the loss of power, banishment. Yet stupidly she clung to her decision. 'You know your punishment, Hall.'

'And you know *yours*,' Isabel responded coldly, holding the photograph in front of Fiona's staring eyes. 'You've been caught stealing — now what *is* the punishment for that? Expulsion, I think. It would be *such* a shame to get thrown out, especially when you've only got one more term to go.'

Prossie smiled wryly, and glanced at the picture. 'I wouldn't worry too much, Fiona, no one ever takes a good photo with their mouth open.'

'Well?' Isabel persisted, her eyes fixed on her tormentor. 'What's it to be? Either I get to go on exeat, or you get expelled.'

David Hall was waiting outside the school anxiously the following morning at ten. He looked worried, his expression only lifting when he saw his daughter run down the front steps towards the car. She had changed, he thought ruefully as he hugged her, she was already growing up, but not away from him, that much was certain.

'Hi, Daddy,' she said, stepping back to look at him. She smiled brilliantly and his heart shifted as he looked into his daughter's lovely face.

'Hello, Knuckles,' he managed to say finally. 'How are things?'

'Fine, Daddy, just fine.'

'And you're getting on with the other girls?'

Isabel's hair swung heavily against her back as she glanced at him. 'No problems.'

'That's my girl,' he said proudly. 'I knew you'd settle down.' He pulled open the passenger door for her, turning as she called out to him and smiling automatically into the camera lens as she took his photograph. 'I knew that camera would come in useful one day,' he said.

'Oh, yes, Daddy,' she replied cheerfully, sliding into the car beside him. 'They encourage photography here.'

5

Virginia stretched out her legs in the plane seat and leaned her head back against the cushion, sighing. The trip to Japan had been exhausting, the people attending her lectures asking predictable questions to which she gave predictable answers. The engine droned on, matching her mood of simmering discontent. Not that the exposure hadn't been good for her, she had been well received on Japanese television although the experts who had appeared with her seemed to think that Hellenic Art was merely a fusion of Greek and Oriental traditions — she sniffed at the idea and closed her eyes, her thoughts turning to her daughter.

An unexpected rush of pride filled Virginia as an image of Isabel came into her mind. At sixteen she had passed the age of clumsy adolescence and was now full grown, five feet six with a neat figure and a mass of brown hair, streaked with her own ash tones. Surrounded by such an impressive framing, Isabel's face was pleasingly slim, and although her nose was a little long, her eyes were brilliant with good humour and intelligence.

My daughter is quite remarkable, Virginia thought with satisfaction. Not that she could have said so to Isabel; it wasn't her style, and besides, she didn't want her to become bigheaded. Virginia smiled to herself; oh yes, she had been right not to spoil her, even though she had wanted to at times. But somehow she had never found the right words or the right moment. An uncomfortable memory nudged her. A year before, she had been lecturing in London and instead of returning straight to Yorkshire, had gone down to Brighton to make a surprise visit at her daughter's school. She had driven along the seafront humming to herself, unusually high-spirited, and when she got out of the car she had been pleased with her reflection in the wing mirror.

The headmistress had been delighted to see her, and summoned Isabel to her office, the girl arriving hot from a game of tennis.

'Hello, Mother,' she said, smiling.

Virginia returned the smile and then added, without thinking, 'Oh, do something with your hair, dear. You look a fright.'

The quick slap of disapproval left Isabel discomforted and she retorted stiffly, 'I was just playing tennis.'

Aware that she had said the wrong thing, Virginia silently cursed herself. She had wanted everything to go well, to surprise her daughter, and now she had ruined everything with just a few critical words.

'I just thought I would drop in and say hello,' she continued stiffly, the words sounding false and out of character. She never did things on the spur of the moment and already regretted her impulsiveness. 'You look well, Isabel, and healthy . . . ' she said, trailing off and turning to the headmistress with relief. 'We've been delighted with her school reports. Is she still making good

52

progress?' she asked, moving on to more familiar territory.

'Excellent, Mrs Hall. Isabel couldn't be doing better.'

'So you're doing well,' Virginia said, turning back to her daughter with genuine pleasure. Isabel was a clever girl, destined to do great things. At least they had that much in common. 'Well, I'm very pleased, dear . . . ' she said, picking up her handbag, ' . . . but I must be going. I've a long drive ahead of me.' Her gaze rested on her daughter fleetingly. 'It's been lovely seeing you.'

'It's been lovely to see you too, Mother,' Isabel replied softly.

Each of them knew the other was lying.

Virginia brushed the uncomfortable memory aside and thought of the future instead. Judging from Isabel's progress at school it was more than likely that she would follow her mother into an academic career, perhaps even continuing where she left off. The thought jolted Virginia, although she had to admit that the idea of retirement was attractive. She was fifty-six years old, and tired of roaming the world; tired of plane journeys and hotel bedrooms; tired of being the expert. No one really liked scholars, she thought suddenly. They admired them, but didn't like them. It had been the same at school, she had friends because she did their homework for them, but parties had been disastrous, boys preferring pretty silly girls to blue stockings.

Until David Hall. In him she had found a pride in herself as he responded to her intelligence, their courtship satisfying but cool, although later there had been real affection and respect. They had been so alike, both concentrating on building up their careers, neither too sure of the opposite sex, neither emotionally adventurous. Both had learned over the years that their intellectual power threatened other people, their intelligence setting them apart — until they met and matched each other, and in relief, married hurriedly.

Yes, Virginia thought, before long Isabel can pick up my torch and run with it and I can spend more time at The Ridings. I can cook, and keep the house nice, and invite people to stay; all my friends can come for weekends and we can have wonderful dinner parties. She wracked her brains, making plans. Of course Eleanor had been marvellous, running the house all these years, but now it was time for her to stand aside. Virginia Hall was the real mistress of The Ridings after all. And David was the master. Oh yes, she decided, things would have to change to enable them to spend more time together — if he would just stop writing all those articles and take more time off. He could even retire.

They had plenty of money, she thought, suddenly irritated. So what were they doing, working themselves relentlessly? Who really gave a damn about Hellenic Art or David's Early Netherlandish painters? Her mood accelerated and she was soon unexpectedly angry, her eyes flicking open — just in time to find someone watching her across the aisle.

'Excuse me, I didn't mean to stare . . . ' the

54

woman said hesitantly ' . . . but I was just wondering . . . you're Virginia Hall, aren't you?'

She nodded briefly.

'Oh, I thought you were . . . I bought your last book and I wanted just to say how much I enjoyed it. My children will be so pleased when I tell them that I've spoken to you. What are you working on now?'

Virginia smiled and answered happily; all thought of retirement and domestic bliss evaporating into the clouds.

★   ★   ★

At that same moment David Hall was standing in the drawing room at The Ridings, Eleanor beside him. He was staring out of the window, the afternoon light fading and the long stretch of lawn scattered with late birds. Unaware that his sister was watching him, David leaned against the oak windowsill and remained immobile even when the clock struck five behind him.

Eleanor was worried about her brother. Perhaps he was anxious about an article he was writing, or irritated with his house guests, a couple of dealers from London visiting for the weekend. Or perhaps he wasn't well. Whatever it was, it was unusual for him to be moody, and unknown for him not to confide in her. At another time she would have questioned him, but there was such a sadness about him that she remained silent, stealing from the room and turning only when she reached the door.

Against the dying light David Hall had slumped,

his head hanging down, his arms wrapped around his chest, a low moan of anguish juddering from his opened lips.

★ ★ ★

'Oh, come on, you know I can't leave you here on an exeat,' Isabel said, watching Prossie as she brushed her hair, the familiar Rossetti print fastened to the mirror in front of her.

In the three years they had known each other the likeness had increased, rather than faded. Tall and languid in her movements, Prossie was a living replica of the Italian's muse, and her heavy-lidded expression and heady sex appeal only underlined her attractiveness.

'I'll just stay here,' she said listlessly. 'I got a letter from my mother this morning saying she might come over, so there's always that to look forward to.'

'You loathe your mother,' Isabel said impatiently. 'And you know she won't come, she never does.'

She was right, neither of Prossie's parents ever visited the school, although her elder brother, Bentley, frequently did, flirting with the girls and taking his sister out to buy make-up and clothes in Brighton, or accompanying her to the cinema where she sat daydreaming through the film and then replaying every role when she got back to school later. A year before, her parents had finally divorced, both remarrying almost immediately, their weddings carefully arranged to take place on the same day.

'Well, which one should I go to?' Prossie had asked Isabel. 'Maybe Mother would be the best bet, apparently her latest spouse is rich and in public relations.' She squinted at the wedding invitation. 'Not that they haven't been indulging in their own not-so-public relations for some time now.'

After repeated telephone conversations with Bentley, they finally decided on a plan of action and set off in his hired Daimler to attend their mother's nuptials in Piccadilly before making a hectic dash up to Stratford for their father's marriage. They apparently arrived breathless, the car screeching to a halt outside the country church, Prossie stealing the bride's thunder as she walked in, full-breasted in purple velvet.

'Well, are you coming tomorrow or not?' Isabel asked, bringing Prossie's thoughts back to the present. 'Daddy's driving down specially and he'll be glad to see you.'

'I might . . . '

'Oh, don't do me any favours,' Isabel replied wryly.

Prossie bristled. 'I don't like being a gooseberry.'

'He's my father, you idiot,' Isabel said incredulously, 'not my boyfriend.'

In the end Prossie decided to join them. Having weighed up the alternative — a sneak visit to the nearby boys' school — she had to admit that the local youths had lost their appeal. Time spent climbing out of windows in the dead of night had been invigorating when she thought she might get caught, but groping hands behind the chemistry lab had soon made the risk seem unworth taking and other diversions had not materialised. Bored, she had tried to persuade Isabel to accompany her, but she was too aware of the likelihood of expulsion to go along with the idea.

'I can't.'

'You're scared,' Prossie said, piqued.

'I'm not, but I don't want to get expelled. Your parents wouldn't give a damn — mine would.'

Prossie narrowed her eyes. 'We could have fun, if only you'd liven up a bit.' She pointed to the stack of books on Isabel's desk. 'You're always reading, or in the damn art room painting away like mad.' She sighed. 'It's a waste of time anyway, everyone knows that only men make great artists.'

'Let it rest, Prossie,' Isabel replied patiently. 'I like painting and I like working and I want to do well in my exams.'

'Well I don't,' Prossie said emphatically, slumping over her desk, her hair fanning over her arms. 'I want to be adored. I want some man to fall in love with me.' She sighed. 'I could just lounge around all day looking sexy and he'd give me everything I needed — '

'Like a brain transplant, you mean?'

Prossie refused to rise to the bait. 'I was born too late, that's my cross to bear. I should have lived in the Victorian times, when men adored their women and painted them. Their images were everywhere.'

Isabel sighed. 'The Queen's beaten you to it, Prossie,' she said drily, turning back to her work.

On the day of the exeat both of them were standing on the front steps of the school when David Hall drove up. Isabel ran to greet him, though Prossie hung back until he smiled and put his arm around her shoulder, affectionate as ever. They spent the day exploring the Lanes, Prossie rummaging through second-hand Victorian clothes, Isabel buying some extra paints and a small canvas.

'Well?' Prossie asked, trying on an antique blouse and turning to face David Hall, her expression seductively challenging.

He glanced at her, aware of how attractive she was, but too wise to flirt. 'It suits you perfectly, Prossie, I should buy it.' He then turned back to his daughter and pointed to her parcel. 'More paints? Don't they give you enough at school?'

She shrugged. 'I go through them really quickly, Daddy, and they ration them in the art room, so I thought I'd get my own.' She studied his face, attuned to some alteration in him. 'Are you all right?'

'D'you think I should I get this one instead?' Prossie asked, cutting into their conversation and interrupting them.

David looked at the blouse she was modelling. 'I prefer the first one,' he said patiently before turning back to his daughter. 'I'm fine. No problems.' His voice was as melodious as it had always been, but it carried some other quality in it that Isabel couldn't place, and she frowned.

'You just seem sad — '

He kissed her hand quickly. 'Me sad! Never! How could I be when I'm with my favourite girl?' He felt Prossie's envy and winked at her, including her in his affections. 'How could I be unhappy with my *two* favourite girls?'

★　★　★

Snow fell heavily on South Stainley, cutting off the main road until the snow ploughs came through from Harrogate and made it passable again. In the week before Christmas Isabel and Prossie made the journey from Brighton to Yorkshire, via London, Prossie changing clothes in the train toilet and emerging, fully made-up, just after Haywards Heath.

They laughed and chatted all the way to London, changing stations and trains and settling down for the long trip to Yorkshire, their bags full and heavy above their heads in the luggage racks. Around them other seasonal travellers slept or argued, children fitful and tired, elderly couples talking in whispers as Isabel pulled out the last letter from her father and read it again, the train rocking under her.

Dearest Knuckles,
Well, when you get this note you will be on your way home. God speed, take care and I'll collect you at Harrogate. I can't tell you how much I look forward to seeing you again, and Prossie. Your mother sends her love also.
Eleanor says that she won't hear another word about your diet and that no one diets at Christmas! I'm afraid you'll be stuffed

full of turkey and mince pies so you better adapt yourself to the idea now or we could have a mutiny in the kitchen. Your mother told me to tell you that she is having some of her friends down on Boxing Day and that they are important — one of them has just invited her to lecture in Germany ... do remember to bring your drawings darling. I want everyone to see what a brilliant daughter I have.

You asked me what I wanted for Christmas, well, I've been thinking very hard about that and I can honestly say that the only thing I want in the world is you coming on Wednesday on the nine-thirty London to Harrogate train.

Cheerio and see you very soon,

Your loving father

Isabel smiled and folded the letter, glanced over to Prossie who was already asleep, then tucked the note into her pocket and stared out of the window. Something tugged at her, a struggling sense of unease that she did not understand but which remained with her like an unseen companion all the way from London to Harrogate.

The feeling only evaporated when David Hall swung the car into the driveway of the The Ridings, the house ablaze with lights, a huge Christmas tree in the window, its illuminated lamps throwing colours across the wintery garden. Isabel leapt out of the car and flung open the front door, the house welcoming and full of

61

noise, music coming from the drawing room, Ivor running barking from the kitchen, and her mother's voice calling out to her from the dining room. She walked in, seeing the table set, a bowl piled high with fruit in the centre, the tang of satsumas in the air, the logs cracking in the hearth.

'Isabel,' Virginia said, kissing her daughter on the cheek and then turning to her guest. 'How lovely to see you again, Prossie,' she said, her glance taking in the make-up and the fitted dress.

Alerted by some second sense, Isabel turned and saw her father standing rigidly, staring straight ahead. Again the sense of dread swamped her, but when he realised she was watching him he walked towards her smiling, and the terror faded.

Eleanor soon found a kindred spirit in Prossie and before long they were both in the kitchen, Prossie watching as the meal took shape before her, her healthy appetite a perfect compliment to Eleanor's cooking. By nine they were all fed, Virginia making a few phone calls in her bedroom, Prossie asleep in front of the television and Isabel sitting with her father in the den.

'Where's Prossie?' he asked.

'Asleep. She does more sleeping than a cat,' Isabel said, curling her legs under her and resting her head against her father's shoulder. 'Do you remember how we used to sit here when I was little?'

He nodded, his arm tightening around her shoulder.

'And how you used to push me along on top

of the library steps?' She glanced over her shoulder. The bust of Dante threw a huge shadow across the ceiling. 'Are you happy, Daddy?'

David glanced at his daughter without smiling. He ached with pain, a long pain which had been with him for many weeks, and which would never fade. Unable to speak, he merely nodded.

'I'm glad,' Isabel replied, apparently satisfied by the gesture. 'I want you to be happy always.'

Both of them looked into the firelight; both of them heard Ivor's snoring; both of them watched the flames — and both felt a dark scratch of anguish which for once they could not share.

★　★　★

At New Year, David and Virginia Hall had their usual large house party, and Prossie agonised over what to wear.

'Wear anything, no one will notice,' Isabel said, pulling on a pair of trousers and a velvet jacket and brushing her hair over her shoulders.

'I could get into this dress before Christmas,' Prossie wailed, tugging at the zip. 'Now what am I going to wear?'

'Try this,' Isabel said, throwing a print dress across the bed.

Prossie looked at it with distaste. 'I'd rather breathe in all night,' she said drily.

By ten the house was full of people, Isabel recognising many old faces from her childhood, dealer friends of her father and some collectors, together with a scattering of intellectuals in huddles discussing their planned lecture tours.

Prossie having already cornered her prey, Isabel wandered amongst the guests alone, admiring the buffet her mother had organised and the flowers bought in from Harrogate, their lush hothouse blooms relieved here and there by the feathers of game birds. The house seemed to welcome its guests too, the high windows brilliant under the hall lights, the corridors filled with the smell of perfume and cigars, a scattering of catalogues on the piano in the drawing room. The magic of The Ridings was very strong that night.

'The house was built over an old monastery,' Isabel explained to a guest. 'There's very little left, apart from the cellars, but it's special.'

'Do you have a ghost?' the woman asked.

Isabel was about to laugh but hesitated, for one instant believing that some spirit *did* walk the house. Shivering, she smiled quickly. 'No, no ghosts I'm sorry to say.'

'I would never have recognised you,' a voice said behind her, as a hand went round her waist.

Isabel spun round. 'Oh hello, Mr Cavendish, how are you?'

The dealer glanced at her keenly from behind his glasses. A different pair for each day of the month, someone had once told her. 'You've grown . . . in all the right places.'

She smiled as another man joined them. 'Mr Thompson, I haven't seen you for a long time. Daddy told me you were opening another gallery in Cork Street.'

Sterling Thompson grimaced. 'What, with those bloody rents? It's just a rumour. Mind you, from what your father tells me you're becoming quite a painter yourself.'

Isabel shrugged. 'I just doodle a bit.'

'No one serious paints 'a bit',' Ted Cavendish said airily, his eyes wandering across the room to see who was arriving. 'If you're serious you have to put your body,' he paused, to let the word sink in, 'and soul into it.' He leaned towards Isabel, the skin of his face gallery white. 'Have you got the body and soul for it?'

'Speaking of body and soul,' Sterling Thompson interrupted, 'I heard Stanton Feller's showing again.'

Isabel was immediately forgotten. 'What?' Cavendish said, calling across to David. 'Hey, Hall, old man, what's this about your friend exhibiting again?'

Unable to hear clearly over the noise, David made his way to the group. 'What did you say, Ted?'

'Apparently Stanton's showing again,' he repeated, sharp with excitement. 'Could you persuade him to exhibit in my gallery?'

David smiled evenly. 'I have no influence with Stanton, you know that. He does what he wants.'

'Oh, but he admires you fearfully,' Cavendish continued, wetting his lips with his tongue. 'I could really do with a favour, old man. I could put in a good word for you with the *Harlington Magazine* editor.'

Isabel glanced at her father, but David's face remained impassive. 'I have reached the point in my career, Ted, when I don't need favours any more.' His voice was low, controlled. 'If you want

65

to talk to Stanton, talk to him direct, don't try and use my voice to carry your words.'

Isabel slipped away soon after, climbing to the top of the stairs and peering down into the hallway as she had done as a child. With solid enjoyment she studied the rich and famous below; Michelous, the wealthy dealer with the French wife; Ted Cavendish, hungry for a success after his last three shows had flopped; Sterling Thompson, too dull to recognise a master talent when the Italian, Portento, came to London. Her eyes scanned the crowd: and lighted on her mother, classical and cool in a blue Joseph dress, talking to Geoffrey Harrod, her manager, and then she spotted Baye Fortunas, the Greek collector who had the finest examples of Hellenic art in Europe, sitting with Portento whose latest collection was all the rage in Rome.

Her eyes drank in the details of the glamorous party: the Savile Row suits; the Leonard ties; the women in Chanel or affecting intellectual scruffiness; the Manolo Blahnik shoes; the Cuban cigars; the 1890 port; and the heady scent of Bal a Versailles drifting up through the high well of the stairs. She watched and forgot she was seventeen, seeing and feeling the same excitement she had sensed as a child; the same thrill of being amongst these special people while The Ridings towered protectively and magically around her.

Only one person was aware of her, for he too wished to be distanced from the scene. With a smile on his face he climbed the stairs, and when Isabel turned she found her father holding out a glass of champagne to her.

'Happy New Year, darling,' he said.

Brighton was free of snow when they returned to school. Isabel glanced out of the classroom window, her lesson forgotten as she remembered the magical night of New Year's Eve, when she and her father had toasted in the year on top of the stairs at The Ridings, Big Ben chiming loud over the radio and the faint peal of church bells echoing over the frozen fields.

She sighed and looked back to her book, but the happy memory kept creeping back into her thoughts. Someone behind her coughed and she turned to see Prossie examining her hair for split ends, and another girl pushing down her cuticles with the end of a ruler. On the blackboard was a string of quotations, the teacher adding more in white chalk.

Suddenly everything seemed in sharp focus, the chalk brighter, the clock ticking louder than usual, the radiator hissing malevolently in the corner. Isabel shifted in her seat, her shoes scuffing the floor, each sound piercing her ears as she glanced over to the door and saw the headmistress's assistant walk in. Her gaze followed the woman, and for an instant she was not even surprised when she looked at her and beckoned.

Isabel rose to her feet and followed her out into the corridor.

'What is it?'

'The headmistress wants to see you,' the woman said, keeping her gaze averted.

In silence Isabel followed, her mouth drying.

The headmistress was sitting at her desk and

glanced up as Isabel entered, her eyes moving across the room to where Eleanor sat. Isabel looked at her aunt in dismay but said nothing, trying instead to distance herself from the bad news she knew would follow.

The headmistress watched her and then began. 'I'm afraid I have some bad news for you . . . '

Stop now, Isabel thought, please stop now.

But she continued. 'You see, my dear, your father is dead.'

The words came too suddenly; before Isabel had a chance to prepare herself; like hail stones on a window.

Your father is dead . . .

Cigar ash by a wing-backed chair. Hair hardly greying, the cuff of a Viyella shirt frayed slightly, the leather buttons on his jacket worn with wear. The smell of old drawings in his den, the shadow of the Dante bust.

The headmistress held her breath and stared at the girl in front of her, wondering when she would start crying.

Arms around her, with big, careful hands. Letters beginning affectionately, 'Dearest Knuckles': the travelling rug on the back seat of the Land Rover where they had hidden a Christmas present for Eleanor. A wine glass extended towards her at an important Private View in Bond Street, offered with confidence, even though she had been terrified of dropping it. A book of old prints with tissue paper in between the leaves, held out for her to see. I was only six years old, Daddy, I could have spoiled them, but you trusted me . . . His hands seemed to reach out to her once more as she stood there, but this time he was not offering her a book, or a piece of sculpture — this time he was offering her his heart.

'Daddy?' Isabel said once, softly and finally. And then she started screaming.

6

Pigeons cooing on the windowledge outside; Ivor barking idly in the courtyard; a winter breeze pushing against the drawn curtains; and the smell of old books left untouched in the study. Isabel paused at the doorway, her eyes burned with dry tears, her gaze resting on the worn back of the leather chair as she moved towards it and laid her hand where her father's head once rested. It felt warm to her touch and for an instant she believed him still alive, until she realised that it was only the pale winter sun which had crept through a gap in the curtains and warmed the place.

Her hand dropped away. She was growing used to disappointment. To loss. But not *this* loss, she said to herself, closing her eyes and leaning against the desk, the old smell of tobacco nuzzling round her. Sights, sounds, smells — she had tried to control them one by one; because if she faced them they wouldn't hurt her any longer. Recognise your fear and face it, her father had once told her, because that's the only way to master it . . . but it didn't quite work out that way, did it? Eleanor might move her father's clothes, his billiards cues and his cigar box, she might cancel his newspapers and magazines, but David Hall refused to be cancelled, or to fade.

I loved you, Isabel said suddenly, disbelievingly. I loved you and you died. She swallowed.

Go on! she willed herself, say it! You didn't die, Daddy, you killed yourself . . . Say the words and they have no power any longer. Go on, Isabel, say them. Say that your father committed suicide. Try the words on for size. Pull them over your head, force them to fit you . . . Oh God, Daddy, why? Why?

The door opened behind her and Eleanor walked in, frowning. The smell of dust and old books was stifling in the study, the bust of Dante, implacably grim, looking down at her. She moved towards her niece, seeing the dry eyes, the whitened face.

'Come on, sweetheart, come and get some breakfast.'

'I'm not hungry.'

Eleanor glanced around. 'I should dust in here — '

'Why?' Isabel countered bitterly. 'No one comes in here any longer.'

'You come in.'

'That doesn't matter.'

Eleanor sighed. 'You have to eat, Isabel. You have to — for his sake.'

'Why? What did he do for *my* sake?' she replied furiously. 'He killed himself. *Killed* himself!' she repeated, her voice shrill. 'Why did he have to do that?'

Eleanor moved towards her but Isabel backed off, rejecting any offer of affection.

'I thought he loved me,' she continued. 'I know my mother doesn't give a damn about me, but he was so kind.' She stopped, frowning. 'Was he pretending, Eleanor? Was it all fake? Or

71

perhaps he was trying to tell me something and I didn't understand.' Her eyes were wide with anguish. 'Did I fail him?'

Eleanor's chest tightened. The shock of her brother's death had been colossal, the village rocked with the trauma, friends and associates rallying around the rigid widow and the distraught child. Virginia reacted by not reacting; she betrayed no emotion in her voice or in her speech. Her daughter she froze out. Keep your distance, Isabel, she signalled with her eyes. Keep away from me. Isabel read the message and felt no rage, only guilt, because in her mother's eyes she read something else — the implication that she was responsible for her father's death.

Then Dr Hunter broke the news. Take, eat, this is my body which is given for you. He broke the truth into manageable pieces to feed the widow and the widow's child. David Hall had killed himself. Not accidental death, as they had thought, but suicide. He had shot himself through the mouth. He had taken his own life, and worse, for his own reasons. And those reasons remained secret.

Virginia looked in Dr Hunter's eyes and seemed calm. She stayed calm while he left and remained calm until she called Ivor in from the garden. Then she picked up a kitchen knife and lunged at the dog. Eleanor sprang forward and caught hold of her arm just before the blade hit the animal. Screaming hysterically, Virginia fought her sister-in-law, all her elegance and poise made ugly as her skirt rode up and she lost her footing, falling clumsily on to the kitchen floor, her head thudding on to the tiles.

By the door Isabel stood shaking with shock whilst Ivor crept under the table and howled. As the unearthly noise continued, Eleanor wrenched the knife from Virginia's hand, threw it into the kitchen sink and knelt down beside her.

'Pass me a damp cloth, Isabel.'

She stood immobile by the door, trembling.

'Get me a cloth!'

Still she couldn't move; still the dog howled. Impatiently Eleanor scrambled to her feet and wrung out a towel before placing it across Virginia's forehead. 'She didn't know what she was doing . . . ' she began, trying to explain. There was no answer and when she glanced up Isabel was gone, the door swinging silently closed behind her.

All that night Eleanor sat next to Virginia's bed. Her time for grief would come later; now she waited on others. As she always did. Throughout the long night Virginia dozed in and out of sleep, tranquillisers taking effect, then lifting, hauling her back into full consciousness. Her eyes were closed, feigning sleep, but Virginia's mind was busy . . . She knows, she decided. She knows. My daughter knows why he killed himself. They were always too close. They kept secrets from me . . . She moved irritably and then winced, touching her forehead.

'You bumped your head . . . ' Eleanor said, leaning over her. 'You'll feel better in the morning.'

Isabel knows, she knows . . . she knows why.

' . . . the child's so upset. Do you want to see her?'

It's her fault, Virginia thought, it's all her fault. Oh God, suicide. How would she explain?

'... she's in shock, Virginia, you have to talk to her. She needs you ...'

The scandal, the disgrace. People will talk, they'll think he was unhappy; that he killed himself to get away from me. They'll talk ...

'Virginia, she loved David very much and she's very unhappy. Please, please talk to your daughter ...'

Little bitch, pushing her hands through the window when she was little just to get her own back. She wanted him for herself, always. She wanted me out of the way so that it was just the two of them ... but now he's dead. He's killed himself and left me ... her eyes brightened momentarily with triumph. But he's left her too ... you've lost ... you've lost, Isabel ...

Moments later a peculiar rest settled on Virginia Hall and she fell into a deep sleep.

The following evening she phoned Geoffrey Harrod and told him that she had no intention of cancelling her American tour. His surprise was obvious, but he was tactful enough not to oppose her decision, after all, what could he say? The whole business was fraught with embarrassment. To think that David Hall had killed himself. It was so out of character, so unlike him ... it made you wonder why.

'Of course I'm delighted, but do you think you're up to it, Virginia?' he asked cautiously. Oh God, he was thinking, don't let her get hysterical. Don't let her break down.

'I'm fine, Geoffrey, but I need to work. Believe

me, I have to work.'

Her voice sounded even, smooth as a frozen lake.

'But could you possibly have everything . . . settled . . . ' He winced at his own clumsiness. 'I mean, can you have everything organised in a week?'

'The funeral's on Friday, Geoffrey,' she replied calmly. The laying to rest of the restless. 'I can leave on Saturday.'

'But what about Isabel?' he replied, surprised.

'Eleanor's looking after her,' Virginia responded coolly. 'They get on.'

'Oh . . . '

'Did you want to say something, Geoffrey?'

'Oh . . . no . . . nothing,' he blustered. God, he hated cold women. They terrified him and there was something unearthly cold about Virginia Hall. He found himself chilled physically over the phone line, and suspecting that he was seeing something of her true nature, wondered exactly what had driven David Hall to suicide.

Isabel wondered about that too. Emotional amnesia made it possible for her to function on that bleak Friday, the day of her father's funeral. Only snatches of memory came back to her; Virginia's calm expression under the black veil, Eleanor's soft weeping in the car as they drove back to the house; and the sun glinting on a spider's web which patterned the drawing room window.

People babbled incoherently, Isabel receiving condolences and avoiding the questioning eyes. Why did he do it? He was so successful, so nice.

He seemed such a thoughtful man . . . why? Why? David Hall's only child, his golden child, walked down the stairs at The Ridings and felt the unkind sun streaming in through the open window; she held her poise as he had taught her to and knew that at seventeen she was the woman he had wanted her to be. But as she came down the staircase she suddenly remembered New Year's Eve — and his betrayal winded her. Instantly her eyes filled and she hesitated, unable to continue. Many pairs of eyes glanced up towards her. Baye Fortunas, having flown in from Romania; Michelous from Greece; and Portento from Italy. Birds of a feather sticking together. They watched Isabel, and she knew it, and with all her courage she clenched her teeth and tilted her head back slightly to stop the tears running down her cheeks. Look for sensation elsewhere, gentlemen, she thought, this house has had enough.

Virginia left silently the next morning like a thief. A note was slid under Isabel's door which said something clumsily comforting — the effort easier on paper than in life. Isabel read it and ripped it into pieces, throwing them out of the bedroom window and watching as they caught on the bare rose bushes underneath. Paper flowers. Slowly she eased herself out of bed and showered, dressing by rote before she went downstairs. She was glad that her mother had left. After all, she thought bitterly, another betrayal was such a little thing to bear.

Eleanor was already in the kitchen, her wide back turned to the door as Isabel walked in. Her hands moved efficiently, cutting bread for breakfast, her hair the same as it was every day, as were her actions. The same, and not the same. Locked into her own bitterness, Isabel sat down at the table and began scratching fork marks into the soft wood. The clock chimed seven and Ivor barked outside at the milkman delivering the usual three pints, the bottles clinking in the cold air.

'I wonder where Mother is now?' Isabel said, as she tugged the fork along the table surface. 'Probably off to impress everyone with one of her lovely talks.' Her bitterness rose like bile in her throat. 'Off to talk about dead civilisations. Well, she should be an expert on the deceased now. After all, if she runs out of statues, she could talk about her own dead.' Isabel's voice took on a fairground barker's tone. 'No more Hellenic sculptures, sorry folks, we've run out, but there's this dead figure here, it's called a David Hall — '

A sudden cry stopped her in mid-flow. Eleanor slumped forwards over the work top and Isabel sprang to her feet, putting her arms around her aunt and turning her round to face her. Eleanor Hall's face was swollen and blotchy, her eyes raw with weeping. Days and nights she had spent weeping for a dead brother, and no one had thought of her grief. Not once.

Shame welled up in Isabel as she rocked the older woman in her arms.

'Oh, don't . . . don't cry . . . '

'He was my brother . . . ' Eleanor said softly. 'He was everything to me. Always had been. He gave me a home, and you . . . ' she blinked, her eyes blinded with tears, ' . . . he trusted me with The Ridings and with his child . . . he made me *important*. Anywhere else I would have been a spinster, but here I was somebody . . . I ran his home . . . '

Isabel nodded, unable to speak, as her aunt clung on to her.

'He didn't mean to be cruel, believe me, that wasn't his intention. I know him.' Her eyes fixed on Isabel. 'I know him better than anyone and I've been thinking, wondering if he was ill, and couldn't face a slow death, or if he was in pain . . . ' She seemed hopeful suddenly. 'Maybe he had a brain tumour, or something like that . . . ' then her voice trailed off, desolate, ' . . . but Dr Hunter said he was in good health. Perfect health . . . He should have been, I always tried to look after him well.'

'You always did,' Isabel said finally. 'You've always looked after all of us.'

She didn't seem to hear her niece and carried on brokenly. 'When our parents died it was awful, but I had David and somehow that made it bearable. Even not marrying, well . . . it didn't seem to matter because I had the best man anyone could want. He wasn't a husband but he loved me. He relied on me . . . I can't believe he's dead.' She caught her breath, and rummaged for a handkerchief. Isabel watched as she blew her nose and wiped her eyes. 'Your father was a good man — '

'I know — '

'Hear me out!' Eleanor snapped, holding

78

Isabel at arm's length and looking into her eyes. 'You are his child, his beloved child, and believe me he loved you so much. You feel betrayed now and unhappy,' she nodded, 'and you have every right, but something happened that neither you nor I understand. Something happened to make David kill himself, and maybe we will never know what it was . . . but we can't betray his memory.'

Isabel frowned.

'I mean what I say,' Eleanor continued. 'He was the best father any child ever had, the best any child could dream of. He gave you your character and your courage and there was never a day of his life that he didn't love you with all his heart. Don't betray that legacy, Isabel, if you did you would destroy everything he made of you, and gave to you. Don't be bitter, don't hate him, wait to judge him. Time alone will explain why he did what he did. Give him the benefit of the doubt . . . he would have done the same for you.'

★ ★ ★

It was the last show of grief Isabel ever saw from her aunt. Instead Eleanor Hall made a series of long telephone calls to Scotland and received several letters within the space of a week. Finally she received a call which left her smiling.

'Blair's coming home,' she announced triumphantly, sitting down beside Isabel on her bed.

'Blair who?'

'Blair, my cousin,' Eleanor replied, as though

she should have known.

A faint flicker of memory nudged Isabel. 'Blair? Blair . . . the one who's a little . . . ?'

'Slow? Yes.' Eleanor nodded.

'But — '

'He's been in a home for years. He was happy apparently, but the place is closing down through lack of funds and I thought that since we need a man to help around the place, Blair could come here.' She glanced at her hands, willing Isabel to speak.

But her niece was dumbstruck. Blair was intellectually impaired, or so she had been told, a man who had lived most of his life in an institution, and he was coming to The Ridings to take her father's place?

'It's a stupid idea!'

'Why?'

'He's not fit — '

'He's not David, you mean,' Eleanor countered perceptively. 'I know he's not, but then he's not supposed to be, is he? I don't want a replacement for my brother, I want to help someone.' She reached for Isabel's hand. 'Oh come on, he's nowhere else to go. We have the money and the room, and besides, your mother will go crazy.'

'She'll be in the right company,' Isabel replied drily. 'Is he . . . Blair . . . is he safe?'

'You have to watch him when there's a full moon,' Eleanor responded, raising her eyes heavenwards. 'Oh, don't be so damned silly, of course he's safe, otherwise I wouldn't think of having him here. He fell when he was a small child — it was a freak accident — and it left him intellectually impaired. He has the mind of a ten-year-old.'

Isabel gave her aunt a sidelong look. 'And?'

'Nothing else.' Her tone cajoled her niece. 'He'll be company for me when you're at school . . . '

'But I'm home most weekends,' Isabel replied, on the defensive.

'Most weekends are not every day,' Eleanor responded gently. 'You have to go back to school and concentrate on your exams, and I have to run the house — and I need help to do that, sweetheart. After all, your mother spends very little time here. The place gets damn lonely, so far away from town. You should see how you would like living here alone.'

'You've got Ivor to protect you,' Isabel said, leaning back against the headboard. 'Mind you, if Blair does come here I can just imagine how my mother will take it. How do you intend introducing him to her guests? As what exactly?'

'As my cousin, what else?'

Isabel nodded and then smiled broadly. 'So when is he coming home then?'

Blair Hall came home to The Ridings at the end of March. The train was delayed, Isabel rubbing her hands together as she waited on the platform, Eleanor interrogating the British Rail staff as to the reason for the delay. Finally it pulled in, and Isabel and Eleanor watched as the passengers got out. They scanned each man's face, looking for a thirty-five-year-old male with the little description they had to go on. Several men passed them curiously, one winking at the attention paid to him, another hurrying past awkwardly. As the train drew out, Isabel glanced over to her aunt and shrugged, a door slamming behind her as she did so.

She spun round quickly in time to see a man jump down from the train, his bag preceding him. He landed on both feet, his knees bending against the impact, his arms extended joyously. Isabel put her head on one side and looked at him, all thought of Blair forgotten, and as she did so he turned and smiled at her.

No, she thought, laughing out loud, not *this* man. This can't be Blair. But he stood, tall, wide and wonderful like a huge, overgrown miracle child. God, you're beautiful, she thought, walking timidly towards him.

Eleanor glanced at Isabel and hurriedly stepped between them.

'Blair?'

He nodded, smiling, two rows of large even teeth. Like a dental chart, Isabel thought delightedly.

'I'm Blair,' he agreed.

She blinked, searching his face hopefully for any sign of arrested development. 'I'm Cousin Eleanor.'

He smiled again, massively pleased. But there was still no sign of his being intellectually impaired.

'This,' Eleanor said, gesturing to Isabel, 'is my niece, Isabel.'

Blair looked appreciatively at her seventeen-year-old face, and Eleanor paled with anxiety. He was the most fabulous man she had ever seen.

His dark hair rested against the back of his collar, his pitch-coloured eyes deep set and evenly browed, his skin weathered by working outside for years. On his six-foot frame his jeans fitted tightly, his denim jacket fashionably worn at the elbows and cuffs, his large hands gripping his holdall easily.

Eleanor had expected to be giving a home to a poor fool, and stood, transfixed, as this Adonis's gaze rested on her innocent niece.

Finally he spoke. 'Isabel,' he said, looking into her eyes with an expression most women would die for, 'do you like frogs?'

7

He brought joy to The Ridings, and laughter and more than that, innocence. Into the rooms where so much pain clung to the walls he blundered and looked and laughed. He pointed at Dante and called him a 'poxy old sod'. Eleanor overheard him and hauled his fourteen stone to one side.

'Don't use language like that, Blair!'

'Like what?'

'Like 'sod',' she said awkwardly. 'It's rude.'

'Why?' he replied pleasantly. 'What does it mean?'

'Oh, hell!' she blustered. 'Just don't use it again. All right?'

All right, he agreed, and used the word 'bugger' instead, until Eleanor stopped him. After a week she had cured him of most of his obscenities, although she could not curtail his energy. If she was up early, Blair was up earlier, walking Ivor so far that he would return, slump in his bed and remain comatose until lunchtime. If there was wood to be cut, lawns to be mown and windows to be cleaned, Blair did it.

But if Eleanor and Isabel appreciated him, the staff did not. The gardener complained, as did the two cleaners, and the garage mechanic had more than a little to say on the matter of Blair servicing the car for free.

'If he's bloody disabled, I'd like someone to hit me on the back of the bloody head too. Aye, and my bloody mechanic.' He scratched his head. 'Disabled, my arse.'

'He has the brain of a ten-year-old,' Eleanor said defensively.

'Ten-year-old what? Computer?' he sniffed loudly. 'He's no more an idiot than I am.'

Isabel raised her eyebrows and leaned against the door: 'I really wouldn't let him hear you bad-mouthing him, Mr Waters,' she said. 'Blair gets very mean if people insult him. He bit a man's finger off at the Home.'

The man stepped back. 'I meant nothing by it. I was just kidding.'

'Oh, he was too,' Isabel continued, 'he was just trying to trim his nails.'

Mr Waters beat a hasty retreat, Blair waving heartily to him as he passed.

'You shouldn't, you know,' Eleanor said, laughing. 'It gets Blair a bad reputation when he's so gentle.'

'On the contrary, it protects him,' Isabel said wisely, watching Blair through the window. 'You know, Daddy would have loved him.'

Eleanor looked over her niece's shoulder. 'I think he was supposed to come here. After all the horrors that have happened, all the unhappiness, he's like a breath of goodness.' She sighed. 'And you're right, David would have loved him. I think maybe . . . ' She stopped, embarrassed.

Isabel glanced at her. 'Go on, what were you going to say?'

'I . . . well, it was just that I thought maybe David sent him to be our guardian angel . . . ' She blushed, feeling stupid.

' "Our Guardian Angel",' Isabel repeated,

glancing back to the garden and watching the big man working. 'Oh, I hope so . . . I do hope so.'

They made an unlikely trio: a middle-aged spinster, a schoolgirl, and a child-like giant. The village talked about them, as did Dr Hunter . . . and Virginia. Eleanor had written to her on her American tour, but, as usual with Virginia, she had been understanding on paper, from a distance, but when brusque reality caught up with her it was quite another matter. She returned to England and phoned from Heathrow. Her voice was combative.

'Eleanor, this cousin of yours. How long is he staying?'

'Blair lives here now,' her sister-in-law responded, knowing full well that under the terms of the will David had left the house half to his wife and half to his sister. They were dual mistresses of The Ridings.

'Yes, but for how long?' The noise of the airport behind her could be heard clearly down the phone. 'Hold on a minute. Geoffrey, get the luggage, will you?' She turned her attention back to Eleanor. 'You see, I can't see the situation working out with this Blair — '

'It's working out perfectly. He's a great help with the house, and . . . ' She paused. She had been about to say that Isabel enjoyed his company; that he had assuaged some of the staggering grief of her father's death. For a moment she had nearly confided that the two of them went walking, the ten-year-old boy's mind inside the man's body making a gentle companion for a bewildered teenager. It looked different to strangers;

86

an older man protecting a girl, but in fact Isabel had decided to protect him.

' . . . he is saving us money.'

That was the right tack, she knew it.

Virginia took the bait. 'Oh really? How?'

'He's doing many of the odd jobs himself and he's saved a fortune on the old Jag.'

In the Heathrow lounge Virginia Hall's face relaxed. Maybe she had been a little hasty, maybe Eleanor needed company and help. Good help. After all, they were giving this man a home, so why shouldn't he help out all he could? It was a fair exchange.

She was suddenly tolerant. 'Well, I'll see for myself when I get back, but it seems like a good arrangement.'

Eleanor put down the phone, smiling.

She had not heard the door of the drawing room open behind her, or the soft footsteps. Her attention was drawn to the garden where she watched Blair trim the edges of the lawn. Clip, clip, clip went the trimmers in his big hands, the sun winking on the long blades, clip, clip, clip, in the still air, peaceful and undisturbed. The day simple as the man was. Then suddenly the noise of a far-off gun made the pigeons spook and fly up from the trees, their wings black against the bright sky as they wheeled upwards. Startled, Blair glanced towards them, using one hand to shield his eyes from the sun, the other tight on the trimmers. He watched them and then lifted the grass cutters and aimed them towards the scattered birds.

'Bang, bang, bang,' he shouted childishly,

whirling round on the gravel path.

'I know how he feels.'

Eleanor spun round. 'God, you scared me! I didn't hear you come in.'

'I heard you on the phone,' Isabel said, dropping into a chair and glancing at a glossy book on the table next to her Hellenic sculpture. Her gaze flickered away. 'Mother's coming back, isn't she?'

Eleanor nodded. 'She'll be home about ten tonight.'

'Well, at least we're spared dinner with her then.'

'Listen, sweetheart, you have to try and understand her,' Eleanor said quietly, sitting down beside her niece. 'She isn't a demonstrative person.'

'She was pretty demonstrative with that knife,' Isabel countered deftly.

'It was her way of showing grief,' Eleanor explained, angered as Isabel shook her head. 'No, come on! Don't do that to me. Don't let your bitterness shut me out. We're in this together, Isabel, and I won't take any kind of nonsense from you.'

Stung, Isabel sank further into her seat, her expression sullen. 'I just dread her coming home, that's all.'

'I know, I don't look forward to it either. But your mother is as she is and we can't change her. She means well, in her own way, and she's grieving in her own way. It's just that it's not a way we can understand.'

'She went off just after the funeral,' Isabel said

incredulously. 'She never thought about how I was feeling.'

'Did you think about how *she* was feeling?'

Isabel turned to her aunt, her eyes sharp, unforgiving. 'Oh, don't give me that. You know I couldn't even talk to her, she froze me out . . . I keep thinking that she was wishing it had been me. If only I had killed myself. She could have come to terms with that. Besides, it would have left her alone with my father.' She swallowed. Truth chokes. 'That's what she always wanted, wasn't it?'

'Yes,' Eleanor agreed, grasping her niece's hand as she glanced at her, shocked, 'but it wasn't what your father wanted.' She took in a breath. 'Forget yourself for a moment and let me tell you about your parents. When David met Virginia he was looking to get married, he wanted a family, lots of children, and someone who would appreciate The Ridings as he did. For years he never met anyone suitable. They came and went, some pretty, some clever, some pretty clever,' she smiled, her recall was complete, 'but none suitable. He could have looked further afield, but although he was adventurous in his work, he was timid with women. So Virginia Aldridge had quite an easy run. I remember the first time I met her. She walked into the hall out there and glanced round . . . ' Eleanor had a mental image of a tall young woman, perfectly composed, with crafted bone structure and fine ankles. ' . . . she talked articulately on his subject and flattered his intelligence.' She paused again. Down all the years came Virginia's voice talking to David in his study. *You have such insight, it's rare to find someone with clarity and insight into their subject.*

'Oh, she was very clever and anxious to be in love.'

Beguiled, Isabel tried to imagine the past as Eleanor continued. 'You see, having thought about it for a while, I think I understand her now. She wanted desperately to love, to be in love, and thought that it would happen when she met the right person, but it couldn't because it isn't *in* her. That's your mother's tragedy, not that she doesn't care, but that she wants to care so much, and can't.'

'Did she love my father at all?'

'In her way,' Eleanor responded. 'They fell in love with each other's minds, and admired each other's intelligence. No passion, only great mutual respect. But as time went on, both were disappointed. David more obviously because his affection was never spontaneously returned; Virginia because she never felt the love she expected to feel. They cooled towards each other whilst maintaining a splendid front. The house cooled with them.' She paused in her story, remembering. 'When we were children this place was busy. My parents argued and made up, and they invited friends round, and people stayed, and we grew up here in an atmosphere of trial and error. I can't say it was easy, but it was possible to *breathe* in that environment . . . ' She glanced towards the window, got up and opened it and leaned against the sill. The claustrophobia of the memory swamped her. 'But in your parents' marriage they choked each other, they sucked the life out of each other and left no air to breathe in. And worse, it was all so chillingly polite.'

The image was becoming clearer in Isabel's mind: her father in his study, her mother travelling. Miles of solitude in between.

'David felt it the worst, I think, because it affected the house too. He saw the decline of his dream and the decline of his dream castle. He found the atmosphere unendurable and looked for escape . . . '

Isabel turned to her aunt. 'He tried to commit suicide then?'

'No,' Eleanor said, glancing out to the garden. 'No, it was more subtle than that. He gave himself a time limit.' She turned, her eyes were suddenly like her brother's, full of kindness. 'He wrote a letter to himself in which he gave himself eighteen months. In eighteen months he would either have sorted out his marriage and his life, or he would end it.'

The words made Isabel flinch. 'Eighteen months isn't a long time,' she said brokenly.

'I found the letter by accident. Ivor caused some damage to the desk in the study and I called a man in to repair it. I had to empty the drawers. Only one was locked, but oddly enough this letter was in an unlocked drawer, tucked at the back.' She paused, clenching her hands. 'I *never* open anything, I've never pried, but this time something nudged me and I was frightened, so I opened it.' She glanced at her hands as though the letter was in them; as though she read from it. 'I knew then how unhappy he was . . . and so I began to watch him . . . I watched him . . . '

Her memory wandered. Footfalls on the stairs at night, lonely vigils over a doomed brother. Glances through open summer windows, concealed watches in the small of the night and the eternal waiting, waiting, for late cars.

'The months rushed past . . . it was obscene how quickly they went by . . . soon it was a year, then nearly fourteen months.' She swallowed, her brother, her beloved David, hurtling towards the end.

'How? Where? How would he do it? I asked myself repeatedly. Would he be away from home, away from The Ridings? Or would I be there with him, ready to stop it, ready to prevent him going over the edge?' Her voice failed her momentarily. 'You have no idea what it was like.'

'But . . . didn't you ever think of talking to him about it?'

'No,' Eleanor said simply. 'You see, he knew that I had found the letter, even though he never mentioned it. He couldn't, he was too unhappy, too embarrassed . . . I don't know. Maybe he would never have gone through with it; or maybe he just needed to know that I was there, looking out for him.' She paused and then smiled wistfully. 'The sixteenth month had just passed when Virginia told him she was pregnant.' Eleanor laughed suddenly, sounding like her brother, a laugh of pure relief. 'She didn't know but she saved him. Or rather, *you* did.' Her eyes filled. 'Oh God, no child was ever wanted so much. David believed it was a miracle, and it pulled him back from the edge. From that time onwards his every thought and breath was centred on his child. You were always his child. I knew then that the watch was over . . . no more wanderings, no more sick terror when he was late home . . . no more.'

'And when I was born?'

'You were the world to him.' She glanced at her niece. 'Sometimes I used to worry that it was too much of a burden for a child to carry, but you were clever and you shouldered it so well. That's why he encouraged you so much, pushed you so far. He was living his dreams through you.' She frowned. 'Don't misunderstand me, Isabel, he would never have been disappointed in you, whatever you had wanted to do, but that's because I think he knew you *would* never disappoint him. He was so lucky with you.'

'I was lucky with him,' Isabel said quietly. 'He spent so much time with me. You know, Mother loves her work, but she never made me interested in the arts. He did though, because he cared so much, and he made it fun.'

'I think you should prepare yourself for something,' Eleanor said suddenly, her tone changing. The past faded, reality coming in like a quick tide. 'Your mother wants to talk to you before you go back to school, she wants to know about university.'

'University!' Isabel echoed. 'I don't want to go. Daddy knows that . . . '

She trailed off. The confidant had gone, her ally had gone.

'Virginia expects you to go to university, as she did, and to read History or Art, and to follow in her footsteps.'

'I want to paint.'

Eleanor sighed. 'I know, I told her. But she pooh-poohed the idea — '

'What right has she!'

'Hear me out!' Eleanor snapped. 'I'm telling you this to forewarn you. There's no point flying off the handle, that way you'll play into her hands. Your mother will be cool and collected, and you must be too. You know what she's going to say — 'Painting is no career, not for anyone, and especially not for a woman. No one makes a good living from painting. You can take your degree and when you've got some security behind you, you can always do it as a hobby.''

'It's not a hobby!'

'Stop interrupting me!' Eleanor said abruptly. 'Let me go on.' Isabel's face set as her aunt continued. 'You know you have talent, you know your father wanted you to train as a painter — he'd asked advice from Stanton Feller and Portento and both agreed you have a special gift — but it's a bad time for painting. People don't commission work any more, except from the greats. They take photographs instead, and have them printed out on canvas to make them look like pictures.' She raised her eyes incredulously. 'The competition is fierce, Isabel, there are scores of students coming out of art schools every year and little or no work for them. And worse than that, people don't respect painters, they think it's the easy option — after all, many people can paint, very few people can be scientists or lawyers.'

''Art ennobles, science explains.''

'What?'

Isabel smiled wryly. 'Daddy used to say that. Whenever people tried to imply that art wasn't important, he just said that. They usually went on to say that civilisation needed doctors to save lives, scientists to discover electricity and engineers to make everything function. They make our lives safer and easier, it's true,' she flicked back her hair from her forehead, ''But artists,' he would reply, 'they give man hope, and beauty, because without that the world is simply clever, but without heart.'' She sighed, her eyes looked almost amber in the late sunlight. 'He could inspire people, couldn't he?' Eleanor nodded. 'Not just me, but so many others.' She stood up and walked over to the mantelpiece and looked at her reflection in the ormolu mirror. 'He said I had green flames in my eyes, four of them, and they were for luck. I had four wishes to be granted in my life . . . ' She paused, glancing over to her aunt's reflection. 'He gave me so much hope for the future, it seems so sad that no one could give him the same.'

At ten o'clock that night Virginia Hall returned. She opened the door and walked into the hall of The Ridings with Geoffrey Harrod in tow. She looked tired, her clothes uncreased but her face waxen, strain showing round her eyes. Was it the trip? Isabel wondered, or the thought of returning home? She paused, glancing down from her vantage point on the staircase, and studied her mother. Knowing something of the past now she found herself feeling a reluctant pity for her, together with the ever-present awkwardness. Not for the first time she wondered why it had to be her father who killed himself.

'Mother,' she said kindly, walking down the stairs. 'Welcome home.'

Virginia smiled. Frost eyes trying to be gentle. 'Hello, dear, say hello to Mr Harrod.'

She treats me like an infant, Isabel thought, turning to her mother's companion. 'Hello, how was the flight?'

'Fine, fine,' he said uneasily, a stocky man in a tight suit, obviously wanting a stiff drink. His hair was slightly untidy, his eyes bloodshot. The travelling had exhausted him.

'Geoffrey's staying here tonight,' Virginia said easily, turning her attention back to her hand luggage. She leaned down and started to undo the straps, her hands shaking slightly. Isabel watched, surprised, her mother's face was impassive, but her actions were unusually gauche. 'Ah, here it is,' she said finally as she extended her hand towards her daughter.

The bribe was duly offered. A magnificent book, just published in America. A wonderful book that any connoisseur would be pleased to have, only the subject was her mother's — Hellenic Art.

'Thank you, it's wonderful,' Isabel said woodenly. Virginia leaned forwards to peck her daughter on her cheek, but at that moment Isabel lifted her head and their foreheads cracked. Both reddened, Virginia backing away rapidly. How clumsy of me, she thought, I was a fool to try and express affection, and in front of Geoffrey too.

'It's my pleasure, my dear,' she said rigidly, turning back to her guest. 'Well, I think we'll just go and have a nightcap.'

You are dismissed, Isabel thought, as she walked back up the stairs into her room and closed the door. Quickly she pulled the curtains closed and tossed the book on to the bed, sitting down at her work table and reaching for a piece of Ingres drawing paper. Laying it out in front of her she gazed at the blank sheet and then picked up a piece of charcoal. One, two, three strokes, and the sketch began to take shape, an outline going where she wanted it to go. After another moment, Isabel leaned back, a sense of power filling her.

She got to her feet and glanced round the big room, seeing the bed by the window, the door to the small adjacent bathroom, the two large wardrobes against the wall and the work table beside her. The table was nearly five feet square, and almost a third of its surface was covered in paint tubes and papers, whilst underneath were the shelves on which she had piled her innumerable sketches. She knelt down and pulled out some of the drawings. The face of her father looked up at her, with a funny note in his handwriting; under another sheet she found a letter he had written to her at school a year before, putting his feelings on paper, always writing to her so that she could re-read the words later, in her own time.

Carefully she replaced the papers and ran

downstairs, going out to the stable block at the back of the house. Ivor barked from inside the kitchen then fell silent. She unlocked the stable door and walked in, smelling the old scent of horse and hay although there had been no horses there for many years. Eagerly she climbed the rickety stairs to the loft and flicked on the light switch at the top.

The huge space was dry and warm and uncluttered although there was plenty in the studio. Down one wall were rows of shelves, on which Isabel stacked her canvases and unused frames, while the wall which faced it was almost entirely made up of windows, admitting the North light. Sighing, she flopped into an old couch and glanced round. Three easels faced her, one supporting an indifferent landscape, one a charcoal head, and the last a large portrait of Eleanor. Critically, Isabel scrutinised the oil painting, looking for faults.

Her art teacher had told her she was gifted, although she had already discovered that from her father and his friends. The woman encouraged Isabel, but it was Portento and Stanton Feller who gave her the insight she needed. Knowing two artists of international calibre she discovered the reality of the painter's life. Not that she believed Stanton's version; but she did trust Portento.

The morose Italian was ugly with an overlarge nose, heavy jowls and protruding liquid eyes which seemed to take in little, but missed nothing. His accent was heavy, his voice without enthusiasm, but his work . . . She had visited

Portento's studio in Florence with her father several times. Geraniums flowered in terracotta pots on the balcony, the brickwork crumbling in patches, summer birds flying across a hot sky whilst the noises of bustling crowds of people floated up from the streets below.

At times the Italian would be disturbed as he worked by a passer-by calling out to him. 'Portento! Portento, come to the window.'

Grumbling, he would throw down his brushes and lean over the edge of the balcony.

'What is it?'

Sometimes a tourist would recognise him and take his photograph; or there would be a new father waiting there to lift his newborn towards the ugly man for blessing; and sometimes a young artist would wave a painting or a contract in glee.

'Wish me luck, Portento. I made it! I made it!'

'You made nothing,' the artist would reply hoarsely. 'No artist makes anything until he's old.'

'As old as you?'

'OLDER!' he would shout, moving back to his work.

Then he would try to carry on painting, muttering under his breath and shouting at the model until, unsettled, he would shake his head with resignation and go back to the window. Sure enough, the young artist would still be there.

'Wish me luck.'

'What, you still here?' Portento would ask, as though surprised. Then his ugly face would soften, his eyes glowing. 'You did good, boy, you did good.'

Isabel thought of him now and wondered. She knew that Portento had been very fond of her father, his presence at the funeral proved that, but could she go to him for help? She frowned automatically, a little afraid of the strange Italian, but if she didn't go to Portento, who was there? Stanton Feller? A wry smile crossed Isabel's face. Oh God, not Stanton, he was such a lunatic. But did that matter? she thought, trying hard to assess him. Her father's opinion of Stanton had been enormous, 'the greatest painter alive today', but what of the man himself?

Was there anything in him to which she could appeal? Oh, she knew he loved women, but what about women painters? She had an uncomfortable feeling that he would find the idea laughable, he usually found a great deal to laugh at. A memory of his freezing Holland Park studio came back to her. Stanton in bare feet and green fingerless mittens, the male model covered in goose pimples, his skin horribly blue and white under the unkind light from the North-facing window.

'Relax, you bugger!' Stanton roared. 'I want a picture of an Adonis, though you've sod all between your legs.'

The model replied savagely, 'Neither would you in this bloody temperature. Turn on the heating.'

'It's lovely and warm in here,' Stanton said, trying to ignore his nose running with the cold. 'If you want heating, it'll have to come off your posing fee.'

'Jesus — '

'Won't help you now,' Stanton responded evenly. 'Which is it to be? A little discomfort or penury?'

The models put up with Stanton because he was famous. And not just for his meanness; his work was legendary. If you posed for Stanton Feller it was more than likely someone would remember your face or your not-so-private parts on the walls of the Royal Academy or in a Cork Street window. And that would mean more work. The life of a model was always erratic, long hours in cold studios spent holding poses, little comfort and little thanks. If the work went well, fine, if it went badly, it meant tempers and withheld fees.

'Don't take it out on me, you bastard,' one of Stanton's male models screamed. 'You owe me money. I worked for it.'

'You didn't keep still for a fucking second! You were useless,' Stanton replied, pouring himself a sherry and topping it up with vodka, his usual mixture.

'Just because the picture went badly, don't use me as your whipping boy,' the man replied, pulling on his clothes. 'You owe me fifteen quid.'

Stanton flinched, put down his drink and went behind a screen to unlock his cashbox. A wealthy man, he was stupidly foolish with money, alternately spending it and hoarding it, his meanness never extended to himself. Carefully he peeled off a ten pound note and a five pound note and then relocked the box. He then walked to the toilet with the model in hot pursuit, holding the two notes over the bowl.

'Aw, come on, Stanton, give me a break.'

'You're a lousy model, with a sagging behind,' Stanton replied. 'But as I do owe you the money, I will pay you as I think fit.' He dropped the money into the lavatory bowl and then calmly urinated over it. The notes sank below the water level and as both men watched them sink, Stanton grabbed the toilet chain.

'Well, aren't you going to rescue them?'

The man blinked disbelievingly. 'Piss off.'

'I already have,' Stanton replied deftly as he made a move to pull the chain.

In desperation the model jumped forward to stop him and then, swearing, dipped his hand into the bowl.

Of course the story could have been apocryphal, but Isabel was inclined to believe it. Yet if Stanton was so disgusting, how could her father have cared for him so much? The cultured David Hall, the kind David Hall, how *could* he have remained friends with such a monster unless, in that monster, there was some semblance of a good man? But then again, what if her father had been wrong? Isabel shifted her position on the couch. What if he had been taken in by Stanton? After all, Eleanor didn't trust the artist, and her mother loathed him.

The thought of her mother stopped Isabel in her tracks and her eyes moved back to the painting. Having been protected by her father all her life, she had little experience of the outside world, except in snatches. But those snatches had been safe; at seventeen the only way a girl could be safe in such circles was to have her protector, and her father had always been that. But now he was gone, and Eleanor could not fill his role.

Neither could her mother. Not that Virginia even wanted the job. She wanted her daughter to follow her, to continue the good name. What her mother offered was a life spent as a perpetual also ran, playing Dr Watson to Virginia's Sherlock Holmes. Isabel's fingernails dug into the couch. No, her father had told her she was unique, a one off. She had her own life to live, not as someone's heir. She had her own beginning and end. I want to be a painter, she thought, knowing the idea was improbable, wildly romantic, hugely ambitious.

'But I want it,' she said aloud.

How long would it take her? How long before she exhibited? And what if she never did? What if it was just a childish dream? What if she had to live the tough reality of the average artist's life, having to take on a job to support her hobby, or follow a career which only left her free to paint on Sundays or holidays, as a little treat. How nice, people would say, it's always good to have an interest.

'No!' she said out loud. 'My father didn't make this studio for nothing. Not for a hobby.'

The word rankled inside her. Hobby. To be an amateur painter . . . No, she was going to prove them all wrong. She wasn't going to take the easy way out and cheat herself and her father. But how could she begin? Apply for entrance to the Royal Academy Schools? To the Slade? She wracked her brains. Neither Portento or Stanton

Feller had attended art school, but had been apprenticed with Salvatore Dimitrious. They had learned the hard way, mixing paints for the master, taking abuse, and watching him.

Isabel had met the old painter when she was a child. Dimitrious had smelt, and he dribbled as he spoke. An old man in a high backed chair with a nun looking after him. Frightened, she had backed away from him.

Her father had stopped her: 'Look at him again,' he had whispered. 'Forget that he smells, that his eyes are clouded with cataracts. He sees . . . ' David Hall had tapped his forehead, ' . . . inside, and he remembers. He thinks of the beautiful women he knew, and his children who sat eating oranges as he worked. He dribbles because he is old, not because he is stupid.'

Isabel glanced back at the ruined, blind painter. His head thrust forwards to catch her words as she moved towards him and placed a bowl of fresh oranges in his lap.

He said nothing, but his hands picked up the fruit and he smelt it, and then he wept, his tears running down the orange peel which was as smooth as the cheek of a child.

8

'Isabel? Isabel? Come down, dear, I want a word with you.'

This is it, Isabel thought as she hurried down the corridor into her mother's bedroom. The window was open, the cool April air rushing in and making the room chilly. On her dressing table was a bonsai tree, tiny and perfect, and on the walls were prints brought back from her many trips. This was Virginia's room, not shared with her husband — they had slept apart for many years — and it was curiously uncomfortable. Isabel smiled and sat on the edge of the bed.

'Oh, don't, dear, the cleaner's just made it.'

Isabel jumped up, scolded.

'Not that it matters,' Virginia said lamely, already cursing herself for her awkwardness. 'If you want to, you can sit there.'

'No . . . I'll sit here,' Isabel said, lowering herself into an easy chair by the unused fireplace. Her mother sat on the dressing table stool and faced her.

Quite a young woman, she thought, appraising her daughter. Handsome too. A little scruffy, but that was to be expected, all children go through an untidy phase. Good features, regular, she should marry well. Not like her, picking David Hall . . . Virginia's smile was like a piece of glass crystal.

'Well . . . so you're all right, are you?'

'Fine.'

'Not too unhappy? I mean, about your father . . . ' Virginia glanced away. A clock chimed below. 'It was very wrong of him . . . to do what he did.'

Isabel's face tensed. No, she thought, don't respond, or she will punish you for it. You need her on your side, don't antagonise her.

'He left us alone, I'm afraid,' Virginia went on, trying to sound plaintive, but failing. All that came out was irritation and a hint of anger. 'But we have the house, and plenty of money . . . '

Fair exchange, no robbery, Isabel thought with a stab of agony.

'Life goes on . . . ' she continued lamely. 'Eleanor copes very well while I'm away, even if she does some odd things. That cousin of hers, for example . . . ' Her thoughts trailed off elsewhere for a moment before she rallied. 'You see, I have to work, dear, it's what I do best.'

'I know, Mother.'

'Yes, well . . . '

Silence.

'It's not just the money.'

'No.'

' . . . but I need the stimulus, and besides the money does help to pay for your schooling.'

Isabel prompted her mother with a smile.

'Speaking of which, we should talk about your future. I was thinking — '

'I want to be a painter.'

'Quite . . . ' Virginia said stupidly. 'However, that can be something to sort out later, when you've got your degree.'

'I want to be a painter.'

106

'After you get your degree you can paint — '

'I want — '

'Oh, for God's sake! Don't say that again, Isabel!' Virginia snapped, getting to her feet and straightening a print on the wall. 'I want you to go to university.'

Isabel's voice was soft. 'No.'

'But you have to. I went to university — '

'Is that the only reason I should go?' her daughter replied quietly. Reasonably. Don't lose your temper. Be wise. The words resounded in her head as though her father were speaking to her. 'Please, Mother, please let me do this, it means so much to me. I can be a success.'

'No one ever makes a living as a painter.'

'But I want to make a name as well as a living,' Isabel reasoned. 'We have the money, you said so yourself. If I went to university you would be supporting me for years, so what is the difference if I train as a painter instead of taking a degree?'

'You come from a good family, that's the difference.'

Isabel frowned. 'What?'

Her mother's voice was hard-edged. 'There is no respect for painters. They're a dirty, rough crowd. No one takes them seriously — '

'Unless they happen to be Portento or Stanton Feller.'

Virginia's eyes flicked pure steel. 'They are the exceptions, and you can hardly want to follow Stanton Feller's example.'

'He's a great painter.'

'He's a vile man,' her mother responded vehemently, her snobbery awesome. 'You *can't* want that kind of life for yourself. I refuse to believe it.'

'I don't want his kind of life, just his kind of success,' Isabel countered. 'Please let me try. What's the harm in it? If I fail, not that I will, but *if* I do, then I'll do as you say. I'll go to university, anything. But let me try this first . . . Oh, Mother,' she said, getting to her feet and walking over to Virginia. 'I could do it, I really could succeed.'

Mother and daughter faced each other, perfectly matched in height and determination. No, Isabel thought, I'm not going to weaken, this is my life I'm fighting for, and my father's dream.

'Isabel,' Virginia said finally. 'I'll do a deal with you.'

The girl listened and waited.

'I'll give you a time limit to prove yourself,' Virginia said carefully. 'You have eighteen months.'

Shaken, Isabel looked into her mother's eyes and tried to read the expression. Does she know? Or was it a random time limit she had picked? Is this her way to punish me for defying her wishes? Or something more disturbing?

'I agree,' she said at last.

★   ★   ★

'Eighteen months! No one could pick that time limit out of a hat,' Eleanor said crisply when Isabel recounted the conversation later. 'Your mother must have known about the letter all along.' Carefully she laid down her shopping on the hall table and took off her coat, her thoughts

108

running on. 'So if she did know, maybe that's why she got pregnant . . . ' A slow smile spread across her lips. 'Your mother might be a remarkable woman.'

'Or a cruel one,' Isabel responded. 'If she did know about the letter, why did she leave it until the time was nearly up before getting pregnant?'

Eleanor's eyebrows rose. 'She was forty when she had you. Perhaps she found it difficult to conceive.'

'And perhaps she waited deliberately. To punish him.'

'Don't assume the worst,' Eleanor said quickly, but without conviction, as she picked up her shopping. Thoughts buzzed in her head. If Virginia had known about the letter, why hadn't she come to her? Why hadn't they joined forces to save David? It would have been so much easier for both of them. If Virginia had known it would have been the normal thing to do, to look for help near at hand. Eleanor shook her head, she can't have known . . . but surely, she must have, or she wouldn't have given herself away to Isabel so obviously. Eleanor rubbed her forehead as a slow anger growled inside her. What the hell are you playing at, Virginia? For years Eleanor had lived with a woman she thought she knew well, but now there were doubts which wouldn't go away. If Virginia had fooled her for so long, she must have fooled David too . . . If she could be so clever at hiding her feelings what else could she hide?

'Can I help?'

Eleanor dropped the jar she was holding and spun round.

'God, I'm sorry, I didn't hear you, I was miles away.'

Isabel smiled and bent down to mop up the jam on the tiled floor. 'It's a good job Mother is too — you've just smashed a tile with that bottle.'

★ ★ ★

School was not hard to leave behind, and although Isabel did well in her A levels, she had lost all real interest in her academic studies. David's death had killed any scholastic ambitions, and though she went through the motions, she longed to follow Prossie into the outside world. Always restless, Prossie had gone abroad with her brother and now they seemed to be travelling the world on a shoestring and bumming off any unfortunate who offered them shelter. Being handsome and amusing, Prossie and Bentley Leonard found a shelter in every port, and regaled Isabel with elaborate stories on the backs of crumpled postcards.

Went to Rome to be a muse, visited Florence but your old friend Portento wasn't interested. Ugly sod. Love, Prossie. Often the postcards included an addendum from Bentley: *Prossie covered in gnat bites, looks hideous, not even the Italians fancy her at the moment.* Then one card rang a warning bell in Isabel's head. *Met that artist, Stanton Feller, in Germany. Ignorant, but thinks I'm wonderful. Seeing him in London when I get back. Love, Prossie.*

After that, nothing. No cards arrived at the

school, and no phone calls. As Isabel's last term at Oakdean drew to a close, she still expected news from Prossie, but had to admit that her silence was not really surprising. Her old friend had gone off and made her own life — just as Isabel intended to do.

Almost one month after the conversation with her mother, Isabel packed her portfolio with all her latest drawings and, shaking with nerves, rolled up the dry canvas of Eleanor's portrait and slid it into a carrying tube. Then she walked down to the hall with her overnight bag and stood, looking like a lost child.

Eleanor saw her from the study doorway. 'Come here, pet, I've got something for you.'

Isabel followed her as she moved back into the study and over to her father's desk. 'Oh, God, I don't want to go,' she said suddenly, childishly.

'Have you got Mrs Harrod's address?' she asked. Isabel was to stay with Geoffrey's wife overnight in Kensington, then after her interview she would take the train back to Yorkshire. It was simple, but Eleanor's heart was banging with nerves. 'Ring me when you get there. Are you sure you don't want me to come with you?'

'You can't leave The Ridings, Blair couldn't cope alone, you know that.' She paused. 'I don't want to go,' she said quietly, her face pale with anxiety, 'I don't think my work is good enough.'

'Nonsense!' Eleanor replied briskly. 'It's better than anyone's. That Stanton Feller's got a surprise coming to him.'

'Maybe I should phone and make an appointment.'

Eleanor frowned. 'No, we agreed that it would be better for you just to turn up unannounced. He's an old friend of your father's, he'll help.'

'But he's so . . . ' Isabel trailed off, suddenly the journey to London seemed terrifying.

'He's a great painter and you want to be a great painter, so stop being so wet,' Eleanor said quickly, turning to the window as she heard a car blasting its horn. 'There's your taxi.' She caught hold of Isabel's hand and pressed a letter into it. 'It's not your birthday until Thursday, but I thought you should have this now. It's from your father.' Isabel's eyes looked disbelievingly at her aunt as she continued. 'The lawyer delivered it yesterday, so he would be with you . . . ' She stopped, her voice failing her, and ushered Isabel into the hall.

Isabel's eyes were huge. 'A letter from Daddy?'

Eleanor nodded. 'He wrote a great many — '

'Where are they?' Isabel asked desperately. 'I want them.'

Eleanor shook her head. 'In the will David said that you were to be given one a year, on your birthday, and at no other time — '

Stunned, Isabel gripped her aunt's arm: 'Let me have them! *All* of them. Please . . . '

'I can't, love,' Eleanor said softly. 'The solicitor has them, and he has to abide by David's instructions. One letter every year, on your birthday.'

Isabel glanced at her father's familiar handwriting and the letter shook in her hand.

'How many are there?'

Her aunt shrugged. 'I don't know, sweetheart.'

112

Resigned, Isabel nodded and gripped the letter tightly, unable to speak.

Moved by her niece's obvious distress, Eleanor guided her to the door gently. 'Come on,' she said, leading Isabel out to the taxi.

Slamming the car door closed she leaned through the open window. 'Blair wishes you luck, so do I, we're all with you, sweetheart, every step of the way.' She paused, 'And your father is too.'

The taxi pulled away before Isabel could answer.

★   ★   ★

She did not read the letter until she was ready for bed. After ringing Eleanor to say she had arrived safely, Isabel ate with Mary Harrod and then was shown to her room. For an instant her rising panic almost made her sick and she sat down, clutching the bedcovers in her hands. I can't go, she thought, he'll be horrible to me, he'll throw me out and say I have no talent. And he might be right . . . She stopped herself, pulling on her courage. No, he'll say I'm good, he'll help.

Her aloneness shook her. In a strange room, waiting for the morning, her clothes seemed naive, her work infantile as she looked at it and then pushed it back into the portfolio with disgust. It was then she took her father's letter out of her handbag, carefully opening the envelope and pulling out the piece of paper. Before she read it she smelt it, and her father seemed suddenly in the room with her.

'Oh Daddy,' she said helplessly and began to read.

Darling Knuckles,
 Happy Birthday, my darling. You're eighteen now, and how pretty I can't imagine, but I just know I would have been so proud of you. Eighteen years old. Quite an age, isn't it? I wonder what you've learned already. A great deal, I know, and some of it too soon. Forgive me for that.
 Can you hear my voice? Concentrate, darling, it's there for you, talking to you. This way I'm with you wherever you are. And *where* exactly are you now? At school, or in the studio, or where? Is Ivor with you? Or Eleanor? Or are there people there I've never known? It doesn't matter, whoever is with you is blessed, as I was, by your company.
 Happy Birthday, my lovely child, remember the four wishes and use them wisely. I miss you, I miss you with all my heart, but with my heart I speak to you now. Never doubt that I loved you, and know that I am close to you always.

Your father,

David Hall

She slept with the letter in her hand.

★ ★ ★

The day was thick with mist and heavy drizzle as Isabel showered and made her way downstairs for breakfast. Mary Harrod was already up, talking very quickly as people do who have a great deal on their mind.

'Cereal all right, dear?'

'Fine,' Isabel said.

'Will you be in for dinner?' she asked, laying aside some post and smiling absently.

Isabel fielded the question deftly. 'It's very kind of you to let me stay here.'

'Oh, it's no problem. I've been friendly with your mother for years, and of course she and Geoffrey are inseparable. Good team work . . . You must never worry, if you need to come down to London again there is always a bed for you here.' She glanced at the post again. 'I have some committee work to do, I wonder if you would mind — '

'Of course not,' Isabel said eagerly, wanting to be on her own. 'See you later.'

After three cups of coffee Isabel decided that she finally had to leave and checked her reflection in the hall mirror, putting on some lipstick and then wiping it off again hurriedly. The result made her lips look unnaturally dark and she felt self-conscious as she walked down Airlie Gardens, putting out her arm timidly to hail a taxi as she had seen her father do so many times. But the cab went past and, mortified, she glanced around to see if anyone had noticed her failure. Apparently no one had, so, for the second time, she put out her hand and this time a taxi stopped. A small feeling of triumph welled up in her as she rode along, although it was soon extinguished by their quick arrival at Stanton Feller's house.

Surprised, Isabel clambered out of the taxi and dropped her portfolio, struggling with her purse to get the money out. The driver waited with a look of resignation and then drove off hurriedly, just missing running over the case. Angrily, Isabel snatched it up and wiped the dirt off with a tissue before walking through the gate at the back of the house. Two bells had written labels beside them: Residence and Studio, and without pausing she lifted her finger to press the second.

Then she stopped. Dropped her finger from the bell and sat down on the window ledge, her portfolio on her lap, her courage failing her.

'GET OFF THE BLOODY ARCHITECTURE!' a voice shouted from above.

Isabel leapt to her feet and looked up. 'Mr Feller?'

'DOESN'T LIVE HERE ANY MORE.'

She frowned. 'But . . . '

'HE'S GONE. DIED SUDDENLY,' the voice bellowed, slamming down the upstairs window.

Isabel felt acutely embarrassed. She had not been able to see the owner of the voice, and he could not see her, but she knew it was Stanton Feller and wondered helplessly what to do next. She could ring the bell, of course, but what could she say? And besides, it was humiliating to have to carry on a conversation in public, especially when he was shouting so loudly.

A minute passed before she plucked up courage to ring the studio bell.

'WHAT!'

She jumped back. 'I have to talk to you.'

'COME UP TO THE BLOODY INTER-COM. I CAN'T HEAR YOU.'

Isabel shuffled towards the mesh. 'I said — '

'DON'T SHOUT, I CAN HEAR YOU ALL RIGHT.'

'I said,' she continued softly, 'that I've come to see you. It's Isabel, Isabel Hall.'

'DAVID'S GIRL?'

'Yes.'

'DON'T BE BLOODY SILLY, SHE'S UP IN YORKSHIRE.'

'No, I've come down to London to see you.'

'CAN'T BE THE ISABEL I KNEW, SHE'S AT SCHOOL.'

Isabel's patience snapped. 'Oh, do let me in, I've come a long way and I feel stupid talking to a damn machine!'

Immediately a buzzer sounded and the door swung open.

Cautiously Isabel moved in and let her eyes adjust to the lack of light. There was some kind of staircase with illumination at the top, and the smell of paint and turps was powerfully strong. As she climbed, struggling with her portfolio and the tube with the canvas rolled up in it, she was met by Stanton's face leering over the banister rail.

'By God, it is too. It's David's little girl.'

Isabel smiled and walked into the full light of the studio, four half-finished portraits staring at her from their easels, a kettle whistling on the table at the back.

117

'Dump your stuff on the couch, Isabel,' Stanton said, leaning back and watching his visitor. 'You're looking good.' His hand went out and he caught hold of her, pulling her to him. Quickly his lips found hers and his tongue tried to prise her teeth apart. Isabel struggled and then punched him deftly in the small of his back.

Stanton released her immediately. 'Good God, mind the bloody kidneys!' he said, rubbing his lower back. 'You could have injured me.'

'I could have done *what?*' she replied, anger raising her voice, her face red with embarrassment.

'Tea?' he asked calmly, as though nothing had happened.

Wrong-footed, Isabel did not know how to react. Common sense told her to run, but her ambition told her to stay. She touched her lips, repelled by him.

'I came to see you — '

'Yes, I can see that,' he said impatiently, 'but do you want tea?'

'Yes, all right,' she replied, unzipping her portfolio and flipping back the cover. 'I want your help.'

He moved towards her and she stepped back. 'Are you a virgin?' he asked.

Isabel swallowed and gestured towards her work. 'Please, look.'

'Oh, I am,' he replied, staring at her.

She stuttered uncomfortably. 'Listen, I want to know what you think.'

'Actually I don't think you do,' he replied, 'it might shock you.'

118

It had been a stupid idea, she realised. His reputation was correct, Stanton Feller was a pig. All she had to do now was get out. She was disappointed, in a strange way not for herself but for her father; he would never have believed that his friend would have acted this way. Her gestures were clumsy, inept, and she fumbled with the zip to close the portfolio as he watched her.

'Oh, don't go so soon.'

'I think I ought to. It was a mistake. You see I was looking for someone else. He was a greater painter, not a seedy old man.'

A slow handclapping started from the other end of the room. Surprised, Isabel glanced round and blinked, unable for a moment to believe her eyes. Dark-skinned from plenty of sun, her hair heavy over her shoulders, Prossie stood draped in a sheet. The artist's muse, at last.

'On the ball, Isabel, on the ball as ever.'

Stanton dropped the act immediately and shrugged, going out of the room as Isabel sat down on the side of the dais and looked at her old friend. Prossie was magnificent, there was no denying that, sexually streetwise and full of warmth. Yet for all her wisecracks, she was obviously devoted to Stanton.

'He's kind, you'll see. He's just being the *artist* now.' Her heavy-lidded eyes rolled dramatically.

'But you and he . . . you're not . . . ' Isabel trailed off, embarrassed.

'Lovers?' Prossie laughed, not unkindly. 'Sure we are.' A toilet flushed in the hallway outside to herald the artist's return. 'The Master's Voice,' she said, gesturing to the doorway. 'I wonder what his mood will be now, lady killer, misunderstood artist, or father figure?'

Stanton walked in and dug his hands into his pockets, standing before Isabel and looking down at her. 'Well, I think I'd better have a glance at your work, don't you?'

'Father figure,' Prossie whispered into Isabel's ear and they both burst out laughing.

He ignored them and lifted the portfolio on to his work table, pushing back a stack of brushes and rags. Isabel studied his face: brown hair thinning on top, aquiline nose, slack jawline, but a well-shaped mouth, now almost attractive as he began to smile. Not at her, at her work.

'Yes, yes, this is good.' He picked up another. 'But this is shit!' he said, ripping it in half.

Isabel leapt forwards. '*Hey!*'

He looked at her sharply. 'D'you want to be a painter, or a hack?' He pushed the torn pieces into her hand. 'Go on then, stick them together again. I said it was shit and it is. You don't want anything below standard.' He glanced back to the sketches. 'Jesus, your father should have told you that.' He lit a cigarette and inhaled, then pointed to the carrying tube on the floor. 'What's in that?'

'A painting.'

He raised his eyes. 'No! I thought maybe it was a horse and cart.'

'Oh, lay off, Stanton, give her a break.'

He snatched up the tube, while Prossie winked at Isabel. Carefully he pulled out the canvas and unrolled it. He said nothing, just pinned it to a board and put it on one of his easels. For a long time he just stared, without speaking, then he picked up a brush and dabbed a little paint on it. Isabel moved forward to stop him, but Stanton pushed her away with his arm.

'What the hell are you doing?' Prossie asked.

'Shut up!'

She ignored him. 'You can't — '

'Oh, go out, will you?' he snapped. 'Both of you! Get out. Don't come back for an hour.'

Isabel opened her mouth but Prossie put her hand over it and jerked her head towards the next room. Silently Isabel followed her, watching as Prossie pulled off the sheet and tugged on a pair of Levis and a checked shirt. Her naked body was fuller than usual, heavier.

When Prossie caught Isabel looking at her, she smiled. 'I'm pregnant.'

'Oh God.'

'No, Stanton,' she said, grinning and linking arms with Isabel. 'You want to see round the house?'

'You're only eighteen, Prossie.'

'Nineteen, don't you remember? I was stupid, that's why I was in your class. The thickhead.' She tapped her forehead, although her tone was ironic.

'How old is Stanton?' Isabel asked and Prossie took her round into the main house.

'Fifty-one.'

'Oh . . . '

Prossie nudged her and smiled. 'What's age to an artist?' she asked, throwing open the double doors and ushering Isabel into a large room,

121

which was light, airy, the walls whitewashed and hung with several of Stanton's paintings. One of them was an impressive nude of Prossie. A huge fireplace filled nearly half of one wall, with seats on either side, a collection of feathers in a glass case on the mantelpiece.

'He gets them from all over the world,' Prossie said admiringly. 'I bought him that one from Japan.' She tugged at Isabel's sleeve. 'Look — he has your mother and father's books.' She stopped talking, her head on one side. 'He still weeps when he thinks about your father sometimes.'

'Really?' Isabel said simply.

Prossie shrugged. 'D'you know why he did it?'

The question was an uncomfortable one. 'No.'

'I wouldn't have thought he would kill himself. Was he depressed or something?'

'No.'

'Sick?'

'No.'

Prossie turned, and seeing the rigid look on her friend's face, changed the subject. 'Bentley got married, you know, to some heiress in Nice. Well, she said she was an heiress, but I think she was just a twenty-four-carat liar.'

'Do you think Stanton likes my work?' Isabel asked, glancing back to the paintings on the wall.

'Oh, yes. Otherwise he would have got rid of you by now. People come every day to see him, they want to be students, although he doesn't take on pupils any more.' She stopped, suddenly wise. 'Oh . . . was that why you came?'

Isabel smiled ruefully. 'Yes . . . I thought . . . well, anyway.'

'You see he has so much work to do, he can't give time to pupils,' Prossie said, genuinely distressed. 'He tried but he gets so angry with them — it wouldn't be fair on you.'

'Yes,' Isabel said woodenly. What else was there to say? Her hopes were finished, torn to pieces like the sketch in the studio. The disappointment winded her, she had been so sure that he would take her on. She had been so sure . . .

'You could take the entry exam for the Royal Academy or the Slade.'

'I know.'

'Or maybe go and see someone else. Like Portento, for instance.'

Isabel thought of the ugly Italian and felt the cold breeze of rejection again. No, not Portento, not so far away from home. Here was where she should be, here or nowhere.

'He may suggest someone else . . . he knows loads of people,' Prossie said helpfully, jumping as the intercom sounded.

'GET BACK IN HERE,' Stanton bellowed.

She glanced at Isabel. 'Follow my lead and we'll eat at the Caprice tonight.'

The painting was still on the easel, but ruined. Isabel looked at it and her eyes filled with a mixture of disbelief and anger. How could he do it? How? Eleanor's features were gone, instead a stranger looked back, the colours altered, the background made fashionable. All her individuality was destroyed; and instead of skill the canvas smacked of slickness.

'What have you done!' she howled, looking at

123

Stanton with hatred. 'That was my picture, you bastard. Not yours. How dare you!' Her eyes moved back to the painting, her chest exploding with rage. 'You've made it mediocre. Worse, you've made it yours and it's *mine*. I thought I wanted to be your pupil, but you can't teach me.'

Stanton caught hold of her arm. She tried to shake him off, but he held on to her.

'Correction, I *can* teach you. You are just the kind of painter I can teach. You stand up for your work, and you know what's bad.' He shook her. 'I ruined your painting, but you had the guts to know it, and to tell me. You want to work with me? You want to be my pupil?'

Angrily, Isabel nodded.

'Right,' he said, pushing one of his own brushes into her hand. 'Now start again.'

They worked unceasingly until late that afternoon, until the light failed. Stanton cursed Isabel and she returned his threats, word for word. She saw how the light altered the tones of Prossie's skin, and noticed how her chin relaxed when she fell asleep. Working on an easel beside Stanton, she drove herself on until her back ached and her hands stiffened with tiredness as she fought to keep up with him. He watched her, pushed her, harder than her father had done, and with less kindness, but he saw in her something unusual and he was artist enough to encourage it.

'Wake up!' he said, tapping the sleeping Prossie with the toe of his bare foot. He always worked barefooted, he said it made him keep in touch with reality; actually it kept him cold enough to stay awake. 'Get back into the pose, darling. You're my muse.'

'I'm tired,' Prossie grumbled. 'Can't we eat?'

'Later,' he promised. 'Later.'

Later came and went. Later came when the light failed and the blinds came down in the studio. The kettle whistled for endless mugs of tea, the telephone was ignored, the defeated footsteps of visitors dismissed as unimportant. Only the work mattered, and in that work Stanton and Isabel communicated. His language coarsened with irritation; she stood up to it. He cursed her for stupidity; she countered with a deft brushstroke. And he knew he had met his artistic match. A lot to learn, of course, but Isabel Hall had Windsor and Newton's Cadmium Red for blood, and blood will out . . .

'So, let's look,' he said finally, laying down his own brushes and glancing at her canvas for the thousandth time. 'What a frigging mess,' he said, glancing to her and catching hold of her hair. Gently he kissed her forehead and added, 'You've a long way to go, kiddo. But I'm game if you are.'

'Thank God,' Prossie said, stretching. 'Now can we eat?'

9

Isabel moved in with Prossie and Stanton Feller. The arrangement was greeted with horror by Virginia but by the time she returned to England she could do little about it as her daughter was already firmly ensconced in Holland Park. Measured outrage poured down the phone and only the timely intervention of Eleanor prevented her from physically going down to London and hauling her daughter home.

'She's over eighteen, you have no legal control over her.'

Virginia was all freezing hostility. 'I should have thought you would stop her. You knew what she was doing — going to that man.'

'She went to see him as a teacher, not a lover — '

'Eleanor!' Virginia snapped furiously. 'This is not a joking matter.'

Her sister-in-law regarded her thoughtfully. She seemed unduly upset, even considering the circumstances. 'She's just learning from him, Virginia, he's taken her on as an apprentice. Besides,' Eleanor added, 'she's quite safe, he's involved with someone else.' She didn't say whom; that would have been too much for her sister-in-law to bear.

'No doubt he is, he's generally running around with some tart.' She rearranged the cushions on the settee in the drawing room, fussing over

126

details. 'I don't like the idea one little bit, and I hold you responsible.' She turned to her sister-in-law, one hand resting heavily on the silken back of a chair. 'David would not have approved.'

Eleanor bristled. She knew better than Virginia what would have met with her brother's approval. Her good temper snapped off like a dry twig in a gale. 'I think my brother would have seen the situation in a clearer light — '

'Your brother!' Virginia snorted. 'What *would* your precious brother have done? I'll tell you what — he would have done nothing. Nothing!' Her voice rose. 'He had no guts, he couldn't stand up to life. He ducked his responsibilities. He killed himself — '

'Why, Virginia?' Eleanor's face was flushed, her hands itching to strike the brittle woman in front of her. '*Why* did he do it? I've often wondered, especially after you told Isabel she had eighteen months to prove herself.' Her voice darkened, she looked suddenly formidable. Not like herself at all. 'Eighteen months was an odd time limit to set, wasn't it? Was there a particular reason for it, Virginia?'

Her sister-in-law's eyes flickered. But she said nothing. The moment when she could have answered swung in the air between them, then passed. Eleanor knew the chance had gone, just as Virginia did.

'We shouldn't fight,' Virginia said with a tight smile. 'It serves no purpose. We have to learn to live together happily here.'

'Especially as half the house is mine,' Eleanor countered, unwilling to let bygones be bygones.

'Yes,' Virginia agreed, the barb prickling under her skin. If David had been sensible, she thought, he would have left the house to her alone and Eleanor would be off in some village cottage somewhere. Her *and* her damn cousin. 'We have to get along. Work together.'

'To what end?' Eleanor asked, not willing to let her off the hook.

'Oh, don't be difficult!' Virginia replied, irritation in her every word. 'I've never got under your feet, have I? I've never interfered in the running of this place.'

'You never wanted to, you were happier travelling.'

'To earn money for us!'

Eleanor laughed. 'Oh, don't take me for a complete fool, Virginia. You know as well as I do that you want power and glory — and being a wife and mother could never have given you that. Your career does though, that's why it's important to you.'

'It's always easier for stupid people to try and undermine achievement.'

The slap stunned her. She hadn't expected it; hadn't even had a chance to register Eleanor's quick movement before the hand made contact with her cheek. Her skin blazed with pain.

'How dare you!'

'Don't ever patronise me again, Virginia, or by God, you'll live to regret it.'

Blair was in the garden when he heard Virginia's car on the gravel driveway. Happily he waved to her but she ignored him and his smile faded, his head hanging as he walked to the kitchen door. Carefully he pulled off his boots, then hitched up his socks and pushed open the kitchen door. Ivor raised his head, his tail wagging twice before he fell back to sleep. Miserably Blair pulled some cheese out of the fridge and began to make himself a sandwich, cutting the bread unevenly.

'Oh, come on, I'll do that for you,' Eleanor said, pushing him aside.

'She didn't wave.'

'Who didn't?' she asked, knowing full well.

'Mrs Hall,' Blair replied forlornly.

To have to come to Virginia's defence was galling, but it was the only way to console Blair. 'She can't have seen you, dear. She said I was to say goodbye.'

He brightened automatically. God, how simple it is for him, Eleanor thought, having a child's speed of recovery. She passed him the sandwich and he picked it up in his hard hands and bit into it greedily. You are so perfect, she thought, that it's probably only fair that you're disabled. Had you been a normal man with such looks you would have been spoiled, and you would have learned to spoil others. Men would have envied you, women would have wanted you, and you would have learned how easy it is to abuse good fortune.

'When's Isabel coming home?'

'Don't talk with your mouth full,' Eleanor said automatically, sitting next to him. 'She's going to be away for a while.'

He stopped eating, his disappointment obvious. 'How long?'

'A few weeks. She'll come and visit us soon though.'

His child's mind ran on. He thought of the girl who had spent time with him; who had stood up for him when someone said something outside the corner shop in the village. It was the last time she had ever had to do that, he thought, puffing up his chest. From then onwards he could stick up for himself — and for her.

He glanced behind him through the window to the studio in the stable block. Sometimes he had crept up there at night and tapped on the trap door, calling softly to her until she let him in. They had talked and sometimes she cried. Blair frowned, he found that difficult to understand, but it had something to do with her father, David. He had learned to listen and nod at times, and at other times she would glance over, her eyes suddenly crinkling with laughter, and mess up his hair with her hand.

'You think I'm crazy, don't you?' she asked.

Crazy, like he was. Two of them crazy . . . Was it possible that they were both crazy? The thought made him smile. He doubted it, he thought it was just another way of her being kind.

'I read the book. Well, some of it.'

Eleanor frowned, puzzled, as Blair put a tattered volume of poems on the kitchen table. 'I didn't give you that.'

'No,' he agreed, 'Isabel did. But that man's wrong — they talk to me.'

Eleanor was getting used to Blair's way of speaking, but she was still frequently confused.

His thought patterns were erratic, flicking from subject to subject, his speech often in shorthand.

Baffled, she asked, 'Who talks to you?'

'The man in the book says that they don't talk to him.' Blair pushed the paperback towards her and found the page, jamming his finger on a passage which read:

For some have heard the sirens' voices
Murmur, with their myriad choices
Murmuring — but not to me.

He paused. 'Well, I'm one of them.'

Eleanor concentrated hard, trying to follow his train of thought, but understanding eluded her. 'One of who, Blair?'

His patience was fraying. 'One of the ones the sirens murmur to!' He tapped his head. 'All day they murmur to me. Louder at night. I used to wonder what it was, but now I know. It's the sirens.'

Eleanor's heart shifted suddenly. She had been told that since his accident many years before Blair had had regular check-ups, and each time he had complained to the doctors about the noises in his head. Tinnitus, they called it, adding in an aside that it was incurable. Not that they told Blair that.

Most of the time he adjusted, but at times he had found the noises unbearable and would sit with his head in his hands, rocking slightly.

Her tone was gentle as she asked, 'Do they murmur every day, Blair?'

He nodded. 'Most days. Sometimes very

131

softly, other times real loud. They don't murmur to *him*,' he said dismissively, pointing to the book, 'but they do to me.'

* * *

As Prossie's pregnancy advanced, her intake of Turkish Delights confounded everyone.

'This kid will be born with its toes curled up,' Isabel said, rubbing Prossie's back as she lay on the bed.

'Oh, God, it aches. Do you think every woman goes through this to have a baby?' She glanced over her shoulder, grimacing. 'Have I got stretch marks? I can't get stretch marks, they'll ruin my figure.'

Isabel peered at her tanned skin. 'Not one. Honestly.'

'Stanton hates imperfection. He'd go off me like that,' Prossie clicked her fingers, 'if I lost my looks.'

'You won't,' Isabel assured her, knowing the awful truth of the words.

Ever since she had come to live with them, she had been well aware of the potent sexual attraction between Prossie and Stanton. It was palpable, so obvious that when they were in a room together she expected to be able to see it. What? A colour? Or a kind of sexual ectoplasm?

'What are you smiling at?' Prossie said, rolling over and pulling her dressing gown round her.

'I was thinking of you and Stanton,' Isabel replied, 'and wondering . . . '

'About our sex life?'

She nodded, surprisingly unembarrassed.

'We enjoy each other,' Prossie said, peeling an orange and giving half to Isabel as they sat on the bed. 'I like sex and he's an old lech.' She laughed. 'We're perfectly matched.'

'But don't you ever feel insecure?' Isabel wondered.

'Insecure?' Prossie repeated, frowning. 'Oh, you mean because we're not married?' She put her head on one side. Orange juice ran down the index finger of her right hand. 'Or because I'm having a baby?'

Isabel shifted her position. It had been tactless to bring the subject up.

'It's none of my business, forget I ever mentioned it — '

'But I don't mind talking about it. No, I don't feel unsafe. He could throw me out tomorrow, but then again I could leave him tomorrow. It's as broad as it's long.'

'But it's not the same. You would be alone, with a child.'

'I'd manage,' Prossie said easily.

'How? On what? You don't have any qualifications, or any money. How could you manage?'

Prossie blinked slowly, like a cat. 'I would cope.'

'How?'

'Dear God, are you my mother or something?' she snapped finally, all indolence gone. 'I would get by. I don't think about it. If I did I might panic.' Her eyes moved towards the pillow next to hers, and she touched it. 'I look at him while he sleeps. He's not too handsome, not too kind, but he's brilliant, and people admire him so much. Besides, I wanted to be an artist's muse and now I am. I don't know how long it will last, but I'm going to make the best of it.' She raised her eyebrows. 'Besides, I love him. I've got it bad . . . ' she parodied, ' . . . and that ain't good.'

'I'm glad . . . and I'm sorry if you thought I was prying.'

'Pry away,' Prossie said gaily. 'I don't mind, I'm glad you're here. You're the only female I could trust to knee him in the balls if he starts anything.'

'I couldn't live with that uncertainty,' Isabel said briskly. 'I find it difficult enough coping with his moods in the studio.'

She thought back to the day's work. Stanton had been irritable because a commission from the Fishmongers' Guild of London had fallen through. He had sworn violently at her, and at a small child who had come for a portrait, kicking his shoes across the studio and finally deserting his sitter. It had been left to Isabel to soothe the child and the child's mother, and she had resented it.

She turned back to Prossie. 'He acts like a spoiled kid sometimes.'

'Because that's what he is,' she replied. 'He has talent and because of that people *expect* him to behave badly. They *want* him to be shocking. And he has too little personality to resist the temptation.'

The following morning he was even more irascible. After she had displeased him for some minor misdemeanour he spat violently, the gobble

134

of spittle landing fair and square in Isabel's paint.

She regarded it thoughtfully, her stomach heaving, then she folded her arms and looked at her tutor.

'What's that supposed to mean?'

Stanton felt momentarily abashed; he had expected her to react furiously or cry, both responses being more usual than this patronising chill. For one disconcerting second he looked at her and saw Virginia Hall standing in her place.

'Oh, Christ, Isabel, don't go all snotty on me.'

'I rather expected that might be *your* next trick. After all, you've used all your other bodily excretions to make a point.' Her words shocked her and she thought of her father. What would he think of her now? Pride that she could stand up for herself? Or sorrow that she was growing up, and out of innocence? But I have to, Daddy, there is no other way.

'You have a very prissy streak to your nature,' Stanton said, turning away from her and pulling out a sheet of canvas. One finger jabbed peevishly at a corner. 'You missed that bit,' he said, delighted. 'When I say I want the bloody canvas primed, I mean primed all over, *and that means the flaming corners too.*'

Isabel took the canvas from him without comment. She hated his shouting, but had managed to adjust to it, accepting his tempers as a necessary adjunct to his tuition. In the four months since she had moved in she had learned a great deal — none of it expected but all of it valuable. Stanton had none of her father's appreciation of art as a culture, he saw it as a

135

talent to be exploited. That was all.

But for all his cynicism, his reputation held steady. Sitters came with regularity, climbing the dark back stairs to the studio, adjusting their clothes self-consciously as Stanton greeted them. He was usually polite, only on the odd occasion did he display childish tantrums to the people who paid him for his work. Normally he charmed them instead, although he did it heavy-handedly, leading women to the raised dais and sitting them down, flattering their clothes and their features, before padding back to the easel, his big dusty feet scuffing the floorboards.

Some of the visitors' eyes rested, mesmerised, on those bare feet. Others pretended not to notice; and Stanton never commented. Instead he worked quickly and skilfully, blocking in a head whilst chatting to the sitter and putting them at their ease. He gauged his customers well; he flirted where flirtation was expected; spoke articulately where intelligence was expected; and was silent when the sitter refused to respond to his banter.

'Dry old sod,' he would whisper to Isabel as he reached out for his palette, the sitter silent on the dais at the other end of the studio.

And if things were not going well, then God forbid that Isabel squeeze out the colours in the wrong order, or in different amounts. The pigments had to be arranged in a semi-circle on the palette, like a gluey rainbow, before Stanton would even pick it up. Then Isabel had to pass him his brushes, one by one, silently. If she gave him the wrong one, he simply threw it back over his shoulder, sometimes hitting her if she hadn't seen it coming. But otherwise, if all went well, the ritual was duly completed and Stanton would begin to paint.

On to the white canvas went the pigment, a brown halo painted round where the head would be so that he could gauge the flesh tones. Stanton's eyes would flick to the sitter, then to the canvas, then back again. Quickly the head took shape, a blur, a dreamscape without definite features.

'Move your chin up a little. Bit more. Lovely, hold it.'

The chin would go up, the sitter's eyes fixed on the artist in front of them. *Make me beautiful*, the women's eyes said. *Make me impressive*, the men's eyes said. Always the same message.

When things were really going well Stanton would carry on painting, continuing beyond the usual hour allocated for a sitting. Concentrating deeply, he would hold his breath, little grunts of exertion escaping his lips in snatches. Then the studio bell downstairs would ring, and Prossie would let in the next sitter, showing them into the lounge where they would wait their turn. And wait, and wait. Yet the sitters seldom complained, even the businessmen, for hadn't Stanton Feller painted Royalty? Being late for an appointment seemed a small price to pay for immortality.

★ ★ ★

The next model arrived half an hour later and walked in, coughing.

137

Stanton walked over to him. 'Put out your arms.'

The man stretched his arms before him. His veins looked purple as Stanton ran a finger down his skin.

'Good,' he said simply. 'I hate bloody dope heads.'

The man was unmoved. 'I'm here early, so where's the food?'

Deftly Stanton threw him a packet of crisps. 'Enjoy,' he said simply, beginning to paint.

The hours rolled on endlessly as Stanton painted and the model held his pose. Flesh the colour of dull pearl strained against tiredness; the model's face bland, without feeling, the limbs white against the dark couch, hands with dirty fingernails rubbing at tired eyes.

'Keep the pose!' Stanton snapped.

At two he scratched himself absent-mindedly.

'God, you bloody peasant!' Stanton shouted, raising his eyes at Isabel.

The hand dropped away immediately; the pose resumed, his attention wandering off into night thoughts as though he slept where he sat. Only Stanton remained busy. When he finally put down his brushes he padded barefooted over to the dais and pushed a ten pound note into the exhausted man's hand.

'Go and have a shower,' he said.

Isabel got up and stood before the canvas. 'Oh . . .' she said simply.

A sleeping man looked back at her. But not the model, someone infinitely more gentle. In that moment, Isabel Hall looked greatness in the face.

10

Isabel's progress was obvious; Stanton was pleased with her but would rather have died than admit it. She was David Hall's daughter, the child of his greatest friend, but more than that she was indebted to him — and he wanted to keep it that way. After all, there was a price to be paid for everything. If she knew she was impressing him then he would lose face, and Stanton hadn't the stomach for that.

He rolled over in bed, Prossie stirring in her sleep. A rush of genuine pleasure filled him. God, she was something, a woman any man would desire. But not when she was pregnant . . . Lifting the sheet off her sleeping form, Stanton looked at Prossie's naked belly, bloated, and at the blue veins in her breasts, the nipples dark and large. He touched her left breast gingerly; she stirred. Again he touched her, his excitement rising. Then suddenly he felt a quick kick against his arm.

Snatching back his hand he glanced at the moving flesh. Bloody kid's a killjoy, he thought wryly, leaning towards Prossie's stomach.

'Listen, buster,' he said quietly. 'Until you get out of there, what *I* say goes.' He tapped Prossie's stomach with a feather-light touch. The baby kicked back fiercely. 'So you want to fight, do you?' he asked, grinning broadly. 'Well, I've got news for you — '

'Is this a private conversation, or can anyone join in?' Prossie said, propping herself up on her elbows and laughing.

★   ★   ★

The Ridings was at its most magical in autumn, the long drive golden with late sunshine and fallen leaves. Blair waited patiently, leaning over the wrought-iron gate, his gaze scanning every car that passed. He counted until he got to thirteen and then lost interest, watching Ivor instead as he ran off after a rabbit in the next field.

Blair had kept up a nearly constant vigil since Isabel had gone to live in London, feeling the unexpected emotion of love-sickness. Was he in love? Only it was a child's love surely. Or so Eleanor prayed. She wasn't certain though; it was so difficult to know what Blair felt. His appearance was what made judgement difficult; he looked like a man, so perhaps he felt like one sexually? Did some kinds of love leapfrog mental age?

Perhaps she was worrying too much, but he seemed changed, and talked about Isabel a great deal, treasuring every one of her letters home. Blair read them avidly, not sharing them with Eleanor, but waiting for the post and stealing them to read alone in the garden. She scolded him for it, and he always handed the letter over, shamefaced, but after a few days he would be up early again, waiting for the post, and the whole episode would be repeated.

'Give me that,' Eleanor had said the day before, having been woken by Blair rising at six to meet the postman.

He hung on to the letter defiantly. 'No.'

'That letter is addressed to me,' Eleanor said calmly.

'And to me,' he countered.

'Then we'll both read it,' she replied, trying hard not to lose her temper as she put out her hand.

Blair hesitated, then opened the envelope himself. 'I'll read it to you,' he said simply.

Her anger seethed as he stumbled through the letter, word for word, agonising over the pronunciation of some names. Eleanor had a quick desire to snatch the letter, but resisted. With Blair only logic mattered; force was out.

'She's coming home tomorrow,' he said finally, passing the dog-eared paper to Eleanor. 'She's coming home.'

'Blair,' Eleanor said thoughtfully, 'you like Isabel, don't you?'

He nodded.

'She's like a sister to you, isn't she?' Eleanor suggested hopefully.

Blair's gaze was honest, open, as he said, 'Oh no, I love her.'

Feeling suddenly lightheaded, Eleanor got up and put on the kettle. The road to hell, she thought ruefully, is paved with good intentions. *He has the brain of a ten-year-old*, they had said, *he's gentle and he'll be no trouble.* Eleanor glanced at the man sitting rereading Isabel's letter. Well, maybe it's my own fault, maybe I was playing God, offering him a good home as though he was a needy animal, maybe my motives were suspect. I wanted company and help with the house and it seemed the ideal solution. A pliable boy in a man's body; someone easy to control. She smiled and shook her head, seeing a grim humour in the situation. Oh, David, she thought helplessly, what have I done now?

When the taxi finally came up the road Blair waved frantically, pulling open the gates and running behind the car as it drove towards the house. Dust blew up around his feet, his brown arms swinging as he drew up to her and lifted her high into the air.

'Hi!' Isabel shouted, laughing. 'That's some welcome.'

He lowered her to the ground, suddenly shy, and picked up her cases. 'Eleanor's waiting for you,' he said, glancing away from her.

Puzzled, Isabel ran towards her aunt and hugged her. 'What's the matter with Blair?' she asked, baffled when Eleanor started laughing.

They ate dinner in the dining room. Blair had showered, washed his hair and plastered it down on his head. Instead of his usual jeans and shirt, he wore a white polo-neck jumper and a pair of dark trousers, and toyed uncertainly with his wine glass.

Isabel was sparky with good humour. 'I'm getting better, I'll show you my new sketches.' She turned to Blair. 'You'll have to sit for me, you're much the best-looking model any painter could dream of.'

He dropped his glass immediately, the stem

snapped, wine pouring over the polished table. Gauche and miserable, he leapt to his feet and ran into the kitchen, the outer door banging closed as he made for the stable block and the studio above. Isabel and Eleanor followed him, the latter glancing through the kitchen window as the studio light went on.

'He'll sit there for hours.'

'Why?' Isabel said, bewildered.

'He's in love,' Eleanor said simply.

'Oh, with who?'

Her aunt turned and looked at her, raising her eyebrows. 'Think, Dumbo.'

'Me?'

'You.'

'Oh, God.' She sat down heavily. 'I thought he was . . . '

'Intellectually impaired?'

She nodded.

'Me too,' Eleanor agreed, 'but boys of ten fall in love hopelessly, all the time.'

'Poor Blair,' Isabel said, suddenly frustrated. 'It's never easy for some, is it? I mean, some people just fall in love and it all works out, and others it never happens for, or it happens with the wrong people . . . '

'What are your talking about?' Eleanor said patiently.

'Prossie,' Isabel replied, glancing away and going back into the dining room.

Her aunt followed her, watching her refill their two glasses and taking the one Isabel offered her. 'Can we talk?'

'Come upstairs,' she said, leading the way to

143

her bedroom. The room was heavy with the scent of late roses. A curtain blew by an open window and the bed was banked high with cushions. Isabel sat down and curled her legs under her, Eleanor resting her back against the headboard.

'So . . . talk.'

'Prossie's having Stanton's child, any time now. He's a womaniser, a vile man in some ways, but she adores him . . . she's quite prepared to have a baby unmarried, even though she knows that he could kick her out at any time.'

'So? That's her problem, not yours.'

'But it's . . . odd . . . that she's so happy.'

A breeze blew the curtain out; it swelled like Prossie's stomach and then fell back. Isabel struggled to find the words to describe the atmosphere between Stanton and Prossie, but once she had come across them talking; his arm had been around Prossie's waist, his fingers pressing into her flesh. She had turned and looked into his eyes, shaking back her hair, her glance certain, without doubt. Slowly she ran her tongue along her lips, then leaned forwards and ran her tongue along his lips also. His hand had tightened on her waist, fingers melting into her flesh. He had said something and she had put up her hands to touch his hair, drawing his face towards hers. The shadows had swallowed them whole.

Eleanor listened as Isabel recounted the incident, slowly, as though the words might bite her. Then she drained her glass.

'Sex.'

'Yes,' said Isabel, 'sex.'

'So you're curious. So what? Who wouldn't

144

be? Besides, you're in an environment where it's important. Stanton Feller always had an eye for the ladies — '

'But why Prossie?'

'You mean why not you?'

Isabel's face burned. 'No, I didn't mean that.'

'Oh don't get me wrong, sweetheart. I know you don't want Stanton, you'd be certifiable if you did — but you *do* want someone of your own.'

She nodded.

'It's difficult for you because of your father. He loved you so much and gave you so much attention that you grew to depend on it, and when that attention ended so suddenly you lost the man *and* the friend.' She touched Isabel on the shoulder. 'Someone will come for you. You're only nineteen, and you have such a lot in front of you.'

Isabel shook her head. She knew it was unfair to confide in her aunt; she knew she had no man of her own; but Blair's unhappiness and her own growing unease made her continue.

'Oh, Eleanor, I *can't* wait, I can't seem to think of anything else. I don't even enjoy the painting any more.'

Her aunt frowned. 'You have to work hard now, you have a chance many people would kill for.'

'To be what?' Isabel countered angrily. 'A famous painter, a success? What *is* that? I don't know . . . all I know is that I'm empty, I miss affection, closeness . . . ' Her eyes filled with sudden self-pity. 'I miss my father . . . '

Eleanor put down her glass and wrapped her arms round her niece. 'What you are feeling is normal, it's all part of growing up, but no one gets everything they want, Isabel.'

'Don't say that!'

'I will say it!' Eleanor snapped back. 'I will say it because it's true. You have talent and you could go a long way. What do you want other than that? To be Prossie? To be pregnant by a man old enough to be your father? To be forever wondering about the future?' She shook Isabel hard. 'No, that's not the way for you. Remember your father, he suffered, he wanted to do so many things and was so disappointed. He wouldn't want to see you like this. You have to succeed . . . Use Stanton Feller, learn from him, and concentrate on what matters now. The rest will follow in its own good time.'

'I'm lonely,' Isabel said finally.

Eleanor glanced away.

★ ★ ★

Blair waited, hoping that someone would come, but no one did. He sat on the couch in his best clothes and felt first foolish, then angry. With a quick movement he ruffled his washed hair and pushed up the sleeves of his jumper, then got to his feet. The studio was warm because the day had been a hot one, and a drowsy bee hummed against the skylight. Carefully he pulled out the piece of paper from his pocket and read it. The words seemed silly now, even to him, a silly poem which Isabel would have laughed at. He

146

tore it into little pieces, then opened the window and let the paper fall into the sleeping garden.

His throat ached with misery. Across the courtyard he could see the light blazing from an upstairs window, Eleanor's window, and he knew they were talking. About what? About him? Perhaps they were laughing . . . no, he decided, Isabel wouldn't laugh at him. Or would she? After being with her clever friends maybe she would, after all if she liked him even a little she would have come out to talk to him, to find out what was wrong. He would have done the same for her; he would have killed anyone for just looking at her in the wrong way.

Temper made him desperate and he began to pace the studio, looking at her drawings and her paintings and wanting to destroy them, to hurt them as she had hurt him. Blair moved towards the easel and looked at a half-finished picture supported there. His eyes narrowed and he cursed Isabel under his breath; cursed her for not comforting him; for not coming to see him; for humiliating him. He looked round hurriedly, finding a bottle of turps and hurling it at the canvas. It bounced against the cloth and fell to the floor shattering into pieces. Angrily he reached for the penknife next to her paints.

'Blair?'

He stopped, dropping his knife guiltily just as he heard Isabel's footsteps on the studio steps.

She paused on the top stair, her head on one side, smiling.

'Hello,' she said easily, putting her arms around him as he moved over to her, his head

147

resting against her own. 'So . . . ' she said kindly as they sat down on the couch, 'why don't you tell me what you've been doing while I've been away.'

He did so willingly, and she responded, offering affection as her father had always taught her to do. Blair didn't know that she had seen him try to destroy her work; that she had hung back and then re-entered, making her footsteps heavy enough to warn him of her approach. He didn't know — but Isabel knew that she had seen the dark side to Blair, and the shadow across the sun.

* * *

Prossie went into labour the following week, doubling up with pain as she posed for Stanton.

He stood, stupidly holding the brush in his hand. 'What's the matter?'

'I've got colic,' she said witheringly, 'what the hell do you think's the matter? The baby's coming.'

The three of them went in the ambulance, Stanton fussing ineffectually, Isabel holding Prossie's hand, Prossie grey-faced and silent. At the hospital she was taken away from them, leaving Stanton pacing the floor and tackling the first doctor he saw.

'She wants me with her.'

'No she doesn't.'

Stanton blinked. 'I'm the father.'

'Congratulations,' the doctor said phlegmatically. 'But that doesn't change the fact that she doesn't want you in there.' He turned to Isabel.

148

'She asked for you though.'

Stanton's eyes narrowed. 'I might as well get back to the pissing studio then,' he said unpleasantly.

'Oh, I wouldn't bother . . . ' Isabel replied, unruffled, 'your muse is indisposed.'

As it was he decided to wait; it was nearly six hours before the child was born. Wearily Prossie raised her head to take the baby, her face glorious with triumph.

'Welcome, little one,' she said and laughed once, loudly, lustily, all the joy of her life given in one breath to her child. 'Welcome, baby.'

Isabel stayed with her until Stanton came in, all sulky and bad-tempered.

'So what is it?'

'A rabbit,' Prossie replied drily. 'What were you expecting?'

He snorted and glanced down at his firstborn then back to the doctor.

'What is it?' he repeated.

Prossie raised her eyebrows indulgently. 'He wants to know if it's a boy, a girl, or a model.'

When mother and baby returned from the hospital Isabel was pressed into service. Prossie, under the impression that she could rest, was soon back acting as Stanton's model, her full figure reclining in a variety of comfortable poses.

Not that Stanton didn't try to push his luck. 'Get your arm a little higher.'

'Get lost,' she replied evenly.

The baby, called Chloë, was neither good nor bad, just a moderate baby. She cried when she was hungry, then Prossie breastfed her and she fell back to sleep; she cried when she was dirty and either Prossie or Isabel would change her; and she cried when she was unhappy.

'Shut up!' Stanton shouted as the baby woke him in the night. 'I've got the Duke of Northumberland coming for a sitting tomorrow, I need to sleep.' He leapt out of bed and glowered down at the baby in Prossie's arms. 'I can't function like this, I'm too old.'

Prossie gazed up at him and winked. 'Too old, hey? Too old for everything?' She got to her feet and padded down the corridor to Isabel's room. Gently she tapped on the door and then walked in. Isabel was fast asleep, one hand hanging over the side of the bed, her breathing regular. Hesitating for an instant, Prossie leaned forwards and shook her until she woke.

Immediately Isabel snapped on the light. 'What is it?'

'The baby,' Prossie said easily, 'wants changing, and Stanton wants his oats.'

'Perhaps you should give the baby some oats and change Stanton,' Isabel said, snapping off the light and turning back to sleep.

Ten minutes later she was awakened by a small fist landing against her chest. Starting, she turned on the light again only to find Chloë lying happily in bed beside her.

The pattern was repeated frequently, Isabel receiving a crying Chloë in the early hours, the baby howling for a few instants before settling and falling to sleep.

Isabel came to look forward to sharing her bed with Chloë, as she found in the baby an ideal

150

recipient for all her affection. In the small hours when the noises had ceased from Stanton's bedroom and the house was quiet, she whispered to the child, tickling her and talking to her, telling her the tales her father had told her. Sometimes Chloë wouldn't settle and Isabel would turn on the light, throwing a scarf over it so that the illumination was soft, and gaze at her. Chloë gazed back, large-eyed, her mouth as full as her mother's, her head supported in the crook of Isabel's arm.

'I'll take you to see The Ridings,' Isabel promised. 'You'll love it there, Chloë. I could push you out in your pram . . . '

The baby gurgled softly.

' . . . and buy you things.' On and on she talked, her ability to soothe the baby far more developed than Prossie's.

'Stanton can't stand having her in bed with us,' Prossie said one morning when she came in to feed Chloë. 'Daddy's grumpy sometimes, isn't he?'

'Some father,' Isabel muttered darkly.

'Oh, come on,' Prossie responded with astonishment, 'you didn't think he was going to change, did you?'

'But you put his interests first, not the baby's.'

'I have to,' Prossie said quietly, 'if I want to keep him.'

★ ★ ★

Stanton was not impressed with Isabel's work and she knew it by the quick grunts of displeasure when he scrutinised her paintings. His eyebrows were drawn down, his mouth set, his hands dug deep into his pockets. Isabel waited for his response, shivering in the cold studio under the unflattering winter light.

Suddenly, exasperated, he threw several drawings on to the floor and trod on them with his bare feet, smudging the charcoal. Isabel watched and swallowed, fighting tears.

'Have you got their number?' he said finally.

'Whose?'

'Andrex,' he snapped. 'This work is only fit to wipe your backside on.'

Isabel glanced away. She had nothing with which to fight; he was right.

'How long did your mother give you? Eighteen months?'

She nodded, she had told Stanton when she came to him that her mother had set her a time limit to prove herself.

'You've no chance, Isabel . . . ' he said, shaking his head. 'How long have you been with me?'

'Ten months.'

'Forget it, go home, Isabel. I was wrong about you, I thought you had talent, but it was just precociousness.' He turned away. 'Sorry, kid.'

Her mouth opened, but no words came out. Nothing, only a dull sense of anguish and disappointment. She had failed, she would never make it — and she knew why. She was unsuited to greatness. All the nights she had previously spent working in the studio, or watching Stanton and learning, she now spent with Chloë. I'm not an artist at heart, she thought miserably. I

152

thought I was, but I was wrong.

'Stanton,' Prossie said, clambering off the dais and coming over to him. 'Don't he so flaming cruel. Isabel's been helping me lately, it's my fault that her work's fallen off. Give her another chance.'

'She hasn't got the talent,' he said simply, as though Isabel was no longer there, 'and she hasn't the fucking heart.'

Prossie winced. 'You old windbag, how long did it take you to learn? Not ten bloody months, I'm sure!' She bent down and picked up the drawings covered in his footprints. 'Maybe it's not Isabel that's at fault; maybe your rotten teaching's not all it's cracked up to be.'

'What the hell — '

'Just listen to me a minute,' Prossie said quietly. 'David Hall *made* you, Stanton, you owe him, and you can't just dismiss his daughter like that — '

He was adamant. 'She hasn't got it in her.'

Prossie stood up to him. 'Do you love me?'

She had regained her figure and her erotic full-blown looks, and she knew it. She also knew that sexually he was bound to her and wanted her above all other women; and in that moment Prossie put her own future on the line for her friend.

'Well? Do you love me?'

Stanton glanced at her in exasperation. 'Don't piss about, you know I do.'

'So do this for me,' Prossie said gently, touching his cheek with her hand. 'Please keep Isabel on, teach her, darling, please, even if it's

153

just for the next eight months. Do this, for me . . . please.'

He hesitated, then moved away without looking at either of the women. 'Eight months then, but that's the lot.'

11

Teddy Gray was not in a good mood, in fact he was burning from having just lost a case. A good case, he said to the barrister, a good case that they should have won with one arm tied behind their backs. Instead a technicality got the man off. It was maddening. Lunch did nothing to soothe Teddy's temper, and by three he was suffering from indigestion. That, compounded by the fact that he had just received a letter from his ex-wife, put the cap on a bad day.

He leaned back in his chair and patted his stomach, still pleasingly flat from all the gym workouts. When you reached forty you had to watch your shape, he thought, already bored by the banal conversations in the locker room. Jesus, he said to himself, he would never have believed that men used shampoo *and* conditioner! He thought that was just for women. Suspiciously he would eye up his companions, bodies tanned from sun lamps, taut stomachs, legs looking like they belonged on frogs. It was laughable — if he could just find someone to laugh with.

The North beckoned him home; it always did, like a mirage, when things got bad. Slate grey skylines, derelict mills, white collars ringed by lunchtime — each seemed almost romantic when he was homesick — when he was there he longed to be back in London. His hand wandered to the intercom and he pressed a switch.

'Yes, Mr Gray?'

He hesitated. 'Nothing. Thank you,' he said, turning the machine off.

Mr Gray. He liked the way his secretary said his name. Made it clear sounding and expensive, just like his clients. Most of them came from the art world after Teddy had represented one of them in court and succeeded in having a forger jailed. He'd been flavour of the month with the Bond Street dealers since then.

They were not really his type, but he adjusted to them as he adjusted to everyone — easily. Teddy Gray was an easy-going fellow, good company, good-tempered, good at his job, and good and fed up. Disgruntled, he rubbed the side of his nose and winced, remembering his sparring match from the previous week. That'll teach me to show off, he thought ruefully, the guy was twice his size. But he hadn't been able to resist the dare.

'I bet you wouldn't take him on,' someone had said as he watched the large Swede work out in the ring at the gym.

Teddy had been an amateur boxer at university, he could throw the odd punch.

'Besides,' the man continued, 'you're too easy-going to have the killer instinct.'

The words rattled in Teddy's head. Two things annoyed him: one, that easy-going generally meant soft; and two, that no one thought he had the bottle to take on the fighter — even if he was twice his size. Suitably provoked, Teddy Gray

156

took off his expensive Leonard tie, his Savile Row suit, slipped off his Gucci loafers, and tried to beat seven bells out of the Swede.

Teddy was flattened in thirty seconds . . . But the attempt did win him some real admiration from his colleagues, and he dined out on the story for several days. Easy-going Teddy, not quite as easy-going as everyone thought. He smiled to himself, his good mood restored, his blue eyes and blond hair the perfect companions to his youthful features. Everything in its place, and everything in order — apart from the deep gash down the left side of his nose where the Swede had knocked him out.

★   ★   ★

'Well, that's the limit. The bloody limit!' Stanton shouted as he read the letter which had come in the second post. 'Prossie!' he bellowed, beckoning to her as she materialised at the studio door. 'What was the name of that solicitor, that guy who sorted out the trouble on Cork Street with the forger?'

She frowned. 'Who?'

'Tall blond guy. He looks harmless, but he's got a good brain.' His patience went. 'You know who I mean! He went out with Carrie Freeman.'

'Oh, Teddy Gray,' Prossie said, adding, 'He's a good-looking man.'

'Whey-faced,' Stanton said flatly. 'Looks like he has anaemia.'

Prossie raised her eyebrows. 'What about him?'

157

Stanton gestured to the letter in front of him. 'There's some bugger forging my work in Italy — '

'Oh, how flattering,' Prossie said excitedly. 'People say you haven't really made it until someone fakes your stuff.'

Stanton gave her a bleak look. 'I want to know where I stand. If this forger's getting paid for my work — *his* work pretending to be *my* work — we, my love, are missing out.'

'So phone Mr Gray,' she said simply.

★   ★   ★

Much to his amazement there was a parking space almost directly opposite Stanton Feller's studio and Teddy pulled his Mercedes into it gratefully. A hard shower rattled on the roof over his head reminding him of the noise of rain on the tin roof of the coalshed behind his grandmother's house in Little Lever, a small town in Lancashire. Little Lever, he thought nostalgically, even the name seemed friendly. He waited patiently; the rain smacked the windows, a woman running for cover and hauling a crying child behind her, a removal van backing out of an entrance. Moving in weather like this wasn't his idea of a joke, Teddy thought, remembering his own removal into his flat on Baker Street. He had little furniture then, just a few good pieces, antiques, the kind you bought, not inherited.

Smiling, he slid down further in the driving seat and thought of his apartment with pleasure. It had taken him years to really settle in and to decide on a style and when he did Philippa altered it. Out went the bachelor Italian leather settees, and in came the cots for the boys. One, two, three kids in quick succession, the flat resounding with crying babies. Out went the Mahler, and in came Jack-a-bloody-nory, out went his pictures and in came the bloody fig trees. Teddy frowned, suddenly piqued. He hated greenery indoors; outdoors, fine, indoors, no. But Philippa had insisted — it reminded her of the country.

'What country? These are *fig* trees,' he replied. 'You're not Greek.'

She bristled, blond hair held back with an Alice band. 'It's fashionable.'

'Who said?'

'They have them in Peter Jones,' she said defensively. Peter Jones, Sloane Street, home territory. The implication was obvious, what would some Northern hick from Little Lever know about décor?

So now Teddy hated fig trees *and* hair bands, but he did like rain. It reminded him of home. He said the word defiantly, watching the shower, feeling good about the world. And then the rain stopped. Just to prove a point . . . Reluctantly he got out of the car and rang Stanton Feller's studio bell. No one answered, but the door was open so he walked in.

The stairs were dark, as they always were. Stanton could have replaced the light bulb, but he said that it gave him an advantage to have his sitters come up blinking and disorientated into the full light of the studio. Teddy came up blinking too and waited until his eyes adjusted before looking around. The place was quiet and cool, a low smell of damp creeping out from the walls. He frowned, hadn't he been told that damp affected paint, made it bloom or something? Yes, he was sure some dealer had told him that.

The cold North light shone down cruelly on the bare floorboards and the messy work table; it made the chair on the dais look shabby and the red cloth thrown over the screen behind seem tired and in need of a wash. But the light was not unkind to the paintings on the easels; they were simply enhanced by the glare. Teddy put his head on one side and looked at the dark-haired girl in one painting; he found her appealing, but a little heavy, a little too obvious for his taste. Prossie's eyes followed him, her lips parted slightly to welcome him. Momentarily disconcerted, Teddy stepped back and moved away from the picture.

It was then that he saw her, curled up, fast asleep on a divan pushed against the wall. Isabel had exhausted herself working most of the night on a picture, and had fallen asleep where she sat. Prossie had found her later, tucking the eiderdown around her and putting a cushion behind her head. She had slept as though bewitched, without moving, her hair half over her face, her hands relaxed.

Teddy Gray looked at her, fascinated. She was obviously very young, her face without make-up, her skin white with sleep. Against the dark red of the cushion, her glossy hair threw up all its different colours, and when she shifted her position slightly, her fine-nosed profile rested like an effigy in a country church.

He thought her incredible and, without realising it, reached out and touched her sleeping shoulder.

'Oh . . . ' Isabel said suddenly, sitting up.

'Sorry,' Teddy explained, lying clumsily, 'you had . . . a fly on your shoulder.'

Isabel glanced at her sleeve, frowned, and then swung her legs over the edge of the divan, her arm clasped round the eiderdown. 'Did you come to see Stanton?' she asked, yawning and then getting to her feet, still clutching the eiderdown. Slowly she looked down the entries in the studio diary, then glanced back to the visitor.

'I'm sorry, he doesn't seem to have you in the sitters' book for today.'

Teddy shook his head, watching her. 'I'm not a sitter.'

Isabel smiled again, obviously still half asleep, then she hitched something up on to her hip and pulled back the side of the eiderdown. The face of a small baby peered out at him. Teddy's smile faded as though he had suddenly seen a snake.

'Perhaps you'd like to make an appointment for another time?' Isabel offered.

He seemed momentarily to lose the power of speech. That this dream creature should suddenly be exposed as Stanton Feller's mistress, and the mother of his child . . . Teddy Gray felt the disappointment as keenly as a knife wound.

Barefooted, Isabel stood looking at him, the baby's eyes also fixed on him.

161

'I have an appointment. Is Mr Feller here?'

A vague smile answered the question, Isabel turning her head and raising her eyebrows. 'I'm afraid he's still in bed . . . ' She trailed off.

'Well . . . could you tell him I'm here?'

'Do I have to?' she responded quietly, moving Chloë on to her other hip. 'He can get very irritable first thing.' She glanced round. 'Wouldn't you like a cup of tea first — it would give him time to wake up.'

Teddy nodded, sympathy now mixing with disappointment. So they had had a fight and she didn't want to face him, he thought, God it was sordid. How old was Stanton Feller? Fifty-odd? And this girl couldn't be more than twenty. Heavy footsteps next door confirmed that Stanton was up.

Unperturbed, Isabel made mugs of tea for both of them and passed one to Teddy. He took it gratefully, avoided looking at Chloë, and walked back to the divan with her.

'He won't be too long,' she volunteered, sitting down and sipping the tea. 'Do you want him to paint your portrait? You have a good face.'

Teddy hadn't been prepared for the remark and found himself unusually shy. 'Why . . . Thank you . . . '

'All your features are very even,' Isabel said sleepily, Chloë burping on her lap, 'except for that cut,' she said, pointing to the mark on Teddy's nose. 'What happened?'

'I got knocked out by a Swede,' he said.

'Oh,' she replied, trying to fathom out what he was saying. 'I knew someone who was knocked

162

out by a melon once, but not a swede. I wouldn't have thought they were heavy enough.'

It was Teddy's turn to be bemused. He sipped his tea, and then slowly realised what she was talking about. 'Oh, I see . . . no, I mean Swede as in Swedish boxer, not swede as in the vegetable.'

Isabel burst out laughing and he joined in, although both of them stopped just as suddenly when the sounds of an argument exploded from the bedroom next door.

'Oh,' Isabel said, colouring. 'I think Stanton might be delayed a little longer than I thought . . . '

She trailed off, the two of them following the incoherent sounds — and then the unmistakable sounds of lovemaking.

'Perhaps I should be going . . . ' Teddy said, more mortified for Isabel than for himself. That bloody Stanton Feller had a woman in here! While his mistress and his child were listening he was making love to some tart . . . He was surprisingly shocked.

'Well, if you must go . . . ' Isabel said, trailing off, embarrassed. 'I could try and call him — '

'No!' Teddy said rapidly. 'I'll phone.'

'But it'll be over in a minute,' she said without thinking, then blushed fiercely.

He thought her wonderful and brave. 'Listen — '

'Isabel.'

'Yes, Isabel.' His eyes were fixed on hers. 'Just tell your . . . '

'Teacher.'

'Teacher,' he repeated, 'just tell . . . ' He

163

stopped short. 'What did you say?'

Isabel smiled. 'I said that Stanton was my teacher; and this,' she said, looking at the baby, 'is Chloë. Prossie's baby. Well, Stanton and Prossie's baby. I look after her . . . ' She paused, aware that Teddy was watching her with a strange expression on his face.

The truth flustered her. 'You didn't think . . . ?' She glanced away. 'Oh . . . '

He shook his head and extended his hand easily. 'Let's take it from the top, shall we? How do you do, Isabel? I'm Teddy Gray.'

★　★　★

Eleanor had spent all afternoon in the garden with Blair. The winter had not been too severe and spring was on its way, but she had been caught out too often before and was taking no chances. The weather might be deceptively mild, but the late snows could still come and kill the early bulbs. She pushed back some hair that had fallen over her face and glanced across the flower beds, watching Blair with the gardener. They were deep in conversation, the old man listening, nodding his head, then replying, his voice coming in snatches across the quiet garden.

Pausing for breath, Eleanor gazed across the lawn towards the heavy bank of trees that marked the boundary. It was such a shame that David wasn't here to see it, she thought, and even more of a pity that Virginia never stayed in Yorkshire long enough to appreciate either the garden or the house. You would think she would be tired now, Eleanor thought, unless she's afraid . . . The thought startled her. What was there to be afraid of at The Ridings?

Only ghosts. Old ghosts from the cellars, built on the old monastery. Or maybe new ghosts? Those who were not long dead. Like David . . . She laid down her trowel and glanced up at the top floor of the house, her eyes resting on the windows of her brother's room. When we were children we used to scare guests with our stories, we used to tell them that the dead monks came walking at night . . . she smiled wickedly at the memory, it had always surprised them how nervous people became . . . but now she wondered if David had joined the ranks of the unrested himself.

A sudden cloud crossed the sun, the lawn shadowed, the window of David's room black. Eleanor's mind wandered back to the time she had found him in his study, inconsolable, and the time she had discovered the letter . . . Her heart fluttered. Too many mysteries! She was getting too old for them. All the wondering; all the suspicions about the reasons for David's death. And what did it matter in the end? He was dead, and she was no nearer an answer . . . She shivered, suddenly cold. Perhaps she should have confronted Virginia, forced her to confess.

Confess what? That her husband was unhappy? Or that she drove him to his death? Was it likely that she would take the burden on herself? Or even admit it? The answer was plain enough — she must feel some guilt and apparently she felt it most acutely in The Ridings. That was why she stayed away so much. The place did not welcome her.

Oh, God, what are you talking about? Eleanor thought suddenly, it's a house, that's all. Just a house . . . But David hadn't thought so. He had loved the place and had chosen his bride in the fervent hope that she would adore it too. It had been his first disappointment to find that Virginia hadn't cared, that his joy of the place was not shared by her. Yet in the end he had been lucky — his child had fallen in love with The Ridings and David Hall had lived long enough to know that.

The sun came out again, and the lawn lightened. Yet they had all left. Isabel for London, to live with Stanton Feller and Prossie; Virginia abroad; David, God knows where — and who stayed behind? A middle-aged spinster and her cousin. Eleanor smiled ruefully. What a pair . . . Her glance moved over to Blair again. Yet it was right that he ended up here, she thought. Only a simple man, who heard the sirens singing, could really appreciate the place. A simple man and an old maid.

All right, she said impatiently, picking up her trowel and working the earth again. All right, David, so be it. But not for ever. We need some young blood, some fresh blood here . . . She glanced at her dead brother's study window and thought for an instant that she saw a shadow move there. She smiled again, less angry, as she whispered under her breath, 'Come on, David, see what you can do.'

The eighteen months were nearly up. But although Isabel tried desperately, her ambition to be a painter no longer seemed to matter as much. The paints and the canvases which had been her obsession were still touched, used, and admired, but somewhere inside herself the will to succeed had gone. She knew the moment when it faded; at the instant she fell in love.

After her run-in with Stanton she had applied herself, but the fierce joy of creating would not come back. It tingled at the edge of her brushes and seemed almost within reach, but when she met Teddy Gray it was as though someone had opened a window and let out the hummingbird. The loss stung her, but the excitement of being in love seemed to be enough, and day by day she worked a little less. The months passed, coming round to her birthday in May when she returned home briefly to the Ridings.

When she arrived she hugged Blair and Eleanor, but fear made her secretive; fear of losing Teddy as suddenly as she had lost her father; fear that the second kind man in her life might be taken from her. Her talent was her own to lose; her future with this man was out of her control.

Eleanor suspected something immediately. Isabel seemed altered, more composed, the strain of the past few months lifted. The despair she had felt with her work had been real, but there was now no trace of it. Why? Eleanor wondered. How could something which mattered so much suddenly cease to be important? Had she mastered her craft? Was Stanton pleased with her? Eleanor hoped so, but did not press her niece.

'Stanton's painting Princess Falina,' Isabel said to her aunt, smiling at Blair, who was as smitten as ever as he watched her, greedily hanging on her words.

'That's wonderful.'

'Yes,' agreed Isabel. The distance between her and her aunt yawned wide. 'He's exhibiting in the Academy again this year.'

So what, Eleanor thought. What the hell do I care about Stanton Feller? I care about you because you've gone through so much. 'How about your work?'

'It's good,' she said, but the enthusiasm trailed behind the voice and both of them knew it. 'I have six months left.'

'I know,' Eleanor said, waiting, knowing that Isabel was about to confide in her.

'Can we go to Skipton tomorrow?' Blair asked, breaking into the moment.

Both women blinked. The chance was gone.

'Sure,' Isabel said, turning back to Blair and smiling. He smiled in return. Like exchanging coins. 'We'll go shopping.'

'For chocolate.'

'For chocolate,' she agreed, looking into the marvellous face. It's so simple for you, Blair, isn't it? she thought, so simple. Or maybe not. His eyes fixed on hers and in them she read another kind of love; not the same as she saw in Teddy's eyes, but the same need was there and it made her push back her seat quickly and leave the table.

Mystified, Eleanor watched her go and then finished her meal with Blair. Isabel walked up the stairs slowly, pausing to glance up at the window where the moon peered in, then rounded the bend on the stairs. In her bedroom the work table was empty, a silent rebuke, and invoking a sharp memory. Where did all that ambition go? she wondered, heavy with unease. Birthday presents lay unwrapped on the bed, and on top lay the letter she was expecting — from her father.

It looked the same as all the others. The letters which came every birthday, as if by magic. Spirited to her, as though her dead father had become flesh long enough to leave a message, his ghost laying down the letter on her bed. In remembrance of me . . . Logic told Isabel that the letter came from the solicitor, and that he was just following her dead father's instructions, but somehow to see David's handwriting, to read his words, to finger the paper he had touched, and to remember him — it was a moment so intense that it left Isabel momentarily almost afraid. What was the purpose of the letters? Were they her father's way of keeping contact with her? Or were they a reminder — lest we forget? But how could I, Daddy? Isabel thought, how could I?

Carefully she picked it up, her heart banging, her throat tight. You would be disappointed in me, Daddy, she thought. You wanted me to do so well and I let it go, I gave it away, for what? She

169

sat down heavily. Teddy had told her he loved her the night before. Slowly, as though he had measured the words and knew exactly what they meant. And he did, far more than she did. He had already gone through a bad marriage and a hard divorce.

'I know you're very young,' he said, touching her cheek. An affectionate, not erotic gesture. She was unreasonably grateful for that. 'But I love you very much, and I could make you happy.'

His hair was so fair that it had looked white in the half light of his car. What will you look like grey? Isabel had wondered suddenly. You'll never look really old, your features are too youthful for that.

'Isabel, I love you,' he repeated. 'I just wanted you to know before you go home tomorrow. Think about it, if you want to carry on with this afterwards, we'll talk.'

Carry on with it? What did that mean? She knew later she should have asked him but she hadn't wanted to look gauche, or say the wrong thing. Did carrying on mean sleeping with him, or marrying him? The thought rattled her. Did she want Teddy the way Stanton wanted Prossie?

I want to be safe, she thought suddenly, and if Teddy means safety, that's what I want. But what about your work? something said inside her. Oh that, she thought impatiently, I can always paint. Yes, you can be a housewife and paint on Sundays. As a hobby. Everyone should have an interest.

Isabel tore open the letter quickly, expecting to find an answer there. After all, her father had never failed her before.

Dearest Knuckles,

Happy Birthday, darling. This is your nineteenth.

You're a young woman now, and how do you look? Is your hair short . . .

'Long Daddy,' Isabel answered automatically.

. . . or long, like it was when you were little? And what are you wearing? I hope it's not a dark colour, you look so much prettier in bright clothes. Not that you aren't perfect in anything.

While I'm writing this, pet, I'm thinking of Stanton Feller . . .

A cold chill ran down Isabel's spine.

. . . he has a great talent, don't be put off by his crude ways. He also has a good heart, way down deep — not that it didn't take me many years to discover it. Ask him for help, darling, if you need to. Your work could be spectacular if you develop it in the right way, with the right people, and at the right time. Remember, you are gifted — it is vital to your happiness that you understand how important that fact is.

Do not go off course; do not lose heart; do not abuse the talent you have. So many others only dream of your abilities. Oh, my love, I don't mean to scold you on your birthday, but as I am not there to talk to you, I have to advise you this way.

The world will be kind to you in stages. You will be a success, and you will be loved, but only when the time is right. Hang on, darling, and work hard. Now is the period in your life when you master your craft. Be wise, be careful and be happy.

Your father,

David Hall

Isabel folded the letter and tucked it inside her case. A cold wave of disappointment crushed her because she knew her father was right. But I love Teddy, she thought. If you were here, Daddy, I could explain . . . And what would he say? she wondered. He would ask if this man encouraged her, and she would tell him that Teddy had no objection to her work. The reply shook her. *No objection. What right has he to object?* David Hall would have responded.

I need him, Daddy, she said. I'm not a man, I need security, a home of my own, children. I need affection. I can't go it alone, struggling, fighting for recognition.

Your mother did, I did.

But you had each other, she replied, talking to herself, as though her father was in the room with her.

No, we were married, but we were each alone.

I don't have your courage, Daddy.

You do, you just want the easy way. You have to work and work, and fight to succeed. And don't tell me it's harder for a woman, I know it is, but your mother did it, so you can too. You can be grateful for her ambition.

'But I don't want to be like her!' Isabel said out loud, getting to her feet, suddenly angry. 'She's a cold woman with only her success to show for her life. I want happiness, fulfilment.' She made up her mind quickly, hardly daring to stop and consider what she did.

Crossing to the mirror on her dressing table, Isabel stared hard at her reflection. The four flecks of green in her eyes seemed more obvious than ever as she concentrated.

'You told me once, Daddy, that I had four wishes . . . ' She paused, almost afraid. 'Well, I want to use one of them now.' She thought of Stanton's studio, his bare feet, the dripping tap, the powerful smell of turps and the tired models. She saw the sheer joy of success, the wedge of money in his hand, and Prossie throwing herself, naked, into his arms and laughing.

Then she saw Teddy Gray — and she made her choice.

PART TWO

PART TWO

12

He slipped off his shoes first, then lay down on the bed next to her. Gently he undid her blouse and bra and slid his hand over her breast, his mouth moving over hers, his tongue searching. His fingers tightened on her nipple and she moaned, her hands reaching out and cupping his face, her eyes fixed on his. But he pulled away from her, undressed quickly, and then with infinite care, undressed her. Isabel watched him in the half light, closing her eyes as his hand stroked her stomach and then moved between her legs. Gently, he explored her, his lips passing over her breasts, fastening on her nipples as she moaned again.

Then he moved on top of her and she reached out for him, pulling him to her, his blond hair mixing with her own, his lips against her cheek as he climaxed. For a while he lay looking at her, and then smiled, asking her what she wanted him to do to her. She blushed, embarrassed, and he teased her kindly, experimenting with her body until she forgot her shyness and begged him to continue, her own orgasm coming as a shock and a delicious sense of release.

Never once did she regret her choice. Never in the small hours of that first night did Isabel regret the decision she had made.

★ ★ ★

'I think everything went very well,' Virginia said without enthusiasm as she walked into the hall of The Ridings with Eleanor.

'Isabel looked wonderful,' Eleanor said, thinking of her niece and smiling. Dressed in a wedding gown of the palest lavender satin, Isabel's hair had been drawn back into a snood, her head crowned with a coronet of freesia, her ivory skin luminous. As she had walked into the church some people had gasped instinctively, the familiarly pretty Isabel Hall transformed into a thoroughly beautiful woman, clasping a handful of flowers, her eyes steady as she walked ahead. Eleanor studied her sister-in-law. Virginia was as composed as ever, wearing a mink hat with a stud at the back which looked like a belly button. 'Do you want something to eat?'

Virginia touched her stomach as though repelled. 'Good Lord, no. I've had far too much already.'

Eleanor doubted it; she had watched Virginia at the reception at the Majestic in Harrogate and unless she was a magician and could absorb food without the use of her mouth, she had eaten little. In fact, Eleanor thought, she looks as though a good meal would floor her. Virginia's fine navy silk suit hung uninterrupted down the straight line of her back, a superb diamond pin glittering importantly on the lapel of her jacket, her legs tapered, the ankles fragile. As she touched her face, her rings swivelled loosely on her fingers, and her wrist bone seemed almost fleshless. Elegant starvation, Eleanor thought, getting to her feet and walking to the drinks cupboard.

'Well, I'm going to have a sherry,' she said.

178

She was happy, her beloved niece was married, and safe. Soon The Ridings would be busy with their visits, and friends, and children . . .

'Mary Harrod looked old, didn't she?' Virginia said suddenly, taking off her belly button hat and following her sister-in-law into the drawing room. The room was cheerful with a fire, the curtains drawn. 'I wonder why Geoffrey doesn't do something about it.'

'Like trade her in for a new model, or get her to have a face lift?'

'I'm serious,' Virginia said, helping herself to a whisky. 'He looks so much younger than her.'

Eleanor changed the subject. 'Portento looked the same though — '

'Hideous man!' Virginia chimed in, critical as ever. 'I can't think why anyone could stand to have their portrait painted by him.'

'The alternative's Stanton Feller,' Eleanor said mischievously.

Virginia's eyes glinted. 'Did you see that . . . girl . . . Prossie Leonard?' she asked, narrowing her eyes. 'I suppose you forgot to mention the fact that she was Stanton's whore? At her age too!'

'At *his* age, you mean,' Eleanor said drily, draining her glass and refilling it. She was feeling good; at peace with the world: even Virginia couldn't rattle her this evening.

'Your cousin behaved well,' Virginia said grudgingly.

'I had him sedated before we left,' her sister-in-law replied wryly.

'Oh . . . I wondered what it was,' Virginia said,

not seeing the joke and stretching out her legs towards the fire. 'He did look a little sheep-eyed when he saw Isabel though.'

Eleanor let the remark pass; she had had a hard time explaining to Blair why Isabel was marrying Teddy and not him.

'He seems a nice boy.'

'Blair?'

Virginia blinked. 'No, Teddy . . . what do you suppose Teddy is short for?'

'Michael?' Eleanor said drily.

'Oh . . . Michael . . . ' she answered absently. 'That's nice. David always said we could have done with a lawyer in the family.' She shifted in her seat, unable to get comfortable. 'Teddy Gray, Mrs Isabel Gray — it's quite a name, isn't it?'

'Quite a name,' Eleanor agreed.

The old ghosts swung between them.

'Do you suppose . . . ?'

'Yes, Virginia?'

Quickly she got to her feet, and wandered round the room, pausing by the piano. 'Do you suppose that David would have liked Teddy?'

Eleanor stiffened; she hadn't been prepared for this and realised that Virginia had drunk a little more than she usually did.

'I think David would have liked him very much,' she said evenly, without turning round to look at her sister-in-law, knowing that if she did so, Virginia would clam up.

'Very much? Or just a bit?'

'Very much,' Eleanor repeated. 'Teddy has a lot of David's kindness.'

'I have no kindness,' Virginia said suddenly,

180

her voice muffled. 'That's been my trouble.'

Stiff-backed, Eleanor kept her eyes fixed ahead. 'You've achieved a lot — '

'Like *what?*' she snapped. 'Fame and money? What's that? Don't you think I'd give it all to get my husband back?' Her voice rose, terrifyingly loud. 'Don't you think I'd give anything to have David walk in this room now?' She stumbled, tipsy, but regained her balance, leaning back against the piano. 'You don't know what it's like to travel all the time. Hotel rooms, talks, thousands of people asking stupid questions. Chat, chat, chat. All that inedible food. Sleeping alone . . . ' She trailed off. Eleanor heard her drain her glass. 'I miss him. I could have helped you know, I should have helped . . . '

It was then that Eleanor made her mistake. She turned, and in turning looked into Virgina's eyes. The effect was immediate; her sister-in-law sobered up instantly and pushed herself upright, her voice returning to normal as she looked down at the piano and said coldly, 'This veneer's lifting. I told you to keep the curtains closed and the sunshine off the piano. It may seem a little thing to you, Eleanor, but it's the little things that matter.'

★　★　★

'Stupid cow,' Stanton said softly to Prossie as she stood behind him, looking at Isabel's early drawings over his shoulder. 'She had a real gift and it's gone.'

'Oh, for God's sake, darling, she's happy. What

181

does it really matter if she's not painting any more? She'll be having babies soon.'

For an instant he looked at her with something approaching dislike. Not that you could teach Prossie how to feel, to care, about painting. Fat bloody chance. She'd sit for you and look marvellous, but if you wanted to talk to her and share your feelings with her, no way. A roll in the sack, and that's your lot, Jack, he thought.

A rush of guilt washed over him immediately. He was feeling peevish but he shouldn't take it out on Prossie. After all, she was the best model he'd had, and damn nearly the best lay. It wasn't her fault he was feeling so flaming depressed. He glanced at the drawing in his hand and, unexpectedly, his eyes filled. It was a waste, a bloody, sickening, waste of talent. He knew Teddy Gray, liked him, even if he did look anaemic, but he hadn't the balls for Isabel.

'I always liked that one,' Prossie said dreamily, leaning over his shoulder, her breasts against his back.

He nodded, too shaken to speak. Oh shit, David, he thought, I wanted your girl to succeed, I really did. And she could have done. I let you down. Sorry old man, sorry.

'A bloody waste.'

'What?' Prossie said.

'I said it was a bloody waste of talent. I'll never see such potential again,' he said seriously.

'Well, she can still paint in her spare time.'

'It's not the same, you stupid bitch!' he snapped, relenting immediately. 'It's not the same, Prossie. You have to *want* to be the best in order to get to the top. She just stopped wanting, it's as simple as that,' he concluded, pushing Isabel's drawings to the back of his desk and turning back to Prossie. 'She could have matched me, you know.'

Prossie raised her eyebrows. 'That good, hey?' she said, her tone lighthearted although his words had stung her. Archly she nudged him with her elbow. 'Surely she wasn't really as good as the Maestro? Not really?'

'Well,' he said, beginning to smile. 'Maybe not *that* good.'

Sure that she had cajoled him into a better humour, Prossie then slid to her knees and began to tickle his bare feet, laughing delightedly as Stanton swatted her with one of Isabel's old drawings.

★   ★   ★

The Baker Street flat was sufficient for their needs, Teddy continuing in his law firm, Isabel trying to work on her painting in the spare bedroom which had been converted into a studio. He had indulged her, delighted that she kept herself busy, but his tone was constantly kind and she knew that however appalling her work was, he would approve. That hurt her; and she felt guilty that it should. After all, he wasn't Stanton, was he?

Marriage was what she had chosen and she didn't regret it. Teddy was loving and easy-going, but not a pushover. He stood up to her when she was irritable and he cajoled her when she was depressed, but he never fired her imagination, and that worried her. Sex was good, life was good, what else was there? she asked herself . . . Knock, knock, came the doubts. One by one, marching into her cosy world.

She found after the first few months that she missed Stanton and Prossie, and when she realised that the eighteen-month time limit had come and gone without her realising it, she wept. No one had even mentioned it, let alone remembered it — although she had a sneaking suspicion that her mother was fully aware of the date. How typical of her not to say anything! Isabel thought, and then felt ashamed, after all, hadn't the day passed without her noticing? The day which should have determined the course of her life; the day which had seemed so important before; the day she had lived for. She remembered coming down to London and staying with Mary Harrod, and Stanton shouting down the intercom . . . Isabel shook her head. There was no one to blame but herself — it had been a dream, no more. A dream a child might have, without substance.

This is my reality, she thought, glancing round the flat and running to Teddy when he came home. Fiercely she made love to him, and he responded like a happy man, and for a while the pain eased into nothingness.

⋆　⋆　⋆

Blair was fiddling with his food, pushing it around the plate sullenly as they all sat in the dining room at The Ridings. Virginia was at the head of the table, Eleanor on one side, Isabel on the other, Teddy and Blair facing each other. It was Christmas and over two years had gone by, years in which Prossie had given birth to her second daughter, Bracken; years in which Virginia had had a minor stomach operation; and years in which Isabel had been a wife. Nothing else.

'Darling, you look marvellous,' Teddy said before they went down to dinner. He touched her bare back, wanting her. He always wanted her. 'I'm a lucky man.'

'Teddy,' she said softly. 'I want to talk to you later.'

He flinched, knowing what was coming. 'Not that again, darling.' His lips moved over hers. Sexual comfort.

'No,' she said, moving away. 'I *have* to talk to you.' She paused, his face was so guileless, indulgent. Except on this one subject. 'It's important that we talk.'

His blue eyes hardened. Their expression said, I have given you a wonderful home, money, affection, love, and I have never been unfaithful. I have asked nothing of you, so why persist? But she did.

'I want a baby.'

'NO.'

His tone startled her. 'Teddy — '

'No, I've told you before, no children.' He paused, breathing in. 'I have three children from my first marriage and I can barely cope with them. I don't want any others . . . Besides, look

185

at your family, do you really want to risk anything?'

She frowned, not understanding.

'Blair,' he said, exasperated.

'Blair had an accident, he wasn't born that way,' Isabel replied hotly. 'You know that, so don't try using it as an excuse.'

'All right, try this for size. I don't want to start another family at my age — '

'You're only forty-two! Stanton is — '

'Stanton is Stanton. I'm me!' he snapped, turning to the mirror and adjusting his tie. 'We've gone through this a hundred times. You knew before we married that I didn't want any more children.'

Isabel glanced down at her dress. A party dress, almost a child's in a way, and that was the trouble. She *was* still a child, so much younger than her husband that he babied her; just as her father had.

'I want a child,' she persisted stubbornly.

'And I don't want to talk about it,' Teddy retorted, catching hold of her arm and jerking her towards the bedroom door.

'I'm not going down!' she shouted. 'I'm not going down until you say that we can have a child.'

'Then you'll stay here all night,' he replied, banging the door behind him.

In the end she had gone down, making her apologies and sitting stiffly without eating much. She tried to be reasonable because she loved her husband; she tried to tell herself that he was being fair; that he *had* told her before they

186

married that he wanted no more children — but she had thought he would change, especially as they were so happy. Surely that counted for something?

She glanced up and caught Blair looking at her and for an instant coloured. He never seemed like a child to her, not for an instant, just a very handsome man. Indeed he was so handsome that he made Teddy look a little pale, a little insipid by comparison. Blair smiled and the thought faded. The child's smile gave him away; that same child's smile Chloë greeted Isabel with when she visited the studio; the same smile Prossie's new baby wore as she lay at her mother's breast.

'What are you doing?' Teddy hissed, looking down into Isabel's lap.

Without realising it, she had cradled her arms and was rocking them. Flushing, Isabel turned her attention back to her food.

Eleanor had seen the exchange and wondered what it was all about. Isabel and Teddy seemed happy, but it was obvious something wasn't right.

' . . . so Geoffrey said, 'Why don't you just take the money and run,'' Virginia droned on, 'so I did. The Americans can afford it.'

Blair bit into a piece of celery hard. The noise ended Virginia's sentence like a vocal full stop.

Her gaze rested somewhere over the top of his head as she continued. 'I'm having a party at New Year, inviting some friends down to the house.' She paused, but no applause was forthcoming. 'Baye Fortunas, for one.'

'Isn't he that Greek millionaire?' Teddy asked, intrigued.

His mother-in-law nodded, glad that someone was suitably impressed. 'He's a very wealthy collector. There might be some useful contacts for you there, Teddy. I'll see what I can do.'

'Excellent,' Teddy replied, turning to his wife. 'Don't you think so, darling?'

'Whatever you say, Teddy,' she replied, 'whatever you say.'

He was irritated when they got back to their bedroom and remained irritated, even when Isabel tried to cajole him into a better mood. Nothing worked, not sweet talk, not sex, nothing; he was angry and disinclined to forgive her. In bed, Isabel waited to hear his breathing change as he fell to sleep, then she crept out of the guest room and ran down to her old room at the other end of the house.

Flicking on the light switch, she glanced round. The same window she had driven her hands through; the same bed by the window; and the same work table with a few neglected pencils on the top. Gingerly she touched the blank paper, a feeling of excitement and intimidation welling up in her as she sat down. Carefully, her heart beating quickly, Isabel began to draw.

For months she had not done any work, her longing for a child her one and only thought. Everything else had come a poor second. And the longing never stopped, although she tried endlessly to fill her mind with other things. She went to exhibitions, to shows, she visited all the people she had ever met with her father, but she was an outsider now, not taken seriously. A solicitor's wife, with a part-time job, working for an interior designer in Soho. Nothing more.

The realisation had made Isabel despair and look round hopelessly for comfort. But there was none. She had made her choice, and besides, what had she to complain about? She was happily married, even though she was childless, there was no grubbing for money for her, no struggles, no strivings for the top, no dreams left . . . Even her father's letters, which still came every birthday, seemed to belong to another time, just as they seemed to reproach her. Isabel had made the wrong choice, she knew it, and the sense of loss and isolation was her punishment.

She didn't want to leave Teddy though. She loved him. So what else could she do? Uncertainly Isabel took a deep breath and began to sketch on the blank page, her palm sweaty as she tried to regain something of her previous self, back in the past when she had known what her life was about; when she had known which road to take.

Work hard and be wise, her father had said, and she hadn't listened, she had thrown away her talent instead — or had she?

For an hour Isabel worked on, but in the end she knew that the drawing was little more than a shadow of her former talent. Stanton had been right, the heart had gone out of her work. Dry-eyed, she pushed the paper away, too weary to cry, too lost to know where to turn.

Silently Isabel turned off the light and went

back to the guest room. She slid under the sheets next to her husband and silently asked his forgiveness for what she was about to do. Then she slept, and in the morning she flushed all her contraceptive pills down the toilet.

13

Philippa walked into Teddy's office and sat down. Having arrived unannounced, her presence unsettled him and his eyes narrowed slightly as he continued with his telephone call. Coolly composed, Philippa simply sat and waited for him to finish. She knew she had nettled him, but she was not going to be put off this time. Having left innumerable messages, which had never been answered, Philippa had now decided to beard the lion in his den — and if the lion wanted to make a meal out of the confrontation, so be it.

Her anger prickled her lips, but as she watched her ex-husband a grudging sense of affection crept up on her. Teddy was not looking at her, but at his notes as he talked, his blond head bent down, his boyish face ageing a good deal better than hers was. Damn you, Teddy Gray, she thought, you'll never look more than thirty-five.

Finally he put down the phone and glanced at her, resigned. 'So what can I do for you, Philippa?'

Her charm school accent shot across the desk, all affection suspended. 'Why don't you answer my calls?'

'I've been busy — '

'And I haven't?' she responded predictably. 'I'm the one who has to look after your children — '

'*Our* children,' he corrected, his own voice taking on a steely tone. Jesus, this was all he needed.

'I'm glad you remember that!' she snapped, opening her Hermès handbag and taking out her cigarettes.

Teddy sighed. 'Do you have to smoke?'

'Oh, don't tell me you're concerned for my health,' Philippa replied bitterly.

'No, mine,' he responded evenly, getting up and opening a window. The chill January air slapped her and yet Philippa sat, defiantly smoking, as the room cooled down several degrees.

'I've got work to do,' Teddy said calmly, 'what's this all about?'

'Your son, Robert,' Philippa replied, trying not to shiver. 'We should discuss his further education. He's thinking of trying for university.'

Teddy raised his eyes. An easy-going man, getting less easy-going by the second. 'Oh, come on, Philippa. Bobbie's lazy, you know as well as I do that university would be a waste of time. Besides, when I last spoke to him, he wasn't keen.'

'Oh no, he wouldn't be!' his ex-wife snapped. 'He knows he can wind you round his finger! He knows you're not going to cause a scene — '

'You make up for both of us in that department.'

She inhaled deeply, smarting. 'During your little chat I don't suppose he mentioned the fact that he wanted to form a rock band.'

'With the word 'Brighton' running all the way

through?' Teddy said, smiling.

Philippa frowned, not getting the joke.

'Actually he did tell me,' Teddy continued, watching the smoke from Philippa's cigarette flutter gently above their heads. 'And I think a rock band might be a good idea.'

'*What!*'

Satisfied that he had infuriated her, Teddy continued happily. 'A rock band might be a good idea, Philippa, if only to let him have some fun out of life.'

'FUN!' she roared, stubbing out the cigarette fiercely.

'Yes, fun,' Teddy repeated, shutting the window pointedly and sitting down again. 'We have three sons, Philippa. Two are very bright and very dull . . . ' her eyebrows rose towards the velvet hair band ' . . . and will, no doubt, make excellent professional careers. Ben was a doctor in his pram, and Henry had the look of a solicitor the first time he had his hair cut . . . ' He paused, teasing her. 'I remember when you brought him back from the barber's in Harrods with his first short back and sides, I thought to myself, There's a boy *born* to the law. He looked so grown up that day, if he'd suddenly lit up a cigar I wouldn't have been in the least surprised.'

Philippa hated to be laughed at and her voice rose an octave. 'You may have no sense of responsibility, but luckily I have. I come from a family — '

' — who are a pain in the ass.'

She blinked hotly, as if to hold back tears. 'My family were right about you! You're common.'

193

She paused, expecting him to flinch as he had always done before when she referred to his background. 'Anyway, I didn't come here to listen to you talking nonsense, or make light of our children's futures.'

'I don't suppose you did,' said Teddy. 'But whatever you intended, Philippa, get it over with quick because you are boring me.' His voice hardened, suddenly irritated by the whole subject of children; his in particular. They didn't like him much, or have any interest in what he did — Philippa had seen to that. They looked down on him too; their mother's snobbishness passed down from generation to generation like a club foot. As they had grown he had seen their disappointment intensify every time they visited him, and in the end he had decided to keep his distance, because no matter how successful he was in his profession, his achievements could never erase the one vital error he had made in being born in Lancashire. The occasional flat vowel, or Northern expression, damned him in his sons' eyes as surely as a prison record. Well they could all go to hell, Teddy thought angrily. He had struggled too hard to be a success to let his children undermine him . . . So now he was no more than an envelope dropping through the letter-box every month, his influence almost entirely confined to a note on a piece of Basildon Bond and a National Westminster cheque.

Teddy leaned forward in his chair. 'Bobbie will be fine, Philippa, believe me. He might start his rock band, and he might not, and even if he did, it wouldn't last long. In the end, he will go to university and get a dull degree to enable him to follow a dull career . . . Oh no, I have no doubts that Bobbie will end up a respectable man. We all do.'

'You sound bitter,' Philippa said, scenting dissatisfaction and hoping against hope it was with his new marriage.

But Teddy was no fool and saw her interest quicken. He also knew how really to upset her. 'Oh, I'm not bitter, I like my life and my success . . . ' he said, smiling youthfully. 'Believe me, I'm a happy man.'

★　★　★

Isabel had been shopping and returned late, dumping her parcels in the hall of the flat and walking into the sitting room. Bending down, she flicked on the gas fire, turned on the lamps and drew the curtains. Then she moved into the kitchen and started to unpack her groceries to the accompaniment of Verdi's *Requiem*. The fridge soon bulged with food, the grill turned on high, a couple of chops already laid out for cooking, a bottle of wine beside them on the white working top.

For months Isabel had been obsessed with the one thought uppermost in her mind. Since the tablets had been so ignominiously flushed down the toilet of The Ridings, she had waited with bated breath; and every time she began to bleed, she wept. Soon her whole attention centred upon the calendar, her every thought for the child who was to come. She never doubted what she was doing, and even though she had some niggles of guilt, she told herself that a baby would cement her relationship with Teddy, not threaten it. She was sure.

But the monthly disappointments had continued; her eagerness to conceive making her sexually voracious, much to Teddy's initial surprise. After a while though, he merely enjoyed his pretty, young wife, who was a welcome change from the judgemental Philippa. His life sweetened and his business progressed well, his Northern suspicion of Southerners understood by Isabel, who was an outsider herself. They were well suited; two affectionate people who enjoyed and understood each other. Teddy could talk to Isabel about his upbringing in Little Lever and she could tell him about her insecurities with regard to her mother, and for the first time in her life she could talk freely about her father.

Teddy encouraged her to confide in him, her naivety and sweetness a welcome change from his first wife's Sloane Ranger confidence. As a result they entertained little, dined out a great deal alone and lived for each other by choice. Only the question of children caused any real arguments . . .

Isabel's mind clicked into the present. Whether there is to be an argument or not, I'm happy at last, she thought jubilantly, I'm pregnant. As though to steady herself, she chopped up some carrots and tipped them into a pan. Names jostled in her head; names for boys and names for girls. Which would it be? she asked herself, laughing softly because she was so happy. What did it matter, boy or girl? She was having a baby. The water began to boil under the vegetables and she turned down the gas, pushing back her hair from her face with the back of her hand. On her way home from the doctor Isabel prepared herself. Which was the best way to tell Teddy? she wondered; words and phrases rehearsed constantly as she crossed Devonshire Place and walked up the Marylebone Road. Would Teddy be annoyed? Possibly. Angry? No, not Teddy, and if he *did* get angry it wouldn't last for long . . .

Isabel jumped as the kettle whistled, her mind running on as she made herself a cup of tea . . . She was worrying about nothing. After all, Teddy was not a cruel man. Or an unreasonable one. She closed her eyes and leaned back against the fridge door imagining how he would hug her to him and tell her not to worry, that everything was all right, that he understood what she had done, and was delighted that she was pregnant. That was the image Isabel hung on to — seeing Teddy happy, surprised by what she had done, but a man who would adjust after he realised how much a baby meant to his wife. Isabel smiled timidly. They loved each other, they enjoyed each other; he would understand, wouldn't he? After all, Teddy cared for her almost as much as her father had done, so he was bound to forgive her . . . It would just be a question of his getting used to the idea.

Isabel put down the cup of tea and walked into her bedroom, feeling at the back of the dressing table and taking out a well-thumbed book she had hidden there. Automatically she smiled at the mother and baby on the cover and opened the pages to a picture of a sixteen-week foetus. Reflectively she touched her stomach and imagined it rounded, then turned over another page and glanced at the drawings of the developing child in the womb.

So deep was her concentration that she didn't hear the front door open and was startled when Teddy called to her. Hurriedly, Isabel hid the book and glanced around, looking for any other incriminating evidence before going to greet him.

He seemed drawn.

'Hi, darling,' she said, kissing him, her arms around his neck, the news already nuzzling her lips. 'How was your day?'

'Not too good. Bloody Philippa came to see me.' He hugged Isabel tightly, his cheek against hers. 'She was nagging me about the children,' he said, his irritation fading as he smelt Isabel's perfume. 'She was going on and going on . . . ' he continued, his thoughts already in the bedroom, ' . . . about the damn kids.' His lips moved to Isabel's neck, his breath burning her, as his words did. 'God knows, they'll be the death of me. I'm just glad they're not babies any more.' His hands moved down her back and then he suddenly lifted her into his arms. She was curiously still. 'You know, darling, I'm so relieved I don't ever have to go through that again. You don't know how glad I am that there's just the two of us.'

Quickly he carried Isabel into the bedroom, too excited to wonder why she was so silent.

★ ★ ★

Blair was still in the garden even though it was dark. For the fourth time Eleanor called for him, pausing to hear if he replied and then calling again. Unaccountably worried, she pulled on a coat and, picking up a torch, called for Ivor. The old dog staggered out of his bed reluctantly and looked up at her.

'I know you'd rather sleep,' Eleanor said, pulling the back door closed behind them and fastening up her coat, 'but Blair might be in trouble somewhere, it's not like him to be out so late.'

The dog padded slowly behind her as they walked towards the stable block, Eleanor glancing up at the top windows to see if the studio light was on. Nothing showed, but, suspecting that Blair might be hiding there, she tried the door. It rattled under her touch, but remained locked. Frowning, she moved on.

The Yorkshire night was deep black, without stars or the sound of owls. Dense night. Eleanor moved along slowly, stopping repeatedly to listen for any sound, and to call Blair's name. But there was no reply in the darkness. Past the bare rose bushes she walked, her coat catching momentarily on a branch, her curse soft in the hostile darkness.

'Damn, look at that!' she said to herself, then turned, suddenly alarmed. In the torchlight glare, Ivor blinked at her and she reached out her hand, grateful that he was with her. 'Good boy, you stay close to old Eleanor now, won't you? There's a good boy,' she continued, wanting to return to the house, and yet not able to. Something made her continue, just as a quick jolt of fear went through her.

'Blair? Blair, where are you?' she cried, alarmed by the sudden noise. 'If that's you out there, answer me. *Blair?*'

★ ★ ★

Prossie was dozing, Bracken lying on her stomach, Chloë on the bed beside her, an overfed Persian cat resting against her feet. In the studio next door Stanton was painting Adriana Markos, a teenage sitter who had been sent by her mother, one of his ex-mistresses. She bore a strong resemblance to her mother and smiled coyly every time Stanton glanced at her.

He chatted away easily, flattered by the girl's obvious admiration of him. Now and again the little Pekinese dog on Adriana's lap barked softly, its owner patting it lightly on the head with one small hand.

'You should stop biting your nails,' Stanton said disapprovingly, taking hold of the girl's hands and studying them. They were pliable in his.

She glanced down, displaying an affecting look of anguish. 'I have such ugly hands.'

'No, you don't. You just bite your nails,' Stanton replied, thinking back. Her mother had bitten her nails too; a small Greek statue of a female, who bleached her hair to make a white halo around her bronzed face. He gazed down at Adriana. 'Don't bite them any more, my dear.'

'Whatever you say, Mr Feller,' she replied, smoothing the dog's head with languorous strokes. 'Whatever you say.'

★   ★   ★

High up in the clouds Virginia slept, her thoughts drifting in and out of reality as the plane dipped for Los Angeles and the promise of the Golden Coast. She stirred in her seat, Geoffrey downing another Scotch next to her, his eyes straying over to the air hostess who was bending over a passenger in the aisle seat. He sighed, thinking of his wife, and then turned back to his companion.

Even asleep, Virginia Hall had control. No sagging jowls, no puffy eyes. Even her skin was disciplined, he thought, not a line in sight even though she must be over sixty. He blinked disbelievingly. Over sixty. He'd never thought of her getting old; just as he'd never thought of her giving up her work, but surely she must be thinking of retiring soon?

His own thoughts jangled uncomfortably. If Virginia retired he was out of a job, a lucrative job which was not too taxing, even though he was beginning to feel his age. Virginia Hall's career had provided him with a good living; he had organised her tours and lectures for nearly thirty years. He frowned. Was it really that long?

The next thought followed immediately — how much longer was it likely to go on? Even with Virginia's drive, her intelligence, and her energy, how long could she continue?

He watched her, thinking of her for the first time as a woman, rather than an academic. She was still handsome, she should have remarried after David killed himself ... Geoffrey's thoughts rattled in the high air. What *had* happened between them? he wondered, and why did David commit suicide? He studied the sleeping woman's face. There was nothing there to indicate cruelty, but then there was an obvious coldness about her which was off-putting.

He hadn't been the only one to notice it; many of her acquaintances remarked on the tension between Virginia and her daughter. Geoffrey felt an unaccustomed stab of pity. It was a shame that they were not close, he knew how much Virginia had wanted Isabel to follow in her footsteps. She had once told him so, in a rare confidence praising her daughter's intelligence and expressing a heartfelt desire that she go to university and on to a glittering career in the arts. But Isabel had gone her own way, and Virginia no longer talked about her child's academic future. For a moment he wondered if Virginia's bitterness was keeping her going. After all, Isabel Hall could have achieved a great deal, instead of settling for mediocracy as the wife of a solicitor who came from up North somewhere.

Geoffrey sniffed, ever the snob. Perhaps it was better that things had turned out the way they had. Isabel would never have had her mother's dedication and if Virginia had retired to live happily ever after with David Hall, he would have been out of a job. He shifted in his seat. Oh yes, that would have been a tragedy as far as he was concerned. Better that he keep encouraging Virginia Hall and making her life easy; that way they were set to travel and work together for the rest of their days. Profitably. He smiled, suddenly content . . . Then the plane lurched and he and Virginia began to fall to earth.

⋆ ⋆ ⋆

Eleanor spun round, breathing heavily as Ivor barked. 'Who *is* that?' she asked, peering at the outline of the figure sitting on the wall by the side of the wrought-iron gates. 'Blair?'

'Yes,' he said simply, dry twigs cracking under his feet as he moved towards her.

Eleanor lifted her torch and shone it into his face. She was angry with him for frightening her. 'What on earth are you doing out here, Blair? You'll catch your death of cold.'

He raised his hand to shield his eyes. 'I was listening.'

'To what?' she said, exasperated.

'Can you turn off the light?' he asked, dropping his arm as she switched off the torch. The darkness trickled over them. 'Listen.'

Eleanor was cold and exasperated. 'Oh, Blair, for goodness' sake — '

'No,' he said firmly, 'listen. Listen to what they tell you.'

In the cold air Eleanor stood next to him and

203

listened patiently. A tree creaked in the slight wind and a fox barked in a far-off field. Otherwise she heard nothing and glanced back longingly towards the house, her hand resting on Ivor's head. 'We should go back, it's cold. I'll make us something to drink.'

But Blair's thoughts were far away from the small, plump woman who stood beside him.

'Something bad's going to happen,' he said simply. His voice was as clear as a lute.

'Blair, we have to go in. It's stupid standing out in the cold,' Eleanor said, sensing something she did not want to feel; some faint echo of his premonition.

He appeared not to have heard her. 'It's all going to go bad.'

Eleanor closed her eyes. So he sensed it too, did he? she thought. You're not such a child. Not so very simple at all, are you, Blair?

'There's nothing wrong,' she said emphatically, beginning to walk away.

He ran after her.

'There *is*!' he insisted petulantly. 'I *know*.'

'How?' Eleanor said, turning to face him.

They were near to the house by that time, and the light from the downstairs windows shone out, illuminating one side of Blair's face.

'Someone told me.'

'Someone told you?' Eleanor repeated, her tone exasperated, although she felt immediately guilty. She shouldn't humiliate him; shouldn't patronise him; he had every right to tell her what he knew . . . and yet . . . 'I don't want to hear any more of this nonsense.'

His eyes filled, bewilderment setting in. She had never spoken to him like that before, brushing him off, making him feel stupid. Blair's mind went back to the time he spent in the Home; they were always laughing at him there — but he was older now, and although he was confused he was also courageous and he stood up to her.

'It's not nonsense!' he blustered. 'I know something bad is going to happen. I heard it.'

'Where?' Eleanor said sharply. Fear made her brittle. 'You don't know anything. Go to bed!'

Shaking with misery, Blair began to cry, his nose running. 'The man told me, he told me.'

'Where?' Eleanor asked harshly, catching hold of his arms and shaking him. 'Who?'

Blair was too distressed to speak, his breaths came in gasps, his shoulders heaving with his sobs.

'WHO TOLD YOU . . . ? WHICH MAN?' Eleanor shouted, her voice huge in the garden.

But Blair could not respond in words. Instead he turned, one hand extended towards the window of a darkened room. He pointed, in the night, towards David Hall's study window.

★ ★ ★

Isabel woke suddenly in the very same instant that her mother's plane began to dip. Her hair stuck to the back of her neck, her hands gripping the bedclothes. Nauseous, she struggled to get out of bed and rushed to the toilet, hanging over the bowl and heaving until she emptied her stomach. Then she flushed the toilet and rinsed her face with cold water in the hand basin, her forehead pressed against the side of the white marble tiles. Something terrible was about to happen, she realised, something fearful. Her hands shook as she wrapped her arms around her body and tried to keep control.

Slowly the nausea subsided and she straightened up, her feet bare as Stanton's always were in the studio. Bare feet, blank heart. The light went on the bedroom, Teddy calling out to her. Then she knew, in that one deadening moment, she knew. Her feet stopped moving and she glanced around. Aftershave on the shelf over the wash hand basin, fluffy peach-coloured towels folded on the bath, and a pair of bathroom scales, the glass dial misted with talcum powder. Automatically Isabel knelt down and wiped it with her hand, her fingers smudging white.

Teddy called out to her again. She heard him rise from the bed, heard his feet coming across the floor towards her. If she closed the door she could stop the moment; postpone whatever demon was waiting for her. But for how long? Teddy stood in the doorway, his good-tempered face questioning, his arms reaching towards her.

And then she told him.

14

The flight finally hiccuped into Los Angeles. Virginia, although severely rattled, showed no emotion whatever as she got off the plane, though Geoffrey's face was the colour of chewing gum. He shambled after her, speechless, marvelling at her powers of control, the coat over his arm trailing its belt along the floor. Virginia went through the formalities patiently and then made her way to the exit, where a fat man stood holding a card with her name on it.

'Thank you,' she said loftily, as she slid into the back seat of the car, 'but my name is spelt V-I-R-G-I-N-I-A, not V-I-R-G-I-N-A.'

The man shuffled in the driver's seat, embarrassed.

'For God's sake, Virginia, what does it matter?' Geoffrey said, irritated. 'We could have been killed.'

Her eyes were flinty. 'But we weren't, Geoffrey, so it *does* matter.' Her hands reached into her bag and she began to check her make-up, her composure terrifying.

'It was awful,' Geoffrey said, leaning back in his seat, his mouth slack.

'Oh, good heavens, what a fuss — '

'A fuss!' he exploded. 'What in God's name are you talking about? We could have been *killed*.' His voice dropped. 'Sorry, Virginia, I'm just a bit rattled, that's all.'

'Evidently.'

'I was thinking of everything I'd lose. You know, my children, and Mary . . . ' He rambled on. 'God, I haven't got that insurance policy up to date for her . . . ' His hands ran through his hair. 'It was a close-run thing. It makes you realise how much you want to live.'

Virginia's expression was unfathomable as she said quietly, 'Did it? It rather made me realise how much I wanted to die.'

★ ★ ★

It was a joke, of course. It had to be. Teddy would walk back in the room and tell her that he was kidding. He'd smile and look all boyish again and they would end up in bed, making love, because that was what they always did. He was never really angry, well, not for long. She knew that, he was her husband after all.

He threw two cases into the back of the car and accelerated into the Baker Street traffic, making for the White House where he had booked himself in for the remainder of the night. And many more nights, until he sorted himself out. For Isabel to have betrayed him, to have lied to him, to have cheated him . . . Teddy's thoughts ran on. He had told her how he felt about children. She *knew* it, he had been fair with her, straight with her, before the wedding. She knew what trouble his sons had caused him. A car horn blasted behind him and Teddy moved back into his lane, changing his mind and making for Knightsbridge instead.

After parking he sat in the car silently, then he banged his fists down on the wheel several times. Nothing eased the explosion in his brain, the realisation that something perfect had been spoiled, for ever. He leaned his head back, dizzy with frustration. She tried to cheat me. She thought I was a pushover. Again his hand slammed down on the steering wheel. People were going to have to learn that he wasn't Mr Nice Guy. He wasn't just a hick from the back of beyond. The lad from Little Lever who had made good in the Smoke.

All I wanted was for her to be happy, and for me to be happy, but it wasn't enough. He swallowed as a cat ran across the road in front of the car and stopped, staring at him . . . Jesus, why did it all have to go wrong? Why? He could never trust Isabel again — he *would* never trust her again. To cheat him! He gasped in amazement. What the hell did she think he would do? The answer came back with all the bitterness of many years' experience. She expected him to accept the inevitable; she expected him to go along with her plan. Mr Nice Guy, Mr Agreeable, Mr Bloody Wet.

Suddenly Teddy started up the car and, lurching forwards, ran over the cat, the car wheels crushing its body into the asphalt road.

★ ★ ★

The studio door was open, the stairs dark, as always. Isabel paused, then rested her suitcase on the bottom step. Voices came from above,

209

Stanton bawling his head off at someone, then the sound of a child laughing. Wearily Isabel rested her head against the door jamb and looked up the stairwell. For an instant she nearly turned and left, but her heart lifted when she heard Prossie's voice, and she began to climb.

She climbed the stairs, each step more difficult than the last, her mouth dry as she rounded the bend at the top which led into the studio. Prossie's back was towards her, Stanton leaning down and blowing on top of Bracken's head, the little girl wriggling and laughing.

Hearing Isabel's footsteps, he stopped suddenly, straightening up. 'Christ, you look like shit.'

Prossie swung round, then rushed over to Isabel. 'What's the matter?'

'I . . . ' She trailed off. 'I didn't know where else to go.'

Stanton's eyes narrowed. 'Where's your anaemic other half?'

Prossie shot him a fierce look and turned back to Isabel. 'Oh, love . . . Tell me what happened.'

'He didn't want it.'

'That's a first for any man,' Stanton said drily.

'Oh, shut it!' Prossie snapped. 'Isabel, tell me properly. What happened?'

Isabel's eyes fixed on her friend. She seemed disorientated, then Prossie realised it was shock. Gently she rubbed her hands and signalled to Stanton who came back with a stiff brandy.

Isabel sipped it tentatively. 'I'm having a baby,' she said suddenly. Defiantly.

Prossie was overjoyed. 'But that's wonderful!'

She turned to Stanton. 'Isabel's having a baby.'

'I heard,' he said, helping himself to a drink and topping up Isabel's. 'So what's the matter, didn't *Teddy* feel *ready* for it?'

'I cheated him,' Isabel said quietly.

Stanton bent forward to hear her clearly. 'Why?' he said, frowning. 'Isn't it his?'

She laughed suddenly, softly, like a child. 'Oh, Stanton, of course it's his.'

'So?'

'He didn't want children, he said he was too old.'

Stanton snorted.

'So I decided to get pregnant and tell him when it had — '

' — been decided for him?'

She nodded.

Stanton raised his eyebrows at Prossie. 'He'll come round, just give him time. He hasn't the balls to be a bastard.'

'No, you're wrong, he won't come round,' Isabel said firmly. 'You see I misjudged him; I thought he would act as my father would have done. I thought he would be kind.' She stopped, guilt and wretchedness fighting for the upper hand. 'I was so selfish — and so stupid.'

'Oh, I don't know, he shouldn't have expected a healthy young woman not to want children,' Stanton said flatly, downing his drink. 'Do you want another one?'

Exasperated, Prossie raised her eyebrows. 'No she doesn't, it's bad for the baby.'

Irritated, Stanton moved off, his feet pounding down the stairs.

Isabel looked at Prossie helplessly. 'I was so wrong to do what I did . . . he told me he never wanted children . . . '

'Oh, pet, don't . . . don't.'

Stanton reappeared a few moments later and leaned down in front of Isabel. 'Listen, kid,' he said, 'sorry as I am, and all that, I would appreciate your shifting out of the studio now, I've got a two o'clock appointment.'

Colouring, Isabel struggled to get to her feet, Prossie standing, furious, beside her. 'You bastard, Stanton! What the hell does it matter about your stupid sitter at a time like this? How could you be so cruel when Isabel hasn't got anywhere to go? She came to us for help, and you're worried about a bloody sitter — '

'Oh, dry up, Prossie,' Stanton replied, picking up his brushes and jerking his head towards the door. 'Who said she had nowhere to go?' He winked at Isabel. 'Your bag's in your old room, kid. Welcome home.' Then he turned towards the easel. 'Now, get out.'

For the next few days Isabel slept fitfully, refusing any sleeping pills in case they harmed the baby. In her old room she curled up on the bed and looked round nostalgically. But the high white walls looked blankly at her, the African mobile over her head still in the unmoving air. Slowly, her gaze moved towards the window. The same white curtains were drawn against the light, making the room seem oddly foreign, and the Indian screen around the wash hand basin looked the worse for wear, Chloë having scribbled incoherently on the black wood.

Only the phone by her bed seemed unfamiliar, and Isabel jumped every time it rang, although it was never for her. As one day followed another Prossie realised that words meant little and left Chloë to comfort Isabel, the little girl curling up beside her on the bed, her thumb in her mouth. Slowly and painfully Isabel realised that Teddy was not the man she had thought him — and that he was not going to forgive her.

'He should ring you at least,' Prossie said, plumping herself beside Isabel on the bed. 'What the hell is he playing at? It's his child.'

'He doesn't want it.'

'So?' Prossie said, stroking Chloë's hair. 'It's still his responsibility whether he wants it or not.'

'I deceived him — '

'Oh, for God's sake,' Prossie replied aghast. 'Stop tearing yourself apart. I can't stand all this breastbeating, you were never so feeble before.' She softened her tone. 'What's done is done, you're pregnant with Teddy Gray's child. That's fact. The next thing to decide is what are you going to do about it. And, more to the point, what he is going to do?'

Isabel shrugged, her movements were heavy. 'I haven't thought about it. I suppose the only way I can make everything all right again is to get rid of the baby.'

Prossie's eyes narrowed. 'Abort it?'

'He probably wants that,' Isabel said, sighing and turning on to her side. 'But I'm not doing it . . . I'm having this baby . . . ' She was suddenly angry. 'Oh, God, what a bloody mess!'

Prossie was quick to notice the signs of

imminent panic. 'Don't worry about a thing. Stanton says that you can stay here with the baby. He says it'll be good for his reputation.'

Immediately Isabel burst out laughing, despite herself. Stanton might seem a hard man, but he was a good one at heart. 'I have to tell my mother and Eleanor . . .' she said finally, serious again. 'I should have told them already, but I couldn't stand the thought of my mother organising everything.'

Prossie wasn't surprised as she thought of Virginia Hall; she would be chillingly efficient, within days Isabel would be booked into the best hospital for the birth, Teddy Gray would receive a solicitor's letter, and the unborn child would have its name put down for the best public schools. Frowning, she glanced at Isabel.

It was obvious how much she had changed, her sweetness subdued by hurt, her liveliness gone now that life had turned on her. Prossie knew how little she slept, too often she heard footsteps in the early hours creeping towards the kitchen, and the sound of miserable retching at dawn. The baby was obviously aware of its mother's distress too; an uneasy infant carried by an uneasy mother, little more than a child herself.

'Phone him.'

Isabel glanced up. 'What?'

'Phone Teddy,' Prossie repeated. 'You have to find out what he wants and get things sorted out, one way or the other — '

'I can't.'

'You can,' Prossie insisted. 'You have to. Think

214

of the baby, Isabel.'

'I thought of the baby more than I thought of my husband,' she replied bitterly.

'All right,' Prossie said, staring hard into Isabel's face. 'But let me ask you one thing — if it came down to a choice, which of the two of them do you want the most? Your husband, or your child?'

★   ★   ★

The office was too warm when Teddy walked in, his head muffled with a hangover. Quickly he opened a window and leaned out, gulping the cool air, his hair blowing slightly in a half-hearted London breeze. He had spent several nights at the White House and then returned home, surprised to find that Isabel had left. Moodily he had checked the fridge for food, and picking up a yoghurt, went to watch a little television. His thoughts wandered off the programme quickly — he had made his decision, if Isabel got rid of the baby he was prepared to give the marriage a second chance. Things might be a little uneasy for a while, but they would straighten out, he didn't want to lose her.

Unsettled, Teddy put down the half-eaten yoghurt and turned the television down. Isabel would have to realise that he was different now; that he wasn't going to be taken for a fool. The problem was that her father had spoiled her. After all, what the hell did she want? He had given her a good home, with no money worries. She had a comfortable life with him, seeing her friends, working part time for an interior decorator to give her an interest. Teddy shook his head disbelievingly, he would like to know what his mother would have thought if she had still been alive. Poor woman worked all her damn life without a break, he thought irritably, she would have thought Isabel had it made.

A sudden thought of the baby tweaked his conscience. His three sons he remembered as infants; just as he remembered the crying, the mess in the house, the sleepless nights, and Philippa constantly irritable and uninterested in him. At first he had liked the idea of being a father, but as time passed he resented the role . . . Teddy's momentary feeling of guilt passed. No, he couldn't consider bringing up another child. It was too late. Isabel had to understand that.

A reasonable man, an easy-going man — if it was all going his way.

★　★　★

Isabel phoned The Ridings that evening, waiting as the bell rang out several times, her palms sweaty. She imagined Eleanor getting up from the table, or rushing in from the garden to answer it, just as she imagined her genuine concern when she told her what had happened. Kindness would be automatic, without reproach. Whatever Isabel had done would be accepted without censure, Teddy automatically cast as the villain of the piece.

The phone continued to ring. Answer, Isabel

begged silently. Her thoughts rushed on. After Eleanor, she would have to tell her mother. Virginia would be composed, she knew that, smiling one of her tight smiles as she assured her daughter that everything would be sorted out. Like spring cleaning; nothing too dirty, too untidy to be organised . . . she might even be pleased, Isabel thought suddenly, frowning. She closed her eyes, dreading her mother's gloating sympathy — well, neither of us had any luck with our men, did we, dear?

The phone continued to ring out, unanswered, and after another moment Isabel replaced the receiver. Everything was in suspended animation, she thought hopelessly, but not for long. Suddenly determined, she got to her feet and reached for her coat.

★　★　★

Twenty years of marriage and three children are not easily forgotten, Philippa thought, pacing the street, her Hermès leather handbag with its gold chain swinging on her shoulder. When she had last spoken to Teddy he seemed preoccupied, and for a week there had been no answer from the Baker Street flat. Not that she had ever rung there before; no, since her ex-husband's remarriage she had never interfered. Deep in thought, Philippa paused by the lights on Brompton Road, a pigeon pecking at the pavement by her feet.

She had to admit that she missed him; for all his irritating ways. Of course they were socially mismatched, but lately Teddy had been doing very well in his practice, so perhaps her family had been a little too hasty in their assessment of him. The lights changed and Philippa crossed the road, still thinking deeply. Oh yes, it was all right for them to tell her to divorce Teddy, but they didn't have to live alone afterwards with three sons to look after. Resentment boiled in her; in the middle of London, how likely was it that a woman of forty-five would marry again?

Philippa's Gucci heels clicked along the grey street and as she remembered Teddy Gray a remarkable transformation took place. The Northern hick suddenly metamorphosed into a man of substance. Selective editing allowed Philippa to daydream happily; Little Lever was expunged, as was Teddy's habit of wearing black socks with a blue suit, or the faint accent which crept into his speech when he was talking quickly . . .

Philippa felt an instant and unbearable pang of anguish and, unable to stand it any longer, hailed a taxi and arrived at Teddy's office minutes later. He seemed hardly surprised to see her, in fact it seemed as though he expected her, and when he offered her a coffee, Philippa's heart soared. As skilful with his mental editing as she was, Teddy told his ex-wife the whole story.

'But that's terrible,' she said, forgetting her coffee as she glanced across the desk. It was annoying, but for an instant Teddy looked hardly older than their eldest son. 'What are you going to do?'

'Isabel will have to get rid of the baby,' he said,

218

glancing up. 'I know that sounds hard — '

'Oh, no.'

' — but it has to be done.' He shook his head. It was easy to talk to Philippa, after all she had known him for a long time. 'I told her I never wanted any more children. I never lied to her.'

'She was wrong to do what she did,' Philippa said softly. There was no need to shout, the point was made.

Teddy nodded reluctantly. 'But she's very young . . . '

The words stabbed Philippa near the heart, but she kept a careful look of understanding on her face.

' . . . and very sweet . . . ' he continued. 'But perhaps a little *too* young for me.' Teddy didn't know quite what to think, but the office was hot and his hangover made him vulnerable to rash notions. He glanced at his ex-wife, at least Philippa would never have pulled a trick like this. She had honour, class. 'Maybe it's not fair of me to expect someone her age not to want children,' he said blindly. 'Perhaps it's all my fault . . . '

Philippa got to her feet and walked round the desk, standing only inches from her ex-husband's chair. The scent of her Madame Rochas was a potent memory for him.

'Listen, darling, I'd be the last person to interfere, you know that, but perhaps you need a little breathing space from each other . . . '

He nodded, boyishly grateful for her advice. 'I think we do, at least until this mess is sorted out.' Teddy paused, the effects of the hangover and his own misery making him maudlin. 'Oh God,

Philippa, what happened? I've made such a bloody mess of my life.'

Immediately she leaned down and took him in her arms, feeling a rush of triumph as he responded and clung to her.

Just in that moment Isabel walked in. Her glance took in the scene with blistering clarity, Teddy stumbling guiltily to his feet, his blond hair untidy, Philippa leaning against the desk, defiant in her velvet hair band and Hermès suit. Victory crackled like an aura around her, and Isabel knew then that her husband was no longer hers.

'What the hell are you playing at?' she snapped, fury in every word.

'Listen, Isabel — '

She cut him off immediately. An angry young woman in a dark dress, ready to sort out her life. 'I came here to talk to you, Teddy, and I don't want an audience.'

'Philippa was just being kind — '

'Kind!' she snapped. 'What in God's name has she got to be kind about? I want her out of here. This situation concerns us, and us alone.'

'Perhaps I should go,' Philippa said, rising to her feet.

But Teddy had already chosen. One way meant difficulties, the other familiarity. In the instant he wavered he moved towards safety, and away from chance.

'No, I want you to stay,' he said to his ex-wife.

Alienated, Isabel felt at first intense rage, then a coolness, and lastly an unexpected pity. The man was dissolving before her eyes, an ice man melting to the touch.

'All right, Teddy, as I can't throw her out bodily — not in my condition — we'll talk in front of her.'

He winced, but said nothing.

'I know that what I did was wrong, but I did it for the right reasons.' She paused. 'No, I won't even say it's wrong, just misguided. I'm having this baby, Teddy, because no man on earth has the right to kill another human being simply for their own convenience.' Her voice was like her mother's, but her feelings were David Hall's. 'I want children, you see, not just one but a few . . .'

He looked away, down at his hands lying, palm down, on his desk. He remembered the sleeping girl in Stanton's studio and his throat tightened. But he didn't stop her, or even interrupt.

'I need a family, not just a husband, Teddy. God knows, I do love you,' she said, her voice failing, her gaze averted from the watching Philippa, 'but that's obviously not enough.'

'It's all rather a mess — '

Isabel swung round to face Philippa. 'Keep out of this! You've no doubt already had your say.' Breathing heavily, she turned back to Teddy. 'Well, what do we do now?'

He felt as though he had been pushed into a test tube, a cork stopper forced into the top to keep out any air. There was no room to move, or breathe, and he struggled to find his voice.

Finally he said, 'Do you want a divorce?'

No, Isabel thought, reeling at the word. No, I don't. I want us to go home and make love and

221

be as we were. I want to feel your body on top of mine and catch the scent of your hair on the pillow.

'Is that what *you* want?' she said brokenly, her voice so quiet it could have been a child speaking.

He nodded. Never said the word; never gave it utterance. Just nodded — and that was enough.

15

Stanton yawned and stretched his arms. The studio was freezing. Barefooted, he padded about, the fluorescent lights humming overhead, his hands in their fingerless mittens alabaster white. He glanced at the canvas on the easel and blew on his fingers to warm them, tucking a brush into the top pocket of his smock, his eyes fixed on the painting. Not bad, he thought grudgingly, little Adriana should be pleased with her likeness. He smiled quickly, she had been very like her mother in the end he thought, recalling their exploits on the couch in the corner of the studio.

His mind replayed their lovemaking and then he shrugged and threw a cover over the finished painting, turning off the studio lights and walking into the dark drawing room. The vague shapes of his paintings looked down at him, a faint light shining at the far end of the wall. Frowning, he moved over to his stereo unit and turned it off, his hand resting momentarily on the warm top of the cabinet. Little Chloë at it again, he thought resignedly.

Carefully he poured out his usual drink, sherry topped up with vodka, took a long gulp, and then burped quietly. He then felt his way, as a blind man might, towards the sofa and slid into it, his hands resting on his stomach. In the distance a police siren raced towards Notting

Hill, and a door slammed on the opposite side of the house. In a minute he would go to bed, he thought, although Prossie would already be asleep with Bracken beside her. He frowned momentarily. God, children everywhere — and another one on the way with Isabel. He shook his head. She was a nice kid. Too nice, or she would have taken that shit Gray to the cleaners instead of struggling on alone. Still, the house was big and she hardly took up any room, so who cared how long she stayed? Besides, she had talent . . . Once.

Taking several more gulps of his drink, Stanton mellowed. The portrait was a success, Prossie was restored to full loveliness and it wasn't so bad having the kids around, even in the studio. If only Chloë would just stop fiddling with the paints everything would be fine . . . If only the Duke of sodding Nottingham, or wherever it was, would pay his bill, everything would be fine . . . If only the frigging dealer would cough up his money, everything would be fine.

Stanton sat up, suddenly nettled by a growing variety of irritations. Putting down his glass he padded into the kitchen and pulled out a chicken, made a pile of sandwiches and heaped them on to a plate. He then put it on to a tray with several glasses and a bottle of wine and went upstairs.

Balancing the tray, he banged his foot on Isabel's door. 'Get up, it's party time!' he shouted, walking towards his own room and waking Prossie.

She rubbed her eyes, Bracken sat up in bed

beside her. Isabel, now heavily pregnant, walked in with Chloë only seconds later.

'Sit down, Isabel, come on, put your feet up,' Stanton ordered. Obediently she sat down, the bed creaking under the weight of three adults and two children.

'Oh, boy, chicken sandwiches,' Prossie said, squinting in the bad light as she reached out for one.

Stanton raised his eyes and offered Isabel the plate. 'Eat up, and don't puke it back either, these things cost money.'

She laughed happily and began to eat. 'So what's this in aid of?'

'Life,' Stanton said simply, pouring out the wine and passing her a glass. 'You look good pregnant, Isabel.'

Contented, she smiled. Prossie reached for another sandwich. 'You know,' she said, speaking with her mouth half full, 'no one makes sandwiches like Stanton. No one on earth . . . '

He looked at her and felt a fast rush of affection and then he looked at Isabel, and was fearful for her. In his own haphazard way, Stanton loved both of them and felt suddenly deliriously happy.

'Here,' he said, pulling some money out of his wallet and passing it to Isabel. 'Go and get yourself something better to wear, kid. You looked a sight today, like something from the scattered homes.'

She hesitated, taken aback, as Stanton wasn't known for his generosity. 'I can't take your money . . . ' she began, her thoughts running on,

225

' . . . anyway, what was wrong with the dress I had on today? It fits like a glove.'

'Sure, like a boxing glove,' Stanton replied, nudging her good-naturedly as he started to laugh. 'Go on, get something special,' he said, then glanced at Prossie. 'Both of you get something. I want to see my girls looking good.'

In the dim light he could not see Isabel's eyes fill, the memory of her father coming back just for an instant in his friend.

★ ★ ★

Isabel went into labour the following day, before she had the chance to spend Stanton's money on a new dress. She clung on to Prossie and gritted her teeth, saying nothing in the ambulance or at the hospital, except, 'Phone Eleanor when the baby's born. Mother's in Italy, so you can't get hold of her . . . ' She stopped, the contractions ripping into her stomach. 'Don't tell Teddy.'

Prossie clung on to her hand.

'Are you sure?'

She nodded, grey-faced, sweat beading her forehead. 'Don't tell him. He never wanted the baby born.'

For ten hours Prossie sat with Isabel, Stanton arriving late after a series of sittings, and having left Chloë and Bracken with a next-door neighbour. He sat, as he had done for the births of his own children, in the waiting room, and smoked a packet of Sobranie cigarettes, losing patience at two in the morning when he took out a small sketchpad and began to draw a pretty

226

nurse. At three he was asleep, two empty Guinness cans on the table in front of him.

Isabel had no idea of time; it was all dissolving into red pain. She clung on to the sheet, then turned and clung on to Prossie, her face pressed against the pillow. Teddy was there one minute, then she realised it was just a dream; he didn't even know the baby was coming; all he knew was that the divorce was under way. Other images came to Isabel but they all faded without recognition, until she thought of her father and smiled.

The baby was born at five. Small, irritable and very fierce, Sybella came into the world and cried out when her mother held her. Nothing like the pliable Chloë or Bracken.

Isabel held on to her anxiously, fearfully.

'She's so cross.'

'Christ, what a noise!' Stanton said, coming in to see the newborn. His eyes opened wide. 'She'll be a beauty, this one. You mark my words.' He winced. 'But a bloody noisy one.'

'She'll settle,' Prossie said phlegmatically, stroking the baby's head. 'She's just startled, that's all.'

Sybella remained startled, and succeeded in startling everyone else. Difficult to soothe, and refusing to be breastfed, she set off all the other babies in the hospital by crying most of the night. In the end Stanton came back with a dummy, but that was soon spat out. Sybella wanted the world to know she was alive, and angry.

Exhausted by the birth and by her difficult child, Isabel turned to Eleanor for help.

'She's impossible. She only quietens when Prossie or Stanton hold her.' She felt a rush of rejection. 'She's happier with anyone but me.'

'You're just nervous — '

'Jealous, more like,' Isabel replied honestly. 'Oh, Eleanor, I can't stand to see how good she is with everyone else; it's as though she hates me.'

'Babies don't hate their mothers,' Eleanor replied calmly, 'but they do know when they're anxious, and that is what Sybella's picking up from you. That's why she doesn't cry with Stanton or Prossie, they're used to children.' She paused, trying to reassure her. 'She'll settle down, you'll see.'

But she didn't, and she had a tremendous personality, even as a baby. Wise beyond her years, Eleanor said, when she came down to Holland Park to see her, trying to encourage Isabel to come back to The Ridings for a while. But the new mother was too nervous to leave the familiar territory, and relied too heavily on Prossie to think of looking after Sybella on her own.

Isabel made one concession though — she and the baby moved to another bedroom at the far end of the Holland Park house, Stanton deciding that enough of Sybella's constant nocturnal howling was enough.

'She's a baby, so what?' he bellowed. 'She's young, she'll recover. Me, I might never get over this lack of sleep.'

Prossie was in full agreement when she explained the situation to Isabel. 'She sets the others off, you see — '

'Do you want me to leave?' Isabel asked defensively.

'Don't be stupid!' Prossie replied. 'I hate it when you act like a martyr — '

'I *feel* like a martyr,' Isabel replied angrily. 'I can't do anything right for the baby. She just keeps crying. I can't understand it, I looked after your children all right, they were no trouble.'

Prossie frowned. 'They're just different children.'

'How different can children be?' Isabel snapped wearily. The broken nights were telling on her; her dreams of maternal bliss shattered by an irredeemably bad-tempered child. She had lost her husband for this baby, because she had been sure that it was the right thing to do. With a pang of guilt Isabel wondered if Teddy hadn't been right all along.

'Just let her settle.'

Isabel turned on Prossie angrily. 'I don't want her,' she said suddenly, cruelly. 'I lost the people I loved, my father and my husband, and I thought she might take their place but she can't.' She glanced at the baby, who was suddenly defiantly quiet. 'We're enemies.'

A month later, when Sybella was only eight weeks old, Isabel took her home for a visit to The Ridings. Sybella slept until mid-journey, and then began to cry, a middle-aged woman in the next seat asking if she could hold her.

Isabel smiled awkwardly, and passed over the child.

Almost immediately, Sybella fell into a contented sleep.

'They are a nuisance, aren't they, when they play up?' the woman said. She could see the familiar signs of exhaustion on Isabel's face, the dead eyes and the nervous gestures. 'You don't want to worry though, the ones who are difficult when they're babies grow up good.'

'At this rate she'll be lucky to grow up at all,' Isabel replied drily.

She slept the rest of the journey blissfully unconscious until the train pulled in and the woman nudged her.

'Time to go home and show your baby off,' she said, holding Sybella out for her mother to take her.

For an instant Isabel hesitated and then smiled as she took her child. At once Sybella began to cry, and she continued to do so until the taxi wound its way up the drive of The Ridings. Eleanor hurried out to the car and opened the door.

'Welcome home,' she said, beaming with pleasure.

The baby's cries drowned out her words as Isabel struggled to get out of the car.

Blair stood behind Eleanor, grinning at her and holding out his arms.

Without another thought she gave him her child, and sighed with relief as Sybella rested peacefully against his chest. His eyes fixed on the baby and for the first time Isabel realised how beautiful Sybella was: dark-haired, blue-eyed, her face already dark-browed, her limbs long and well-formed. There was no hint of Teddy Gray in this child; no hint of an unhappy coupling . . . No, she was a heavenly changeling — just like the man who held her.

Blair would not be parted from Sybella and

learned very quickly what she needed to keep her sweet-tempered. Nappies were changed, feeds prepared, and baths run willingly, the child/man transfixed by the infant.

Not that Isabel wasn't anxious.

'I worry about him. I mean he's not a father, so how can he cope with her?'

'He just does. He remembers what we tell him and wants to do everything for her,' Eleanor responded easily. 'Don't worry, Blair would die rather than risk that child, or let anything happen to her.'

Virginia thought otherwise and was vocal on the subject. Returning from another trip to America she descended on The Ridings full of criticism and outrage. From her old familiar vantage point at the top of the stairs, Isabel had watched her mother arrive. Her hair was precisely styled, but much greyer than Isabel remembered, her face composed, and her dark grey suit exquisitely tailored. Walking into the hall Virginia paused, drawing off her gloves and her coat and waiting, perfectly balanced on her court shoes, for the confrontation to begin.

'Hello, Mother.'

She glanced up, her eyes taking in the change in her daughter. Isabel seemed older, more aggressive, her voice a little sharp, her hands deep in the pockets of her trousers.

'Well hello, dear,' she said. They exchanged kisses without contact. 'I hear there is some trouble with the baby.'

'She's just fretful, that's all,' Isabel said defensively.

231

'Eleanor's been a fool to let that overgrown moron look after her — '

'Blair doesn't look after my baby, I do,' Isabel replied coldly. 'He just helps, that's all.'

Virginia regarded her daughter thoughtfully. Her marriage ruined, all for the sake of a child. Children, she thought ruefully, had a lot to answer for. 'Help or otherwise, I don't think he is the person to bring up my grandchild — '

'Oh, and who is, Mother?' Isabel replied, her voice freezing with enmity. 'You? I hardly think so, you had precious little to do with my upbringing.'

Virginia paled. 'Perhaps if I had had more to do with it, you would have turned out better,' she answered. 'You could have done so well, Isabel, and instead . . . ' Her voice trailed off, as though her daughter's actions had been too heinous to mention, 'you got married to the first man who came along — '

'Have you ever wondered why?' Isabel asked, interrupting her mother and facing up to her. 'Because I wanted to be loved.'

Virginia glanced away, almost amused.

'That makes you laugh, doesn't it, Mother?' Isabel said. 'Well, it wasn't so bloody funny for me. When my father died, I had no comfort from you, so I took it where I found it.'

'Don't blame me for your shortcomings — '

'Shortcomings! For a child to want its mother to love it?'

Virginia's eyes blazed. 'I loved you as much as I could. Just as I loved your father — '

'Well, it wasn't enough for me, and it

232

obviously wasn't enough for him.'

'What do you know about it!' Virginia said savagely, all composure suddenly gone. She was momentarily terrifying. 'You're such an expert on love, are you, Isabel? Well you explain to me why you couldn't help your father, or hold on to your husband. Go on, I would be fascinated to hear your explanation.' She paused, gathering strength for the kill. 'You want to blame me for your father's death, well, I'm not taking responsibility for that. It was his life and his choice to end it . . . and as for you, if you want to squander your brain, end your marriage, pass your child over to any Tom, Dick or Harry who is good enough to take her off your hands, well, don't expect me to stand by and approve.'

'I don't give a damn for your approval!' Isabel replied hoarsely, hating her mother. 'What the hell does your approval mean?'

Virginia caught hold of her daughter's arm, her fingers pinching the skin. 'Do you think I don't know what you're feeling? That I don't know the disappointment? The humiliation? I had to stand by for *years* and watch while you and your father excluded me. And it hurt. If your daughter does the same to you, perhaps it's poetic justice.'

Isabel tried to shake off her mother's grip. 'You're a cruel woman, that's why no one loved you — '

'Stop it!' Eleanor said suddenly, walking into the hall and standing up to both of them. 'That's enough, all the recriminations in the world won't bring David back. We have all to work together now to give this child a happy home.'

Virginia dropped her daughter's arm and her face relaxed; she looked frighteningly composed. 'You're right, there is no point looking back. Sybella is our first concern, and Isabel's future is our second. After all, you can't go on living in Holland Park — '

'But I am, Mother.'

Eleanor saw Virginia take in her breath, fighting not to lose her temper. She wanted Isabel home, at The Ridings, where she could control her, but she had a battle on her hands.

'I think it would be better for both of you. After all, you were happy here as a child.'

'Sybella is not me.'

'No,' Virginia conceded, 'but she is in need of a good home and a permanent one. Camping out with a person such as Stanton Feller is *not* the environment in which I want my grandchild.'

'But it is the environment in which I want my child,' Isabel countered flatly, 'and Sybella is *my* child, not yours.'

Virginia looked carefully at her daughter and then glanced away, apparently resigned. 'We'll talk about this another time. Everyone is overwrought at the moment.'

With that she went upstairs to her room, knowing that Eleanor and Isabel watched her go. Only when she had closed her door did Virginia let out a shaky sigh and pull off her shoes, her body trembling. She was terribly tired, and the argument had shaken her, especially as the trip had been wearying and once or twice she had faltered while giving her speeches. Even Geoffrey

234

had noticed and he usually missed most things. She was getting old, she realised sadly, as she sat down heavily on the edge of her bed, unzipping her skirt and unfastening her blouse. Age was slowing her, stopping her in her tracks, just as age would render her incapable and keep her here, at The Ridings, with her memories. Virginia glanced down at her naked body. Her skin sagged slightly without clothes and her mind was losing its firmness too . . . before long the trips would stop and she would have to remain here for the rest of her life. Guilt and memory rattled like pebbles on a frozen lake as Virginia's composure suddenly crumpled and she buried her face in the pillow and wept.

Downstairs Eleanor faced her niece. 'You were too hard on her.'

'I don't want her interfering in my child's life,' Isabel said flatly.

'She's getting older.'

'So?' Isabel countered. 'You're getting older, but you don't try to interfere. She wants me to stay here, ready for her old age.' Isabel glanced round. 'If I come back with Sybella she will have us both on tap for when she retires, and although she considers me a failure, she will be happy to think she can live vicariously through my child.' Her face was set hard. 'No, Eleanor, that is not how it's going to be.'

'You're jealous,' her aunt replied.

The words slapped Isabel. 'What?'

'You're jealous,' she repeated, defying her niece's anger. 'You think Sybella prefers everyone else to you and you're terrified that she might turn to your mother. That would be the final straw, wouldn't it? For your mother to take your child.'

Isabel blinked. 'But Sybella is *my* child!'

'Yes, and never forget that you are Virginia Hall's child too, and much as you dislike the idea, there are similarities between you. She knows how you think because she has already experienced rejection, whereas you feel the rejection of your husband and child deeply because you have only known acceptance until now.' She reached out her hand to her niece. 'You should try to understand your mother, Isabel, you could help each other.'

'I don't want to help her,' Isabel said calmly. 'I don't trust her, or like her. And I don't want my child to be influenced by her.'

'Your father — '

'Is not here to speak for himself,' Isabel said bluntly. 'Don't ask me to forget the past because my mother is suddenly getting older. Age doesn't alter what happened, and something happened between my mother and my father that caused him to kill himself.'

Eleanor was exasperated. 'You don't know that for sure!'

'Neither do you,' Isabel replied, 'but you've always suspected it.'

Her aunt did not reply.

'The past is not past, Eleanor,' Isabel said softly, 'because it always affects what we do in the present. I don't want my child to spend too much time with my mother. Believe me, it would not be wise.'

Be wise, be careful. Her father's words came back and for an instant they seemed to mock her.

16

Isabel's divorce came through speedily, one of the advantages of being married to a solicitor she thought wryly as she read the form which told her it was all over. Decree Absolute. The End. Her face was reflective as she folded up the paper and placed it amongst her things, then walked down to the studio. Music was playing from the room next door, Prossie nursing a sleeping Sybella in her arms.

'Change lobsters and dance,' Isabel said enigmatically.

'Huh?'

'I was just thinking — I can remember when I used to nurse Chloë for you. We've switched roles.'

'No, just children,' Prossie said deftly, gesturing for Isabel to sit down. 'That bloody Greek bitch has just been to collect her portrait,' she whispered. 'Stanton thinks I don't know he was knocking her off in there.'

Isabel raised her eyebrows. 'Oh no! I don't know how you stand it.'

'It's like living with a permanent dieter,' she replied, tongue in cheek, 'you have to forgive the occasional pig-out.'

Tactfully, Isabel changed the subject. 'D'you think she'll stay asleep?' she asked, glancing at her daughter.

'For ever, or for another hour or so?'

Isabel leaned towards Sybella and peered into her face. 'At least it's not as bad as it used to be, at least now she lets me hold her for a while.'

'She just picked up all the trauma, that's all,' Prossie said, shifting her position. Sybella slept on. 'All the upset with Teddy was bound to have some effect.' She paused. 'Do you miss him?'

'No,' Isabel said simply, 'to be really truthful the only man I ever miss is my father. As for the rest, you can't trust any of them.'

'But Stanton cares for you.'

'In his way,' Isabel agreed, 'but I could never live with someone like him. I'd be too jealous.'

Prossie's expression was sympathetic. 'You'll find someone soon. Besides, your marriage wasn't a total failure, you have Sybella.'

The two women looked at the sleeping child. She was already a favourite model for Stanton, her striking face appearing time and again in his work.

'Do you think I'll ever get the hang of it?' Isabel asked, rushing on to explain. 'You see, I thought I'd be such a good mother. After looking after your children, and finding it so easy, I thought that having a baby of my own would be . . . simple.' Her hair fell away from her face as she leaned her head back against the sofa. 'I thought I would make a good wife too. I wished for that, you know.' She glanced at Prossie shyly. 'I made one of my four wishes that I could be happily married. And I was . . . for a while . . . It's funny, but I'm not too smart about myself. I wished for things that weren't right for me, and gave up the one thing I could do well.'

She looked at her child.

'I became a poor mother when I could have been a good painter. I gave up my career for sex and safety.' She laughed, but there was no bitterness in the sound. Just resignation. 'I gave up my talent, and I was punished for it.'

'Quite bloody right,' Stanton said, walking into the room and sitting on the arm of the sofa. 'So why not try again?'

'You once told me you had to want to succeed in your guts; it had to really *matter* to you.' Isabel shrugged. 'It must never have mattered enough to me or I would not have let it go.'

'Maybe it's just lurking in you, waiting to get out again. Like glandular fever,' he said helpfully, watching Isabel as she got to her feet.

'Maybe,' she agreed, 'but I'm not looking for it. If the time comes when I feel I can paint again Fate will determine it, not me.'

The following evening Isabel had arranged to go to the theatre with Mal Harris, an old dealer friend of her father's, and she asked Prossie to babysit. Prossie agreed willingly, plonking Sybella down on the couch next to Bracken and waving through the studio window as Isabel left. She turned at the gate and smiled broadly, the evening warm and high with the sound of birds. She looked young and pretty in a floral dress, her slim legs tanned, and her expression eager as she hailed a taxi to take her to the West End.

The play was indifferent but she was happy, unconcerned, and Mal was good company, making her laugh in the interval when they went to the bar for a drink, Isabel's thoughts no more

240

serious than a child's. At ten-thirty they returned to Holland Park, Isabel insisting that she could walk the remaining fifty yards to the studio on her own.

'I'll be home in a minute, Mal. Don't bother to drive me to the door. Besides it's a one-way street.'

'You sure you'll be all right?'

Isabel nodded. 'Of course I'm sure, it's only a few yards ... I had a lovely evening, Mal, thanks,' she said, waving as he pulled away from the kerb and disappeared into the late traffic.

Humming under her breath, Isabel swung her handbag and glanced up at the street lamps. The night was not dark, more like dusk, the shapes of the houses black against the deepening sky. She had gone past several houses when she heard the footsteps behind her. Probably someone exercising their dog, she thought at first, then realised the steps were too quick for that. Closer they came, then closer, and it was only when an arm closed round her face and neck that Isabel suddenly realised what was happening.

Hands reached under her skirt; others groped at her breasts as she struggled, frantically trying to loosen the grip round her throat, her knees buckling as she began to fall. The pressure on her throat increased, a glimpse of a man's face pressing close to hers as she slid on to the pavement. Immediately they began to drag her, her bare legs and elbows scraping the ground, as they pulled her towards the alleyway between two of the largest houses.

Her hands reached up and clawed at the air,

fighting for breath, then she managed to kick the man who was holding her round the throat. He swore violently and let go, leaving Isabel gasping and drawing in great gulps of air, on all fours in the street. But as she tried to get up, he kicked her.

'Fucking cow!' he shouted, one boot landing in her stomach as she fell backwards.

'Bitch!' the other man screamed, his own foot aimed at her head.

She could feel the soft night air on her face and on her bare breasts and legs, and thought for an instant that she heard singing as one of the men smashed her right arm against the ground. Pain exploded inside her as the fingers of her right hand curled inwards like a burning leaf.

Along the cold street she was dragged, the men still trying to get her away from the street lamps and into the darkness of the alley. Under the towering houses she passed, pulled along, her head bouncing on the flagstones, the smell of dog excrement in her nostrils. Then, mercifully, she began to fade, her mind turning off before her eyes did, their expression fixed for a lingering moment on the magnolia tree blooming over her head.

17

Lights. Green doors. Faded cream paint on corridor walls. Smell of disinfectant. Swishing of cotton skirts passing. The creak of a trolley. A far off phone ringing. Pain. The cold steel bars of a stretcher touching the skin.

Isabel winced, mewed like a kitten, and moved her arm away from the stretcher bar. A light shone over her head. White light; almost as white as heat. Like pain, like fire, burning. She moaned, her eyes failing to focus properly as someone began to push her along. Over her head went the line of lights, the sudden bend of a corridor making her roll slightly on the stretcher, her arm again brushing the steel bar. She blinked — even blinking caused her pain — and slid backwards into her own thoughts, thinking of herself as a child in a pram, pushed along.

'Daddy . . . ' Isabel said softly.

But when a nurse bent down to hear what she said she turned away, her eyes fixing instead on the dark mass of red on the pillow next to her.

'Keep your head still,' someone said. Not unkindly, just emphatically. Keep your head still. Keep still, be good. Let us do what we want with you.

The kicks replayed in Isabel's mind, over and over again. The men's feet, in crêpe-soled shoes, kicking out. Again the memory came back. Her head banging on the cold pavement, her bare

243

legs drawn up, her hand clenched. Again the kicks resounded, and Isabel sobbed quickly as hands fixed around her head to keep her still. People holding her down. Panicking, she began to struggle, thinking she was back on the Holland Park pavement . . .

'Let me go!'

'Hush . . . hush. Be still now.'

'Let me go . . .' The words exhausted her and her mind trailed off, her body giving way.

Cigar ash by a wing-backed chair. Hair hardly greying, the frayed cuff of a Viyella shirt, leather buttons on his jacket worn with wear. The shadow of the Dante bust.

'Daddy?' Isabel said again softly.

'Your father will be here soon,' the nurse replied, not knowing that he was dead, and that his daughter was merely returning home in her head. Taking the only route she knew.

The world will be kind to you in stages . . . be wise . . . darling, be wise . . .

The pain shot through her suddenly. She gasped, trying to move her right arm. A whole world of pain exploding inside her. Her stomach seemed as though it was tearing and bleeding inside her, her head grinding with images and red fire, the right side of her face stiff with dried blood. She tried to open her eyes again, but the lids remained closed and as she attempted to move her right arm the limb only flinched, her fingers turned inwards towards the palm like the legs of a dying crab.

Reality winded her. Again she tried to move her fingers. A flicker, no more. A ghost of feeling.

244

'My hand . . . ' she said softly, then stopped as the tears came.

Slowly, they ran down her face, making little white trails through the dried blood. Fighting hysteria, Isabel fixed her attention on her tears and behind her closed eyes she lay quietly. Stop fighting. Stop struggling. It will all be over soon, she thought. Blindly she lay. Blind and quiet. Still. Making no movements, but hearing everything.

Be calm, be wise, her father said suddenly.

'Yes,' she replied, eyes closed. 'Yes, Daddy. Yes.'

An old woman had been Isabel's saviour. Looking out from the first-floor window of her flat she had seen Isabel being beaten by the two men and immediately phoned for the police and an ambulance. Then she had replaced the receiver and opened the window, leaning out on to her balcony and calling out to the men to stop. Her figure, backlighted by the room behind her, looked fragile, but her voice rang out aggressively across the street. Soon other lights went on, a few people coming to their doors, only to close them hurriedly again when they saw what was happening.

By that time Isabel was no longer aware of anything. She didn't know that the men had run off, startled by the shouting woman and knowing that they had been seen. She didn't know that they had reached the end of the street and parted to give themselves a better chance of escape. She didn't know that they never looked back . . . Unconscious, she lay exposed and bleeding on the pavement, people staring at her body from behind drawn curtains, her privacy violated by a dozen hungry eyes.

Finally an old woman hurried out into the street, laid a blanket over Isabel and took hold of her hand. Two minutes trickled past. The blood from Isabel's facial injuries pooled beside her, a dark bruise mottling her face from her forehead to her cheek. Under the street lamp, she looked like a sleeping child who had been playing with paints.

★   ★   ★

'Is she a relative?' the nurse asked when Stanton arrived at the hospital.

'What the shit has that got to do with anything? Isabel Hall is my pupil, but she also lives with me.'

The nurse's expression faltered.

'Not as my lover!' Stanton explained impatiently. 'But with us.' He pointed to the seated Prossie. 'She is a very close friend. We care for her,' he added lamely.

Shortly afterwards a young doctor emerged, smiling.

Stanton's face set. 'How's Isabel?' Dr Andrews glanced down at his notes.

'She's got a subdural haematoma — '

'A what? For God's sake speak bloody English.'

'Miss Hall has got a clot on the left side of her brain which can only be resolved by surgery.'

'What kind of surgery?'

246

'It will only take about an hour.'

Stanton turned to Prossie. 'Did I ask how long it would take?' He glanced back at Dr Andrews. 'I asked what *kind* of surgery it was.'

The doctor coloured and his voice hardened. 'The surgeon uses a burr hole — it's a kind of drill — to bore into the skull.' He continued, brutally frank. 'Then they suck out the clot which is causing the pressure in the patient's head.'

Stanton's face turned ashen.

'They *drill* into her head?'

'It's not an unusual procedure.'

'Unless it happens to be your head,' Stanton replied coldly. 'Is it safe?'

Dr Andrews hugged the case notes close to his chest as he replied, 'All surgery carries a risk.'

'So it's dangerous?'

'I didn't say that.'

'You implied it.'

'Miss Hall has a serious head injury caused either by a kick to the head, or by her skull hitting the pavement as she fell . . . '

Prossie's hand went up to her mouth, but her eyes were steady. 'Go on.'

'The clot is affecting her right arm — '

'She's a painter,' Stanton said disbelievingly. 'She's a bloody painter for Christ's sake! She needs her right arm and hand to work perfectly. She *needs* it . . . ' He trailed off, seeing the horror of Isabel's tragedy as though he was suffering it himself.

'She should recover the full use in time. With a lot of work.'

'How long?'

Dr Andrews paused. 'Six months to a year ... at the moment we have to take things one step at a time. After the operation, Miss Hall should start to recover because getting rid of the clot gets rid of the reason for the weakness in her arm. When she gets stronger, we will start working on recovering the full use of her arm.'

'What about her face?' Stanton asked suddenly. 'Is her face marked?'

'Only bruising,' Dr Andrews replied.

Stanton nodded. 'Thank God ... Bruises fade.' Another thought struck him. 'The operation on her head — will they have to shave off her hair?'

'Only on the left hand side.'

'Oh, so that's all right,' Stanton replied bitterly. 'Being bald on one side isn't so bad.'

'It will grow back,' Dr Andrews replied coldly.

'Sure.'

Dr Andrews hesitated, then glanced at Isabel's notes. 'What about her family?'

'We'll look after the baby.'

The doctor nodded. 'But she keeps asking for her father.'

'Her father,' Stanton said finally, 'is dead.'

★ ★ ★

Eleanor was in the garden when the telephone rang. Quickly she got to her feet and hurried in, pulling off her work gloves and lifting the receiver. Blair hovered by the open window, listening.

'Hello?'

'It's Prossie.'

'Oh hello, dear, how nice to hear from you.'

The summer light danced on the silver and darted along the polished sideboard. Happy light.

'Eleanor, I tried to get hold of you last night, but there was no reply.'

'There should have been,' she said easily, 'but the phone's been out of order. The engineers only came to fix it an hour ago.' She paused, suddenly alerted. 'Why? Is there anything wrong?'

Prossie's voice was soft. 'There's been an accident.'

'Accident?' Eleanor echoed. 'Oh God, not Isabel?'

'She's been beaten up — '

Eleanor sat down, her weight leaning heavily against the cold radiator, her legs shaking. 'How . . . how is she? Where is she?'

'She's in Charing Cross Hospital, in Intensive Care — '

'Oh God.'

'They operated on her immediately — '

'For what? What happened to her?' Eleanor said shrilly. Blair rushed round the house and banged the front door as he came in. He stood beside her as she talked down the phone. 'Tell me what happened.'

'There were two men — it was a bungled rape attempt.' Prossie paused. 'I'm so sorry, Eleanor, but they beat her up . . . '

Eleanor moaned. Slow motion horror climbing over her.

'She had a blood clot in her head, but the operation's relieved that. They say she'll be all right, and that she'll get back the full use of her hand.'

Eleanor's eyes stared ahead, the words making impact one by one. Like stones on greenhouse windows. 'Her hand?' Pause. 'Which hand?'

Wait, wait for the bad news. So much of it.

'Her right hand.'

'It would be,' Eleanor said softly, her eyes filling. Blair watched her, his face creased with misery. 'Will it get better?'

'They say so,' Prossie said, hurrying on. 'She'll be fine, you'll see. Honestly, they said she's making great progress.'

'I'll tell Virginia,' Eleanor said, her hands shaking as violently as her legs. 'Don't worry about that, Prossie, I'll tell her.'

'Where is she?'

'Milan at the moment,' Eleanor replied, nausea building up in her. 'How does Isabel look?'

'Her face is bruised, but nothing's broken. She has a little scar above her lip, but that will fade.' Prossie paused. 'She'll be OK, they didn't rape her.'

'No,' Eleanor said woodenly. Blair tugged at her arm, his eyes brilliant with anger.

'Did they catch the men who did it?'

Eleanor glanced at him, her nausea fading. 'Blair asked if — '

Prossie had heard the question. 'No . . . no, they got away,' she replied. 'The police are still looking for them.'

Blair's eyes were full of tears. 'I'll kill them,' he said suddenly, banging his fist into the palm of his left hand. 'I'll kill them.'

Eleanor stopped shaking, Blair's imminent hysteria bringing her out of her own shock.

'Prossie, I have to go. I'll come down to London straight away — '

'You don't have to, we can cope.'

'No,' she said kindly. 'I want to be there.'

'Well come and stay with us at Holland Park,' Prossie said.

'But . . . ' Eleanor glanced at the man next to her. 'I was going to bring Blair with me.'

There was no hesitation as Prossie replied. 'Fine. Then you can both stay here.'

⋆   ⋆   ⋆

After receiving the message left for her at her hotel, Virginia phoned from Milan about an hour and a half later. She was irritated at being bothered by Eleanor, any intervention from Yorkshire unwelcome in her tidy schedule, and reluctantly put in the call to England with the operator. Tapping the toe of her shoe on the carpeted floor, she took off one of her earrings and held the receiver to her ear, the faint sound of someone vacuuming coming from the next bedroom.

'Virginia?'

Eleanor's voice was artificially low, distorted by the long distance line.

'Yes. What is it?'

'It's about Isabel.'

251

Virginia's eyes flicked towards the window; a bird settled on the wrought-iron balcony and then flew off.

'What about Isabel?'

'She's been hurt.'

'Hurt?' Virginia repeated, irritatingly calm. 'How?'

'She was beaten up.'

'Is she in hospital?' Virginia said evenly. 'She should be. I want her to have the best care. It's important. She should be in a good hospital.'

Her sentences were staccato. The only sign of her shock.

Eleanor took in a deep breath. 'She's in Charing Cross Hospital — '

'I want her to go private.'

'She can't be moved at the moment, and besides, Charing Cross is better equipped to deal with neurosurgery.'

Ask how she is, Eleanor thought bitterly, ask how she is. What the hell does it matter about the hospital? Your child's welfare should come first. God, why can't you be human . . .

'What do you mean — she can't be moved?' Virginia asked briskly, her fingers running over her forehead.

'They removed a blood clot which was causing pressure — '

'Where?'

'Her head.'

'Her head,' Virginia repeated, her hand dropping from her face. Milan sun hazed outside the window. 'What happened to her head?'

'She either hit her head on the pavement when

252

she fell, or the injury was caused by the men . . . kicking her.'

'They *kicked* her?'

'Yes, and . . . her hand's affected. Her right hand.'

'Permanently?'

'No . . . they say that with work it will improve, but it will always be slightly impaired.' Eleanor's voice failed. 'She's a painter — this would have broken David's heart.'

'The painting doesn't matter!' Virginia said dismissively. After all, Isabel had lost interest anyway. 'Why was she beaten up?'

Eleanor's voice was steady. 'Apparently the men tried to rape her, but failed. They beat her up when she was only a few doors away from the studio — '

'She should never have been out at night! I always warned her this kind of thing could happen.'

'What does that matter now, Virginia?' Eleanor asked angrily. 'She has to go out sometimes.'

'She should have been at home — with her daughter,' Virginia snapped.

The thought swung between the two of them like a spider's web.

'Who's looking after Sybella?'

'Prossie.'

'Prossie! That tart of Stanton Feller's?' Virginia's voice rose violently on the line. 'We're talking about my granddaughter here, not one of Prossie Leonard's illegitimate brats.'

Eleanor winced. 'I'm going to London today,' she said desperately, already knowing what

Virginia was thinking. 'I'll bring Sybella back to The Ridings and look after her here.'

'I'm coming back.'

No, Eleanor thought, no. Stay away. Please God, keep her away from this child.

'I don't think — '

'I DO!' Virginia snapped. 'I'll be back in London tonight and I'll bring Sybella back to The Ridings.' Her face softened; for an instant she looked almost young. 'I'll look after her for Isabel. It will be one less thing for her to worry about.'

★   ★   ★

After the operation Isabel seemed to rally, but a few hours later she started to deteriorate and late in the afternoon Dr Andrews became concerned. When he shone a light into her eyes, her pupils did not dilate and her arm flopped heavily back on to the bed when it was raised. Quickly, he did a variety of tests, calling in the surgeon who had performed the operation.

'She's comatose,' Mr Elliot said.

Dr Andrews nodded. 'She was doing so well — '

The surgeon glanced towards the doors of Intensive Care. 'Are her relatives here?'

'Her mother's due later tonight, and Stanton Feller's in the waiting room.'

'The artist?'

Dr Andrews nodded. 'The same.' His gaze flicked back to Isabel, and he felt an overriding sense of disappointment. 'I don't fancy telling him about this, he's an awkward bastard.'

Stanton had cancelled all his sittings that day, and Prossie had gone back to Holland Park to take care of the children, although he phoned her hourly with reports.

He had just spoken to her when Dr Andrews walked into the waiting room.

Stanton got to his feet, his eyes narrowed. 'What is it?'

'I'm afraid — '

'What?'

Behind him the door opened and Eleanor walked in with Blair. She nodded towards Stanton and then faced the doctor.

'I'm Isabel Hall's aunt — how is she?'

'She's in a coma.'

Stanton sat down heavily and closed his eyes. 'Christ.'

'What's a coma?' Blair asked innocently.

Surprised, the doctor glanced at the handsome man standing next to him, then saw from the look in his eyes that he was honestly confused.

'I'll explain later, Blair,' Eleanor said patiently, turning her attention back to the doctor. 'How long?' she asked. 'How long will she stay like this?'

He had no answer and said simply, 'We don't know.'

Inexplicably Eleanor's hands suddenly lost all feeling, the bag she had been holding falling to the floor. Blair bent down and picked it up, but when he passed it to her she didn't even respond.

Dr Andrews continued hurriedly. 'It could last only days — '

Stanton lifted his head up. 'Or?'

'Weeks.'

Eleanor's face was expressionless, and Stanton helped her to a chair as Blair stood defensively beside her.

'We want to see a specialist.'

Dr Andrews bristled. 'Mr Elliott is very well known — '

'Listen, kid, I'm very well known, but I know bugger all about the brain.'

Eleanor's clear voice calmed him. 'Stanton, please, don't . . . ' she said, turning her gaze back to the doctor. 'I would like to speak to Mr Elliott, would that be possible?'

Dr Andrews reluctantly dragged his eyes away from Stanton and looked at the woman sitting in front of him. Eleanor was simply dressed, her soft greying hair in loose waves, her feet neatly placed together. A caring woman, and a calm one; a woman who was holding on to her control.

'I can arrange for you to see Mr Elliott, of course,' Dr Andrews said, smiling briefly, 'if you would just wait here.'

Walking out, he closed the door softly behind him.

'I feel so fucking responsible,' Stanton said suddenly, his head in his hands. 'I should have taken better care of her.'

Surprised by the confession, Eleanor studied him carefully. His hair was thinner than she remembered, his large, paint-stained hands pressing against his forehead.

Touched by his genuine distress, she reached

out and tapped his arm. 'Stanton, it wasn't your fault, you've done so much for Isabel. She was — *is* — so happy with you and Prossie.'

'I feel I let David down,' he said blindly, apparently not hearing her. 'I should have made her continue with her work instead of marrying that prat Gray. But I didn't.' He dropped his hands, his voice hard with anger. 'She was so unhappy when the marriage broke up, then she had so much trouble with Sybella.' He fixed his eyes on the floor. 'Bloody kid leads her a hell of a dance . . . you know, she never went out, and for once she just wanted a break. A night out . . . ' He stopped, seeing her at the studio gate, a young woman in a summer dress, waving. 'It's not fair,' he said hopelessly. 'It's not bloody well fair.'

Mr Elliot was helpful, but could tell them little more than Dr Andrews had done. Isabel was in a coma. No, he didn't know how long she would remain in that state. The conversation was brief, and unsatisfactory, and when he left Stanton turned to Eleanor, jerking his head towards the door.

'Behold, the medical profession. The blind leading the blind.'

'They do their best,' Eleanor said calmly.

Stanton shrugged and looked across to Blair. He had heard about him from Isabel, but had never met him before, and was struck by his silence, and his size.

'So you're both coming to stay with us at the studio?'

Eleanor dragged her thoughts back to the

practicalities. 'Is that all right . . . Prossie said — '

'It's fine,' Stanton assured her. 'Do you want to come back with me now? I'm going to swop over with Prossie, she's coming back here.'

Eleanor smiled weakly. 'No, I'll stay until Virginia arrives.'

Stanton grinned bleakly. 'Jesus, that's just what we need! The Earth Mother — '

'Whatever you say,' Eleanor snapped, 'Isabel is her child — '

'A fact she conveniently forgot whenever it messed up her career.'

Eleanor faced him defiantly; whatever she thought of Virginia was her private business, to the outside world they were family, and a family protects its own.

'She's just not maternal.'

'You can say that again,' Stanton responded, then changed his tone. 'Oh Eleanor, I'm sorry. I've got a big mouth. Forget what I said.'

She smiled half-heartedly. 'I know you don't mean any harm, Stanton, but I'll still stay here until Virginia comes.'

He nodded and then glanced at Blair. 'D'you want to come back with me?'

Blair's dark eyes flickered as he moved towards Eleanor and stood by her side protectively. 'No. I'll stay with her. We're family.'

Stanton returned to the studio alone, parking his Volkswagen van and resting his head back against the worn car seat for an instant to collect his thoughts. He felt exhausted, physically and mentally, hardly able to consider the long list of cancelled appointments, his mind constantly returning to Isabel. She had looked so small in the hospital bed, her head bandaged, her remaining hair covered up, her character gone. Switched off.

He closed his eyes, fighting unexpected tears. Sickened, his mouth dried with a mixture of anger and disbelief. Isabel, David's child, a clever kid who had gone through so much; who had squandered a rare talent. For what? A marriage which hadn't worked and a child who didn't even seem to like her . . . He suddenly raged against the Fates, calling down every god on his own head, his words bouncing around the van uselessly.

But nothing helped and after another few minutes he got out, slammed the door and made his way to the studio.

At the top of the stairs Prossie stood, her face white with rage.

'That bitch Virginia Hall,' she said vehemently, 'has just taken Sybella away.'

18

Prossie leaned towards Isabel and listened. Her breathing was steady, her face still. Suspended between sleep and life. Or life and death. Sitting down again, Prossie sighed and glanced out of the window, a few London pigeons winging across a blank sky. June is the cruellest month, she thought suddenly, adapting the poem from schooldays. Prossie frowned, trying to remember the next line, then leaned towards Isabel.

'How did it really go?' she asked. 'April is the cruellest month . . . ' She paused. ' . . . breeding . . . breeding . . . breeding . . . lilacs out of the dead land!' She was triumphant and smiled at the still figure on the bed. 'You see, I remembered, so I can't have been that stupid, hey?' Her smile faded. 'I hope it's true, then we can breed you like a lilac out of the dead land.' Prossie's fingers ran along the length of Isabel's right arm. 'We'll get you fit, you wait and see, you'll be just fine.' Her hand enclosed Isabel's. 'Oh, love, I wish you could hear me. I wish you could.'

For an instant she nearly broke down, but then she sighed, pushing back her hair and leaning on to the bed, her vitality at odds with the still figure in front of her.

'Chloë was asking after you, and Bracken went into your room to look for you.' She thought of the empty bed in Holland Park and hurried on. 'Sybella's fine . . . ' Fine? Was she? How fine could she be with Virginia Hall? Prossie frowned, struggling to keep the hard edge out of her voice as she continued. 'She's eating well and sleeping . . . ' Was she? There had been no news, except what Eleanor could tell her.

All Prossie knew for certain was that Virginia had taken Sybella back to The Ridings, asking Eleanor to stay on in London for a while to be near to Isabel. Eleanor had wavered, faced with the awful dilemma — should she stay or should she go? After all, what could she say to Virginia? That Isabel's greatest fear was that her mother would take over her child? How could she possibly say that?

So Virginia took her grandchild home as her daughter lay in a coma, unable to do anything to prevent it. Not that Virginia neglected Isabel; she phoned the hospital twice daily to enquire after her progress and spoke to the doctors frequently. But what else could she do? she reasoned. Wasn't it far better that she looked after the baby until her daughter recovered? *If* her daughter recovered.

Prossie shifted in her seat, scratching her leg thoughtfully. 'D'you remember school?' she asked Isabel. 'That fat cow Fiona who put you through so much?' She laughed softly. 'God she was a sight . . . ' Her thoughts ran on. 'Remember how you wanted to be a painter?'

She bit her lip. Damn, of all the things to say, why did she go and say that? She glanced at Isabel's right hand and reached out for it, lifting it against her face, warming it with her body heat.

'You have to get well, Isabel. You have to, you've got your baby . . . ' She thought of the fretful Sybella and the battle royal there would be to wrest her away from Virginia, and suddenly she wondered if Isabel could cope with the trauma. Maybe she was better enclosed in that secret place she now inhabited; shut off, where the world could never get to her. Maybe it was better that way. No more disappointments, no more deaths, divorces, losses, struggles. No more sacrifices. Nothing, except blankness and the opportunity of death.

Gently Prossie laid down Isabel's hand. The fingers rested lightly on the sheets and for the first time she noticed that the pink nail polish was chipped. She thought back to how Isabel had taken such pains to apply it before going out that terrible night, to look pretty. She had been so happy, sitting on the end of Prossie's bed and blowing on her nails to dry them . . . Now her nails were spoiled, a few broken off when she had clawed for her life, the others uneven.

Prossie's eyes filled, her own hand covering Isabel's as she slept on, oblivious.

★ ★ ★

Sybella also slept, but she was in a large coach-built pram outside the drawing room window at The Ridings. At first when Virginia had brought her home she had been difficult, fractious and crying often, but after a couple of days she settled. Her eyes watched her grandmother carefully, her well-defined brows

262

arching before she smiled, her slim arms thrashing about in the pram. Virginia found herself enchanted by Sybella, and surprised as she realised guiltily that she had never felt the same way about her daughter.

She glanced down into the pram and wondered why. Sybella was pretty, but then Isabel had been a stunning baby and a very attractive child. Her intelligence was not that remarkable either — after all, neither of her parents was stupid. Virginia leaned towards the baby, casting a shadow across the child's face. Immediately Sybella awoke, her eyes widening, her mouth sulky and then welcoming with a smile.

Virginia's heart shifted. That was why she loved her. Here was the one person who did not judge her; the one person to whom she could give affection and receive it back, without question. The past did not matter to Sybella, and as Virginia Hall cradled the child in her arms, she felt only a sense of relief and a fleeting freedom from guilt.

⋆ ⋆ ⋆

'I don't understand,' Blair said sullenly. 'Why can't she wake up?'

'Because she's ill,' Eleanor replied patiently although her tone was a little sharp now that she had repeated herself several times.

At the other end of the dining table Stanton cut into his cheese and chewed some bread thoughtfully, only half hearing the conversation,

263

his thoughts concentrating on Blair's remarkable profile.

'But if she doesn't want to get well . . . '

'It's not that!' Eleanor snapped finally, glancing towards Stanton for help.

'Isabel's lost,' he said simply. 'When she finds her way out, she'll come back to us.'

'Lost?' Blair echoed. 'Where?'

Stanton leaned forwards and tapped the side of his head. 'In here,' he replied.

Blair considered the information. 'Can't we help her to find her way out?'

'Maybe. If we talk to her.'

Eleanor pushed her plate away. She felt ill at ease in Holland Park and wanted to go home; yet she worried that in leaving Isabel she was shirking her duties. After all if her niece woke up, she should have someone there. Someone close . . . She glanced at Blair. Perhaps she should send him home, but how would he cope? Could he find his way back to Yorkshire alone? And if he did, how would he get on with Virginia?

Impatiently, she flung down her napkin, and Stanton glanced towards her in surprise.

'What's up?'

'How long do you think this will go on?'

He shrugged. 'I dunno. We have to wait.' His eyes narrowed. 'Why? What's bothering you?'

She paused, uncertain whether to confide in him or not. Then she jumped in. 'I'm worried about Virginia looking after Sybella. She's not . . . good with children. I don't know if she can cope.'

'Oh, believe me, she'll cope,' Stanton said

drily, reaching for the wine bottle and refilling his glass.

'But what about the baby?'

'She'll have it all organised, and besides, Sybella's too young to know what's going on.'

'She's ten months old, that's not too young.'

Stanton watched her over the rim of his glass. Then slowly he laid it down. 'What's this really about?'

'Isabel was always worried that her mother would get hold of the baby — '

'She's looking after her, for Christ's sake! She hasn't kidnapped her.'

'All right, Stanton, have it your own way,' Eleanor said stiffly, looking down at the table. 'But if David had still been alive I wouldn't have worried. Virginia is another matter.'

'If David had still been alive, none of this would have happened,' Stanton responded flatly. 'If David was here Isabel would never have married Teddy Gray — '

'Why?' Eleanor asked, startled.

'Because she would still have had enough affection in her life not to rush off looking for it.' He leaned back in his chair, kicking off his shoes. 'David would have made her keep faith; she would never have given up the painting if he'd still been alive.'

'But if she really wanted to paint she would have carried on — '

'No, Isabel needed the back-up she always got from her father. When David killed himself he pulled the rug out from under her feet and she didn't have the emotional strength to go it alone.' He scratched his chin thoughtfully. 'So she did what all women do, she went in search of love, then she tried to secure it with a child — which is when the whole bloody lot went down the tubes.' His voice dropped. 'This coma is her way of healing herself; she wants some peace, so she's ducked out for a while.'

Eleanor shook her head vigorously. 'No, not Isabel. She always faced everything. She has great courage.'

Stanton pushed back his chair and walked towards the window. Blair watched him suspiciously as he drew back the curtains and looked out.

'Every time I see that gate, I see Isabel,' he said flatly. 'I see her waving, and then I think of her in that hospital bed and see all that hope gone . . . Gone.' Stanton shook his head, his eyes still on the empty gate. 'Eleanor, do you know why David killed himself?' he asked suddenly.

She stared at his back, but said nothing as he continued.

'You see, I wonder what drove him to it. After all, he was so close to Isabel I can't see him hurting her unless something terrible happened.' He turned, the lamplight made his features blur. 'So why did he do it?'

'I don't know,' she said simply, folding her napkin and rising. 'I'm going to bed.'

'Was it something to do with Virginia?' he asked, seeing her flinch. 'It was, wasn't it?'

Eleanor pushed her chair back against the table. 'I don't know,' she said emphatically, unwilling to confide. 'I have no idea what

266

happened to make him kill himself. Only David knows that.'

'And David is dead.'

She nodded.

'And his daughter is almost dead.'

Eleanor's eyes flashed. 'Isabel will recover — '

'Will she? Maybe she has too much of her father in her. Maybe she'll let herself slip away — '

Eleanor's voice was high-pitched, and so shrill that Blair was startled out of his seat. 'My niece will live! She inherited only the strengths of David Hall, not the weaknesses.'

'He was a weak man, you're right,' Stanton said calmly, seeing Eleanor's face flush.

'HE WAS NOT WEAK!' she howled. 'He was gentle and good, and if you had really been a friend to him you wouldn't talk about him like that.' She banged her hand down on the table, rattling the plates. 'How *dare* you judge him, Stanton Feller! How dare you judge a man who was worth ten of you. You may be clever and successful, but you'll never inspire the kind of love David inspired. He was good . . . good . . . ' she said, her voice faltering, 'and Isabel loved him so much and missed him so much. She would have done anything to save him.'

'Enough to die for him?' Stanton asked simply.

Lying awake that night Eleanor gave up all thought of sleep and crept down to Isabel's empty bedroom where she wondered about what Stanton had said about Isabel — *Enough to die for him?* — and she prayed that it wasn't true that her niece wanted to die in order to return to

267

the one person with whom she had been safe. Eleanor turned on the bedroom light, the African mobile fluttered over her head, the white curtains blank as hospital sheets. Down the corridor came the sound of a cistern emptying as Prossie drew a late bath, the pipes knocking.

Eleanor glanced round and looked into the mirror. A woman, in late middle age, looked back at her, her expression bewildered. Slowly, Eleanor felt down her right arm, closing her eyes and trying to imagine it immobilised, her fingers clenching and unclenching. Then she traced the outline of her head, her mind rerunning what the police had told her. Isabel had been kicked in the head. Kicked. Feet landing against bone and hair, and under it, brain . . . Eleanor shivered. Two men had stolen Isabel's life; wrecked it as surely as a man pouring acid over a photographic print.

She could be repaired, but at what cost? And how effectively? And how much would it matter to her child, now indulged in The Ridings? Or to herself? Oh God, Eleanor thought, snapping off the light, please God, do something. Her thoughts spun round frantically, her mind going homewards as she cried out, 'Oh, David, *do* something. She's your child, do something.'

★ ★ ★

'You must have seen him,' Eleanor said, facing Prossie at breakfast. Chloë watched her thoughtfully, Bracken crying from her high chair. 'He was here last night.'

Prossie looked at Stanton helplessly. 'Did you see Blair go out?'

He shook his head, and picked up the paper. 'I'm off to the hospital,' he said, slamming the door behind him.

Eleanor turned to Prossie. 'Blair only has the mind of a ten-year-old, he can't manage out there alone.'

Prossie leaned towards Bracken and wiped her face. 'Honestly, I've told you all I know. He was asleep when I came in. I looked in to check, and when I looked this morning he was gone . . . ' She paused, her hair was hanging down her back, thick and heavy. 'He might just have gone for a walk, Eleanor. Don't worry unnecessarily.'

But Blair never went out alone, and both of them knew it. Eleanor sat down, exhausted, her eyes wide with tiredness. Prossie looked at her and pushed a cup of coffee across the table.

'We'll look for him,' she said simply, surprised that Eleanor did not respond. 'We'll find him.'

They trundled around the streets looking for Blair while Stanton went to the hospital, slid into Isabel's room and stood awkwardly by her bed, a bunch of violets in his hand.

'I brought these,' he said, putting them down on the table beside her. 'Prossie sends her love, and the children . . . ' He trailed off, uncertain of how to continue, but reluctant to stop talking.

Talk to her, the doctors had said. Sometimes it helps. Sometimes it brings them round. Stanton smiled, well, talking had certainly helped him in his life; talking a dealer into showing his work; talking to get a woman into bed; and talking to

269

get a patron to buy. All talk, all show, all clever stuff . . . but not this kind of talk. Heart talk.

He sighed, uncertain and embarrassed, and pulled out a chair. He would never have done it for anyone else. Not for any friend, or any lover. But old ties went deep, and Stanton felt bound to David Hall as much as his sister or his daughter did. He felt committed, so he kept visiting Isabel. Although she could not hear him, or see him, or know he was there, he visited her, and he longed to say the one thing which would make her move, or smile, or crawl out of that bloody hell hole she was now jammed in.

Jesus, David, he thought, why the hell did you die like that, and what the hell did those men do to your child? And why do we punish the people who deserve it the least? Stanton glanced towards Isabel. White-faced, silent, no longer pretty, only asexual, subhuman. Gone from the world of men. Christ, he thought, illness is ugly.

'Isabel?' he said softly. 'Can you hear me?'

There was no response. Only a vase of flowers and a bunch of violets withering fast on a hospital locker.

'Your father and I go back a long way . . . we met when I first went to art school. We went out with the same girl . . . ' He closed his eyes, somehow it was easier to talk when he couldn't see her. 'She thought David was sensitive and that I was a bum.' He laughed, surprised that the sound was genuine. It careered round the silent room. Tomb quiet. 'I wanted to marry her . . . well, I thought I did. But it was only an idea.' He glanced at her hands. He did not see the chipped polish, only the hands of a painter, the fingers locked into immobility. 'You could have given me a run for my money,' he said sincerely. 'You have such talent.'

His eyes moved towards the window, then lingered for an instant on the tap dripping into the wash hand basin.

'We went to Florence once, your father and I. He was looking at all the paintings, and I looked at all the girls.' He stopped short. 'That's bullshit, Isabel, I pretended to look at the girls, but the paintings chewed their way into my heart. They were the first things that made me want to cry.' He paused. 'Talent doesn't die, kid, just faith, and hope ... they die,' he said, touching the violet petals. 'Just faith and hope.'

Her face was closed off, no laughter, no turning to smile at the studio gate. Nothing, only a wall of silence over which no one ventured until the wanderer returned. The silent zone; the realm of the nearly dead.

Stanton shivered, but continued. 'Come on, girl, get a move on. You could have it all back, you know.' His arm moved across the still sheets, his large, stained right hand gripping hers. 'I'll teach you — You could show me up, and how. By hell, you could knock me into a frigging hat.'

Speak, he willed her. Speak, Isabel.

She slept on.

'I loved your work, even that stuff I tore up — I only did it to make you angry, to make you show me how good you could get. You're too young to give up. Too bloody young — and I miss you.'

He remembered her hair falling over her face as she bent down, all shades under the light; he saw her raise her arms and grimace, lifting a heavy frame; and he saw her struggle with her work, her eyes reddened and tired, her beauty suspended. You are a painter, he thought wearily, and work comes first. Love later, if at all . . .

But how could he tell her that?

'Prossie cries for you . . . ' he continued. 'She cries when she thinks I don't know, and she's started smoking again.' He ran his fingers through his hair. 'If all this stress doesn't kill her, then she'll get emphysema.' He smiled grimly. 'I'm painting Lena Norman,' he went on, 'the biggest whore in London. Her tits sag like a pair of empty tights, and you should see her skin — I have to put her under the sunlight to blot out the pockmarks . . . '

Silence.

'She says she's forty, but her hands are an old woman's hands. You can always tell from the hands, remember that, Isabel. Look at their hands, it's a dead giveaway.'

Talk to me.

'Her voice is like a man's too. I wouldn't be surprised if she'd had a sex change. Remember that Dr Rickles we had round for dinner? He does sex changes, I'll ask him . . . '

Nothing.

'You aunt's uncomfortable at the studio. I can tell, she wants to be home.' He tugged at some broken skin around his index finger. 'She's not happy with us. And Blair's . . . '

Missing, he thought, moving on quickly.

'I looked out your last painting yesterday, and I hung it up in the studio. It's a bitch, I have to tell you, but with a little repainting it could be something. I thought more darkness in the background might help . . . '

Go on, he willed her, defy me. Tell me to stuff myself and my suggestions. Get mad, like you did that first day.

Nothing, again nothing.

'And her dress should be lighter.' He stopped. Looked into her face. The zone of the nearly dead. Gone. 'Isabel?'

Talk to them, sometimes it helps.

'Isabel, say something . . . please . . . '

But there was nothing.

Only sorrow. And silence.

She had gone away; gone home.

'Isabel?'

* * *

The policeman had found Blair wandering down the Portobello Road. He had seen him, and watched him for a while suspiciously as Blair hurried along, hunched up, a big man in shirt sleeves, staring at everyone who passed him on the street. That was what had alerted the officer, the way Blair scrutinised the passers-by, some hurrying past him, others simply staring back, streetwise and aggressive. On the other side of the street, the policeman paused, then followed Blair, his eyes never leaving the big man.

It became apparent very soon that Blair was not looking at women, only men, and although

273

he was behaving in a strange way, it was obvious that he wasn't drunk. Drugged then, the officer wondered, crossing over and falling into step behind Blair. As they approached a row of shops, Blair hesitated and glanced round, then, seeing two men talking together outside a pub, he hurried over to them. They glanced up, one man frowning as Blair began to gesticulate frantically, the other getting to his feet.

The policeman could smell trouble and quickened his stride, arriving beside Blair just as he was about to throw a punch, his victim dodging backwards against the table and knocking over a pint of beer.

'*What the hell!*' he snapped, glancing at the officer. 'This maniac was about to hit me.'

The policeman held on to Blair's arm. He could feel the muscle under the skin and wondered fleetingly what would happen if he decided to make a run for it.

'What's all this about, sir?' he asked calmly.

Blair's eyes fixed on him, and then he frowned.

The officer frowned too, aware that there was something odd in the man's behaviour. 'Well, what's going on?'

'They kicked Isabel.'

'*Who?*' one of the men shouted, turning to his companion. 'This guy's off his bloody head. I don't even know an Isabel.'

The policeman still kept hold of Blair's arm, relieved to feel the muscles relax. 'Who's Isabel, sir?'

'She's sick.'

He nodded patiently. 'Well, perhaps we should go and look after her. Where is she?'

'She's lost.'

The officer frowned. 'Lost? How long has she been lost?'

Blair rubbed his forehead, his tone impatient when he replied, 'She's lost in her head.'

'She's not the only one, mate,' one of the men responded drily.

The policeman motioned for him to be quiet and looked hard at Blair. The expression in his eyes told him what he wanted to know — the man was either simple or sick. Either way, he wasn't safe wandering about alone.

'Where do you live, son?'

Blair frowned, he couldn't remember the right address and mumbled incoherently about the studio in Holland Park.

The officer pressed him. 'Do you know the name of the road?'

'No.'

'OK, who do you live with?'

'Eleanor,' Blair replied, narrowing his eyes with effort. 'We live in Yorkshire ... but we're staying with someone here.'

The officer sighed. 'Who?'

'He's a painter,' Blair said, suddenly childishly gregarious. 'He paints famous people, all kinds. He was Isabel's teacher — when she was well.' He paused, all sudden clarity. 'He's called Stanton Feller.'

From then on it was simple. The policeman, knowing where Stanton lived, just walked him home, Blair now docile and chatty. He told the policeman all about The Ridings and about Isabel, biting his lip hard after he described how she had been hurt.

'They kicked her,' he said angrily. 'I'll kill them for that!'

The officer looked at Blair's strong hands and wondered . . .

Under the summer trees they walked, Blair alternately confiding and then bewildered, his handsome face tanned, his eye guileless. The officer walked beside him, and when he rang the bell at Stanton's studio, he was relieved to see two women at the head of the stairs waiting to greet him.

'Thank God,' Eleanor said. 'Where have you been?'

He looked shamefaced and shuffled his feet without answering.

The policeman glanced at Blair and then said, 'He was looking for the two men who apparently attacked someone called Isabel — does this make any sense, ladies?'

Prossie looked at Eleanor, who raised her eyes and then glanced over to Blair. He loved Isabel; they all knew that, and in his own childish way he was trying to punish her attackers. Simple, to a child. But Blair didn't know who her attackers were — no one did. In his eyes, any two men could be the ones. Any two innocent men . . . Eleanor's eyes strayed to Blair's hands hanging passively by his side. She had seen him work in the garden, lifting massive weights without effort; she knew the strength there. He loved like a ten-year-old, all passion and no control; and he

276

thought like a ten-year-old, with no sense of moral right or wrong. Combined with his strength, such feelings could be lethal.

Eleanor glanced at the policeman. 'Don't worry, officer, we're going back to Yorkshire tomorrow.'

He nodded. 'Well, make sure you do. I know he's not . . . ' he shrugged, embarrassed, ' . . . that bright. But he could cause trouble. The police are handling the case, I suppose?'

Eleanor smiled fleetingly. 'Yes, they're doing a fine job . . . It's difficult, you see, but they haven't got a good description to go on, and my niece is . . . unable to help them at the moment.'

'Don't you worry, they'll find them,' he said kindly, then added, 'I hope Isabel recovers.'

For an instant they all stood uncomfortably in the cool studio, her name swinging between them like a pendulum.

Eleanor took Blair home to Yorkshire the following day, as she had promised. They rode the train back, and Blair ate several sandwiches before falling asleep, his head lying heavily against Eleanor's shoulder. Virginia had not been pleased to hear that they were returning, and her face when she saw them was stiff with irritation.

She swung open the front door of The Ridings and stood back for them to enter, a winter smile flashing across her lips, her eyes searching for something to criticise.

'I phoned the hospital only an hour ago,' she said, closing the door. 'There's no change.'

Eleanor nodded, thoroughly tired, and walked towards the stairs. She had not told Virginia the reason for their hurried return; she had merely said that she needed a break and that she would return to London after a few days to be with Isabel.

'I think I'll just go up to bed — after I've had a look at Sybella.'

'I'd rather you didn't!' Virginia snapped abruptly, then modified her tone. 'She's asleep.'

'I only want to look at her,' Eleanor replied steadily, moving off, her feet already turning towards the makeshift nursery where the baby now slept.

Thwarted, Virginia turned her frustration on to Blair. 'Well, young man, I hope you've been behaving yourself.'

He smiled half-heartedly: he felt uncomfortable with Virginia. 'I've been good.'

'I'm glad,' she replied sharply. 'Well, you better get a good night's sleep, there's plenty to do in the garden. You've had your little holiday for now — tomorrow it's back to work.'

*   *   *

The apple tree hung haphazardly against the outside wall, falling away from its rusty hoops, the brick rust-coloured in the late evening sun. Behind the stable block, Ivor barked, and a slow pigeon landed on the sundial. All down the drive, a scattering of fierce weeds crept up between the gravel, dry dust blowing in the breeze, an old branch creaking by the library window.

Two weeks had passed, two weeks of phone calls, and of communal waiting and listening.

Sybella flourished with Virginia — Geoffrey Harrod was amazed when she phoned and cancelled her next trip explaining that her granddaughter needed her. He asked after Isabel and was told what everyone was told — no change — and then he had to listen to Virginia talking about Sybella for the next twenty minutes. Her voice was lighter, almost feminine, as she chatted on, irritated only when he tried to bring the subject back to work.

And Eleanor returned to London; she stayed at Holland Park and she visited Charing Cross Hospital — and nothing changed. She talked to Isabel, as Prossie did, and as Stanton did, every day. They combined their wills and ran an emotional relay together, as one tired the other picked up the baton and carried on. But the stress told on all of them, and when they were not at the hospital they spoke little to each other.

One thing was decided though — that Isabel should never be left alone. There would always be one of them there — just in case she woke. Even though, as the days passed, each of them privately began to wonder if she ever would. Daily they attended her: they brushed her hair; washed her face and saw to all the little details for which the nurses didn't have time. The other, sadder duties the hospital performed for Isabel: a catheter was put in; she was cleaned after she had a movement; and heart and mind were monitored constantly, her body moved and turned like an overgrown baby.

And Isabel never objected. Not once. Slowly the bruises on her face and body began to alter colour and then start to fade, the stitching above her lip tightening the wound together as it healed.

'I don't think you'll have a scar,' Eleanor said gently. 'So that's something, isn't it?'

Prossie came in to relieve her three hours later, then Stanton arrived.

He was quick-tempered, and had obviously had a couple of drinks. 'I'm pissed off with all this.'

'You're just pissed, you mean,' Prossie replied. 'Oh, come on, Stanton, you know what we agreed. Someone stays with Isabel all the time.'

'My work's suffering,' he said petulantly.

'No, it isn't!' she snapped, glancing towards Isabel and dropping her voice as though she could hear. 'You know as well as I do that Eleanor spends twice as much time here as we do — '

'She doesn't have to work. I can't go on with this permanently.'

'It's not going to be permanent!' Prossie retorted hotly. 'Isabel could — *will* — wake up any time now.'

Stanton's expression was hard. 'Maybe we ought to instead.'

'And what is that supposed to mean?'

He rubbed his neck with his hand, discomforted. 'I mean, perhaps we ought to wake up to the situation and see it for what it is. Isabel might never wake up, for Christ's sake! She could lie there like a vegetable for the rest of her life.' He stopped, suddenly repentant. 'Oh shit, go on home, Prossie. I'm sorry, I'll stay with her.'

She got to her feet and stood before him,

gently kissed him, then pulled his head down towards her so that her lips rested against his forehead. His skin was warm, living flesh.

'Isabel will wake up,' Prossie said softly, her voice deep and certain. 'She *will* wake up. Believe me.'

An hour later Stanton was fast asleep, his head lolling forward on his chest, his open-necked shirt hanging out of the back of his trousers, his shoes kicked off. After talking to Isabel for nearly half an hour his eyes had closed, and in the quiet evening hospital he had dozed off.

So although she was only a foot away from him, Stanton did not see Isabel's left arm move slightly, or the flicker of her eyes under the closed lids.

He slept on.

Inside her head Isabel saw the staircase in The Ridings and the stained-glass window above her head.

Stanton shuffled in his seat, then fell back to sleep.

A quick breeze caught at the metal weather cock over the stable and suddenly Isabel found herself in her studio, the painting of Eleanor on the easel.

Softly, Stanton snored.

Her eyes moved behind her eyelids as Isabel watched. Through the rooms she moved, like a ghost, everything familiar and safe, and when she reached the door of her father's den her fingers gripped the handle and she went in . . . He was waiting for her and turned to greet her. He smiled and stood up, opening out his arms and laughing as she ran to him, her face pressed against his shoulder.

Stanton's eyes flickered as he dreamed.

Isabel was laughing soundlessly, and her father was laughing too.

'You're not dead! You're not dead!' she repeated. 'I knew you wouldn't leave me.'

He hugged her for a moment longer and then held her at arm's length, studying her. His eyes behind the tortoiseshell glasses were unchanged, his deep voice loving.

'I came to say hello, darling, but I can't stay,' he told Isabel simply, touching her face.

She frowned, her stomach churning with fear. 'Don't go, Daddy, don't go.'

'I have to,' he said quietly.

The room faded around them; they were no longer standing in the den of The Ridings, they were suspended, outside reality.

'Don't go!' Isabel cried out helplessly, grabbing hold of her father's arm. 'Please, take me with you.'

'You have your own child now, and your own life. You have to stay, Isabel,' he said kindly.

Desperately she clung on, but she could feel him fading, being pulled away from her. 'Oh, God, please stay, Daddy!'

His body slipped from under her fingers, but his voice continued strongly. 'I love you. I always have. Go home, Isabel, go home to your child and make a future for yourself.'

In panic Isabel cried out to him, 'Wait for me, Daddy! Wait!'

'Go home, sweetheart, I'll never leave you,

and when the time comes you can stay with me . . . Go home now — and don't be afraid.'

In that moment Isabel's eyes opened her mouth opening too. She cried out, the sound so weak that it was little more than a sigh. Then she filled her lungs with air and her voice rang out defiantly in the hospital room.

And Stanton fell off his chair.

19

Isabel left hospital a fortnight later, making the long journey up to The Ridings in a private ambulance, her weak right arm aching, her left hand holding it tightly against her stomach. Since coming out of the coma Isabel had experienced frequent headaches, her memory poor, a thought beginning with clarity, then smudging and losing its thread. But she struggled against the limitations of her injuries defiantly; she spoke to the police; she did all the physiotherapy exercises she was told to do, and when no one was around, she took off the bandages and winced when she saw the stubble on the left side of her head.

Unbeknown to her, Stanton stood by the bathroom door in the hospital and watched her. 'That's a bloody awful five o'clock shadow you've got there,' he said, teasing her.

She turned and put out her tongue — a childish gesture which made his heart shift.

On only one point was Isabel's memory exact. The attack. Over and over it replayed in her mind. She heard the men's voices, and remembered smells, details, textures. The feel of the cold pavement; their crêpe soles; their hands; and the magnolia tree. She remembered, but she wasn't afraid.

She knew that her father had pulled her out of the coma, and she was determined to repay him.

The first horror of disappointment had faded only minutes after she woke. Yes, she had wanted to go with him, but he had been right, she had a child who needed her, and a life to live. Isabel frowned and glanced out of the ambulance window. What kind of life, she wondered, her heart banging. What was coming for her? A sudden rush of hope flared up — she was alive, she was young, the world was hers, if she could just rejoin it. And in order to do that, she had to get better.

It was no easy matter. The injury to her right arm and hand wearied her, the injustice hammering in her head. It could have been her left hand, that wouldn't have been so bad . . . but her *right*. She was a painter, it was so bloody unfair . . . She blinked, her eyes fixed on the road ahead. *She was a painter.* Am I? she asked herself, I thought I'd given that up, I thought it didn't matter any more. Her head pounded with the effort to rally her thoughts, suddenly surprised at how much she wanted to work.

The ambulance moved swiftly towards York-shire, and Isabel dozed intermittently. Perhaps things would change now, perhaps Sybella would like her more. Isabel winced — ashamed to admit that she was afraid of seeing her own child. But was Sybella hers any more, she wondered. After all, Virginia had been looking after her for weeks, and by all accounts, she was thriving at The Ridings . . . Still, it was good for her to be away from London, Isabel thought, trying to crush the feeling of jealousy — no child should be brought up in London.

She tried hard to quell her feelings of anger towards her mother and to concentrate her thoughts on her hand instead, fumbling with her bag and pulling out a soft squash ball. Carefully she laid it in the palm of her weak hand and tried to fasten her fingers around it. She grunted softly with exertion, sweat beading her forehead. Her fingers flickered but hardly gripped the ball, her palm sticky. Agonisingly slowly she tried again, then in frustration, threw the ball back into her bag.

It was all going to be a lot harder than she thought. The recovery and the relationship with her child were going to test her to the limit. Another thought followed on with a rush of pure joy. But she was alive! Isabel Hall was alive — she had come back from the land of the near dead and she had a story to tell. And by God, people were going to listen to her.

The ambulance drew up outside The Ridings and Eleanor ran out, guiding Isabel to the front door where her mother stood waiting. Unsteady on her feet, Isabel paused and smiled at Virginia, her eyes moving to the child in her arms. Cautiously, she extended her left hand to Sybella, and her face broke into a smile when the baby laughed and caught hold of her finger.

'Look, she's welcoming you home,' Eleanor said, her arm around Isabel's waist. 'She's missed you.'

'You look quite well,' Virginia said, walking into the drawing room, her arms still around her granddaughter.

Isabel sat down and reached her left hand out

for her child. 'Please, Mother.'

Virginia hesitated. 'Can you manage her?'

The moment yawned between them, until Eleanor took Sybella and laid her in Isabel's lap, propping a cushion behind her niece's right arm.

'Of course she can,' she said, winking at Isabel. 'Look at that, the baby's as comfy as you like.'

She was, for a time, but soon Sybella's eyes strayed back to her grandmother and after another minute Virginia picked her up.

Isabel's face flushed; the sense of failure acute as she struggled to her feet. 'I think I'll just go upstairs and lie down for a while.'

'You do, dear,' Virginia replied, 'I'll bring you something to eat on a tray.'

'No, I'll come down,' Isabel replied calmly. 'I want things to be as normal as possible.'

Her progress up the stairs was slow, and though Eleanor followed her she never offered to help. She knew it was a matter of pride for her niece to do it alone. As they reached the landing, Isabel paused, glanced up at the stained-glass window and smiled, before moving on.

Finally she reached her room and lay down on the bed, glancing round.

'I thought you said that Sybella slept in here.'

Eleanor smiled. 'She did. But she's in the room next to your mother now, so that we can hear her if she cries in the night.' She sat down on the bed next to her niece. 'Be honest, you could hardly look after her at the moment, could you?'

Reluctantly, Isabel shook her head. 'No

287

'. . . but I want to look after her, Eleanor. I *must*.'

'All in good time,' her aunt replied calmly. 'Get yourself well and then you can look after your daughter.'

Isabel's mind wandered. 'She seemed pleased to see me, didn't she?'

'She *was* pleased to see you, sweetheart — as we all are.'

Blair was especially delighted and found innumerable reasons to be close to Isabel. When she came down for breakfast he made her tea; when she went into the garden, he shadowed her; and when she tired, which she frequently did, he was the first by her side. One afternoon, only weeks after Isabel had come home, she sat in the garden by the drawing room windows, Blair beside her, chewing a piece of grass.

'How d'you feel?' he asked.

'Better,' she replied, leaning her head back against the seat, the fingers of her right hand limp.

'So why aren't you working?'

Isabel opened her eyes. 'What?'

'You should be doing this.' He got on his knees before her and opened and closed the fingers of his right hand. 'Where's the ball?'

She could hardly be bothered to move, the sun was warm and Sybella was asleep in the pram next to her.

'Oh, not now. I'll do it later.'

'No, let's do it now!' Blair insisted, pulling out the ball from the bag next to Isabel's feet. He placed it carefully in her right palm. 'Go on, squeeze.'

She sighed, then she saw the look on his face and tried to move her fingers. They resisted, stubbornly.

'Go on, try harder!' he insisted.

'I am trying!' Isabel snapped, her face colouring with effort. 'My hand just doesn't work that well.'

'Try again!' he said.

Her temper snapped suddenly, Isabel hurling the ball down the garden with her good hand.

He gazed after it impassively. 'Well, I know your left hand works, can you do that with your right?'

Despite herself she laughed, and watched him as he returned with it.

'Did they shave off all your hair?' Blair asked, passing her the ball.

Isabel touched the headscarf round her head. 'No, just on the left side, where I had the operation.'

His eyes fixed on the scarf. 'Can I see?'

Embarrassed, Isabel hesitated. 'Oh, Blair, I don't want you to — '

His thoughts were already running on. 'You see, someone once told me I'd lose my hair when I got older, so I wanted to know what I'd look like.'

His logic was so childlike that her embarrassment faded and carefully Isabel took off the headscarf. The breeze felt cool on her exposed head as she raised her left hand self-consciously to her scalp.

Blair scrutinised the bald patch, his brow furrowed, and then reached out his hand and touched it. His fingers were gentle as he laughed. 'It feels all prickly,' he said, his curiosity immense. 'Will it stay like that?'

Isabel smiled at him. 'No, it'll grow back, like the other side.'

He considered her for a long moment and then said seriously, 'That's good, your head will look more even then.' He leaned back on the grass, his knees bent. 'When do you think I'll go bald? When I get older?'

She smiled down at him and nudged him playfully with her foot. 'You're impossibly vain, Blair,' she teased him. 'And besides you know you'll be as handsome bald as you are now.'

He smiled, hugely satisfied.

Isabel inched back to health agonisingly slowly, and sometimes her impatience made her difficult. Angry with her appearance, one morning she cut off her hair on the right side, dropping the mass of waves down the toilet and tying a red scarf over her head. Then she pulled out her make-up and leaned towards the dressing-room mirror, struggling to apply her eye make-up with her left hand. But the attempt was a failure, and, frustrated by her own clumsiness, she banged her good hand down on the table top, her right arm lying helplessly on her lap.

Eleanor heard the noise and walked in.

'What's the matter?'

'What's the matter!' Isabel shrieked. 'What the hell do you think is the matter? I can't use my arm. I can't put on my make-up.' She pulled off the headscarf. 'Oh God, I feel like a freak.'

Eleanor looked at her spiky hair and pity

welled up in her. 'It will grow back, sweetheart.'

'And this?' Isabel said, pointing to her right arm. 'What will happen with this?'

'Not much, if you don't keep to your exercises.'

Isabel paused, swallowing her anger. 'I've been doing them, Eleanor. They don't work.'

'They do!' she insisted. 'It's just slow, that's all.'

'How slow?'

She shrugged. 'I don't know. But you'll get the use of your arm back.'

'I can't remember things,' Isabel said, glancing away. 'I start a conversation and forget things . . . ' She trailed off. 'My concentration's gone. I thought I'd get better quicker than this.'

Her helplessness affected Eleanor, but she didn't show it. What Isabel needed now was support, not pity.

'What other exercises do you have to do for your arm?'

Rousing herself, Isabel glanced round the room. 'I have to pick up something, and gradually build up the weight.' Her eyes rested on the bookshelves. 'They said I can do it with books — go from a paperback to the *Encyclopedia Britannica*.'

Eleanor smiled and got to her feet, passing her niece a paperback copy of *Oliver Twist*. 'Go on then, take it.'

Isabel smiled back. 'That's not fair, it's a long book.'

'Listen, you're lifting it, not reading it.'

Sybella gradually warmed to Isabel, but she

was obviously still more comfortable with her grandmother. She was always delighted when Virginia entered a room, and grew restless if left with her mother for too long.

Isabel felt it badly, the rejection winding her on top of her other problems. She saw her mother monopolise Sybella and a boiling anger filled her. Often suffering from headaches she would walk into a room and find Virginia holding her child with two strong arms. Her head throbbed with disappointment as she experienced a curious sense of being an interloper and left. Logic told her she could not look after her child, her arm reminded her of that daily, but there was something more. Even if she worked and worked and recovered her full health she knew that the time had passed for her and her child. Sybella was happy at The Ridings; happy with Eleanor and her mother; happy in a big house; happy in a safe garden; as happy as Isabel had once been as a child.

It was then she realised that she had been deluding herself into thinking things would change. Sybella was better with her grandmother than she ever would be with her mother. The knowledge savaged her, but it decided her also. There had to be another life for her. She was a single woman, she had to look ahead . . . Isabel sighed and leaned back against the bedhead, fighting depression. *What* life? *Where?* She pulled hard on her courage . . . Come on, girl, come on. So it wasn't what you expected, so what? You have to think of something else now. Your child is safe and happy, that's the important thing, now you have to remake your own life.

For the next few weeks Isabel concentrated on her exercises. She rose early and did a warm-up, changing into warm running clothes and jogging slowly round the garden, Blair calling encouragement, Ivor barking beside her. Then she would eat her breakfast, paying meticulous attention to her diet, toning up her body which had softened while she was so ill. Over and over again she tired herself until she couldn't think clearly and would fall asleep in her room, waking later when she would immediately pick up the squash ball and begin to work her right hand.

After that, she began with the weights. *Oliver Twist* gave way to Raymond Chandler, then *War and Peace*, Isabel straining, her muscles shaking with effort. She kept herself so busy that at night she was too tired to think, and she did it deliberately so that she wouldn't have to answer the unanswerable question — what is it all for?

By late November Isabel's hair had grown back, her short cut shiny, the golden streaks still highlighted after the long summer in the sun. Her body was strong again too; all the hours of pushing herself paying off, her muscles fit, her right arm nearly fully recovered, some strength even returning to the fingers. And still she never asked — what is it all for? Instead she spent any spare time with her child, although Sybella continued to look to Virginia for the maternal comforts — and Isabel had to concede that, until she was fully recovered, Virginia was better equipped for that role.

The tension between the two women never

faded, but a mutual respect grew between them. Virginia no longer went on her lecture tours, she wrote books and articles at home instead, where she could be with Sybella, and watch Isabel. Many times she had seen her daughter lean against the garden wall and clutch her head, knowing she was in pain; many times she had heard her counting as she lifted the weights; or found her rubbing her muscles after exercising in the early hours when she couldn't sleep. Her courage impressed Virginia, but it made them no closer; they were as estranged as Isabel was from her own daughter.

Then one afternoon Isabel stood by the kitchen window and looked out. Rain puddles formed in the courtyard, an empty hanging basket swinging by the back door. Finally, as though she could resist the temptation no longer, she reached out for the key to the stable block, swearing as it slipped out of her right hand and she had to bend to retrieve it. As she walked outside, the rain dampened her hair and made her T-shirt cling to her shoulders.

At the entrance to the stable block she paused, then unlocked the door and pushed it open. The smell of horses came out to greet her and she smiled nostalgically, walking in and climbing up the stairs towards the studio above. The heavy trap door creaked as she opened it, her right arm aching with the exertion. Sweet summer smells, trapped for months, wafted across the bare boards, dust hovering, old papers yellowed with age, propped up against the work table, and a bunch of paint-stained rags thrown down where she had left them years ago. Isabel's feet scuffed along the dusty floor, leaving a trail as she moved further into the studio.

The memories threatened to choke her; the time her father had had the stable converted for her; the time Portento had come to look at her work; and the thrill of her first painting. She touched the empty easel, sad with dust, and thought back to the picture of Eleanor, her hand hovering almost as though the canvas was still within reach. Her eyes roamed around, she saw the old couch where she had sat that night with Blair, and the discarded portfolio she had taken with her the day she first went to see Stanton.

The memories and the dreams weighed on her heavily and she was suddenly tired, her head aching. Clumsily she sat down, a cloud of dust coming up from the neglected couch, her thoughts wandering aimlessly. A few minutes passed. Then slowly she got to her feet, her left hand wiping the dust off the work table as she glanced round. Finally seeing what she wanted, Isabel snatched up the yellowed piece of paper and pinned it to a board before placing it on the easel.

Then she picked up a pencil. And stopped. Her heart banged, her right hand aching already, her damaged fingers cramped in the unfamiliar position.

A minute passed.

Then another.

Then slowly, achingly slowly, Isabel began to draw.

20

The thing Isabel could never come to terms with was that her hand would not obey her head. She knew how to draw, but her hand refused to listen to her; she saw pictures in her mind, but they never made it on to the paper; and worst of all, she knew that although the talent was still strong inside her, the means of expressing it had gone. The thought was hard to accept and she refused to reconcile herself to it. If her bloody fingers refused to obey her, Isabel thought bitterly, she would work them until she *forced* them to do what she wanted.

She glanced down at her right hand, so familiar to her that she knew every line and crease in it. Patiently, she traced her life line with her left index finger, turning over her wrist and wincing at the effort. Six months to a year, the doctors said — *it will take six months to a year to recover most of the use of your hand, Miss Hall. If you're lucky.*

Isabel leaned her head back against the couch in the studio. Well, a year had passed now, a year of treading water, of working. She closed her eyes — Sybella was nearly two, and was already walking and talking a little. A very striking child, precocious though, because she had been spoiled. Isabel pulled off her earrings and dropped them into her pocket, rubbing her lobes thoughtfully. It would have been hard to stop

Sybella being spoiled when they all doted on her so much. Virginia could see no wrong in her, even though Isabel had often been concerned about her daughter's quick temper, and as for Eleanor and Blair — well, to them Sybella was simply perfect. Good-looking, intelligent, happy, spoiled. She wondered fleetingly if they were right and she was wrong. Perhaps she was too hard on her daughter; after all, why was it that only she saw Sybella's failings?

Time would tell, she thought, glancing over to the easel in front of her and smiling cautiously. That was better, she thought, that was more like her old self. The image of her mother looked back, and next to it, one of Blair. Clear, precise drawings, lacking a little in detail certainly, but with feeling and some real power in them.

Isabel rubbed her hand and felt a sudden feeling of disappointment as she tried to remember what she had been thinking about. What was it . . . ? She scratched round her thoughts, then sighed in exasperation. Her memory was still bad at times, that was something which was very slow in improving. A bird landed on the windowledge and made her jump, and a horse neighed in a nearby field as she turned back to the easel.

She had made her decision the previous night. In the darkness she had been brave, but when the dawn came up Isabel's courage had faltered. I have to go, she said to herself repeatedly, I have to go. I have to leave here . . . Another thought followed immediately. Why? You are safe here, there are no dangers, it's comfortable and your child is here. Stay . . .

Isabel pushed the pencil she was holding behind her ear and thoughtfully scratched her knee. Safety. Yes, there was safety at The Ridings, and good memories. It had been a safe haven for a while, but she had to go back into the world. The time had come. Sybella would be looked after here by her mother and aunt, and she would visit frequently. She had no ties, nothing to stop her. Only a lack of courage.

But what if something happened? Isabel asked herself, answering herself almost immediately. What can happen? Another attack? No, lightning, like luck, never strikes in the same place twice. So what else? Failure? Another unhappy marriage? Or no marriage at all? What was there waiting for her? Loneliness . . . ? She sighed and thought of her father. He had forced her back into the world, back into life, but he wasn't here now to encourage her, that she had to do for herself.

Isabel thought back, recalling the words she had heard so clearly, her father's words: *Don't be afraid*.

He would never had said that if it wasn't true. If there was anything fearful waiting for her, he would have warned her. Isabel shook her head, her courage rising. It was all right to go, her father had virtually told her so.

So how would she make her first move?

Eleanor knocked on the trap door and then pushed it open, struggling into the studio. Her plump knees scraped the steep steps, her soft hair dishevelled as she stood, hands on hips, facing Isabel.

298

'So, what gives?'

Her niece glanced up at her and smiled. 'I dunno. You tell me.'

Eleanor sat down on the couch next to Isabel and smoothed her skirt with her well-rounded hands. 'You're unsettled — '

'I always am.'

She raised her eyebrows. 'No, this is something different.' She glanced over to the easel and looked at the pictures hanging there. 'Oh, that's good, Isabel. You've come a long way.'

'Am I as good as I was?' her niece asked, glancing down, afraid to look into Eleanor's face.

She hesitated for an instant. 'No, sweetheart, you're not quite as good as you were.' Isabel took in a sharp breath, her aunt's hand touching her shoulder gently. 'I've never lied to you, have I?'

'No.'

'So it would be wrong for me to start now.'

'I suppose.'

Eleanor took hold of Isabel's right hand and looked at it carefully. 'Such a poorly little hand, wasn't it? And it took so much to make it better.' She glanced into her niece's face. 'You're a fine painter, Isabel, but you can get better — in time.' She folded her niece's fingers one by one into her right palm. 'But you're ready to try again.'

Isabel's eyes filled. Her aunt had the same perception as her father. She had needed help and it had come.

'Where do I go?'

'You go back to where you started,' Eleanor answered simply.

'To Stanton?'

'He's a great teacher, and he's fond of you — just as Prossie is. You'll be all right there. Believe me.'

Isabel hung her head; she had missed them more than she would admit and the thought of being with them again was comforting.

'But do you think Stanton will take me back?'

'Oh, Isabel, don't be stupid,' Eleanor said, getting to her feet. 'He's waiting for you.'

He was too, only the reunion was not comfortable. Stanton was in a foul mood, Prossie meeting Isabel at the top of the studio as though nothing had changed. She looked older than she had only a year before, and her body suggested yet another pregnancy.

Happily she hugged Isabel and then stepped back, looking at her.

'You look good,' she said warmly, although there was a faint undercurrent of envy. 'I've missed you.'

'Me too. But we kept in touch.'

'Only by phone,' Prossie replied, walking past the studio and into the lounge beyond. The same huge paintings of her looked down from the walls. Only they were of a younger Prossie, with a different quality. 'I missed your company. We had a girl here for a while, to help with the kids, but I got rid of her.' She dropped her voice conspiratorially. 'I think Stanton was screwing her, so I got pregnant again.' Her hands touched her stomach quickly. 'Men, hey?'

Isabel shook her head disbelievingly, as Prossie continued. 'I think I look tired with this one though, I can't understand it. Perhaps things will get better. Certainly Stanton's being very attentive.'

'He always is when you're pregnant,' Isabel said, following Prossie to her old room. The African mobile fluttered over her head and made memory surge back.

'Oh, he's being really good . . . he loves kids,' Prossie replied, adding gently, 'How's Sybella?'

'Pretty and spoiled.'

'Oh.'

'Yes, oh,' Isabel replied, dumping her bags on the bed. She looked at the curtains. 'You changed them, they used to be white.'

'Times change,' Prossie replied, 'I think white's too babyish.' Her voice dropped. 'Listen, don't mention it, but Stanton's in a mess. He owes money — '

'I'll pay rent.'

'Don't be daft!' Prossie replied, lifting her eyebrows. 'What he needs is someone to help with the work. The portraits.'

'But — I'm not as good as I was. I was coming to ask if he would teach me again.'

Prossie glanced around, as though afraid that Stanton would walk in. 'Believe me, after the crap he's seen lately, you'll be a miracle.' Her hand went to her mouth and she burst out laughing. 'Sorry, I don't mean it that way!'

Isabel laughed too, the old familiarity making her feel at home. 'Don't worry, I get the point. If Stanton needs help, he's got it.'

He walked in soon after, stood in the studio, threw his shoes across the floor, ripped a drawing in half and then leaned back against the work table, frowning. Without responding in any way, Isabel looked back at him, apparently impassive. He had rushed through the drawings she had brought with her, criticised many of them, sworn at her, and generally made her feel untalented and stupid.

'Look at this shit!' he said, flinging a portrait of Blair to one side.

'I've had to struggle — '

'Yeah, so it seems. Thing is, was it worth it?' he goaded her unmercifully, so glad to see her that he felt like a thirsty man spotting a wine bar in the desert. Not that he was going to tell her that.

Stanton's eyes flicked from the drawings back to Isabel. Her short hair suited her, the fragility she had presented in the hospital now gone; a steely determination in its place. You live and you learn, he thought wryly . . . His eyes roamed to Isabel's right hand, the same right hand which had been so useless for so long. He noticed that she worked it constantly, whether from nerves or habit he didn't know, but her fingers kept opening and closing without pause.

'So you think you're ready to work again?'

'Yes.'

'What if I said you were no bloody good?'

'I wouldn't believe you.'

Her eyes were hazel, green flecks in the pupils. Quick eyes, eyes to make you think.

'Listen, Isabel — '

'No, you listen, Stanton,' she replied, cutting him off in mid-flow. 'I've been a fool for most of my life. I had a talent and threw it away to get married, and then wondered why it didn't work out.' She lifted her hands to prevent him from interrupting, 'I had a child, OK? Well, my daughter is happy with my mother, so I have no real role left — except the one you're going to give me.'

'ME!' he howled.

'Yes, you,' she replied evenly. 'I can be good, very good. You said that I hadn't the stomach to be a painter, that you needed to *want* to be a success to achieve it. Well, I want that now.' She pointed to her portfolio. 'All I have and all I hope to achieve is in that case — '

'Then you'll starve.'

'BULLSHIT!' she shouted at him. 'You know I've got the talent and you know I can succeed. Don't underestimate me, Stanton. I've been through hell, and I won't let anyone stand in my way now.'

He raised his eyebrows and pointed to his paints. 'I've got problems.'

'I heard.'

'I need help.'

'So?'

She made him say it.

'Listen, kid,' he said finally, 'what say we work together?'

She nodded and picked up a brush.

★ ★ ★

Still lacking some confidence, Isabel confined most of her work to the background of Stanton's portraits and became expert at painting in draperies, landscapes and the occasional country house. She worked hard, and rested her arm and hand frequently, the ubiquitous squash ball pressed into service, her fingers tightening and relaxing automatically around it. Then, when she felt ready, she would slip the ball back into the pocket of her painting smock and pick up a brush again.

For months Stanton had been running behind with his portraits, and now several irate clients were demanding delivery of their pictures. Fast.

'Yes, I do understand, Lady Sherwood, but Mr Feller has been very busy lately,' Prossie said over the phone to one such client.

She was unimpressed. 'But I want my painting, and, if you remember rightly, it was promised to me last month. I've been very patient but there is a limit. I'm having a dinner party at the end of the week and it's important that I have the portrait for then.'

Prossie glanced over to Stanton. 'Lady Sherwood is having a dinner party — '

' — to which we won't be invited.'

She ssshed him and put her hand over the phone. 'Listen, she wants that damn picture for Friday — and we need the money, so talk to her.'

Reluctantly, Stanton wiped his hands on his overalls and took the phone from Prossie. His voice was honeyed, charming.

'Lady Sherwood, how nice to hear from you — '

'Stanton, I need that painting.'

His eyes hardened, but his voice remained treacle. 'And you shall have it. I can't think what the problem is, it must have been some confusion at this end. You see, the portrait's been ready for some time.' Prossie narrowed her eyes as he continued. 'In fact, it's only the frame which needs sorting out.'

Lady Sherwood was suitably mollified. 'So I can have it for Friday?'

'I'll bring it round myself,' Stanton said, ringing off and turning to Isabel. 'Right, get the bloody old cow's painting on the easel.' She did so and he scrutinised it thoroughly. 'You take the background — I want a soft landscape — and I'll do the old bird's hands.' He turned round and picked up his palette, passing Isabel hers, and winking. 'First one to finish gets a drink.'

They worked on the painting for the rest of the day and well into the night when Prossie put her daughters to bed and came back into the studio with her sewing. In complete silence she laid out her pattern on the dais and set to work, her scissors cutting the heavy cloth she had bought, her fingers nimble as she hand-stitched the hem. Around twelve-thirty she made some food, and they all ate together although they said little, Stanton and Isabel concentrating on the painting, Prossie frowning over some complication in the dress pattern.

At two she pulled off her nightdress and, totally unselfconsciously, stood naked in front of the studio mirror before holding up the pattern against herself. Her legs were long and well formed, her stomach only just showing the curve of pregnancy — under the white light she threw off her years and seemed almost ethereal.

'Put your bloody clothes back on, Prossie!'

Stanton snapped good-naturedly. 'You're ruining my concentration.' His eyes flicked over to Isabel's half of the painting and he pointed to the background. 'What the hell is that?'

'A tree.'

'A tree!' he said drily. 'I've never seen a tree like that.'

Isabel was not about to be put off and stood her ground. 'Listen, I paint what is real. If you don't like the damn tree, take the matter up with God, not me.'

Prossie finished her pattern around three o'clock, and, after checking that the children were asleep, she went off to bed, trailing the newly made dress behind her like a wedding train. Isabel watched her go and paused, her arm aching, then she reached out for a bottle of turps. Making sure that the top was secure, she gripped it tightly and raised her hand, bending her arm at the elbow, then lowered it slowly, several times.

Out of the corner of his eye Stanton saw her, but said nothing, only sighed with relief as she began to work on the background again.

At three, he said suddenly, 'What about a dog?'

'Huh?'

'A dog,' he repeated. 'Lady Sherwood likes dogs — and if we please Lady Sherwood she might recommend us to all her lovely rich friends.'

Isabel looked at the painting and put her head on one side. 'Listen, this picture has to be dry by Friday — '

'So we paint in a small dog.'

She smiled ruefully. 'OK, what kind of dog?'

By Friday morning Lady Sherwood's portrait was finished — but it wasn't dry. In horror, Stanton tried everything to make the paint set, finally resorting to the use of Prossie's hairdrier. He stood in bare feet, frowning grimly, waving the drier back and forwards over the sitter's features. Lady Sherwood's eyes seemed to watch him reproachfully.

'Well?' Prossie asked Isabel timidly, as she crept into the studio. 'How's it coming?'

'It's still wet.'

'Oh God,' Prossie groaned. 'What are we going to tell her?'

'Stop whispering!' Stanton snapped, looking over his shoulder. 'Have we got another of these things?'

'I've got a small hairdrier,' Isabel volunteered.

'Get it,' Stanton replied, glancing at the clock. 'I'm supposed to deliver this at six.'

'It'll be dry,' Prossie said optimistically, her fingers crossed behind her back.

At seven-fifteen Stanton delivered the painting to Lady Sherwood's house in Rutland Gate, Knightsbridge. After terrorising the butler he was allowed into the dining room and permitted to hang the portrait himself, his client walking in just as Stanton was about to descend the step ladder.

He smiled winningly, although the smell of drying paint was powerfully strong. Maybe only to me though, he thought. After all, I'm only inches away from it, the guests won't be eating their flaming dinner at the top of a pair of step ladders.

Lady Sherwood was massive in pearl silk, her eyes twinkling girlishly. 'Oh, Stanton, it's beautiful.'

He accepted the compliment gracefully, his heart banging as she came closer. Relax, he thought to himself, the painting's out of reach, she can't get her fingers on it up here.

'You shouldn't have struggled to hang it all by yourself, Stanton.'

'It was my pleasure,' he said gallantly, still at the top of the ladder. 'I like to do the job properly.' Especially when the picture's still wet to the touch, he thought drily, imagining half of Lady Sherwood's face, together with her dog, being wiped off with a little injudicious handling. 'Besides, it looks good hanging here.'

Lady Sherwood frowned slightly. 'Well, you see . . . actually we were going to put it in the drawing room.'

Stanton's face set. His mind whirled uncomfortably and then he decided on the only course of action to avert disaster. At the top of the step ladder he banged his foot. The steps wobbled impressively.

'That is the limit!' he exclaimed, his voice carrying impressively. 'I've never been treated like this by anyone before. By anyone — and I've painted members of the Royal Family.' He was sure by now that his voice was audible to her guests in the next room and carried on confidently. 'Lady Sherwood, this portrait was created for this space. If you move it, you will have destroyed a work of art.' He turned round and leaned towards the painting, as though he was about to take it down. 'I would rather take it back than let it be hung somewhere unsuitable.'

Stunned by his outburst and more than a little embarrassed, Lady Sherwood moved to the base of the steps and looked up at Stanton helplessly.

'I didn't mean to offend you,' she muttered softly. 'Please, Stanton, leave it there. I promise I won't move it.'

He appeared to hesitate and then turned back to the painting, his arms outstretched.

'No, I think I'll take it — '

'Oh, no! No!' she said, beside herself. She had been telling everyone about her portrait for months and the American Ambassador was in the next room, just waiting to see it. The humiliation would be too much to bear if Stanton Feller took the painting away from her, what would she say to people? How could she explain?

'Oh, Stanton, I swear, in God's name, that I will never move the painting.' She looked at him appealingly. 'No one shall ever touch it — except you.'

Prossie sat by the studio window and waited, with Isabel on the divan beside her squeezing the squash ball in her right hand. Chloë was on the floor, scribbling on some pieces of paper, Bracken pulling the tail of the large stray cat which had moved in with them a week before.

'We have to think of a name for it,' Isabel said suddenly.

Prossie looked at her absently. 'What?'

'That cat,' Isabel replied.

'It's got a name. It's called 'You Too'.' She grinned. 'Stanton thought of it. He said it makes sense, after all, he kept calling for the kids, and then saying, 'Oh, and you too.' So it stuck.'

Isabel looked at the cat. 'You Too!'

It turned round immediately and she laughed, and stroked it. With relief she realised that she felt comfortable and happy again, secure back in Holland Park. At first she had wondered if the appalling memories of the attack would spoil the place for her, but other, happier, memories proved stronger: like the day she first came to see Stanton; Prossie having the children; the time spent working in the studio; and the energy of the place.

She yawned and rubbed her eyes. 'I wonder how Stanton's getting on?'

Prossie frowned and wiped Bracken's mouth. 'God knows, but he'll cope. He always does.' She laughed deeply. 'When I watched him put the portrait in the van I had visions of half the picture getting wiped off on his sleeve!'

Isabel laughed. 'So much for Lady Sherwood — the first recorded case of an artistic frontal lobotomy!'

Half an hour later Stanton returned to the studio with a magnum of champagne and a substantial cheque, which he had to rescue out of Bracken's mouth a minute later.

'To our fabulous success, wealth and happiness,' he toasted, raising his glass, 'and Happy birthday for tomorrow, Isabel,' he said, adding gently, 'You did well with that painting, it looked good.'

She smiled, feeling happy, her hand opening and closing on her lap.

21

Isabel woke slowly on the day of her birthday and stretched her arms out, relishing the moment. She was twenty-five years old, she had survived a failed marriage, a divorce, an attack, and she was still strong. Smiling, she thought of The Ridings and of her daughter, looking forward to visiting home the following day, and seeing everyone again. A bird sang outside the window, and the smell of coffee came up the staircase, the snap of the letter-box sounding downstairs.

My birthday, Isabel thought again, and with rising excitement pulled on her dressing gown and padded into the kitchen. Prossie squealed with pleasure and pushed several presents into her hands. The little girls crowded round her, and You Too jumped on to the table and upset the milk jug.

'Happy birthday,' Stanton said, walking up behind her, pecking her on the cheek and handing her a box.

She took hold of it and nearly dropped it. 'God, that's heavy,' she said, pulling off the wrappers. Inside the parcel was a steel dumb-bell weight, engraved with the legend: A DUMB-BELL, FOR A NOT SO DUMB BELLE.

She kissed Stanton and began to laugh, lifting the weight with her right hand, her arm muscles straining, her hair flopping over her forehead.

Prossie watched her, and saw her happiness and the calm look in her eyes. She's recovered, she's herself again, Prossie thought gratefully as Isabel lifted her arm again, bending it at the elbow, the sunlight flashing on the metal dumb-bell and reflecting in the hazel of her eyes.

'There's something else for you,' Prossie said finally, putting Bracken down and pulling a letter out of her dressing gown pocket. 'It's from Eleanor — she said you'd be expecting it.'

Isabel put out her hand, her fingers closing over the letter eagerly. 'I was expecting it . . . Thank you.' She paused. 'I think I'll just go and get ready, OK?'

Stanton watched her go, the children following her, and then he turned back to Prossie. 'Who's the letter from?'

'Her father.'

'Her father!'

She nodded. 'Apparently David Hall wrote her a letter every birthday, and the solicitor delivers them to Eleanor every year for her to pass on.'

'That's ghoulish,' Stanton said, biting into some toast, and grimacing. 'God, it's soggy! The bloody cat's upset the milk again.' He put down the toast with disgust and looked back to Prossie. 'Don't you think it's a bit macabre?'

She thought for a moment. 'Not really, I think it was very clever of David Hall. The letters are important to Isabel. They keep his memory alive for her.'

With a wicked look in his eyes, Stanton moved towards her and lifted her hair, kissing the side of her neck, his hand sliding inside her dressing gown to cup her breast. 'Well, when I die, don't expect any letters from me.' His mouth moved over hers greedily. 'I'll just come back to haunt you . . . You'll feel ghostly hands on your body . . . ' He knelt down and pulled the top of her nightdress open ' . . . and ghostly lips . . . ' He kissed her stomach gently. 'I shall be the Phantom of the Orgasm.'

★ ★ ★

Isabel sat down on the side of her bed and opened the letter. Her father's handwriting was familiar, welcome, as she began to read:

> Dearest Knuckles,
> Happy Birthday, darling, and good fortune for your new year. Your best year, I hope, because I know you will have deserved it.

The strangeness of the words made Isabel frown. It was almost as though her father knew what she had gone through — or maybe he did. She weighed the letter in her hand. It had been written nine years ago — her thoughts wandered. Had her father written the letters at different times? Or all at once? Sitting in his den, had he composed all of them in one afternoon, or one evening? Or were they written on the day he killed himself? She could picture him writing, then folding up the sheets of paper and placing them in envelopes, and marking the year on the front. Year after year, birthday after birthday,

314

keeping the lines of communication open between a dead father and his living child.

Isabel's hands shook suddenly and for a moment she didn't want to read on, but forced her eyes back to the page.

I have something to tell you, sweetheart, which will not be easy for you . . .

No, Daddy, no, she thought. Stop now . . . but she still read on.

. . . but I must explain. I know how often you will have wondered about my death. It must have seemed such a cruel thing for me to do, and so unexpected. After all, darling, I loved you with all my heart, and with all my life, so how could I leave you?

I'm writing this while I am still alive — although I know that when you read it I will be dead and all the unanswered questions will still be there. So, darling, on your birthday I give you the present of truth. It is a bitter present, in a way, but one I owe you — just as I owe you an explanation.

You, my love, are not my child . . .

Isabel dropped the letter. It fluttered in the air and fell like a dying sparrow. No, she thought helplessly, not now, I don't want to know . . . I've had enough pain. Enough . . . She got to her feet and walked to the window, looking out at the studio gate. But the words stared back at her

315

— *You are not my child* — and when she glanced away, up into the heavy clouds, they were there too. Her feet moved across the bedroom floor and stopped beside the letter. Slowly and determinedly, Isabel ground the heel of her shoe into the paper, watching as it crumpled, its corners curling upwards like a dry leaf.

Her breathing was laboured; the tinnitus from which she had suffered since the attack whistling in her head. Automatically she lifted her hands and clasped them over her ears, but the noise seemed louder then and, in despair, she sank to her knees.

The letter lay, soiled and crumpled, beside her. She looked at it, then, stretching out her right hand, she picked it up and began to straighten it, her arm aching, her eyes pricking with tears. The words danced in front of her; they blurred; they smudged; but they remained.

. . . you can't know how much pain it causes me to write these words and I can only hope it does not cause you as much to read them, because you must know that I love you completely, and that will never change, whether you are my child, or not.

But Isabel, when I found out . . . when I discovered that you were not my child. *Not* my lovely child, my clever child, the child I adored so much and who had made my life so valuable . . . it was too much for me to bear. I was wrong, I *am* wrong, to do what I shall do, but, sweetheart, the world's light has gone out for me.

I am not your father in reality, or in blood — but in heart, darling, no man was ever closer to his child.

Truth is always painful. Life is too. Forgive me for what I did, but understand . . . Isabel, remember what I have always told you. You have courage, talent and a great heart — go with my blessing, and take on the world.

All my love, my darling,

David Hall

Isabel left for Yorkshire that afternoon. She travelled in silence, her eyes seeing nothing of the countryside which passed by the train window, her hands folded on her lap. Towns passed, the light faded, a sudden shower splattered the windows, then a fleeting late sunset. And the train roared on. Beside her a woman did the *Times* crossword, a businessman worked on his notes, his eyes tired behind glasses, his hair in need of a wash.

The train moved on. Go on, Isabel willed it, go on, take me back, take me home. Take me to my mother. She imagined Virginia's impassive face and wondered about her. Wondered how she could live with herself, and be so moralistic. Bitterness stung her lips as Isabel felt for David Hall's letter in her bag. Her fingers closed around it and, comforted, she slept for a while.

Her head was aching when she arrived at the driveway to The Ridings. She paid off the driver and swung open the heavy wrought-iron gates herself, wincing with the effort, her feet grinding on the gravel. The lights were on in the house, one burning out from the library, another from the drawing room.

She'll be in the library, Isabel thought to herself. She'll be working on some talk, or some article, her head will be bent down . . . Isabel's feet moved quickly . . . She'll have put Sybella to bed and gone back to work, and when everything's quiet, her clever mind will be thinking up a clever phrase which will look good on paper.

Anger made Isabel quicken her steps, her heart banging in her chest. She could imagine her mother's expression, the critical tone to her voice. My mother, the paragon of virtue, the liar, the cheat — the whore.

Frantically Isabel jerked open the front door, and ran in. She stood in the hallway as Eleanor came out of the drawing room about to speak, but pausing when she saw the look on her niece's face. For an interminable moment Isabel waited and then Virginia Hall walked through the library door.

'Who is my father?' Isabel said, her voice dark with rage.

'What?' Virginia faltered, her hand clenching the pen she had been writing with.

Isabel moved further towards her, waving David Hall's letter in front of her mother's face. 'Who is my father?'

'Don't be absurd,' Virginia said unconvincingly. 'You know perfectly well who your father is.'

318

'I got a letter from David Hall today. In it, he explains why he killed himself.' Virginia's face paled and Eleanor listened, horrorstruck, as Isabel continued. 'He committed suicide when he found out that I wasn't his child . . . '

Eleanor took in her breath.

'So what I want to know, Mother,' Isabel continued mercilessly, 'is the name of my father.'

'Your father was David Hall — '

'Don't lie to me!' Isabel shouted, frantically shaking the letter in front of her mother's face. 'He told me — '

'He wasn't in his right mind,' she blustered. 'Otherwise he wouldn't have killed himself.'

'He killed himself because he found out!' Isabel replied, her face distorted with anger. 'You betrayed him, you slept with someone else, you had someone else's child — who is he?'

Virginia turned to go, but her daughter sprang forwards and gripped her arm. 'I swear to God, I'll make you tell me.'

Immediately Virginia shook off Isabel's arm, her face suddenly composed again. Confident, as she looked from Eleanor to her daughter. 'David Hall was your father.'

'No! He never lied to me.'

Virginia's eyes flickered, but her daughter knew what was going through her head. She knows I can't prove it; she knows it's just his word against hers, and he's dead. Isabel felt suddenly beaten. She's won again — and now she thinks she is safe.

'Mother, please,' she said softly, her voice breaking. 'Please, I have to know who he is.'

Virginia hesitated, then in one quick action she snatched the letter and tore it into pieces, dropping the scraps on to the hall floor.

Triumphantly she faced her daughter. 'I have nothing to tell you, dear,' she said evenly. 'Nothing at all.'

Isabel looked at the torn letter. 'Oh, Mother,' she said softly. 'If only you had done that before I read it.'

A little later Eleanor made her niece a light meal and took it up to her room. She set it down beside the bed and glanced towards Isabel who was nursing Sybella. Her face was pinched with tiredness and stress, but for once her child slept soundly in her arms.

'Eat something, sweetheart,' Eleanor said, 'just a little.'

Isabel shook her head. Her eyes looked enormous, and temporarily blank, as though she had exhausted all her emotions. 'The photocopy is in my bag,' she said simply.

Her aunt took it out and began to read David Hall's words, then she frowned and placed it on the bedside table. 'I can't tell you how sorry I am.'

Isabel did not look up. 'Did you know?'

'No.'

'I'm glad,' she said, smiling faintly. 'I would have hated that.' Carefully Isabel moved Sybella, her right arm aching as she leaned against the bedhead. 'Do you know who he . . . my father . . . is?'

Eleanor shook her head. 'No.'

'Any suspicions?'

'None,' she replied, although her mind turned to Geoffrey Harrod. He and Virginia had travelled together for years, they had had plenty of opportunity to have an affair . . . her thoughts ran on, bitterness bubbling inside her. Her brother had been betrayed by that cold woman; not only did she not love him; she had committed adultery too. Eleanor's lips pursed. Virginia Hall, you have a lot to answer for — and you *will* answer for it.

'You know she's going to get away with it, don't you?'

Eleanor looked at her niece. 'What?'

'She's going to stick to her story. She's going to say that my father — David Hall — was not in his right mind when he wrote that letter. She's going to insist that he was my father, and do you know why?'

Eleanor shook her head.

'Because she knows that we can't prove otherwise,' Isabel replied, hugging her daughter to her. 'I never wanted her to get close to my child,' she said softly. 'God forgive me, I never trusted my own mother — and now I know why.' She glanced at her aunt. Her eyes had lost their dullness all at once; she was fighting back.

'I want you to look after Sybella for me, Eleanor. I want you to help me to bring her up. Will you do that for me?'

'But what about your mother?'

Isabel smiled grimly. 'I know my mother. Guilt will force her out of this house, back to work. And when it does, we'll know that David didn't lie to me.'

She used his name; not Daddy any longer, but David instead. And in a peculiar way, it seemed to make him more of an ally.

'I have to go back to London to make a career for myself, Eleanor . . . ' Isabel kissed the top of her child's head. Tenderly. 'I have to succeed, for Sybella, myself, and David . . . ' She stroked her child's dark hair and nuzzled her cheek. 'God, I love her . . . but she's better here with you,' she said brokenly, holding Sybella out towards her aunt.

Eleanor hesitated and then took the child in her arms. Isabel smiled as she did so.

'I put her in your safe keeping,' she said quietly. 'I leave her to you.'

The following day Virginia was busy on the phone and by mid-morning she had organised a lecture in London that weekend and a tour in America the next week. Geoffrey Harrod was delighted to hear from her, she seemed eager to get back to work, her voice slightly raised with excitement. Eleanor watched her. I thought I understood you, she thought, but you are too clever and too deep for me.

Her exit was proof of her guilt, and they all knew it. For once Virginia Hall's actions were obvious and it damned her in her daughter's eyes.

Throughout that painful day they avoided each other, and only when Virginia was about to leave did she instigate a conversation.

'Well, dear, I suppose it's about time I got back to work, now that you're fit to look after your daughter again.' She pulled on her calfskin

322

gloves, her throat tightening. She loved Sybella, and for a while she had almost deluded herself into thinking that she could keep her. Even The Ridings had become more welcoming — but not for long — no, old sins and lost dogs always come home.

She glanced at Isabel who was holding her daughter tightly, and her heart ached. I do love you, Sybella, she thought . . . Then she turned and walked to the door.

'I'm home in a few days. I know you and Eleanor can cope.'

Isabel's voice was cool, contained. 'We can cope, Mother.'

Suddenly Virginia rushed back, hurriedly kissing Sybella and touching Isabel on the cheek, then she turned and walked out.

★ ★ ★

Isabel hid the torn pieces of David Hall's letter carefully behind her favourite photograph of Sybella — the one she always carried with her — and tucked it into her bag. Slowly she checked around the bedroom and closed the door, walking down to the kitchen, her mind preoccupied.

When she walked in, Blair looked at her and smiled, and Eleanor raised her eyebrows.

'So you're off again, are you?'

Isabel nodded. 'I'll be back next weekend.'

'We could go fishing,' Blair offered.

She ruffled his hair. 'You could go fishing, and I'll watch,' she replied, glancing towards the high chair where Sybella sat and winking at her daughter. Sybella laughed happily. 'You be good for your auntie, little one, won't you? Mummy will be back soon.' Isabel tickled her daughter under the chin and then kissed the end of her nose. 'Love you, baby,' she said, straightening up. 'I've told the taxi to wait at the gates, Eleanor,' she explained, hurrying on. 'I'm just going for a walk in the garden before I go.'

'I'll come with you — '

Eleanor put out her hand to stop Blair, her understanding complete. 'No, let Isabel go on her own. We'll see her again next week.'

The garden smelt strongly of lilacs, hanging voluptuously over the brick walls, their heavy heads bending down as though they were whispering to each other. All along the flower beds, bees droned hazily in the early summer, and the rusty weather vane over the stables creaked in the warm breeze. In the drawing room, a curtain blew out from the French doors, and as Isabel rounded the bend of the house, a shadow moved across the study window.

She turned, half saw it and smiled, lifting her face to the sun. And under the silent sky she made the second of her four wishes.

'Daddy . . . David . . . I'm off again, back to London. I know what I want to do now, and no one is going to stop me.'

Her right hand clenched and then relaxed.

'I remember you told me that when I was a baby you held me up to the moon and asked the gods to give me the heart of a hunter . . . ' She paused, the words seemed to give her courage.

'Well, I'm making my second wish now. I wish to succeed, David . . . and I wish for the heart of a hunter.'

PART THREE

22

London
Two years later

Ted Cavendish stood at the window of his gallery in Cork Street, one hand in his pocket, another scratching his nose thoughtfully. Beside him stood Sterling Thompson, his toupé shining ethereally red-gold in the sunlight coming down from the overhead skylights. Several customers pottered in the gallery behind them, but they were only vaguely interested in the selection of 18th-century Dutch drawings on display and soon left.

Cavendish blew his nose discreetly on a pink silk handkerchief. 'Bloody Wimbledon,' he muttered darkly, 'it's always the same as this time of year. No flaming customers.'

Sterling turned to him. 'I remember when I first set up my own gallery, I had a private view and no one turned up ... ' He paused for dramatic effect. 'It was only the following day that I found out it was the women's finals.'

Ted Cavendish gave him a slow look, then changed the subject. 'So what's new?'

'Baye Fortunas has just come out of hospital after another back operation,' Sterling replied, 'and Portento has just had his haemorrhoids done.'

Cavendish laughed loudly. 'How do you find

out these delicious bits of gossip?'

'I had lunch with his surgeon at the Garrick the other day,' Sterling replied, pleased to have Ted Cavendish's approval. 'You'd be amazed what doctors tell you — '

'Will the operation incapacitate him for long?'

Sterling frowned. 'I don't think so, he does lots of them all the time.'

Cavendish frowned, and then raised his eyes heavenwards. 'I meant Fortunas, you bloody ass, not the doctor!'

Hurt, Sterling pursed his lips. 'I'm sure I can't follow half of what you say, Ted, and I don't think you should be so irritable.' He paused, thinking of something to say. 'Anyway, do you remember David Hall's girl?'

Cavendish's heavy-lidded eyes flickered with interest. 'Isabel?'

Sterling nodded. 'Yes, that's her.' He warmed to his theme. 'I saw she was exhibiting the other day at some gallery in Chelsea. Not one of the big ones,' he added, his tone patronising, 'but then she's only a beginner.'

'Didn't she marry that solicitor, Teddy Gray?'

Sterling nodded.

'Then what happened? There was some scandal, or something, wasn't there?'

His face shining with animation, Sterling leaned towards his companion. 'She was raped, you know — '

'Raped? I thought it was just a mugging.'

'No,' Sterling insisted, knowing that rape made a better story, 'she was raped all right. Two men, blacks. They were never found.'

'I remember when David and Virginia Hall used to have parties in that marvellous old house in Yorkshire, and I noticed Isabel then — she was a good-looking girl.'

'Lost her looks now though,' Sterling said, even though he hadn't seen Isabel for years. 'She had a kid too.'

Ted Cavendish's eyebrows rose. 'She got pregnant from the rape?' Sterling nodded. He wasn't too sure about the details, but the story was a good one. 'Well, well, well . . . ' Cavendish continued. 'So poor old Isabel's had a rough ride of it, has she? I must say she certainly leads a very colourful life — wasn't she living with Stanton Feller at one time?'

'There were three of them,' Sterling said, licking his lips and smoothing down the front of his waistcoat, 'all together in that house in Holland Park. A *ménage à trois*.'

Ted Cavendish mused for an instant and then turned to Sterling, his face bland. 'So what were her paintings like?'

'Good . . . if you like that kind of thing. But then, how can she hope to make a success of her life, with her reputation?'

Baye Fortunas was at that moment walking along Redcliffe Gardens. He glanced at the address he had written down and then pushed open the gate of a run-down house, stopping to read the names on the bells before pushing the one marked 'I. HALL'. The buzzer sounded inside, followed by a woman's voice coming over the intercom.

'Hello?'

'Isabel? Is that Isabel Hall?'

There was a pause at the other end.

'It's Baye, Baye Fortunas,' he continued, frowning when there was no response. 'Don't you remember me? I was a friend of your father's.'

The door swung open and he walked in, pressing the light on and making his way up the stairs. The woman's voice, disembodied, came down to greet him.

'I'm on the top floor, number six.'

Slowly he made his way up and then paused outside the flat, breathing heavily.

The door opened and he walked in. Isabel was standing with her back against the light beside a large canvas. For an instant he blinked, unable to see her, and then she moved and he walked towards her with his hand outstretched. She took hold of it, and he noticed that her grip was weak, which surprised him until he remembered her accident. Her smile was cautious but warm, her long hair drawn back into a heavy plait, her skin fair and without make-up. Only her eyes expressed her strength and they looked at him frankly. Baye Fortunas had not seen David and Virginia Hall's daughter for a long time and he was surprised to find that she impressed him so much.

The dog which moved out of the bay window impressed him too. Growling softly, the Doberman advanced towards the Greek until Isabel caught hold of its collar and frowned.

'It's all right, Sim, he's a friend.'

The dog immediately sat down, and Baye eyed

it thoughtfully. 'That's a very alarming-looking animal.'

Isabel smiled and stroked Sim's back. 'He makes me feel safe — he's very protective.'

Baye nodded and glanced round the room with feigned nonchalance. Isabel watched him, remembering the man from her childhood — olive-skinned, with dark shadows under his eyes, wearing a mohair suit and carrying a cashmere coat over his arm. He smelt of Paco Rabane and his hands were carefully manicured. As she showed him to a seat she wondered about his fabled collection — and wondered why he had come to see her.

Not that she was prepared to show her curiosity; no, better wait for him to make the first move. He noticed her reserve and smiled to himself. So like Virginia — in some ways.

'I saw your work in the Capital Gallery,' he said, accepting the glass of white wine she offered him. 'Are you making a living?'

Isabel sat down on a chair next to him. She knew what the question really implied — Baye Fortunas could see that the flat was not a real studio; he had guessed that she was struggling; but she wasn't going to make it easy for him by admitting it.

'I get along nicely, Baye,' she replied calmly. 'How are things with you? I heard you bought some nice Samuel Palmers the other day.'

'How people talk!' he said, affecting annoyance but secretly delighted. 'I was lucky, that's all.' He changed the subject deftly. 'How's your mother?'

'Fine,' Isabel replied evenly.

'And your daughter? You have a little girl, I know.'

She smiled warmly. 'Sybella's well and happy. She's three and a half now.'

His thoughts wandered. 'My children are all grown up, but not one of them has given me grandchildren . . . '

Isabel crossed her legs and leaned back in her chair. 'Give it time,' she said quietly.

'I suppose you're wondering why I'm here,' Baye said finally, realising that she wasn't going to ask. 'Well, I've been looking at your work, Isabel, and I like it. I would like to see some more of it.' He paused, the room was warm, too warm for paintings, she should have a proper workplace. 'I thought you lived with Stanton, at his studio.'

'I *worked* with Stanton,' she corrected him. 'For a while, but I thought it was time for me to go it alone.' Again, the warm smile.

She's a good-looking woman, Baye thought suddenly.

'So I moved here. Nearly eighteen months now, and of course I still have the studio up in Yorkshire.' Her mind went back to The Ridings, and to the studio over the old stables. She had done some good work there.

'He's still a force to be reckoned with . . . '

Isabel glanced up quizzically.

'Stanton,' Baye explained. 'Yes, he's a hell of a painter, even after all these years he's not lost his touch.'

'He taught me a lot, and he was very good to

334

me,' Isabel said, adding, 'He still is — we do some work together occasionally.'

'I know, Mrs de Souza told me,' Baye replied thoughtfully, dropping the name of one of America's oldest families with consummate ease. Walter de Souza had built up his fortune from casinos, then lost it in bad investments, then remade it by establishing a hotel chain. His son, Irving, had married a penniless girl with no obvious talent or looks, but she did have voracious ambition, and within a decade they had doubled the de Souza fortune.

'She saw a portrait you did with Stanton and she was asking after your work.'

'That's nice,' Isabel said pleasantly, refusing to become excited. She knew how often such talk was idle chit-chat, even when it came from people as powerful as Baye Fortunas.

'We wondered — Mrs de Souza and I — if you would like to come to dinner and bring some of your work with you. We would arrange transport, of course.'

Isabel's heart quickened.

'I would be delighted, of course. When?'

'A week on Tuesday?' he asked, getting to his feet as if she had already agreed.

'That would be fine,' Isabel said easily, walking with him to the door.

'I'll send the car at seven-thirty then,' Baye said, moving out in the corridor, 'and I'll get someone to phone you later this week to organise the transport.'

When he had gone Isabel stood in the middle of the room, Sim by her side. Critically she assessed the painting on the easel, picked up a brush, and then laid it down again, her mind running on. What should she show Mrs de Souza? Portraits or still lives? Should she show them in frames, or bare? Perhaps she could get something else finished by next week . . . she stopped suddenly, her hand resting on the top of Sim's head, his eyes fixed on her.

Carefully, Isabel glanced around her. The flat was far from ideal, she knew that. But it had been all she could afford at the time. Her two easels, a work table and a divan were the only pieces of furniture, that, and Sim's basket. Outside the window everything was equally bare; one of the last surviving elms stood like a lonely sentry and an empty windowbox displayed nothing other than a daily sprinkling of crumbs for the London sparrows.

Beside the studio room there was just a single bedroom, a bathroom and a kitchen, although some welcome attic space did provide storage for new, or discarded, canvases. The flat was functional, no more. There was no hint of the woman who lived there, no clues to her personality — it was a workplace, that was all.

All Isabel's luxuries and comforts were at The Ridings, London was merely her base, not her home. Here she worked, read, studied, exercised. Here she washed her hair late at night, reading the Art Review pages of The Times, and here she phoned Eleanor or Prossie when she felt lonely. She made friends, but kept her own counsel, Sim being her closest companion, and she painted day and night.

The two parts of her life became totally separate: London meant being an artist and working; Yorkshire meant being a mother and relaxing. Neither overlapped; indeed, Isabel kept her Yorkshire life a closely guarded secret, just as she kept her London life divorced from The Ridings. It was the only way she could function efficiently.

I have been here for two years, she thought, studying the painting again. What the hell have I achieved in that time? Her right hand opened and closed automatically. Not much, she decided, sitting down with Sim's head resting on her lap.

She was getting tired of being poor. Starving in a garret had only a limited charm, Isabel realised, and reputations took a lot of starving to achieve . . . She smiled wryly and leaned her head back against the divan, her eyes tracing a fine crack in the plaster over her head — it would be nice to have a patron like Baye Fortunas or Mrs de Souza; such people liked to encourage young artists. Or did they? How many times had she heard of painters being encouraged and fêted only to find themselves out of favour when the patron's whim turned to someone else?

Only the other week she had bumped into a fellow painter, Freddie Michaels, who told her how he had been hired by the owner of a well known supermarket chain, who turned out to be gay. When Freddie didn't perform, he was out.

'Bugger art,' he had said to her ruefully, 'if you get my drift.'

Isabel frowned, trying to shake off her misgivings. Mrs de Souza had a good reputation as a patron, and as for Baye Fortunas . . . she thought back, trying to remember what David had said about him.

' . . . He has a sharp eye for colour, not so much for form. I would trust his judgement on technique, but he might be a bit woolly on composition.'

Isabel smiled, feeling that somehow she already had an advantage over the Greek. But Mrs de Souza? No, she knew nothing about her. Nothing at all.

Which was where Stanton came in. Calling round later that night at the Holland Park studio, Isabel found Prossie in bed, her face relaxed in sleep, the three little girls asleep beside her, You Too sitting on the windowsill. Tiptoeing silently out of the bedroom, she made her way to the studio, and stood at the back whilst she watched Stanton block in the composition of a nude.

When he had finished, she coughed and he turned.

'Stop doing that! I can't stand people creeping about, it puts me off. I know immediately someone's behind me.'

'Sure,' she replied phlegmatically, 'after all, I've only been here for about twenty minutes.'

He said nothing, but dropped his brushes into a jam jar and then half filled it with turps. The smell was momentarily overpowering.

'So where's Orthos?'

Isabel put her head on one side. 'You think I

338

don't know who Orthos is?' she said smiling. 'Well, I happen to have heard somewhere that he was one of the dogs Hercules killed.'

Stanton was miffed. 'Clever old you,' he said grudgingly. 'But you didn't answer the question. Where is your little canine chum?'

'At home. I thought he could guard the flat while I was out.'

Stanton swirled the brushes round in the turps; the paint soon muddied the clear liquid. 'I thought the whole point of having that mutt was to protect you?'

'I came by taxi, Stanton,' she replied wearily, 'and Sim doesn't like taxis much . . . Besides, some cabbies won't take him.'

'I can't think why,' he said drily, pouring himself a drink. 'Want one?'

Isabel shook her head. 'No, I just came for a chat.'

'At ten o'clock at night?' he queried. 'What did you want to chat about — insomnia?'

Isabel raised her eyebrows. 'Baye Fortunas came to see me today, he's asked me to have dinner with him and Mrs de Souza next week.'

'Don't have the beef,' Stanton said immediately. 'Her bloody chef's a Filipino and he's useless.' He leaned towards her conspiratorially. 'Someone told me he's one of those faith healers in his spare time. You know the ones, they perform psychic operations with rusty knives — I tell you, when he started carving the joint I thought the bloody thing was going to rear up and kick us all to death. Sunny de Souza — '

'Sunny?'

He nodded. 'Yes, she was christened Theresa . . .'
He made a face ' . . . but as Mrs Rockerfeller was
called Happy — '

'She called herself Sunny!'

'You're a quick learner, kiddo,' he said
approvingly, his expression curious. 'So are you
supposed to be taking some paintings with you
for her to see?'

Isabel shrugged. 'That's the point, I don't know
which ones to take. I don't know what kind of
things she likes.' She trailed off, suddenly irritable.
'The whole thing might be a washout anyway.'

'Why? Are they having it in the garden?'
Stanton replied deftly.

'God, I hate it when you're in this mood!'
Isabel snapped, slumping down on a chair next
to the dais. 'Can't you go back to being bloody-
minded for a while? You're much easier to talk to
that way.'

Stanton leaned against the work table, his
arms folded. 'All right if you want the cold facts,
here they are. Sunny de Souza is a woman with a
mission — to be able to breathe through her
nose unaided — '

'What?'

He put up his hands to stop her interrupting.
'She is never seen without two things — a Chanel
handbag and a permanent cold. In the winter she
has flu jabs, in the summer she is a martyr to hay
fever, and in between she has rhinitis, which, as I
am sure you know, is an inflammation of the
lining of the nose.' He paused. 'I won't be offended
if you want to take notes.'

Isabel's face was impassive.

'Anyway, in the pursuit of anyone who can cure her from her snotty nose, Sunny de Souza has often been exceedingly grateful to people who have recommended doctors, or remedies, which have alleviated her symptoms — that is, people who have stopped her nose from running like a tap with a faulty washer.' He paused. 'In fact, Portento gave her some herbal remedies to take three times daily with eye of newt, or some other such crap, and as a reward she commissioned a portrait of each of her four grandchildren.'

Isabel frowned. 'What about you?'

'I . . . was not so lucky,' Stanton said carefully. 'I did go to dine with her, but after she had wheezed and dripped her way through two courses, I made my excuses and left — '

' — much poorer.'

'Well, money isn't everything,' he replied grandly now that Isabel's assistance had helped him to extricate himself from his financial mire. Overdue debts were now settled, and late paintings delivered. 'Mind you, Sunny *is* very rich, so I would do your best to get in with her. She also knows many influential people in London, dealers *and* buyers.' Stanton finished his drink. 'If you want my advice I would take your portraits, Isabel. The big, impressive ones. I think she might go for those.'

'Anything else?'

Stanton sighed. 'Just a handkerchief.'

★ ★ ★

In the end Isabel chose three portraits and fiddled with them continually until they were collected the day before the dinner was arranged. With even more attention to detail, Isabel set about deciding what she was going to wear for the occasion. She had brought back various clothes from Yorkshire and ended up with most of her wardrobe on the bed in the flat. In her underwear she stood in front of the mirror, her hair newly washed and hanging down to her shoulders, her face skilfully made up.

If I was painting a portrait of me — as another person — what clothes would I give myself? she wondered, picking up a light summer dress and holding it against her body. It looked drab and was quickly thrown to one side, a pair of white trousers and a silk shirt joined it soon after . . . Panic set in about half an hour later, Isabel still not decided, her hair by that time more than a little out of place. In desperation she pulled on a velvet suit, then tugged it off again and hurried into a plain navy dress, zipping up the back and looking at herself. Pleasantly surprised, she put on a pair of fine navy tights, high-heeled navy shoes and a heavy gold necklace. Then carefully she reapplied her lipstick and combed her hair.

Only then did she look in the mirror again. A young woman stared back, a good-looking young woman who was well dressed and composed. A young woman who had some of her mother's poise. But what of her father? Isabel turned away, snatched up her handbag, and walked out.

Sunny de Souza lived in a house in Belgrave Square, with a gilded harp in a first-floor window easily seen from the road. Isabel hesitated, then rang the bell. The butler let her in immediately, showing her into the drawing room where Baye Fortunas was talking to a young man in a dinner jacket and an older man leaning on a walking stick.

'Ah, our young artist,' Baye said, smiling at Isabel and then turning to the older man. 'This is Miss Isabel Hall, Irving.' He glanced back to Isabel. 'And this is Mr Irving de Souza — '

' — and I'm Gyman,' a voice said behind her.

She turned and smiled warmly, extending her hand. Gyman de Souza was about thirty, not much over five feet ten, with brown hair and a mole on his left cheek.

'I've been looking at some of your work. It's lovely.'

'What!' Irving de Souza said irritably, his balding head bending down towards his shorter son. 'What kind of a compliment is that?' he said, turning to Isabel. 'My son is hopeless socially,' he continued. 'I apologise for him — your work is very fine. Very fine indeed.'

Isabel smiled, but felt acute embarrassment for Gyman de Souza and avoided his eyes, her attention conveniently diverted by the woman who had just walked in. Sunny de Souza glided towards the group and then paused, striking a pose by the fireplace, her arms outstretched along the Georgian mantelpiece.

'I thought a portrait posed just so,' she said, her voice deep, like someone with a heavy cold. 'People have always said my arms were magnificent.'

343

Isabel studied her, mesmerised. Her skin was plumped up with collagen, giving her the appearance of a raddled cherub, and her hair was arranged into a rigid blond bob, although it was sufficiently swept back from her ears to display a pair of vast black pearls. In a black organza dress, black stockings and black shoes, she looked like a bird caught in an oil slick.

'Miss Hall . . . may I call you Isabel?' she said, parting company with the mantelpiece and walking towards Isabel. 'I just know we shall be friends . . .'

Then she sniffed.

Isabel bit her lip fiercely.

'Baye has shown me some of your work. Lovely, lovely.' She squeezed Isabel's arm and led her to a sofa. 'One should surround oneself with talent, and beautiful things.' One magnificent arm gestured to the room in which they were seated. A pair of French gilded torchères flanked the mantelpiece, a Heppelwhite table, and two Chippendale chairs all seemed ready to take a bow. 'One can never have too much beauty. I was Egyptian before, you see . . .' She sniffed again, her son staring at his feet avidly as she dropped her voice, ' . . . in one of my past lives.'

Rapidly losing interest in the conversation, Baye began to talk to Irving de Souza, leaving Gyman and Isabel beside Sunny as she continued enthusiastically. 'I have a wonderful little woman in Clapham who tells the future. Have you had your aura done?'

Isabel smiled half-heartedly. 'Pardon?'

'Auric alignment — it's wonderful.' She patted her organza chest. 'For the heart and the chakras, and the opening up of the soul.' Sunny smiled, blew her nose, and continued her conversation. 'Baye tells me he knew your father very well.'

Daddy, Isabel thought gently. 'Yes, yes, he did. My father was — '

'A very clever man, as is your mother, I hear,' Sunny said, interrupting her. 'She goes all over chatting about lovely stone things, doesn't she?' Her artificially full cheeks swelled up as she smiled. She looked for all the world as though she was storing nuts. 'Not that I care for Roman art — '

Gyman de Souza was suddenly galvanised into life. 'It's Hellenic actually.'

Sunny looked at her son and blinked slowly. 'What, darling?'

'Mrs Hall lectures on Hellenic Art, not Roman.'

'Does it matter?' Sunny asked.

'Only to a Roman.'

Isabel felt a strong hand on her arm as Sunny leaned to her. 'My son has a fine brain,' she said proudly, 'but he can be a little shy. Nothing wrong with that, nothing at all, indeed some people find it charming.' She leaned across Isabel to her son. 'I'm just telling Miss Hall all about you.'

'Good,' he said, staring at his shoes again.

The dinner was superb, principally, it seemed, because Sunny's Filipino chef had left for Hampstead.

345

' . . . for the Admiral's Walk,' she explained. 'All Arabs and plaster columns.' Her eyes flicked towards her husband. 'Irving, darling, who was that awful man who bought a house in Admiral's Walk? Oh, you know who I mean, he put heroin up his nose — '

'Cocaine,' Gyman corrected her.

'Well, cocaine then, darling,' his mother conceded, sniffing. 'Gilly Bentley told me that it rotted his proboscis, and after a while he used to spend all his time with a runny nose.'

Gyman sniggered next to Isabel.

Sunny's expression set like concrete. 'Mine is a longstanding problem, *not* caused by drugs, you little creep,' she said, then smiled gaily at Isabel again. 'Just hay fever, that's all.' She dabbed at her nose with a handkerchief. 'It's in my aura, apparently.'

Isabel continued her meal, stealing furtive glances at her surroundings. She recognised the Paul Storr silver on the Borghese table, and a Venetian chandelier shining down on an Aubusson carpet; just as she could appreciate the Guardi paintings and the Grinling Gibbons carving over the fireplace. Sunny de Souza had superb taste.

Finally Isabel's eyes roamed to the gilded harp in the window, Sunny following her gaze. 'Do you like it?'

She smiled at Sunny and nodded.

'I bought it in Florence, from a dealer who was crippled with angina.' She dropped her voice again. 'Depleted chakras.'

'Bad circulation more like,' Gyman said drily.

'Darling, how could you know? I felt,' she gripped the organza front of her dress, 'his trauma. Past life regression would have helped him — have you been regressed?'

Only since dinner, Isabel nearly replied, but resisted the temptation and changed the subject instead. 'I noticed the harp in the window when I first came to London. I used to wonder if anyone played it.'

'*DARLING!*' Sunny shrieked to her husband. 'Little Isabel noticed our lovely harp. She saw it in the window.'

'Good thing someone appreciates it,' he said, smiling shortsightedly down the table. 'I can't stand the thing myself.'

'She wondered if anyone played it.'

'The only time that thing gets played is when the maid slips with the duster.'

Sunny laughed childishly. 'He's so witty.' She beamed. 'I fell in love with him because he made me laugh, and because he was — is — a marvellous lover . . . he was — is — such a virile man.'

Isabel sipped her wine, uncertain of how to respond, and for the remainder of the meal she simply listened, because she knew that was what Sunny de Souza wanted. Finally Sunny rose and motioned for Isabel to follow her out of the dining room.

'Oh, good, now we can chat,' she said, leading her into a walnut-panelled library where Isabel's paintings were displayed on three carved antique easels, lamps carefully arranged around them. They looked superb.

'I like this one,' Sunny said, smiling to show her perfect teeth. 'But Irving thinks this one . . . ' She gestured to a portrait of an allegorical figure. 'I believe you work with Stanton Feller?'

'Sometimes,' Isabel agreed.

Sunny sniffed. 'He's a brute of a man. No manners,' she said, 'and his language!'

'He's got a good heart though,' Isabel said, rising automatically to his defence. 'It's just his way.'

'I can't think how any of our dear Royal Family can stand him around — do you think he swears in front of them too?'

'Only if provoked,' Isabel said, smiling.

'Well, I like this one,' Sunny decided finally, offering Isabel a very good price. 'Is that enough?' Her face hardened, the collagen cheeks turned to cold stone. 'I can't go higher, I warn you now.'

'It's fine. Thank you,' Isabel said, aware of the change in the woman and of her power. Sunny de Souza acts like a fool deliberately, she thought with sudden understanding, just to give herself time to suss people out. Clever.

'I'm so glad we've managed to do business,' Sunny said, taking Isabel's arm, 'because I'd like a portrait for darling Irving's birthday.'

⋆　⋆　⋆

'How is 'Darling Irving'? — the bald old fart,' Stanton said bitingly when Isabel called in to see him at the studio the following day.

'Ignore him, he's just jealous,' Prossie replied,

struggling to her feet and hugging Isabel. 'I think you did really well, love, and you never know what it might lead to.'

Stanton couldn't stop. 'Did you meet Gyman?' he asked. 'I've got a theory about him, his parents treat him so bloody badly and he takes it so bloody patiently that one day Sunny is going to find a cure for her rhinitis by having an axe smashed into her face.'

He sniffed, to make the point — Prossie and Isabel laughing despite themselves.

★ ★ ★

Gyman de Souza phoned Isabel that Friday, asking her out for dinner and suggesting that he knew certain people who might be interested in her work. Unwilling to offend him or his mother (who she was sure had suggested the date), Isabel accepted and the following Monday they went to the Caprice in Mayfair.

'It was an awful evening, wasn't it?' he said, downing his second martini.

Cautiously, Isabel refused to comment.

'I really do like your pictures,' he went on sheepishly. 'I have a friend in the Elizabethan Theatre Company.'

It was a successful experimental company which had made something of a reputation for itself and Isabel listened carefully.

'He said he'd like to have a look at your stuff — if he likes it he might commission you to paint the cast members of this year's company.' He paused. 'They don't pay much. Sorry . . . '

Without thinking, Isabel put out her hand and touched his. The action was spontaneous and he nodded, as though she had actually articulated her feelings in words. 'I suppose you think I'm a real wet?'

'No. It's hard on you.'

He looked up, relieved. 'You're right, it's awful, what with my father and his hotels, and my mother — she's even better in business than he is. They think I'm a fool.'

'Your mother doesn't.'

He laughed softly, without any emotion whatsoever. The noise shuffled uneasily inside Isabel's head.

'My mother is not interested in me; she doesn't see me for what I am.' He breathed in, as though he was about to face her. 'This evening was her idea — '

'I thought it might be.'

He sighed. 'She knew about your father and mother, and she decided you were socially acceptable — even if you were an artist!' He made a face. 'She thought you and I might get on — I suppose she thought she might even get the portrait cheaper that way.' Quickly, Gyman continued. 'We can get on — but not in the way she thinks.'

He smiled, a child's smile, almost as Sybella smiled when she knew she had made herself understood.

'You see, I want you to understand!' He dropped his voice, suddenly furtive. 'Mother doesn't know I'm gay. Or rather, if she does know, she doesn't want to — if you see what I mean.' Again, the dead laugh. 'I can still help you though, if you want help that is. If you think you would like me to — '

His insecurity made her heart ache. 'Gyman, I'd like any help you can give me,' she replied easily. 'To tell the truth, I'm bloody hard up and I'm sick of it.'

He brightened. 'I thought your family had money — '

'They do,' she replied, 'but I wanted to go it alone. So I ended up alone and *poor*.' She pulled a face, and he smiled, comfortable with her. 'I know I could go home; just as I know I could go back and work with Stanton, but I want to prove myself my own way.'

She paused and he looked at her curiously.

'Why do you do that?'

'What?'

'Open and close your hand all the time.'

Isabel smiled. 'I don't realise I'm doing it.' Her eyes moved to her right hand. 'I had an accident, and I was very ill for a while. My arm and my hand were affected and I had to work hard — I still have to work hard — to keep the full use of them.'

'That must be a bore — You paint with your right hand, don't you?'

She nodded. 'Yes, but for a while I didn't paint at all.' She carried on talking, surprising herself. 'For a while I gave it up. I got married and had a baby instead.'

He watched her. 'What happened?'

'Divorce. He didn't want the baby, you see — so now my aunt looks after my daughter.'

He frowned, trying to understand. 'Is that hard for you?'

Isabel folded her arms and leaned forward on the table. She was surprised to find that she liked Gyman de Souza and was at ease with him. The sexual barriers had been hurdled; they were no longer strangers.

'It should be harder than it is,' she admitted, 'but it seems I'm not really the maternal type . . . I know that sounds terrible, I would never have believed I could say it, let alone feel it, but somehow motherhood is not enough for me. Sybella — my daughter — is happy with my aunt, and she seems to be at home where she is.' Isabel sighed, trying to articulate her feelings. 'At times I want her so badly I could scream; I want to rush up to Yorkshire and run away with her and take care of her for ever . . . but it's not possible, or rather it *is* possible, but I don't choose to make it reality.'

He was momentarily nonplussed. 'But it sounds as though she's better where she is, and you're better where you are. If you gave up your work you would be miserable, and if you brought her to London you couldn't cope.'

'I feel as though I swopped her,' Isabel said gravely, 'for my ambition. As though I have made her second best — I discovered I was a failure as a mother, so I wanted to prove I could be a success with my work. I made the choice for both of us, and I wonder sometimes if it was mine to make . . . It wasn't her fault that she wasn't happy with me.'

'Do you regret having her?'

352

Isabel flinched, then considered her answer carefully. 'God forgive me, but if I had my life over again, I would never have had that child.' The words shocked her and she rushed on. 'That's the real guilt I carry, and one day I'm sure I'll pay for it . . . ' Her voice failed.

The restaurant continued to fill up with people, smoke rising, voices rising also, a whole mass of brilliant people leading brilliant lives.

'You've already paid for it,' Gyman said firmly. 'And what your child doesn't know can't hurt her.'

Isabel's eyes searched his. 'How could any child live with that knowledge?'

'She won't have to, if you don't tell her.'

'Oh, I won't tell her,' Isabel said gently, 'but some day, someone will.'

'Not if you keep it a secret,' he insisted. 'Can't you do that?'

She glanced at him and smiled distantly. 'Maybe . . . we're a family who are good at keeping secrets.'

23

Ivor got to his feet and padded out of the sunlight and into the shade by the side of the house, his tongue lolling out of his mouth. Grey-muzzled and slow in his movements he was tired and wanted to sleep, his stiff legs weary as he slumped beside the brickwork and dozed, a nearby blackbird pecking at the smooth grass of the lawn. After another moment Blair sat down beside him, stroking the dog's head and puffing importantly on a cigarette, his dark eyes black as burnt treacle in the shadowed light.

Totally content, he watched Eleanor weed, Sybella tugging a little wicker trug behind her, her thick hair tied up in bunches. She chattered constantly, her little hands busy, her head often cocked to one side, her socks slipping down her legs. An engaging child, she was totally indulged by Eleanor and Blair. They offered their affection without hesitation, and Sybella responded eagerly, ready to please.

Piggy-back rides on Blair's shoulders had her squealing with pleasure, as did riding in his wheelbarrow, the gravel path round the house made into a racetrack by their repeated circuits. Her eyes were large like her mother's and missed nothing. She remembered conversations too well, sometimes repeating things at painful moments, and when the phone rang she would answer it, then drop it, immediately losing interest. She bored quickly, constantly in need of stimulation — and of company.

So she was never far from Blair or Eleanor and when Isabel came home at the weekends she spent most of her time with her, healing the rift between them in stages. Of all of them, Isabel could see her daughter's progress the most clearly because she was not with her every day. She knew the speed of Sybella's brain and the charm which bordered on precociousness; the pursed lips, the hands placed on the hips when she didn't get her way. Eleanor indulged her by laughing, and she *was* funny, but she was also clever, and that was what made Isabel watch her daughter carefully. Because in her child, she saw the makings of another woman . . .

To all intents and purposes, Virginia Hall and Sybella Gray were totally different. Virginia had little charm; Sybella was delightful with people of all ages. Virginia had no sweetness; Sybella could be tender at times. But Virginia's quiet poise was often reflected in Sybella when she was denied something. It was as though the child realised she could not have her way and that sulks would be useless, so she blanked herself off — she wasn't moody, it was more impressive than that — Sybella was in control.

'She'll have to go to school soon,' Eleanor said one Saturday when Isabel was up from London. 'She needs to be with other children and she's too bright to be with us all the time.'

Isabel pushed some details across the kitchen table. 'I've already sorted it out. She's going to my old school, in the village. She starts in September.'

Eleanor nodded. 'Good,' she said simply. 'I'll tell your mother when she phones.'

'Is she calling tonight?' Isabel asked, knowing full well that Virginia seldom phoned at weekends when her daughter was at home.

They avoided each other as much as possible, Virginia in particular dreading any more confrontations with Isabel. She had good reason to. Since her daughter had read the letter from David Hall she was determined to discover the identity of her real father and tackled Virginia repeatedly, telephone conversations always ending with the same words.

'Oh, Mother, one other thing . . . '

'Yes, dear?'

'Who *is* my father?'

Virginia never replied, although at first she had stuck to her story and insisted that David Hall was Isabel's father. It soon became apparent, however, that her daughter neither believed her, nor was prepared to let her off the hook. So Virginia stopped making telephone calls to The Ridings when her daughter was there; and if Isabel did answer, the conversation always ended the same way, with the same question — which was never answered. Stalemate.

Eleanor brought Isabel's wandering thoughts back to the present.

'Your mother said she might phone tonight, but she wasn't sure,' she said, then changed the subject deftly. 'But let's not talk about her, sweetheart, what about you? How are things? I know you told me about the de Souza woman, but what about your personal life — have you met anyone?'

Isabel leaned back in her seat, putting distance between herself and her aunt. She dreaded the question, even though she knew it would be asked most weekends.

Eleanor saw her hesitation and waited patiently for the answer.

'I don't want to meet anyone,' Isabel said finally, 'I don't feel ready for it. After Teddy, and the attack — '

'Which was three years ago.'

'I know!' Isabel snapped, getting to her feet and walking over to the fridge. A selection of Sybella's drawings were blutacked on to the door. 'I just can't face it. I have to make the break in my career first — '

'But surely that doesn't mean giving up your social life?'

'I'm not giving it up!' Isabel countered. 'I see Gyman de Souza quite often, and I spend a lot of time with Prossie and Stanton — '

'It's not the same as having a man of your own — '

'What the hell would you know about it!' Isabel snapped angrily, then clapped her hand to her mouth. 'Oh God, Eleanor, I didn't mean to say that. I'm so sorry.'

Her aunt shook her head. 'Isabel, I know I'm an old maid, I know I didn't marry, but we're not talking about me, we're talking about you, and you need a man to be happy.' She put up her hands to stop Isabel interrupting her. 'Having a career is one thing, but it's not the beginning and end of life. You should be having some fun.'

'I can't,' Isabel said simply, her fingers running

over Sybella's drawing of a cat. 'I just can't . . . I don't know if it's all because of what happened with Teddy, or because those men tried to rape me . . . But I just don't want a man near me.' She turned, her eyes calm. 'When the time comes . . . but not now. I couldn't cope with an affair if it went wrong.'

'And if it went right?'

She smiled. 'I might give up painting again!' She rolled her eyes. 'Oh no, I think I'll stay celibate for a while yet.'

Eleanor studied her niece, noticing the nervous action with her right hand. 'How are you anyway?'

'Good.'

'No headaches?'

'Some,' Isabel replied, taking Sybella's picture off the fridge door.

'How's your concentration?'

'It comes and goes,' she said, smiling half-heartedly.

Eleanor knew she wanted to change the subject; she always did when it came to the question of her health, but she pushed her nevertheless.

'What about your arm?'

'Fine.'

'Are you sure?'

'Sure.'

'But there's nothing else you're worried about?'

Isabel put down the drawing on the kitchen table, her eyes fixed on the crayon cat. 'I don't have periods any more.'

'What?'

She repeated it carefully, and the words grew

in front of her. Let out of their cage of secrecy, they ran amok. 'I don't have periods any more.'

Frowning, Eleanor gestured for her to sit down. 'Since when?'

'Since the attack.'

'You haven't had a period since the attack?' Eleanor asked disbelievingly. 'Oh God, Isabel, why didn't you tell me?'

'I told the doctor,' she said, glancing away again, 'but he said it was due to shock and that they would come back in time.' Her hand still fingered the drawing. 'They haven't though — not for three years.'

'And you haven't been to see anyone else for a second opinion?'

Isabel shook her head. 'Not for eighteen months. No.'

'But that's ridiculous!' Eleanor snapped. 'Something has to be done.' She scrutinised her niece's face. 'Why on earth did you hide something as important as this?'

'I wanted to forget everything that's happened to me!' Isabel said, her voice rising. 'I wanted to push the whole bloody horrible memory to the back of my mind, the attack, the illness, the recovery — you have no idea what it's been like.' She stopped, her face flushed. 'Then when I found out about Daddy — David — that was the end.' Her hands clenched. 'I don't want to hear, feel, or experience any more trauma. I don't want to know what's wrong with me.' Her eyes were fierce. 'The periods will come back in time. The doctor said so. It's just shock, that's all.'

'Isabel — '

She got to her feet, determined. 'No, don't say any more! I don't function like a woman, because I don't think or feel like one. When I do, the periods will start again . . . ' She paused; she knew she was trying to convince herself as much as her aunt. 'I'm happy again now, Eleanor, I'm settled and safe again . . . Just let me get on with my work. Please. Just let me be. I can only go one step at the time, and at the moment I'm content.' She let go of the drawing suddenly; the edge of the paper had cut into her finger and made it bleed.

But Eleanor was not to be put off so easily. 'No, Isabel, I won't let it drop. You either go and see the doctor, or I'll get the doctor to come and see you.' Her voice was hard. 'If you don't give a damn about yourself, I do. I care about you — remember it was me who damn near brought you up. You are as much my daughter as my own child could have been.' She paused, then gently put her arm around Isabel. 'We'll sort it out, sweetheart, whatever it is, we'll sort it out.'

'But what if they say — '

'Whatever they say, it will be better for us to know.' She smiled. 'We can sort it out, we always do, don't we? You can't hide from life, Isabel, or from men. You had a terrible time of it, I know that and I understand, but your work is not enough.'

'I'm happy at the moment,' Isabel replied, looking into her aunt's eyes and pleading for time. 'Can't we leave it for a while? Just a little longer, just in case . . . just in case it's bad news?'

Eleanor hesitated, then said quietly, 'Do you

remember what David told you? He said, *Be careful, and be wise*. Do you remember that?' Isabel nodded. 'Well, sweetheart, be wise — you can't let him down. Please.'

★ ★ ★

Gyman de Souza was more than a little surprised to hear, only a month later, that Isabel was having an affair with one of the leading actors of the Elizabethan Theatre Company. Apparently, although she was not flaunting the association, she was not hiding it either, and soon the lovers were hot gossip. He was surprised because the actor in question, although not married or otherwise engaged, was not known as the reliable sort. Charming, good company and egotistical, he was the kind of person Gyman would never have matched with Isabel. But then, he mused, one never knew with women.

After working hard for several months, Isabel was getting together a good selection of theatre portraits. The pay for the commission, as Gyman had foretold, was not high, but the theatre name and reputation gave Isabel exposure and publicity, and she was grateful for it. Inch by inch she was climbing up the artistic greasy pole, slowly and carefully; while in her private life, she was becoming reckless — and no one knew what had caused the change in her.

★ ★ ★

'About bloody time,' Stanton said, peering at the label on a bottle he was holding before pouring himself a measure of sherry. 'I was wondering if little Isabel had given up sex altogether.'

Prossie frowned. 'But it's not like her to be sleeping with an actor — and it's all so sudden. Isabel was never capricious before.'

'Maybe she should have been,' Stanton replied, glancing over to Prossie. 'Artists have to experience the sins of the flesh to paint well.'

'Funnily enough, I don't think she did it to improve the quality of her work,' Prossie said drily. 'No, there's more to it than that. She used to tell me that she didn't want men around her and that she wasn't ready for any kind of relationship, and now — to pick some actor and have such a public fling.' She shook her head. 'It doesn't add up.'

'Maybe she was seduced by his Laertes,' Stanton replied, nudging You Too with his bare foot. 'She probably couldn't resist him in those tights.'

'No,' Prossie said thoughtfully, 'something's happened to her. Something happened which triggered all this off. There's a reason for it.'

Stanton dropped on to the bed next to her. 'Yeah,' he said, pulling her to him, 'the reason is she's human.'

★ ★ ★

In her studio flat Isabel lay back on her bed and glanced at the half-finished portrait of Tom Hoffman, then she turned and looked at the original, who was lying beside her. He smiled, kissed her tenderly, then began to undress her, pushing her back against the pillows and kissing and stroking her. Willingly, Isabel held on to him as he slid on top of her, one of her hands moving into the small of his back and another lingering amongst the hair at the nape of his neck. Tenderly he laid his head against hers, his face against hers, profile to profile, and her fingers seemed to dissolve into his flesh so that all sensation was mixed and joined between them, his pleasure her own.

He talked to her, describing her body and making her more beautiful than reality, making her some other Isabel who existed only for him. He made her listen, his words licking at her ears, his hands moving over her body, and each time she glanced away he caught hold of her head and turned her face back to him, so that her eyes looked into his.

Afterwards Isabel went into the bathroom to bathe. She was just pulling on her underwear when he opened the door and stood there, watching her.

'What are you doing?'

She smiled. 'Getting dressed.'

'No,' was all he said, and extending his hand, led her back to bed.

Hurriedly he rolled her on to her stomach and massaged her neck and shoulders with oil, his hands working down to her buttocks and thighs. Moaning, he entered her again, his portrait watching them from the other end of the room.

★ ★ ★

Portento had just returned to England from Florence for the opening of his new exhibition. A selection of paintings leaned against the walls of Sterling Thompson's gallery in Cork Street ready to be hung. The ugly Italian stood, his arms folded, his eyes fixed on the large tempera painting of a stallion with two women which he considered his masterpiece. Flustered, Sterling hovered next to him, his toupé not quite as centred as usual, his face covered with a fine film of perspiration. Behind him stood two porters ready to hang, or not to hang, the picture. One glanced at his watch and sighed extravagantly.

Sterling swallowed and turned to Portento, trying to explain. 'I just don't think that this one fits in with the exhibition — '

Portento scowled. 'You English dealers have no balls.'

'Which is more than can be said for the horse,' one of the porters murmured deftly.

'It's just a little too lusty for me,' Sterling continued lamely.

'D'you want a painter, or an interior decorator?'

'Portento,' Sterling said, his tone affectionate, although he was feeling less than kind, 'you know I live for your work, you have a huge following here. Probably bigger than in Italy.' Portento shot him a questioning look. 'Well, maybe not bigger, but just as appreciative.' He looped his arm around the Italian's shoulder. 'You see, they think of you as a man carrying on the traditions of Raphael, and as such they don't expect to see' — he gestured to the horse with

364

his other hand — 'such magnificent, but out of character, works.'

'But — '

'You see,' he said, rushing on, 'we don't want to deplete the strength of your show. Colour and line and heart,' he said, warming to his theme and oblivious to the Italian's contempt, 'are the important things for us to protect. You have a great eye, Portento, a great talent . . . ' he paused, to make the final point, ' . . . and as such you should not disappoint your followers by altering your basic concepts to go for more obvious effects.'

Portento gave him a very slow look, then shrugged.

'So don't hang it,' he said, walking out of the gallery.

Relieved, Sterling glanced over his shoulder to the porters.

'Dump this animal in the basement,' he said coldly.

'Bagsy the manure for my roses,' one of the men said as they carried it downstairs.

★   ★   ★

Portento was walking down Bond Street deep in thought when Isabel spotting him and crossed the road to greet him. The Italian had his hands deep in his pockets, his paint-soiled white boiler suit incongruous against the backdrop of expensive shops. He passed Chanel, Gucci and Löwe without so much as a glance in their windows, and was just drawing level with

Agnews when Isabel finally caught up with him.

She tapped him on the shoulder and he turned.

'Bella Isabella,' he said, kissing her on both cheeks. 'You look wonderful.'

'I feel good too,' she replied honestly. 'I didn't know you were in London, Portento, although I know the show opens on Thursday, Sterling sent me an invitation.'

'Sterling!' he said with contempt. 'That fool has just refused to hang one of my paintings. The best one.'

Isabel frowned, dropping into step beside him. 'It's not like you to let him.'

'Oh, it doesn't matter to me, I have another buyer for it,' he replied, putting his head on one side. 'Do you think I'd have let him get away with it otherwise?'

Laughing, Isabel walked by his side.

'When I first came to London in 1951 I thought it was one of the most wonderful cities on earth,' Portento said, shrugging his shoulders. 'Now it's filthy, and the drains stink. I think your government fell out of love with London.'

'You're too romantic,' Isabel replied easily. 'Cities decline the longer you know them.'

'Such a cynic!' he laughed, stopping and turning to her. 'So what is your life like? I hear from Stanton and from others that you're doing quite well.'

'Quite well,' she agreed.

'You're doing portraits for the Elizabethan Theatre Company?'

She nodded.

'That's good publicity for you,' he said, changing the subject. 'How's Sybella?'

Isabel wondered momentarily if he was making some kind of point, and then realised that he was simply being polite.

'She's a little girl now, Portento, and very bright.' Isabel paused, shading her eyes from the sun with one hand. 'I suppose all mothers say things like that, but she *is* a clever child.'

'So is her mother, and her grandmother,' he replied. 'And your father was a very intelligent man.'

David Hall was, she thought, but as for my father . . . who knows? He could be anyone. He could be a stupid man, or a reckless one. He could hate the arts, and love business; he could be mean with money, and without principles; maybe a drunk, or a profligate; maybe a man who lived alone, or abroad; maybe married now, his daughter forgotten — if he ever knew about her at all.

'Isabel?'

'Sorry, Portento,' she said. 'I was thinking about my father.'

'I cared for him a great deal, you know,' the Italian continued. 'David was very good to me, and he helped me when I needed it, always writing articles about my shows and taking people to see the paintings. He cared so much, if he believed in you. He was a very kind man, and you were lucky to have him as your father.'

Yes, Isabel thought, even though I was just borrowing him for a while. She glanced at the Italian and smiled, wondering what he would say if he knew the truth. How would Portento view the respected Virginia Hall then? How elegant and fastidious and clever would she seem to him? Isabel frowned. And how much interest would the art world show in her if it became common knowledge that she was not David Hall's daughter? Without his name and reputation, how quickly would she lose the little headway she had made? Oh no, Isabel thought, this is another secret I have to keep.

'You must be in love,' Portento said suddenly.

She smiled. 'Why do you say that?'

'Because you're only half listening to me, and because you glow like a woman in love.' He raised his eyebrows. 'Well, am I right?'

Isabel nodded.

'Is he a painter?'

'No!' she said vehemently, laughing. 'He's an actor.'

'An actor . . . ' the Italian repeated, rubbing his nose with his finger. 'They are fun, but unreliable. You be careful. Some are hard men who break women's hearts.'

'Not only hard men break hearts,' Isabel said enigmatically, taking Portento's arm as they walked on.

★　★　★

'Virginia Hall' the poster declared outside the ballroom of a large hotel in Singapore, and under her name the date and time of the lecture. It had all been arranged by Geoffrey Harrod, as usual, Virginia's reputation attracting a great many academics as well as some of the more esoteric press. Virginia and Geoffrey had arrived the night before, dined with the British Council and exchanged gossip, Virginia composed in grey silk, Geoffrey perspiring in a lounge suit.

The freak weather had caught everyone out, and the ballroom was already smouldering before half the guests were seated, hundreds of fans hurriedly pressed into service down both sides of the room, the floral decorations on the tables limp in the heat. Having politely informed the management that she was not going to give a talk in any temperature over ninety, Virginia retired gracefully to her room until things were sorted out.

In fact, the temperature was merely an excuse for her to be alone. Shutting the door behind her, she leaned against it and exhaled, her temper rising like the heat. To think that her daughter was running around with some tupp'ny ha'p'ny actor! she fumed. A nobody. Hadn't she any sense? Or any pride? Virginia opened the mini-bar and reached for the gin bottle, then changed her mind and poured herself a Perrier water instead.

An actor! What was Isabel thinking of? I suppose she never believed her mother would get to hear of it, Virginia thought, draining her glass. But she had of course, from some kind expat in Singapore relating the information from London like an over-zealous gossip columnist. The woman had been tipsy and silly, though if she expected to see Virginia nonplussed she was disappointed. She merely smiled coolly and said,

'Yes, he's a fine actor, and he has such promise.'

Fine actor! Such promise! Who the hell was Tom Hoffman? Virginia fumed, refilling her glass, the bubbles in the Perrier water fizzing against her tongue. Why couldn't Isabel have had an affair with Gyman de Souza? if she had to have an affair at all?

Virginia breathed in, composing herself. There was no point upsetting herself before the talk. Her daughter was obviously a fool — she had already proved that with her marriage to Teddy Gray, and she was now compounding the felony by mixing with the theatre crowd. Virginia's eyes filled for an instant in hot fury. Damn the girl, she was ruining her life — she would have to have a word with her, mother to daughter . . . the thought tingled like an electric shock as Virginia imagined the scene. How could she talk to her daughter about her morals? How could she? Suddenly David Hall's face loomed up before her and she swallowed.

What I did was a mistake, she said to herself, just a mistake . . . But she couldn't shake his image in her mind. Nor could she forget the look on his face when he had found out about Isabel. Virginia's hand clenched the cover on the bed. He had been so much more affected than she could have imagined . . . She had been a fool losing her temper so uncontrollably and lashing out, but he had driven her to it:

'Stop it, Virginia, before you say something you'll be sorry for,' he had said calmly, as their argument escalated.

'Say something I'm sorry for!' she repeated

hysterically. 'Well, I've done something *you'll* be sorry for, David Hall!' Virginia shouted. 'If you don't want me, someone does.' Her voice swung towards him dizzily.

'Shut up!' David replied angrily, turning away from her and walking to the door.

So, long past gentleness, Virginia stopped him by force, throwing the words after him like a noose.

'I had an affair, David.'

But it wasn't enough, and he still didn't stop.

He was almost out of the door when she added: 'I had an affair and I had a child. Isabel is his child, not yours.'

Then David stopped and turned, and his face was altered so unutterably that it haunted her days and nights from that moment on. Something had gone from him, something which she would never see in him again . . . joy, and peace.

Virginia closed her eyes, the feeling of incredulity washing over her. Why had she told him? To hurt him? To force him to feel something for her? Things had been so distant between them for so long, no affection; no lovemaking. All David's love centred on his daughter instead of his wife . . . Virginia winced. She had wanted to make him jealous, to make him realise that even if he didn't want her, other men did. I told you to make you jealous, but you didn't care! You never even asked me who the man was. Virginia began to shake, long years after the event, the memory as agonising as that night when David found out . . .

It was a mistake, David, that was all, just a mistake, she repeated blindly, the old taste of guilt sour in her mouth. I was a good wife, and a good hostess to your friends and your house, you respected me, David, she thought plaintively. You respected me . . . until you knew. In one instant, our marriage was over.

For six months you punished me, David Hall, she thought bitterly. You lived with me and every time you looked at me, you hated me. Even the house seemed to cut me out. For six long months, I waited for the argument which never came. No reproaches, no anger, nothing. Silence . . . Virginia's jealousy uncurled dangerously. Your punishment was that you didn't care about my adultery — that was not important to you. No, David, what really mattered was the knowledge that Isabel was not *your* child.

Six months, Virginia said to herself again, why did you wait for six months? Then when I thought you had forgiven me, you killed yourself. Her hand clutched the bedcover fiercely, her nails digging into the pale silk. Why did you wait, David? To punish me? Or because the truth was suddenly too painful? Why?

It was such a perfect punishment, David, never letting me know if you had confided in Isabel. It drove a wedge between us which was impossible to overcome. Did she know the truth? I wondered so often. Had you told her? When she looked at me strangely, I wondered. And when you died and I thought it was all over, the letters started to come . . . Oh yes, David, every one of my daughter's birthdays opened the old sore and made me wonder. Would it be this year, I'd ask myself. And when it wasn't, I would feel relief, until I realised there was always another year — and another letter.

Virginia's eyes snapped open. No punishment was ever so perfect or so savage — even extending beyond the grave. But to what end, David, she asked. To what end?

But there was no reply and the unanswered question simply hummed like the fan spinning incessantly over her head.

24

Breathing heavily, Prossie paused outside Isabel's studio flat, then rang the bell. From inside came the sound of Sim's violent barking, and then silence. Frowning, Prossie rang the bell again and waited, knowing that Isabel was in the flat and wondering why she didn't answer. The sun beat down from the skylight overhead, as a woman entering her flat on the floor below let Prossie in. As Prossie reached the top floor Isabel was peeping round the door. 'Oh, hi, Prossie. How's things?'

'Good, I just thought I'd pop round and have a chat,' she said, although both of them knew this was no idle visit. 'Can I come in?'

Isabel smiled awkwardly. 'I'm . . . just in the middle of something.'

'I won't be long,' Prossie replied, leaning against the door frame. 'Those stairs damn near killed me.'

Chewing her lip thoughtfully, Isabel stood back to let Prossie enter. Sim growled, then, recognising the visitor, wagged his tail and walked towards her. Prossie stroked his head. The studio was full of portraits, some on easels, some propped up against the wall, the largest facing Prossie.

'That's good. Anyone I know?'

The sound of running water came from the bathroom beyond. Both women glanced towards the door.

'The original's in there,' Isabel said, trying to

make light of her embarrassment. 'Tom Hoffman.'

Prossie smiled half-heartedly and turned as the bathroom door opened and a man wearing only a pair of trousers and shoes walked out. He glanced curiously towards Isabel.

'This is Prossie Leonard,' she said, introducing them, 'my oldest friend.'

'And prettiest, I would imagine,' Tom replied easily, drying his wet hair with a towel. 'I recognise you from some of Isabel's drawings. You know, I don't suppose anyone's mentioned it before, but you look a lot like Jane Morris. She was Dante Gabriele Rossetti's model.'

'I know,' Prossie said patiently, 'I was nicknamed after his painting of Proserpine.'

Tom's eyes flickered, the electric atmosphere between the two women finally getting through to him.

'Well, I'll leave you girls to talk. I have a show tonight.' He pulled on a jumper, picked up his jacket and walked to the door. 'I'm playing Laertes . . . if you would like tickets any time, just give me a buzz and I'll fix it up for you.' He glanced over to Isabel and blew her a kiss. 'I'll phone, darling.'

Prossie waited until the door closed and then sat down, struggling to get comfortable on the old settee. Still in her dressing gown, Isabel made them both some coffee and came back into the studio, sitting beside Prossie and passing her the cup.

'Thanks.'

'No trouble.'

Prossie sipped her drink.

'That's good.'

'Instant.'

She sipped again. 'Still good. Stanton says I make all coffee taste like burnt Coke.' She smiled, changing the subject. 'He's not your type.'

'Stanton?' Isabel replied innocently. 'Oh, I know. I never fancied him.'

'You know who I mean,' Prossie persisted. 'Tom Hoffman . . . he's a real smoothie.'

'I like him.'

'He's not your type — '

'You said that already,' Isabel said sharply. 'But I really don't see what it's got to do with you.'

'I care about you.'

'People always say that when they're overstepping the mark,' Isabel responded, then hung her head. 'Listen, I didn't mean that, but I don't want you to interfere, Prossie. I know you've done a lot for me — you and Stanton — but keep out of my private life. Please.'

'I'm not prying, love, I have no right,' Prossie said, leaning forward awkwardly and putting her cup on the table in front of them. 'But this guy's on the make, you could do better for yourself, Isabel — '

'I don't want to marry him. I just want a bit of fun, for God's sake!'

'But why him?'

'He was there,' Isabel said simply, glancing away and pulling her dressing gown tight around her body.

Prossie studied her carefully, surprised by the admission. There was a new hardness about

Isabel, a brittleness which had not been there before, and it made her anxious. Carefully, she pursued the topic.

'Convenience isn't the best basis for a relationship,' she said softly. 'I just don't want you to be hurt. Look how cut up you were after Teddy ... and then Sybella.' She watched Isabel's face, trying to read her expression. 'Sex isn't the be all and end all.'

'Really? So what is?' Isabel responded coldly. 'Don't tell me that your relationship with Stanton is a meeting of minds.'

'I never said it was!' Prossie retorted angrily.

'No, you never did, and I don't suppose it ever occurred to you that it was strange for a nineteen-year-old girl to be shacked up with a man old enough to be her father,' Isabel said, getting to her feet and looking down at Prossie angrily. 'You come here and try to lecture me about morals, and you're not married, and you've got three kids. Hell fire! You don't even see your brother any more. You're a fine one to talk about relationships.'

'Listen, Isabel,' Prossie said sternly, her eyes sharp with anger. 'I love Stanton and he loves me — that's fact. We enjoy each other in bed — that's fact, and we have our kids — that's fact. And frankly, I don't give a damn what people think. But you — you're the smart one, the one with the big career, the one who could take on the world, so why are you blowing it on a crap actor who's only out for what he can get? Sleeping around isn't your style,' she said more softly. 'And besides, you could get pregnant and really screw everything up again.'

Isabel's eyes flickered. Prossie saw it and stopped talking, then extended her hand towards her friend, the palm turned upwards. For an instant, Isabel merely glanced at it, then clasped it tightly in her own and sat down, her eyes fixed on the floor.

'I won't get pregnant again, Prossie. You see, I can't.' She stopped, took in a breath. The light made her skin achingly white. 'The doctors ran some tests, it's a result of the attack . . . ' Long white words, dragging their feet. 'The injury to my head caused a fracture at the base of my skull . . . ' She touched the back of her head and winced, almost as though it still hurt, ' . . . and some kind of malfunction of the pituitary gland . . . ' She paused again. 'Medical words, and jargon. Long words to complicate things — I'm sterile,' she said simply. 'Sterile.'

Prossie closed her eyes. 'No.'

'Oh, yes.'

'Something can be done.'

'No, nothing.'

'Something *must* be done.'

'Prossie, for God's sake, nothing *can* be done!' Isabel snapped. She had had the same conversation with her doctor when she had played the role Prossie was playing now. She had listened, argued, and then finally accepted. 'I've had tests, and it's confirmed. I've come to terms with it. Well, I'm coming to terms with it . . . I have Sybella, after all, some women never have any children.' She paused, how easily she lied now, pretending that it hardly mattered. No more children, after having given birth to Sybella there would be no more to follow, she was to be the first and the last.

'Isabel,' Prossie said, touching her friend's shoulder, 'I'm so sorry.' Useless rage welled up in her as she looked at Isabel. Why her? After so much heartbreak and pain, why her again? Isabel's hair hung down against her cheek, shadowing her skin. She looked young still, almost as she had done at school, the bloom was there, but with it some little trace of helplessness. Not defeat, just a reluctant acceptance of something beyond understanding.

'So that's why you got involved with Tom Hoffman?' Prossie asked finally.

Isabel turned her head slowly and looked at her. 'I'd been so careful for so long, not wanting to get involved. I'd suspected something, but I'd wanted to let sleeping dogs lie — I suppose I had to find out eventually. But when I did, it changed me . . . it released something.' She shrugged and smiled slightly. 'So I decided to experiment.' Her hair fell back from her face, her earlobes soft and pink in the afternoon light. 'I threw caution to the winds — and I'm enjoying myself.'

'But . . . ' Prossie hesitated, wondering how much she should say, ' . . . what if it doesn't last?'

'How can it?' Isabel replied, raising her eyebrows. 'The company goes on tour in a month, and Tom will go with it. The affair will end then.'

Prossie shook her head. 'Don't try and con me, Isabel, I know you. You're not hard, you'll be hurt. You're not the kind of woman who's into casual sex.'

'So what do you suggest?' Isabel countered, pulling her hand away from Prossie's. 'That I ask him to marry me? Oh, come on! You know as well as I do that it isn't that kind of relationship. I can't get pregnant, so that's the end of one worry. I was afraid of men, and I avoided them. Well now I've gone out and slept with the first man I was attracted to, so what? What the hell is so bad about that? I'm not sleeping around, Prossie, and even if I was, what the hell business is it of yours?'

'You have talent — '

' — and feelings too!' Isabel replied angrily. 'I hate all this crap about 'You have talent, so you're special' — why? It's the luck of the draw, it doesn't make you immune from frustration. Painting doesn't kill libido. Hell fire, Stanton's living proof of that. For years I didn't want to get involved with anyone, and now I have, you're all up in arms,' she snapped suddenly. 'I'm having an affair, I'm not on the game, Prossie.'

'Listen — '

'No, you listen! I lived with my mother and her holier-than-thou attitudes for years and it was all a con — look what she turned out to be.'

Prossie had no answer. She knew that David Hall wasn't Isabel's father, just as she knew that Virginia refused to tell her daughter who her real father was. God, how complicated life was, she thought suddenly.

'Isabel — '

She put up her hands to silence Prossie. 'Shut

up,' she said, then smiled. 'Please, don't tell me what to do, or warn me, or try and say anything to influence me. I don't want to hear it. This is my life, and if I make a bloody mess out of it, then it's *my* mess.' Her eyes twinkled. 'Let me enjoy myself for once. If I don't care how long it lasts, why should you?' She glanced away, concluding the conversation, and pointed to Prossie's shopping bag. 'White wine? I thought Stanton only drank red.'

Prossie shrugged and relaxed. 'He says red wine makes him fart.' She began to laugh affectionately. 'Stupid sod.'

★   ★   ★

Sybella slept in the room next to Eleanor, Isabel's old playroom, and now that she went to school the floor was littered with little piles of drawings and books. When Eleanor chastised her, she would move them, but later they would be taken out, drawings coloured in, books read with loud confidence, and then dismissed when boredom set in. Blair came and sat with her often, reading with her, although he was not allowed to smoke in the playroom, his crumpled cigarette packet crushed into the back pocket of his jeans.

He told her about the sirens singing in his head, and because Sybella had a good imagination she listened to him, then put her fingers in her ears and insisted that she could hear them too.

'You can?' he asked, delightedly.

'Yes, yes, I can!'

His smile was luminous. 'Sometimes your mother can too,' he said, wanting to include Isabel in their conversation.

A little flash of jealousy winked in Sybella's eyes. 'I bet she just says she can hear them.'

Blair frowned, then shook his head. 'No, she really can.'

Sybella glanced away, her tone nonchalant. 'She never told me she could.'

Blair frowned as he lost confidence, a little nugget of doubt swelling moment by moment. 'Isabel *can* hear them . . . ' he repeated finally. 'I'm sure she can.'

★ ★ ★

Tom Hoffman left for Leeds the following month. He told Isabel he would write and telephone her, and she nodded as though she believed him. Limpid with lovemaking he promised to keep in touch, and made vague plans for returning to London the following year when he was due to be cast in *Coriolanus*. Being the actor he was, he believed his lines, and, wanting to be kind, he thought he was doing the best for Isabel, cradling her in his arms as the light began to dawn on their last morning.

She ran her fingers over the muscles of his stomach, listening to his words without taking in their meaning. As the light intensified she studied his body, and as the minutes passed her scrutiny became more intense, but without passion. Committing him to memory, she

382

wondered how surprised he would be if he knew her thoughts. Their lovemaking had been exotic, experimental and intense, but at that moment in her life, in that period of trauma, almost any man would have served the same purpose.

She sighed and leaned her head on his chest. His legs moved under the covers for the last time, one of his arms around her shoulder. Tenderly, Isabel kissed his stomach, the faint scent of warm skin, peculiar to him, was stored in her memory, as was the dark line of hair which ran down to his groin, and the blue of the veins that ran along the inside of his thighs. I shall not miss you, she thought with relief, but I am grateful to you.

He continued to talk, to make plans which would never come to pass, and to suggest meetings which would never occur. In the never-never-land of that soft dawn, Isabel lay in his arms, her thoughts wandering, her gaze moving towards the portrait on the easel. She dozed intermittently in dreams, her mother coming to her, her daughter running down the back lawn of The Ridings, and Blair standing on the station platform the first time she had ever seen him. In Tom Hoffman's arms she absorbed the affection he offered; she tucked it away in her mind and body, cell after cell taking a portion of loving so that by morning her body was nourished, and when he finally got up to leave she found it easy to smile and let go.

★ ★ ★

'Can't say I will, and can't say I won't,' Gyman de Souza said enigmatically to Sterling Thompson. 'She might agree to do it, and then again I might not agree to ask her.'

Sterling winced, his toupé obvious under the gallery light. He hated Gyman, as he hated all homosexuals, even though half of his colleagues and buyers were that way inclined. Woofters, he called them disparagingly, bloody woofters.

'Gyman, couldn't you just ask Isabel if she would like to exhibit for me?'

Gyman shrugged. 'Why should she? You weren't interested in her before — '

'That was before she was successful,' Sterling responded naively. 'Now she's really beginning to make her mark. That piece in *The Times* made quite a difference, and being Virginia Hall's daughter helps.'

'Isabel is also David Hall's daughter.'

Sterling frowned. 'Yes, yes, I know that. But David's dead — '

'His reputation isn't,' Gyman responded deftly, glancing round the gallery and then looking at Sterling again. 'How's trade? I heard you were struggling a bit.'

Sterling's first impulse was to slap the little poof, but then he remembered how rich Sunny de Souza was and resisted, smiling instead.

'You know how the art world is, Gyman, up and down, up and down.'

'Only sometimes more down than up, hey?'

Convenient deafness came over Sterling and he ignored the remark, pressing on gamely. 'Listen, I want to exhibit Isabel Hall's work. With her family name and her talent, I could really help her career — '

'How noble of you, Sterling,' Gyman said suavely, 'and there was I, thinking you wanted her to help yours.'

'Will you ask her?'

'She'll take no notice of me, so you're wasting your time, Sterling. Isabel Hall is her own woman,' Gyman replied. 'So if you want something from her, ask her yourself.'

'She might refuse.'

'She might.'

'You could — '

'No!'

Sterling conceded defeat.

Gyman relayed the whole conversation to Isabel later that week; she listened and laughed, and shrugged it off, although certain phrases stuck in her head. *With her family name.* The gilded name of Hall. The entrée to the galleries which others did not have. Isabel smiled at Gyman, but her thoughts wandered. Even the protection of her name hadn't saved her from some humiliations: the drunken dealer at Savory's who made a pass at her; the Iranian collector who told her that her work had 'no class', and the cigar-smoking gallery owner in Cork Street who had looked at her paintings and dismissed them with the line, 'I'll remember your pretty face a lot longer than your work.'

Such rejections smarted, but they only made Isabel more determined. Every time her confidence wavered she swore she would make each one of her detractors eat their words. With interest. When I am a success, she said to herself, when I am a success, they will come to me.

Her second wish seemed to be granted. The heart of the hunter was in her. Nothing seemed to stop her, no setbacks to deter her for long. Rejection, humiliation, weariness — Isabel felt all of them, but her eyes remained fixed on her aim and she never veered from it. Only achievement would make sense of her life; only success would absolve the failed marriage, the problems with her child, and the attack.

She smiled at Gyman, her right hand opening and closing on her lap automatically. It was an action that had become second nature to her over the years, together with her own brand of will power. Push yourself, Isabel, push yourself. Get fit, get strong, get out there and fight.

And David had fought with her. His most recent letter had come to lift her spirits and her heart. It arrived bearing the familiar greeting.

Darling Knuckles,

Happy Birthday. Good wishes for the year, and for every month, week, and minute of it. How is your life, sweetheart? Hard going? Well, that's the only way to learn, isn't it? Resilience is what you need to succeed, remember that.

There is something I should explain, Isabel, because I know that you must be wanting an answer to a question I left unanswered . . .

Isabel paused — was the answer in the next words? The answer to the question she repeatedly asked Virginia. Would she now finally find out who her father was?

I don't know who your father is.

Isabel stopped reading suddenly, a vague suspicion plucking at her senses. He didn't know! How could he not know? she thought furiously . . . yet he had never lied to her before, so why would he lie now? Her eyes moved back to the letter.

How strange, when I just wrote that I felt a physical pain, as though even the words could cause injury. I hate to admit that someone else is your father when I still feel as though you are *my* child, even though I know otherwise — Love has no logic.

But love lasts. Remember that. Love is the only thing on earth that can not be burned, buried, drowned or murdered. It endures. As my love lives on — for you, and in you.

Happy birthday, darling, this will be a year which will try you, but I will be with you every step of the way.

David

' . . . do you still miss him?'

Her thoughts came back to the present suddenly. 'I'm sorry, Gyman, what did you say?'

'I asked if you still miss your father?'

How can you miss someone you have never met, she wondered. How you can miss someone who you have never known? Do I miss my father? No, but I miss the man I took as my father; the man who behaved as my father. I miss him every day, and oddly the ache never fades. I miss him now, she wanted to say, more than I ever did. I want to talk to him now, more than I have ever done. He is a part of me that is constant; the best part; the part that struggles and wants to please him still. To make him proud of me.

'Yes,' she said gently, 'I miss David Hall.'

25

The Ridings
Eleven years later

Virginia paused at the front door and then turned. Her glance was quick, brief, almost automatic. Even past seventy, she had the quick walk and sharp control of a woman half her age, and an acute eye for detail which had never faded.

'Why is that dog bed still here?' she asked.

Eleanor turned and glanced at Ivor's old bed in the far corner of the hall, in the shadows. She had aged obviously and was now stout, her feet slightly swollen in flat shoes, her cheeks soft with spare flesh. Her jawline was slack, her neck creased, in direct contrast to the sharp line of Virginia's profile. But Eleanor's hair was still waved from her weekly trips to the hairdresser's in Skipton, and her voice was, if anything, a little firmer.

'I can't bring myself to move it, Virginia. It reminds me of the old boy,' she explained, the implication being obvious. The bed stays.

'Silliness,' Virginia replied, turning back to the door. 'I don't suppose Sybella's coming to see me off?'

'She said she'd try to get back.'

Virginia nodded, then walked out to the waiting taxi.

A hundred, or was it a thousand trips, Eleanor thought, and she never changes. No softness, no surrender, and no answer to her daughter's constant question. After a while, Eleanor had ceased to expect one, although Isabel never gave up. Who is my father? she would ask. And never find out ... The taxi door slammed shut, Virginia's hand raised regally at the window, before it drove off. She has gone, Eleanor thought, closing the door behind her, the feeling of pity more than she would have wished. More than Virginia deserved.

But maybe, in the end, she had been punished enough, Eleanor thought, walking into the hall. Her daughter had remained estranged from her, and Sybella, the child on whom Virginia had placed all her hopes, was changed beyond recognition. A shadow fell across the window and Eleanor glanced up, saw Blair, and waved. He returned the gesture and continued to rake the flower bed. Only he remains the same, she thought, seemingly no older, and no wiser.

Absent-mindedly, Eleanor plumped the cushions on the sofa and glanced round. Her eyes took in the familiar pieces of furniture, the paintings, the piano, the photographs, all the often-dusted, often-handled pieces of the Hall family, all in their place. Her eyes fell on the photograph of David, and she studied it curiously, wondering how he would have aged. As it was, he was locked for ever at middle age, his hair only beginning to thin and grey, his face fully fleshed, his eyes, behind the tortoise-shell glasses, bright with intelligence.

Eleanor sighed, suddenly tired, and then sat down. Her legs ached, and even though she had two cleaning women to help her with the house, the work was exhausting. A stray cobweb caught her eye and she glanced away, irritated, her hands stretched out on the cushions beside her. Footsteps in the hall announced Sybella's presence and for an instant Eleanor hesitated, then slowly she turned to look at her charge.

Sybella stood in the doorway, her hands in the pockets of her jeans. Five foot six, with Isabel's eyes and Virginia's arrogance, she seemed to demand attention by her very presence. Her face was narrow, her jaw firm, her long mid-brown hair tied back in a ponytail; she looked unusual and knew the power of her own fascination. That was the danger in her, and at the age of fifteen she had all the sexual awareness of a mature woman.

'Hi, sweetheart,' Eleanor said, smiling.

Sybella walked over to her and plonked herself down on the sofa beside her. 'God-awful day at school,' she said simply.

Eleanor stroked Sybella's fringe back from her forehead. 'What happened?'

'More prep. I can't do French, I told them.' Her tone was sulky. 'Miss Philips hates me.'

'She's just trying to get the best out of you, sweetie,' Eleanor said, knowing full well that Miss Philips was only another in a long line of teachers who had despaired of Sybella.

She was lazy, that was the problem. Smart, yes, worldly, too much, but lazy. Not for the first time Eleanor wondered if she had failed her, but it had been so difficult bringing Sybella up. The rules had changed since she had raised Isabel. Her niece had been a good child, which was remarkable given her parents' unhappy marriage and her father's suicide; but she had escaped her childhood relatively unscathed, whereas Sybella seemed to have inherited the worst faults from each of the Halls. From Virginia she inherited pride; from Eleanor, stubbornness; and from Isabel, fierce ambition — but without her mother's discipline. It was difficult to see what, if anything, she had inherited from Teddy Gray — he was never in contact with his daughter, and to all intents and purposes, had no part in her life.

Indulged from babyhood, Sybella had responded to affection, but instead of being more selective as she grew older, she had gravitated to anyone who offered love — of any kind. Eleanor and Isabel had worried about it when she was only ten years old, but when she matured so rapidly they became seriously concerned. Reason she was oblivious to; if anyone challenged her on how she behaved, she responded with a series of emotional recriminations. Her mother didn't love her enough to live with her; her father didn't love her at all, and never even wanted to see her . . . On and on the litany went, every woe used as a stick with which to beat her nearest and dearest.

And no one was beaten more than Isabel. At thirty-six she was a respected portrait painter, not that famous to the public at large but sufficiently talented for everyone to agree that it was only a matter of time before she reached the top of her profession. She had achieved so much through hard work and determination, putting her career not before her child but on an even footing. The trouble was that Sybella never forgave her mother for not putting her first, and she resented Isabel bitterly.

The bitterness was further exacerbated by the fact that Sybella was not as obviously talented as her mother, and the jealousy Isabel had felt for Virginia was now repeated in the next generation.

'She's only young,' Eleanor had said a few years earlier to Isabel. 'Give her time.'

'How much time? She should be getting better marks at school. That report was rubbish,' Isabel said and paused, pushing the paper away from her. 'Maybe I should send her away to school.'

Eleanor glanced at her niece in surprise. 'You hated boarding school!'

'I know I did, but it helped me. The discipline might help Sybella too.' She glanced at Eleanor and frowned. 'I'm worried about her. If we don't do something, she'll get out of hand.'

She did, only months later. In fact, she arranged for a girl at her school to go out on a blind date, saying that she knew a man who was keen on her. The schoolgirl was flattered and impressed, and when she saw the very handsome Blair she couldn't believe her luck — until she realised a few minutes later that he was intellectually impaired. Shaken, the girl had been mortally embarrassed and had taken out her humiliation on Blair, who had run home with her taunts still ringing in his ears. Only after considerable coaxing from Eleanor, did he tell her what had happened.

Sybella lied, of course, and swore that there had been a misunderstanding, but Eleanor didn't believe her, and neither did Blair. Her cruelty was shocking, and it took all of Sybella's charm to coax herself back into Blair's affection. She managed it because he had a short memory, but Isabel had a very long one. Hating cruelty of any kind, she punished Sybella by cancelling her trip away the following weekend, and Sybella punished her by 'forgetting' to pass on an important message from Baye Fortunas.

Other people saw the beginnings of trouble in Sybella, especially Stanton. On a visit to The Ridings with Prossie and the children, he found himself monopolised by the thirteen-year-old girl, and for once veered away from flirtation.

'That one is a dangerous female,' he said darkly to Prossie.

She glanced over to him, surprised. At the age of sixty-nine he was in good shape, the fitness bug having caught up with him. After a heart scare, Stanton exercised regularly, taking the doctor at his word that sex was good therapy, and indulging as often as he could. Although he had lost more hair and his face was ageing, his body was holding up well — as was his interest in the female sex.

'Sybella is thirteen years old,' Prossie said, her tone exasperated, although she also saw something in the girl which was far removed from her memories of Isabel at the same age. 'How can a girl her age be dangerous?'

394

'I tell you, she'll get in trouble unless she's kept on a very tight rein,' he replied, then stared hard at the wash hand basin in front of him. 'Jesus Christ, this crack was here the first time I ever visited this house — and that's over forty years ago.' His finger traced the fine black line from the soap dish to the plug.

'Oh God, Stanton, how *can* you remember something like that?' Prossie asked impatiently.

He raised his eyebrows. 'Because I was the one who cracked the basin by dropping a bottle of vodka on it when I was climbing back in after a night out.'

Prossie grinned. 'With David?'

'Oh yes, David was quite a boy in his youth.' He regarded the basin lovingly. 'We got pissed with two bar girls who worked down at the Red Lion in South Stainley — mine was called Millie, and she had wiry red hair and a mole under her chin with a white hair growing out of it . . . I used to wonder what it would be like to pull that hair out with my teeth.'

Prossie groaned and padded back into the bedroom, calling to him over her shoulder, 'D'you think I should have a word with Isabel about Sybella?'

Stanton shook his head. 'No . . . Anything we could tell her she already knows, believe me.'

Baye Fortunas had a similarly low opinion of Sybella, although Gyman de Souza, who had remained a close friend of Isabel's, was not convinced. He had known Sybella since she was a baby and recognised in her some of the problems he had with his own family. A child who is less clever than its parents is always either an object of pity, or a candidate for rebellion. Being the first, he hoped to find Sybella in that position too.

'She's old for her years,' Baye Fortunas said, putting on his glasses and peering at one of the Ming Chinese vases which Sunny collected. 'And she's not a bit like her mother — or her grandmother.'

'Good thing, I never could stand Virginia Hall. Cold as ice.'

'But clever,' Baye replied, straightening up and bowing slightly as Sunny came in.

She moved over to him, her collagened face held at a flattering angle, her hair supernaturally blond. 'Darling, Baye, darling.' She kissed the air by his left cheek, repeated the performance on the right side, stood back, looked at him and sniffed delicately. 'Hay fever,' she said, by way of explanation.

'I've got the name of a reflexologist for you, Sunny,' Baye said sympathetically. 'He might be able to help.'

'Don't they massage the feet, or something?' she said, smiling distantly at her son as though surprised to see him there. 'I have such sensitive feet, do you think it would be traumatic?' She glided to the Noke settee and arranged herself. 'Should I wear Jimmy Choo or Manolo Blahnik?'

'Pardon?'

'Mother wants to know what kind of shoes to wear,' Gyman explained carefully, catching the astonished look in Baye's eyes.

'You take your shoes off when you're having a treatment, Sunny,' he explained patiently. 'Each part of the foot corresponds to a part of the body, so if the therapist manipulates a certain area — '

' — it could be very erotic,' she said, interrupting him. 'There's something faintly naughty about the suggestion.'

Defeated, Baye changed the subject. 'I'm calling in to see Isabel tomorrow, do you want me to give her a message?'

'Just ask her if she's changed her mind about selling that pastel, will you? The one of the young girl.'

'Sybella.'

'Yes,' Sunny said absently, 'Sybella.' Her mind wandered back to the exquisite pastel she had seen in Isabel's studio.

'I'd like to see the girl in the flesh though, just to know what kind of child Isabel Hall produced.' Her eyes flicked over to her son. 'Invite them both over for dinner will you, darling? Dear Isabel and little Sybella.'

When little Sybella heard about the invitation that weekend she was less than enthusiastic. Folding her arms, she leaned back against the kitchen table and regarded her mother sullenly. Isabel ignored her and began to prepare dinner, her usual routine on Friday evenings after travelling up to The Ridings from London.

As she chopped the vegetables she hummed to herself, apparently unconcerned by her daughter's bad mood. Over the years Isabel had learned not to react to Sybella's sulkiness; if she ignored it, her daughter couldn't keep it up for long.

This time was no exception; after a few minutes of silence, Sybella moved over to the sink, leaned against it, and looked hard at her mother.

'Why do we have to go?'

'How many times do I ask you to do anything for me, Sybella?' Isabel countered, nudging her daughter aside and putting a pan down on the cooker.

'That's not the point — '

'Actually it's *exactly* the point,' Isabel retorted calmly, turning to Sybella. 'I never ask anything of you, perhaps I should, but now I want you to come to London with me so that we can go to the de Souzas' for dinner. Sunny is an important patron — '

'I know that,' Sybella replied, interrupting her mother and running her finger along the edge of the sink, 'but I don't like Gyman, and his mother's awful.'

Isabel sighed inwardly, but her face was expressionless. Where her daughter was concerned, there was always an argument; nothing was ever done willingly. Whatever Isabel wanted, Sybella resented. The overhead light shone down on her daughter and shadowed her eyes — she looked older suddenly, and long past childhood. I wonder what David Hall would have made of you, Isabel thought, knowing for certain that he would have been alienated by Sybella's selfishness. And yet he would have loved her charm and made excuses for her — using the eternal argument of a difficult childhood and Teddy Gray's rejection of her.

Isabel frowned. Would talks in the den have helped her child? Would David Hall's gentleness and attention have made some other person out of this girl?

As though suddenly aware of her mother's scrutiny, Sybella glanced at her fiercely. 'I don't want to go to the de Souzas'.'

'I don't want to hear any more about what you want, Sybella,' Isabel replied determinedly. 'You have more than enough of your own way up here, now you can do something for me. You're not a child any longer — it's time you made an effort.'

'I don't want to make an effort with your friends!' Sybella replied hotly. 'What good are they to me? I don't want to be a bloody artist — '

Isabel caught hold of her daughter's arm. 'Don't swear at me! I've had enough of your bad moods. You're coming to the de Souzas' with me, and that's final.'

Later that night Isabel went up to her daughter's room. She had written her a letter, in much the same way David Hall had written, and continued to write, to her. The letter set her feelings out on paper, whilst valiantly trying to open up some lines of communication with her child. When she had finished it, Isabel went upstairs and knocked on Sybella's door.

There was no reply. It was obvious when she opened the door that the room was empty so Isabel walked in. The walls were hung with pictures of Madonna and heavy metal rock bands, a battered mobile hung over the bed. It was the same one which had hung over Isabel's bed at Holland Park, and which had been a gift for Sybella when she was seven. Touching it gently with her fingers, Isabel pushed the mobile round in the still air and watched it, her mind wandering.

She used to watch it in very much the same way when she was living with Stanton and Prossie, studying and helping to look after their little girls. Long before Teddy Gray and Sybella. Isabel sighed at the memory — she had loved those children, finding them easy to be with, and easy to love. They had given her an image of motherhood which was so seductive that she had destroyed her marriage to bear her own child . . . The mobile continued to move overhead, without Isabel's touch.

Sybella had been such an angry baby, and was still angry, and what was worse, there had been no other children to soften that rage. Isabel's eyes followed the mobile. How long had it been now since she first discovered she was sterile? Eleven years. She blinked, surprised by the length of time which had passed. The mirror cheated her — she seemed hardly changed from the twenty-five-year-old who had been told that she could never bear another child — but it had been eleven years, and in those years she had stopped grieving, and even the dull ache of disappointment had become intermittent — besides, she had learned not to dwell on what she couldn't have, and instead consoled herself with her achievements.

The mobile swung overhead . . . and for an instant Isabel wondered what had happened to Tom Hoffman. She had never heard from him again after he left London with the Elizabethan Theatre Company; indeed, it seemed that few people had, his career sinking into quick obscurity. And what about Ben Pease? and Phillip Osborne? Isabel wondered, thinking back to the affairs she had enjoyed over the years. Affairs of the heart, and of the body. Affairs to assuage frustration and temporarily fill the little pockets of loneliness which sometimes became intolerable.

But not affairs of the soul. None of them were that. Isabel found that no man was totally compatible with her. They had past wives or present children; she had the demands of her career and Sybella . . . On the rare occasions Isabel had introduced someone to her daughter, she had been flirtatious. What could she say to her about this? And how much of it was in her imagination? The problem was an old one for Isabel. What kind of advice could she offer her child? She was never sure and there wasn't a husband to help her. No, Teddy Gray had never shown any interest in his child.

She knew she could ask Prossie for help. As the mother of three girls, her old friend would probably have some sound advice. But Isabel was too private to confide her worst fears, and besides, by actually giving voice to them, she believed they might come true.

Prossie, she might begin, I'm worried about Sybella, I think she's going to get into trouble.

I'm sure she's promiscuous.

Isabel shook her head. Wasn't it tempting the fates even to say such things? And besides, what proof did she have?

Sitting down on the side of the bed, Isabel closed her eyes. I've failed you again, Sybella, she thought. I gave you an erratic upbringing and now I'm suspecting you of God knows what . . . Her thoughts wandered recklessly. I wanted a happy child to love, she thought, one who would make sense of my decision, one who would compensate for the loss of my husband — and instead I have Sybella.

The letter was still in Isabel's hand. Encouraging words to help her, which hopefully might mean as much to Sybella as David Hall's words had meant to Isabel. And yet, even as she had written them, she had felt foolish, suspecting that the note would be seen as an emotional tool, and that the words, no matter how painfully written, would be dismissed as trite.

If only I could talk to her, Isabel thought helplessly as she remembered her last birthday. A letter had come from David Hall, as one did every year, but this time it had seemed as though he was trying to communicate something specific to her. His words had been almost prophetic.

Darling Knuckles,

Thirty-seven years old today. God, I bet you're something to behold! Your mother was in her prime in her thirties and forties. Is the world kind to you at the moment? Or angry? Perhaps a mixture? I don't think so,

402

darling, I think perhaps you are a little confused.

How had he known?

Did I ever tell you about the time Stanton and I went to a circus in Liverpool? It was a ragged hole-in-the-corner affair, with a barker who had lost an arm in the war. He kept calling out to the punters and trying to get people in, but he was no good, because he cared too much. His desperation was making other people uncomfortable so he was doing the one thing he didn't want to — he was frightening them off.

So what is that supposed to mean? I know what you're thinking — well, sweetheart, it means that sometimes we lose things because we try too hard to keep them . . .

My love, my love, how I miss you. How I wish I could be with you. But I am, sweetheart. Go into the den and look for me. I'm at the window or in the chair — somewhere — and I'm watching over you. Always

For ever,

David Hall

Sometimes we lose things because we try too hard to keep them . . . the phrase came back to Isabel as she sat with the letter in her hand. From mother to daughter. She hesitated, but

403

finally placed it on the table beside Sybella's bed, where it wobbled and then fell on to the floor. Impatiently Isabel knelt down to pick it up and then noticed something taped underneath the table. Hidden.

Her hand moved towards the container, shaking more savagely than it had done for years. Gingerly her fingers touched the packet, then snatched it up as she looked at it, her eyes burning.

Sybella, her fifteen-year-old daughter, was on the pill.

26

'Come here!' she shouted down the stairwell as she heard the front door slam an hour later.

Blithely Sybella looked up, then her expression changed when she saw Isabel's face. She had rarely seen her mother angry and was suddenly afraid of her.

'Come here, Sybella, I want to talk to you,' Isabel called out, watching as her daughter walked up the stairs, her face a mixture of fear and defiance.

Finally she stood facing her mother. 'What is it?'

Isabel struck her once with the back of her hand, and Sybella rocked off her feet to fall against the landing wall.

'How long have you been on the pill?' Isabel asked, waving the packet in front of her daughter.

Sybella's eyes were wide. 'I'm only looking after them for a friend — '

'Don't lie to me!' Isabel hissed. 'You are fifteen years old. Fifteen! How long have you been taking it? And who are you sleeping with?'

'Not long. No one,' Sybella replied, getting to her feet and trying to get out of her mother's way.

Isabel gripped her arm fiercely. 'How long?'

'Four months.'

The truth winded her momentarily. 'Who are you sleeping with?'

Sybella glanced away. 'No one.'

'WHO?'

'You'll be angry if I tell you.'

'God help me, if you don't I'll beat it out of you.'

Sybella averted her eyes from her mother and mumbled, 'A boy in the village.'

'Who? At the school?'

'Yes, at the school.'

Isabel shook her daughter, her patience gone. 'You're lying! Who is he?'

'Blair.'

Isabel dropped her daughter's arm, stepping back and looked at her as though she no longer knew her. No, this is not my child, this *can't* be my child.

'Blair?'

Sybella nodded, her eyes filling. 'He made me — '

'STOP LYING!' Isabel howled. Eleanor came hurrying along the corridor. 'What on earth is happening?'

'Sybella's on the pill,' Isabel said blankly, disbelievingly, hardly caring to trust her voice with the next words. 'She's sleeping . . . with Blair.'

Eleanor's hand went up to her mouth. 'Oh God.'

'It's all your fault!' Sybella blurted out suddenly, turning on her mother. 'You never cared for me.'

'Oh, shut up!' Isabel snapped, pushing her hair back from her face with both hands. 'You've had more than your fair share of love, so don't try

406

and offload your problems on to me.' Her eyes were blank with anger. 'I'm not going to feel guilty for what you've done.'

'But what about Blair?' Eleanor said hoarsely. 'He's only a child.'

Sybella was about to say something and then glanced down at the floor, keeping silent.

'We have to keep this a secret,' Isabel said coldly, staring at her daughter. 'You know what will happen if anyone finds out?' she asked her aunt. 'It's illegal to have sex with a girl under age. If this becomes public knowledge Blair will be jailed.'

'He won't!' Eleanor said, startled. 'He's disabled. He's not responsible for what he did.'

'Maybe, or maybe not. But do you want to risk it?' Isabel asked her aunt.

'No! No . . . we have to make sure no one finds out.'

Isabel turned back to her daughter. 'Do you have any idea what you've done?'

'He made me do it — '

'DON'T SAY THAT!' Isabel shouted. She knew Blair; and she knew her daughter. And she knew which of them to believe. 'You stay away from him from now on — '

'We'll have to send him away,' Eleanor said pitifully, avoiding Sybella's eyes. 'God knows what it will do to him. He won't understand why.'

'Blair's not going anywhere,' Isabel countered, her voice steely. 'Sybella is going instead — to boarding school.'

'You can't send me away!' her daughter blustered.

'I should have done it before, but it's not too late.' For a moment Isabel came close to loathing her own child. To use Blair, kind, baffled, silly Blair, was unforgivable. And cruel. 'You've had it too easy, Sybella, but no longer. It's time you were disciplined. We've all spoiled you too much.'

Isabel turned and began to move away down the stairs, Sybella running after her, crying hysterically.

'Mum, Mum!' she pleaded, using a word she had not uttered for years, her panic making her childlike. 'Oh, please, Mum, don't. I'll be good, I promise . . . I'll do whatever you say . . . '

Her voice wailed plaintively down the stairwell, as her cries grew more and more desperate. With iron determination, Isabel kept her eyes fixed firmly ahead as her daughter called out to her. Her face betrayed nothing, but when she reached the den and closed the door she slumped, her right hand opening and closing like a broken machine.

* * *

Another secret wove itself into the worn bricks of The Ridings. Secret on secret, holding the walls together, fixing the windows in their frames, securing the gravel in the meandering drive. Whispers of things unspoken, of promises, threats, and betrayals. Their size did not matter. Some were huge and heavy with age; some bold;

408

some unexplained; and some hung and clung like bladderwrack on a sea wall.

A hundred secrets kept house there, and The Ridings took them in. The magic of the place transformed its owners into guardians, so that each of the family hugged its own hidden knowledge, either in guilt or out of protection for the others. But whatever the reason, they all kept silent.

Virginia was told why Sybella had been sent away to school, but she was not told about Blair. He remained at The Ridings, hopelessly lost, his whole world leaving in the taxi with Sybella, all his longings going with her. Baffled and angry, he kept away from Eleanor and Isabel and even slept in the studio, knowing he had done something wrong, but not understanding why. His heart ached with confusion, Sybella leaving without saying goodbye, all her promises nothing but lies.

She had whispered to him that they could run away together; she had taught him delights he had never known. He had been shy, but she had coaxed him and told him they were doing nothing wrong. With her lips nestling against his neck she had made him promise that he would keep their meetings a secret or, she said, Isabel would send him away. He had tried to argue with her, to explain to her that Isabel would never do anything cruel — but he had been wrong. Although he had kept the secret, Isabel had found out somehow and punished him by sending Sybella away.

He brooded in the dark, in the studio. He

wandered in the garden and replayed images in his head of his lovemaking with Sybella. He remembered her breasts and her slim legs, and the way she knelt over him, her hair falling into his face. A hot flush of embarrassment always followed such memories, followed by a rush of almost unbearable longing for her. But she was gone; the person who had taken him into the realms of ecstasy was gone. Sent away — by Isabel.

So he brooded, and he watched and waited, and he swore that he would punish Isabel as she had punished him. One day he would make her suffer by taking away something she loved. One day she would feel the agony he was feeling, and she would know why.

* * *

'You must never let Mother know that it was Blair,' Isabel said, watching him through the window. 'It wasn't his fault, and he can't be punished. It was Sybella's doing.' She glanced over her shoulder towards Eleanor. 'I told Mother that she had been sleeping with a village boy, but that we didn't know whom, and could hardly press everyone to find out. It would be bad for the family name, I said.' Isabel's voice was chilled. 'She was outraged about Sybella at first, but as I said, some traits are inherited.'

Eleanor winced as Isabel continued dispassionately.

'I thought it might be a good time for confessions. So I asked her who my father was

410

again.' She smiled, her right hand resting on the windowledge. Blair moved around the garden, but did not look up. 'She refused to tell me, of course. Jesus! What a bloody mess.'

'Oh, love, what can I say?' Eleanor asked, getting to her feet and walking over to her. 'I should have known something was going on.'

Isabel put her arm around her aunt's shoulders. She was getting older, and such dramas were not fair on her. 'You did a marvellous job with my child, Eleanor. If anyone is to blame, it's me,' she said kindly. 'You must never reproach yourself for anything; whoever brought that child up — you, me, or my mother, whoever — they would have had problems with her. She's amoral, you see. Somewhere down the line she inherited a lack of kindness and a lack of morals. Trouble is, we'll probably never know where she got it from. From my mother? Or my father?' Isabel said, pausing and glancing at her aunt. 'I have a hunch it was him, but I'll never know, will I?'

'She could just be going through a bad patch.'

'No,' Isabel said emphatically. 'No, if it was just a childish experiment, Sybella would have slept with a boy her own age. This was planned.'

Eleanor drew away from her niece and stared at her. 'Do you know what you're saying?'

Isabel nodded. 'Yes. I've thought it out, you see. Sybella is jealous by nature and she wanted to take what I had. And Blair cared for me. So she took him — and besides, he was easy to manipulate.'

'It's horrible.'

411

'It's Sybella.'

'Thank God she's at school now,' Eleanor said, trembling suddenly.

'Thank God,' Isabel repeated. 'I wish David was here.'

Eleanor nodded. 'I know.'

Isabel seemed not to hear her as her thoughts ran on. 'It never gets any easier, does it?' she asked. 'So many problems.' Her hand went to her forehead and she frowned suddenly.

Alerted to the danger signals, Eleanor touched her niece's arm. She had seen the old familiar signs recurring, the headaches and the muddled thinking which had been so prevalent after the attack returning in the weeks since Sybella had been sent away.

'Are you all right?'

'Fine . . . ' Isabel said listlessly, although the pain in her head was increasing even as she spoke, ' . . . it's just strain, that's all. Nothing important.'

'Did you go for your check-up?'

'Yes, I went last week,' Isabel said patiently. 'I always do, Eleanor. I have my check-ups and I do my exercises and I keep myself fit.' She paused, suddenly exhausted. 'But my mind wanders sometimes, you know. My concentration goes . . . '

'You've been under a lot of stress over the last few weeks.'

She nodded, silent agreement. 'It's annoying, because I'd been a lot better lately. I thought all the symptoms had finally gone . . . '

Eleanor smiled half-heartedly. 'Don't let it get

412

on top of you,' she said, immediately wincing at the inadequacy of the cliché. God, she didn't know what to say. After the shock of Sybella, no one knew what to say any more. 'You should go on holiday somewhere, just for a break — '

'I've too much work on at the moment. That new patron, Ivy Messenger, has commissioned another portrait.'

'Just a week would do you good,' Eleanor persisted. 'Really, Isabel. Sybella's safe at school, and everything's fine here. You've got the money, go away and enjoy yourself for once.'

The idea was tempting, and Isabel hesitated. 'Where should I go?'

'Abroad?'

Isabel frowned.

'All right, try somewhere nearer home. The Lake District perhaps?' Eleanor suggested hopefully. 'It's out of season and it'll be quiet now. No tourists.'

'I suppose I could go up there,' Isabel murmured to herself. A week's holiday would be a rest, a chance to recharge her energies. The work could wait for once.

She returned to London and then made the arrangements hurriedly, deciding to go away that weekend — committing herself before she had time to change her mind. Then she began to pack, singing quietly in the bedroom as she laid her clothes into a suitcase. Trousers, anoraks, boots, and a selection of thick jumpers, were all piled into the case. At the last minute she put in a cocktail dress — just in case. Satisfied, Isabel picked up the baby photograph of Sybella and laid it in her case next to the one of David Hall. The two of them looked up at her impassively.

Feeling cheerful, she imagined what she would do, and visualised long walks in the peaceful countryside, away from London and The Ridings. The idea was seductive and when Isabel glanced into the mirror to comb her hair she was surprised and pleased by the image which looked back at her. She stared at herself for a long time, unusually vain, her eyes searching her skin for signs of ageing. There were few. The odd faint line, but otherwise a fine complexion, her eyes as brightly alert as they had been when she was a child. She touched her hair, suddenly self-conscious as she wondered how she looked to men, and realised with a shock that she was lonely.

Her thoughts were interrupted by the phone ringing at her side. Quickly she picked it up. Prossie's voice was muted, too muted, like one fighting anger.

'Prossie, hi!' Isabel said, happily. 'I was going to ring you tonight.'

'Can you come round to the studio?' Prossie asked, again using an unusually still voice.

'Why? What's the matter?'

'Sybella's here.'

The front door slammed shut in the house next door and made Isabel jump. 'Prossie, what did you say?'

'I said your daughter is here,' Prossie replied chillingly. 'I want you to come and get her.'

Isabel arrived at the Holland Park studio only minutes later. Climbing the old stairs she peered

414

upwards, but saw no one and so she paused at the head of the stairwell, calling out. Prossie materialised like a dark shadow, flicking on the light in the studio and facing Isabel.

She looked fierce, tall and dark, and unusually hostile.

'Sybella's gone,' she said simply. Her eyes were faintly pink. Like someone who had been crying a while earlier. 'But your mother's here.'

'My *mother*?' Isabel repeated incredulously, following Prossie as she walked out of the studio and into the huge white lounge.

Virginia was standing by the far wall under a nude painting of Prossie, Stanton draped over a window seat, glancing out into the neglected garden. Confused, Isabel looked at her mother and wondered what she was doing there. After all, she had despised Stanton Feller for decades and had never once visited the studio, even with David.

'Why are you here, Mother?'

Virginia looked tired. Drained of that burning energy so typical of her. 'I came . . . to get Sybella,' she said simply.

Isabel's head buzzed, a peculiar sense of unreality swamping her. 'But how did you know she was here?'

Stanton moved in his position by the window. His bare feet brushed the floor like a bird's wings.

'I guessed,' Virginia said helplessly.

'You *guessed*?' Isabel repeated uselessly. An unpleasant thought scuttled at the back of her head. '*How* did you guess Sybella would be here, Mother?'

Virginia faltered momentarily, then turned to the figure seated by the window. 'Stanton told me.'

Isabel's throat constricted painfully. Her hand went to her neck and she felt a pulse beat under her fingertips.

'Why did he tell you, Mother? Why didn't he tell me?' Her voice echoed in her head like the noises on the street the night she had been attacked. Footfalls, pain, magnolia blossom. Suspended voices. 'Why did he tell YOU, Mother?' she asked again. I'm wrong, she thought, please let me be wrong.

Virginia faced her daughter, but there was no defiance left in her. Instead she looked older, all pretence dissolved. A woman about to slip into old age as she was forced to admit to the folly of her youth.

'Mother, tell me why Stanton contacted you. I want to know!'

Virginia opened her mouth to speak, but no words came out. For someone who earned her living by speech, she was horribly silent.

They could have stayed frozen like that for ever, except that Prossie suddenly moved across the room. She passed Isabel, passed Virginia, and made for the window where Stanton sat. Then she hit him violently across the face, putting all her weight behind the blow, her hand made into a fist. The sound of the punch was loud in the still room. Fist on flesh. Isabel's stomach lurching as Stanton rocked, lost his balance, and sprawled on to the floor, his bare feet jerking upwards.

416

Breathing heavily, Prossie pointed to Stanton, then glanced at Isabel and said chillingly, 'Behold your father.'

Behind them, Virginia Hall began to weep.

27

Pressing the front door key of The Ridings into Prossie's hand, Isabel watched her friend leave with her three daughters, then sat down in one of the chairs in the drawing room and scrutinised her mother. Virginia stopped crying after her first hysterical outburst and composed herself. Having washed off most of her careful make-up, she looked her age, and her nose was swollen and red as she searched her handbag for another handkerchief. She glanced towards Stanton.

He had recovered himself enough to pour them all a drink. Isabel left hers untouched, although Virginia downed hers immediately and held the glass out for a refill. Expressionless, Stanton poured another measure and then slumped on to the window seat again. The light began to fail, the huge paintings of Prossie fading in the dimness, the glass display cabinet like a large transparent coffin in the room.

No one spoke, although Virginia cleared her throat several times, her eyes flicking over to her daughter in a silent plea. Say something, she begged Isabel. Please shout or say something. But don't just sit there, without any recrimination. Don't do what David Hall did; don't punish me by silence.

By contrast, Stanton felt nothing but disbelief. He had slept with Virginia just once, after they had both got drunk at a party. He had made a pass at her, expecting her to rebuff him as she usually did, but this time she didn't. She had been stiff, almost frightened, the sexual act accomplished while she was almost fully clothed. A one-off screw, so insignificant he had almost forgotten it . . . except that now and again he had felt some guilt when he was with David Hall. But it had faded, and when David died it had gone altogether. After all, there was no point dwelling on the past.

Stanton's eyes moved towards Isabel furtively. He caught her looking at him, and flinched. Fierce and unwelcome embarrassment set in. He had fancied his own daughter; made a pass at her the first time she had come to the studio. Jesus! he thought, draining his glass, what a frigging mess.

Stiff with tension, Isabel sat in silence. *Who is my father?* she had asked so many times, her own imagination trying to conjure up some idea of the man who had given her life. But of all the people she had considered, Stanton Feller had never come to mind. She remembered everything she knew about him — the way he treated his models, the bad language, the women, the coarseness — and held up against David Hall he seemed more gross than ever before, his kindness counting for nothing against the enormity of his deceit.

Of all people, Mother, why him? Why Stanton? Isabel wondered. What had he got that David Hall lacked? She stared at both of them, trying to understand their betrayal of the man she loved above all others. Was it just for sex? Was that it?

419

Just gratification? Isabel wondered, glancing over to Virginia. How *could* you sleep with this man, when you had David Hall? How could you give birth to Stanton Feller's child, instead of David Hall's? How could you do it, knowing that the action would hurt David so much? You killed him, she thought savagely, you and Stanton were responsible for the death of David Hall. As surely as if you knifed him, you killed him.

Her gaze moved from her mother to Stanton and she took in her breath. I am his child, she thought suddenly, studying Stanton, their eyes meeting and holding for a long instant. *My father* . . . Her thoughts wandered. So that was where her talent came from. But what else had she inherited from her real father? Some of his faults? Yes some, she realised, at the same instant recognising so many of his traits in Sybella . . . Of course, it all made sense now, promiscuity was in the blood.

'Did you know I was your daughter?' Isabel asked him finally. The words were businesslike. Crisp as clean sheets.

He shrugged. 'Not until your mother told me this afternoon. Sybella was getting on my tits, and I couldn't reach you, so I phoned Virginia. I knew she was at the Hilton — '

Isabel's eyes were suspicious. 'How?'

'There was a piece about her in the paper,' Stanton said defensively. 'Fucking hell, why the third degree? I had to get hold of someone, and you weren't at the studio.' His eyes flicked towards Virginia. 'After all, Sybella's her granddaughter — '

Isabel's expression was stony. 'And she's my daughter — '

'I told you, I couldn't get hold of you!' Stanton snapped, his tone sharp with impatience. 'I just wanted someone to come and get that bloody girl out of my hair!'

Isabel listened to Stanton with disbelief. That the fastidious Virginia Hall could have had an affair with such a man seemed impossible.

'Mother,' she said, turning back to Virginia, 'how *could* you sleep with him?'

'Why the fuck not!' Stanton asked, exploding into rage, his vanity threatened.

Both women ignored him. 'It only happened once.'

'So what, Mother?' Isabel countered. 'It's not the quantity that matters, is it?'

'Don't look at me like that! I know you hate me, well, David hated me too when he found out — I've paid for my stupidity, believe me,' she said helplessly. 'I didn't want you to know . . . I tried to keep it a secret. I tried to protect you the only way I could. Even when you came to live here I didn't tell you. After all, if Stanton didn't know, how could you find out?' She glanced away, shamefaced. 'I'm not proud of what I did . . . I just thought it was better that you didn't know.'

'You nearly drove me out of my mind for years wondering who my father was!' Isabel said heatedly, turning back to Stanton as another thought suddenly occurred to her. 'Wait a minute — why did Sybella come here today, Stanton?'

He raised his eyes, irritation obvious. 'She had a crush on me.'

She laughed once, mirthlessly. The noise bounced off the walls like a clap of thunder. 'Oh God, like grandmother, like granddaughter — how do you do it, Stanton?'

He flinched. 'It wasn't my fault, you should look after that bloody girl better. I always said she was trouble.'

'That 'girl' happens to be your granddaughter,' Isabel said evenly.

Stanton groaned. 'I never thought of that . . . ' He slumped further into the window seat, his eyes trailing back to the studio gate. 'D'you think Prossie's really angry with me?'

'Is that all you can say?' Isabel snapped.

'Shit! What do you want me to say?' he bellowed. 'That I'll adopt you?'

'You don't have to — another man took me on, someone better than you could ever hope to be.'

'I'm no bloody saint, I never said I was!' Stanton hissed, glancing away from her. 'You've turned out all right. Come to think of it, I did all right by you even before I knew you were one of mine.'

'ONE OF YOURS!' Isabel screamed, getting to her feet. 'Is that all I am to you? One of your pack of kids? How many are there, Stanton, I mean, apart from the three you had with Prossie?'

His voice was hoarse. 'Don't tell me how to live my life, kid.'

'Who could? Who ever dared?' she countered

angrily. 'Nothing matters to you, Stanton, even this. All you're worried about is that Prossie has left you high and dry — '

'I care for her.'

'Bullshit!' she replied hotly, facing up to her father. 'She's convenient because she runs the studio, poses for you, and turns a blind eye when you fool around — '

'That's enough!'

'You're right there,' she said, snatching up her coat and glancing towards her mother. 'I hope you'll both be very happy. You deserve each other.'

'I'm not staying here!' Virginia replied quickly, moving towards the door. She glanced at her daughter with a question in her eyes, silently willing Isabel to come with her, but Isabel ignored her and after another instant Virginia walked out, stiff-backed.

'Looks like you're on your own now, Stanton. The harem's all gone,' Isabel said bitterly. 'But not for long, I bet. No doubt you'll find another bed warmer by tonight.' She moved down the stairs in the semi-dark. At the bottom, she turned and looked up at her father.

'You *killed* David Hall — I just want you to know that. I want you to know it, and remember it.'

He said nothing in reply, merely letting the trap door slam closed in her face.

★ ★ ★

The Ridings was full of teenagers and noise. Down the lawn ran Chloë, Bracken and little

423

Eloise, Prossie walking after them, stern-faced and silent. From a distance, Blair watched them, mesmerised by the motley crowd of people who had descended on the house. Only Sybella remained away, returning to her school voluntarily after the traumatic events of that afternoon at the studio.

Reluctantly Isabel had gone to visit her, forcing a confrontation. In silence Sybella accompanied her mother to a hotel lounge, and sat with her arms folded as Isabel ordered afternoon tea.

Her voice steady, Isabel began to talk.

'You and I have to come to an understanding,' she said calmly. 'I've been a failure as a mother, I know that. Well, I'm sorry, apparently the Halls don't make good parents, except for David Hall — and he was a father by default.'

Sybella watched her mother, her interest caught.

'You're not a child, so I won't treat you like one, Sybella. Stanton Feller is my real father, and your grandfather, as you know . . . ' The girl winced. 'Just don't expect anything from him, or you'll be disappointed. If you want to see him as your grandfather, fine, do as you wish, you will anyway whatever I say.' She paused. 'I love you very much. I love you, but I can't make you happy, so I'm going to change tack.'

Sybella watched her mother carefully.

'I can live out the rest of my life castigating myself for ever for my faults, and my feelings, but I'm not going to. I'm thirty-seven years old, and I've had more than enough problems of my own, Sybella. I want to be happy. That's selfish, isn't it?' She carried on without waiting for a reply. 'But you see I can't live like this any longer, it's not enough for me. I wanted more children, but as you know I can't have any more — perhaps one day, when you're older, you'll realise what that means — so I've decided what I'm going to do with my life. I'm going to set up a school, Sybella, an institute for gifted children. I'm not too good at being a real mother, but perhaps I'll be a better substitute parent.'

Sybella glanced down at her cup.

'I know you've had a lot to contend with. You feel rejected by your father, I understand that. But I felt rejected too,' Isabel said, confiding in her daughter for once. 'He left me because I insisted on having you ... ' She paused as Sybella realised for the first time the sacrifice her mother had made for her. 'And God knows, even with all the problems you've given me, I would never go back on that decision.' She fiddled with the spoon in her saucer. 'Sybella, all I can say is that I understand you. I don't condone the bloody stupid things you've done, and I don't want you to waste your life. But it is *your* life, and I can't follow you around around constantly, cleaning up your messes ... I can say don't sleep around, and don't waste your abilities, but the choice is yours. So now I say just this — I'm here whenever you need me. Whatever good that is, I'm here.' Her eyes remained fixed on the table. 'Don't throw away a bad mother, Sybella, when you could have a powerful ally.'

Isabel paused again. The words had been painful and difficult to say, and suddenly she was tongue-tied. Gingerly she glanced at her daughter, and then watched in amazement as Sybella's eyes filled.

'Oh, Mum,' she said simply, taking hold of her hand.

★ ★ ★

Virginia couldn't sleep. A sheaf of unread papers lay on the bedside table next to her, a chilled glass of white Bordeaux left untouched. Her eyes were closed, but the images were in sharp focus — as were the sounds. She had been ready to go shopping before the lecture and when Stanton phoned her mouth had dried automatically, her thoughts spinning backwards down the years. The phone call was brusque, he had been impatient, and impertinent, demanding that she collect her granddaughter from the studio. Virginia swallowed, the saliva balling up in her throat. Her granddaughter, and his also . . . Sick with anxiety, she had hurried over to Holland Park, knowing Stanton's reputation and horribly afraid that something might already have happened. He was Sybella's grandfather, she thought hysterically, her *grandfather* . . .

Not that he knew that. In fact, there was no affection in his voice at all; nothing to indicate that they had ever been anything but acquaintances. The call had been not from a lost love, but from a man who was in a fix. And that had hurt. Come and get her, he had said. I can't got hold of Isabel, so I thought you could help me out.

And I thought you could help me out once,

426

Virginia thought bitterly. Once, years ago, when my husband fell out of love with me, and my daughter loathed me, and there was nothing except the dull comfort of a clever career.

I thought you could help me out, she repeated to herself. David had been so distant, so detached, almost haunted, and she had wanted to get him back. Embarrassed affection was offered, but ignored, her husband turning more to his sister than to his wife. She had tried to make him love her; had tried to love him more; but there was nothing left, so she had become angry and had tried to make him jealous instead . . .

I thought you could help me out, Stanton had said.

Well, I thought you could make love to me and make my husband jealous, Virginia thought, but it didn't work out that way, did it? And now you're ringing me without even remembering that we had sex, without even knowing that one act resulted in the birth of a child, and a man's death.

Virginia ached with the memory. When she arrived at the studio and told Stanton the truth he had been shocked, but had rallied almost immediately. In fact, in a way, she thought he was pleased to know that Isabel was his child. And that had hurt . . . Their lovemaking meant nothing to him, even though it had cost her everything. Virginia smiled wryly. I didn't even enjoy having sex with him, David, she thought. Stanton's hands were not your hands, and his mouth wasn't yours, and he wasn't the man I wanted . . . Her eyes remained staring upwards, unseeing. Tears dried in the corners of her eyelids; they dried and remained fixed, like the image of Isabel standing in silent accusation in that moment before she spoke. In the moment she knew what her mother had done.

★   ★   ★

Eleanor reeled when she was told that Stanton Feller was Isabel's father, then, realising how shocked Isabel was, she rallied and welcomed Prossie and her children unconditionally. Of all people, she thought to herself. She glanced out of the kitchen window and saw Prossie's girls enjoying their unexpected holiday in Yorkshire; and her mind went back to Isabel's childhood and to David. Eleanor sighed deeply and wondered what the future held . . . Prossie did too, not that she was pressurised in any way. No questions were asked about how long she was staying, or where they would eventually go.

Prossie had no money, and no hope of finding a job. For seventeen years she had lived with Stanton Feller. He had been her one and only lover; in him, she saw everything she had ever wanted. But she could not come to terms with the fact that he was Isabel's father. Every time she thought of Stanton, she thought of him in bed with Virginia Hall, and closed her eyes against the image. No, it was too painful to contemplate — besides, she found it impossible to think of returning to live with Isabel's *father*.

So she hovered in mid-air, like a dancer taking a leap. Only she didn't land, she just hung suspended, like one of Stanton's damn mobiles, and waited for some wind to blow her someplace. True to form, Stanton did not phone her; he was the injured party, as she had deserted him. But if he expected Prossie to phone, he was disappointed; her anger, once disturbed, took a long time to settle again.

The most dramatic result of the confrontation was that Virginia moved to America, taking an apartment outside New York City, and Geoffrey Harrod began to spend more time in the USA than at home with his wife. Poor Mary Harrod, Isabel thought with real sympathy, remembering the busy, abstracted woman with whom she had stayed when she first visited Stanton.

'Do you think your mother will stay away?' Eleanor asked Isabel.

Isabel nodded. 'Yes, I think she's had enough of England and us.'

'Are you serious about this Institute idea?' Eleanor asked idly, although her curiosity was burning her.

Isabel nodded, beginning to slice some bread for tea. 'Of course I'm serious, I'm making some real money now and I want to give it a go. I'd like to leave something valuable behind — I've an immortality complex,' she said, laughing.

'I think it's a great idea,' Prossie said, strolling into the kitchen with a letter in her hand. She frowned, then tore it up. 'From Stanton,' she said simply, as she dropped it into the pedal bin.

'But a school would cost a fortune to build, wouldn't it?'

Isabel looked at her aunt. 'Uhm, it would cost a fortune — most of which I don't have. But I think I can raise the money if I can get some backers.'

'It's a bad time for anything speculative, with the recession and everything.'

Isabel raised her eyebrows. 'It's always a bad time,' she replied evenly, putting the plate of bread on the table in front of the girls. 'There's no such thing as a *good* time, for God's sake. You know that. I want to do it, and I'm going to.'

'Then go for it,' Prossie said emphatically. 'What can you lose?'

'Just all my money, that's all,' Isabel replied drily.

'If you wanted to, you could put up the house as security,' Eleanor said quietly.

Isabel turned to her aunt and shook her head gently. 'No, never. This house stays in this family, for ever . . . I could never sell it. It would be like selling a child.'

'Oh, in that case I've got three spare!' Prossie said cheerfully, looking at her daughters round the table. 'Take your pick.'

The routine was quickly established. In the week, Isabel returned to her studio in London, as she had always done, and worked on the series of portraits for which she charged handsomely. Baye Fortunas and Gyman de Souza recommended her frequently and Isabel's social contacts continued to open up — a process which was vital for any portrait painter who hoped to make a lucrative career.

Having decided to set up an Institute, Isabel was surprised to find that she recovered some peace of mind. The idea might take time, and would be difficult, if not impossible, to achieve — but she had a future, a purpose to her life, and that rejuvenated her. At the weekends, she returned to The Ridings to relax. In the South, she pursued her ambitions; in the North, she revelled in her extended family.

Although she didn't need to, Prossie earned her keep by looking after the house. The two daily women were relieved of their duties and she filled her time running The Ridings with Eleanor. They got on well together; neither was argumentative, and both loved the place without feeling that either of them had to be in sole control. Only Blair resented the new arrivals, seeing in Prossie a competitor for Eleanor's attention, and a further indication of Isabel's heartlessness.

He boiled in lonely silence and even kept his distance from Prossie's girls, now attending the local school.

'I'm glad in a way.'

Isabel nodded, already understanding what Prossie was thinking. 'I know what you mean. After Sybella, you would never feel comfortable letting him be alone with the girls.'

'I shouldn't be suspicious of him, should I?' Prossie said, mortified. 'I shouldn't even say it.'

'Why not? we can say anything to each other. There are no secrets any longer,' Isabel said, suddenly relieved. No, there were no secrets between them. Everyone at The Ridings knew about Sybella and Blair, just as they knew about David Hall and Stanton Feller. For a moment the relief was so intense Isabel took in her breath.

'What is it?'

'Nothing, Prossie,' she said, smiling, 'I just had the most marvellous feeling, that's all. 'Scuse me, a minute, will you?'

Wandering off, she pushed open the door of the den and walked in. The same peculiar euphoria continued as she glanced round and then bent and opened up the oak portfolio cupboard. Gently she pulled out one of the sheafs of drawings David Hall had collected and touched the sketched faces, her fingers hardly brushing the surface of the page. Then she looked up at the bust of Dante, fierce and silent on top of the bookshelf.

Turning, she rested her right hand on the back of the old leather chair, feeling the slight indentation where David Hall had rested his head so many times — then she thought of her mother and felt an unexpected jolt of pity.

'I know you said you never knew who my father was, David,' Isabel murmured softly, 'but didn't you guess it was Stanton? Didn't you ever think it might be him?'

The room was silent. Only a late breeze scuttled against the windowpane.

'I can't hate Mother,' Isabel said, surprising herself. 'I hated her for so long, but I can't any longer. She's older and she's run away from us because she's ashamed. As for Stanton — I'm sorry about him. Not just for myself, but for you. You cared for him so much.' She hesitated, remembering how Stanton had taken her in when her marriage had failed, and how he had sat beside her bed in the hospital. 'He's not you, but he has some kindness . . . but then you

432

always knew that, didn't you? Otherwise you would never have loved him.'

Sliding into the leather chair, Isabel rested her head in the indentation.

'One part of my life is closing now, David. I can feel it,' she said. 'Even Sybella and I finally have an understanding. We're almost friends . . . ' She closed her eyes and concentrated. 'I'm going to wish again now, David. This is my third wish — I want to build the Institute. It's for you. A school you would have wanted for children, somewhere the gifted ones can go and learn, where the other kids won't laugh at them.' Her voice was high with enthusiasm. 'I'm going to build big studios and get great teachers — people like Portento could come and lecture — and all the children will be taught the same way as you taught me. With kindness . . . ' She opened her eyes, it was as though she could see the building in front of her. 'It will be your monument, and my thank you.'

Her hand moved along the back of the chair and for an instant she felt him with her as she spoke.

'You gave me the gift of truth, and for that I thank you. I now know who I am, and who my father is. I also know what to do with the rest of my life.'

Be careful, be wise.

She heard the words — either they were spoken in the room, or in her head — but Isabel heard the words and smiled.

'Yes, David, I will.' Then she altered one word, and said, to please him, 'Yes, Daddy, yes, I will.'

PART IV

28

Ivy Messenger was sitting in her wheelchair, a magnifying glass in one hand and a book in the other. Her house, on Chelsea's Cheyne Walk, was busy with activity, only her room was quiet. She had lived for the past two years in this one room with its adjoining bathroom, ever since she had broken her hip in a fall. Her forced seclusion did not irritate her, quite the contrary; Ivy Messenger found that her exile on the first floor had opened up her social life most agreeably. Now people visited her to gossip, and provided she kept them well fed and watered, they kept her well up to date with events in London.

She shifted her position in the wheelchair and peered at the colour plate in the book she was reading. At the age of eighty-six her skin had lost most of its elasticity and her arms were brittle-boned and fragile. Only her hair retained much of its quality, full and ash blond, as it had always been, surprisingly youthful over the ageing face. Impatiently, Ivy squinted at the page again. Cataracts had been a nuisance to her, and although her eyesight had been improved by surgery in her seventies, the sight of her right eye had now gone completely.

Her left eye was good though, and scanned the page thoroughly, her brain showing no signs of ageing; neither did her voice, as imperious and sharp as it had been in her youth. Thoughtfully

Ivy Messenger laid down the magnifying glass and remembered the visitor who had come to see her that morning. She had never liked Sunny de Souza, and made a point of having several open boxes of tissues around every time she visited. Not that she couldn't appreciate Sunny's intellect — having been enormously successful in business herself, she could always admire another's acumen. But she didn't have to like the woman — and she didn't have to like her son either.

Ivy slammed the book shut and listened carefully. She was expecting another visitor any time, and was looking forward to seeing him. Indeed, she had even made a special effort with her appearance, insisting that her nurse help her into her corsets and lace them up the back.

'But, Mrs Messenger, they can't be good for you — '

'This is a Messenger Corset!' she had snapped, holding on to the bathroom door frame for support. 'They've helped women with back problems for years.'

Cowed, the nurse strapped her into the pink and white confection, Ivy breathing in as she tied the ribbons. The Messenger Corset had made her a fortune after her husband died in the war. Not that he had left her penniless — a small annuity could have made her comfortable for life. But Ivy wanted more. So she dug out her mother's old patterns and set to making the first Messenger Corset. Her quick mind and remarkable sales pitch did the rest.

Within two years the Messenger Corset was

worn by fifteen per cent of British women, was exported abroad to Europe and the United States, and Ivy Messenger was its ambassador. Her rigid stance and svelte figure were the perfect advertisement — her appearance put down to the corset rather than the vigorous diet she followed. Ivy smiled to herself.

'What's so funny?'

She glanced up at the man who had walked in. 'I was thinking of my underwear,' she said, deliberately shocking him. 'It's good to see you, Max.'

He kissed her lightly on the cheek then pulled up a chair and sat down next to her. The room never changed, he thought, the same dark red silk paper on the walls, the same Russian icons lighted overhead, and the same heavy Edwardian furniture. 'You look well, Ivy.'

'You look better,' she replied, studying her guest.

She had known Max Henderson for almost ten years, since he was in his early thirties and making a name for himself in business. What business? she used to ask. This and that, he used to reply easily, dodging the question. Such charm, Ivy thought, taking his hand, always such charm.

'I've got a new picture, Max,' she said eagerly. 'I got it yesterday. It's by an artist called Isabel Hall — she's got real talent.'

'The name sounds familiar — I think Gyman de Souza mentioned her to me.'

One thin hand gestured to the corner where an easel stood displaying a portrait of Ivy.

Max rose to his feet and walked over to look at it. He was tall, over six feet, and heavily built, his tailored suit discreet and well fitting. Ivy admired the cut of it, as she studied him and watched his head jut forward to scrutinise the portrait. His dark hair was cut short, his eyes over high cheekbones surrounded by fine lines that creased deeply when he laughed — like the ones round his mouth. Max Henderson was not a handsome man, but he had presence and charisma, and that made him irresistible.

'It's good, Ivy,' he said at last, turning back to her. 'The likeness is there, and your personality. Judging by what's on show at the Academy the painter should do well — she's got damn all competition.'

'Apart from Stanton Feller.'

Max laughed shortly. A big laugh, which suited a big man. 'I saw him at dinner at Baye Fortunas's the other week — he never changes, does he?'

'The man is a pig,' Ivy said dismissively, 'but a great talent. I think Isabel paints like him.' Her eyes moved back to the portrait. 'Mind you, she should do — he trained her.'

Max regained his seat next to Ivy and unbuttoned his jacket to make himself comfortable.

'It's funny, but I've been thinking of getting some pictures for the new house,' he said idly.

Ivy pretended innocence, but she knew that Max Henderson had made a killing in America and had returned to England wealthy enough to buy a house on Bishops Avenue — just as she

440

knew that Isabel was trying to make money to set up the Institute . . . Carefully, she fed him the bait.

'She's very up and coming, you know. Her father was David Hall and her mother's Virginia Hall.' She paused, and noticed the flicker of recognition in his eyes. 'Isabel's had a bad time of it, an attack which affected her for years. It damaged her hand. Her painting hand.' Max listened, but said nothing. 'But she's perfectly all right now. In fact, she's a very pretty little thing,' Ivy said, ringing for drinks. 'I want to help her, Max. People are so damn unadventurous that they keep commissioning Stanton Feller, and he doesn't even need the work.'

'I'm not sure Caroline could stand Stanton Feller in the house anyway!' Max replied, laughing again.

Ivy frowned at the mention of Max's wife. Deceptively winsome, Caroline seldom accompanied her husband to functions, her shyness used as a perpetual excuse to dodge her marital obligations. Shadowy Caroline; the enigma.

'How is your wife?'

'A little . . . ' one of Max's large hands waved in the air 'troubled.'

'Troubled?' Ivy repeated loudly. 'What the hell is that supposed to mean, Max? I hate it when you talk in code! I'm old, I haven't got the time to decipher conversations, I could die before you finished the explanation.'

He laughed, just as she knew he would. 'Caroline's very frail. She gets depressed easily.'

'She should work,' Ivy responded, changing

the subject immediately when she saw the look in Max's eyes. 'Would you like me to arrange for you to meet Isabel Hall? You could talk to her about your new house and the paintings you want.'

His heels dug in immediately, resenting the sales pitch. 'No, I don't want to make it a formal thing.'

'Just in case you don't like her work?' Ivy replied mischievously.

Max smiled. 'You know exactly what I mean, you old witch,' he said, teasing her. 'I don't want to come to one of your soirées and feel obliged to commission her because 'we both know the right people'.'

'Don't be so damned childish!' Ivy responded, tapping him on the knee. 'That's how business is done.'

'Maybe,' he said, glancing away to signify that the subject was closed. 'So, what have you been up to?'

Ivy knew the rules of the game, and also knew that she had aroused his curiosity in Isabel. So, satisfied with her progress so far, she answered him happily.

* * *

Isabel ran along the path in Kensington Gardens, timing herself. She loathed exercise, but she still forced herself out every day, a stopwatch in her left hand, and a battered squash ball in her right. As her feet pounded the path her fingers contracted and relaxed round the ball, her eyes fixed ahead.

The process had kept her in good shape over the years, and also kept her mentally astute. Easily tired, Isabel found that she became confused if she worked for long periods, but if she went out for a run, her brain cleared automatically — although she never ran at night. Generally she set off in the early mornings around six, when the mist hung over the park and only a few cars made their way along Kensington Gore. She liked the early city, and the smell of wet grass under the sprinklers, and the shrouded Albert Memorial, just as she liked the few regulars who called out a greeting to her.

By seven, she was usually running up Kensington Church Street, stopping to buy a paper and leaning against the church wall to read the headlines. But this morning Isabel was strangely out of step, her feet faltering, her mind wandering as she ran. Irritated she pushed herself, then froze when she heard feet running behind her — she spun round, brushing her damp hair out of her eyes.

A large man in a jogging suit ran up to her and stopped.

'What do you want?' she snapped, startled.

Max frowned. 'Isabel Hall?'

'Yes.'

'Ivy, Ivy Messenger said I might find you here.'

Isabel relaxed, feeling suddenly rather foolish. 'I'm sorry . . . I'm a little nervous about people coming up behind me,' she said awkwardly.

Suddenly remembering what he had heard of her attack, Max cursed himself for his

443

thoughtlessness. 'I'm sorry.' He extended his hand. 'I'm Max Henderson.'

Isabel smiled and shook hands with him, wondering how she looked, and then wondering why it mattered. 'What can I do for you, Mr Henderson?'

'I wanted to talk to you about some paintings,' he said, dropping into step beside her. 'I've just moved to a new house on the Bishops Avenue and I want to commission some work.'

She smiled up at him and then glanced away, feeling an overwhelming attraction for the man. 'What kind of pictures were you looking for?'

He shrugged. 'Forgive my ignorance, but I'm not sure. Ivy was determined to introduce us at one of her dinners — God forbid — and I was too much of a coward to accept. I would hate everyone to know now boorish I really was.'

Isabel smiled easily, liking the way he poked fun at himself.

'I thought that the dining room and drawing rooms needed some 'important' pieces.' He laughed, the sound was loud and infectious in the morning air. 'That's what they call them, isn't it? Important pieces?'

She nodded.

'Well, that's what I need. I saw your portrait of Ivy Messenger, it's good.' He paused again, Isabel was having to hurry to keep up with him as he walked on. 'I'm sorry, the word 'good' doesn't convey much, does it? But I appreciate your skill. Perhaps you could paint my wife?'

Isabel would wonder for years afterwards why the words hurt her so deeply. My wife. She hardly knew the man, minutes earlier she had been running alone, and yet the words tore at her when he said them. My wife.

'Of course . . . ' she said lamely.

'We dismissed the idea of commissioning Stanton Feller. Although I believe he taught you?'

Isabel glanced away, across the damp gardens. 'Yes . . . yes, he did.'

'It's raining,' Max said suddenly.

Automatically, she looked up at the lowering sky.

'So what do you think, Miss Hall?'

'About what?'

Max raised his eyebrows. 'About coming to look at the house and painting some pictures for us?'

She smiled easily. 'Fine. Whatever you say.'

'Thursday, around five?'

She nodded.

'We're at number eleven,' he said, turning to go. 'Thank you.'

'No . . . thank you,' Isabel murmured, watching as he moved off.

She continued to watch him for a while as he stopped walking and began to jog. A big man in a tracksuit, running in the early rain.

★   ★   ★

Sunny de Souza sneezed three times and then dabbed at her eyes with the corner of a handkerchief, Baye Fortunas watching her. Beside them sat Ivy Messenger in her wheelchair, one thin arm extending a package of Kleenex.

'Darling Ivy, so thoughtful,' Sunny said, taking several tissues. 'I can't think how I got this cold.'

'It's the same one you had last week, and the week before,' Ivy said mercilessly.

'I'm thinking of trying acupuncture again,' Sunny said plaintively.

'Try a couple of corks. One for each nostril,' Ivy said deftly, winking at Max.

He laughed and turned away, pushing her towards the window and passing her a sherry. 'You shouldn't be cruel,' he admonished her.

'Listen, it's the only benefit of old age,' Ivy replied. 'You can say what you want.'

'I saw Isabel Hall yesterday . . . '

Ivy's eyes quickened.

'She's coming over to the house on Thursday.'

'Good.'

'You approve?'

'Of course. She won't disappoint you.'

No, Max thought, Isabel Hall couldn't do that. A picture of her flipped up in his mind. A slim young woman in a running suit, her hair tied back, her fringe damp with perspiration, her eyes bright with intelligence and sadness. His stomach lurched uncomfortably — and he felt inexplicably guilty.

'Will Caroline be there?' Ivy asked him.

He frowned. 'Oh yes, she wants to talk to Isabel about the paintings.'

'Taking an interest.'

'Yes, taking an interest,' he agreed, knowing that the old woman saw more than he was willing to admit. 'Caroline is very good in the house.'

'People usually say that about dogs when they

446

stop fouling the carpets,' Ivy replied, smiling slyly.

'You don't like my wife, do you?'

'My dear Max, I don't see enough of Caroline to form an opinion one way or the other.'

'She's shy.'

'So you say.'

His expression hardened, all ease gone. He didn't like his wife to be criticised and at that moment Ivy could see the other side of Max Henderson — and was momentarily awed by him.

'Isabel will do some wonderful work for you,' she said, deftly changing the subject, and glancing down at her hands. 'You know that she's trying to set up a school, an Institute?'

He looked surprised.

'She wants it to be for gifted children — somewhere where they can get specialised training in art. You know, a bit like a glorified apprenticeship out in the country somewhere. I personally think she's mad, but I like her so much I'm trying to help her to raise funds.'

Max frowned. 'Something like that would cost a fortune to set up.'

Ivy nodded, and shifted her narrow hips in the wheelchair. The famous Messenger Corset dug into her skin . . . The afternoon light was fading, the gold leaf on the icons glowing supernaturally in the shaded room. 'I know it will, but she's very determined. She's like her mother in that — '

'Who's like her mother?' Sunny asked, butting into the conversation.

'Isabel is.'

Sunny frowned. 'Oh, I think she's like her father, David Hall. His suicide was *such* a shock.'

'Isabel Hall's father killed himself?' Max asked, intrigued. 'Why?'

'Oh, no one really knows,' Sunny replied. 'But he was always highly strung. He stabbed himself — '

'He shot himself actually,' Baye Fortunas said, joining the group at the window. 'In a field, well away from the house. A farmer found him.'

Max listened, transfixed. 'Thank God his daughter didn't find him.'

Sunny glanced at him suspiciously, and then glanced at Ivy. The dim light made her look tiny in the wheelchair, but her one good eye was bright with interest.

'Yes . . . it was a good thing,' Baye answered, knowing that Max Henderson had unintentionally given himself away. 'Isabel was very much affected by her father's death. They were very close.'

'David Hall has always been the most important man in her life,' Sunny offered. 'She's not married, you see . . . well, she was, but now she's divorced . . . '

Max stiffened, sensing the undercurrent in the conversation.

'Although she does have a daughter, Sybella. A very attractive girl, but troublesome. Rumour has it that there was some kind of scandal with her a little while back — '

'You know how people talk,' Baye said, trying to curtail the gossip.

'Stanton Feller's mistress, a woman called Prossie, lives with Isabel ... ' Sunny offered. 'Well, she lives with Isabel's aunt in Yorkshire. She moved up there when she fell out with Stanton. Took her three daughters with her — can you imagine?'

'The artistic circle is different to ours,' Baye said tactfully.

'And so much more exciting! Rumour has it that Stanton Feller has a lady butler now, and that she undresses him and dresses him like a valet.' Sunny sneezed. 'He's such old roué.'

'But he can still paint,' Baye said coldly, glancing over to Max.

His face was calm, without expression, but he took in every word that was said. He wanted to know more about Isabel Hall, but could hardly make his interest more apparent. So he waited, knowing that Sunny de Souza would be unable to stop talking.

'Isabel was married to that lawyer — oh, what was his name? He went back to his wife, who used to be Philippa Welsh — don't look at me so dully, Baye, you know who I'm talking about.'

'Isabel was married to Teddy Gray.'

Max filed the information away.

'Yes, Teddy Gray! That's the man. He had a heart attack last year, and he's not that old. Portento saw him a little while back and said he still looked only thirty — even after a heart attack. He said it even improved him. I put it down to good genes myself.' She sneezed again. 'He and Isabel weren't suited. I can't think what she saw in him.'

Ivy glanced up at them from her wheelchair and smiled. How the silly woman prattled on, but Max was watching her, and listening. Oh yes, Ivy thought, how hard you are listening. Picking up every piece of news about Isabel Hall. Storing it away. Clever Max Henderson — uneasy Max Henderson.

'Isabel's doing awfully well now though,' Sunny continued. 'I discovered her, you know, and Gyman's in love with her, has been for years . . .'

Your son is homosexual, Ivy thought incredulously.

'And I had my darling Irving painted, before he died . . .'

It would have been difficult to paint him afterwards, Ivy thought drily.

'He *adored* Isabel too,' Sunny said, then corrected herself quickly. 'Well, in so far as he adored anyone other than me. We were blissfully happy . . .'

Irving de Souza had a mistress in Madrid and an illegitimate daughter in Canada, Ivy thought to herself.

'You'll like Isabel, everyone does,' Sunny said to Max. 'Except for some of the dealers. They think she's a little lightweight — but then what can you expect? It's always harder for a woman to get on. Even these days, after women's liberation . . .'

My head is splitting, Ivy thought, casting a pleading glance at Max.

He understood immediately and pushed her chair into the centre of the room, sitting beside

450

her on the sofa. 'Sunny de Souza has a lot of energy,' Max said, in a low voice.

'Yes, and she's only just coming to the boil,' Ivy replied evenly. 'In another few minutes she would have had Isabel's reputation cooked to a nicety.' She glanced at Max. 'Don't worry, I never recommend anyone unless they have talent — Isabel Hall will do a fine job for you. She takes her work very seriously.'

'I wonder why her father killed himself,' Max mused.

'My dear boy, you will never find out,' Ivy responded. 'The Hall family is a very strange one. They have many secrets, and they keep all of them to themselves.'

★　★　★

Isabel dressed herself carefully for her appointment on Thursday and took a taxi to Bishops Avenue. A late sun blazed over the house, making it formidable, new money surrounded by white pillars; so different from The Ridings. She rang the bell, and was ushered into the drawing room, Max Henderson arriving a moment later.

She turned to face him, and saw in his eyes that their attraction was mutual. The knowledge wrongfooted her:

'Mr Henderson, hello.'

He smiled uneasily. 'Welcome, Miss Hall — would you like a drink?'

'Not just at the moment,' she replied, glancing round. The drawing room was furnished in a typically English Colefax and Fowler style. Pale beige silk walls ran into carefully pelmeted curtains, a pair of French windows leading out on to a patio. In the hearth a real fire burned; two chintz sofas flanked the hearth, and several carefully arranged vases of flowers topped occasional tables, a set of Monkey Band figurines in pride of place in a Georgian cabinet. The room was in careful taste, but it seemed to have little in common with Max Henderson.

'These are very collectable,' Isabel said, glancing at the little statues of the monkey musicians. 'They're charming.'

'My wife — ' he hesitated, the word took on a low voltage of its own, 'has collected them for years. I'm not too keen on them myself.'

Isabel smiled and turned away, as embarrassed as he was.

'I was thinking,' Max continued, turning the subject back to business, 'that we needed a painting in here — something to give the room a focal point.'

Isabel smiled, wondering where his wife was. 'What kind of painting?'

'Caroline,' the name was out, 'thought that a landscape might do nicely.'

'I don't do landscapes, Mr Henderson,' Isabel replied quickly, a little too quickly, almost as though she was passing judgement on the suggestion. 'I mean, I'm a figurative painter — if you want a landscape, I can recommend someone though.'

He looked at her, and she returned the look. Both of them felt the same sense of anxiety, the strength of their attraction making conversation stilted. Go home, Isabel thought to herself, get out now. Before anything happens. He's married to Caroline; the woman who created this room; the woman who collects the figurines. Get out while you still can.

'Well, it doesn't have to be a landscape,' Max continued evenly. 'It was just a thought. I'd be glad to hear what you suggest.'

Isabel leaned down and picked up her portfolio, laying it on the sofa and opening the pages. A selection of photographs of her work lay on display, and he glanced at them. 'Sunny said how good you were — she wasn't lying,' he commented, flicking over the pages. 'I like this kind of thing,' he continued, pointing to a painting with several figures in costume. 'Would something like this go well in here?'

Isabel glanced down at the picture and nodded. He stood very close to her, only inches away, both of them very aware of their proximity.

'Where would you put it?' Isabel asked, smiling and glancing over at the marble fireplace. 'There?'

He nodded. He hadn't thought where to put the painting; until that moment he hadn't even considered what he wanted. Unusually awkward, Max found his pulse rate quickening and wished Isabel would leave; at the same time knowing that if she did, he would miss her.

'I wanted you to look at some other parts of the house,' he said suddenly, closing the portfolio and walking to the door, Isabel following behind. Now that she was no longer so close to him, he regained his poise and began to talk more easily.

'The top landing needs something to give it character,' he said, mounting the stairs, Isabel walking one step behind him. The smell of fresh paint and newly laid carpet was strong, the hall and staircase as unmarked and perfect as a mausoleum.

'Well, what do you think?' Max asked her as they stopped on the landing of the first floor. On either side of them were doors, a window at the end of the corridor looking down to a newly landscaped garden.

'Caroline thought that some tables and a few wall lights might be enough, but I was wondering about a mural.' He laughed suddenly. The sound was overloud, and yet Isabel smiled. 'I'm finding this very difficult,' Max admitted. 'You see, I don't know anything about art — I was hoping my wife would be here to help out.'

Isabel smiled sympathetically. 'You're doing very well, believe me.'

'I am?' he asked, seeming even more amused. 'Well, it's more luck than judgement.' His eyes moved down the hallway. Its ghostly sterility jangled on his nerves. 'I want the place to look older; to look lived in — you know what I mean? I want some paintings to give it some character, and a mural down here — do you think that might work?'

Isabel nodded, relieved to be on her own territory again. 'Yes, it could do.' She walked down the corridor, glancing round her. 'If I painted a pastoral scene, with lots of figures, using the old methods, it would look aged — '

'That's what I want!' Max said, running one

454

hand through his hair, obviously relieved. 'I want the house to stop looking like a flaming hotel.'

'I know exactly what you're looking for and I can do it. No problem.'

He nodded his head, convinced. 'Good, now come and look at this,' he said suddenly, taking the stairs up to the second floor.

Isabel followed, hurrying to keep up with him, and arrived on the next landing a moment later. There were only two doors on this floor, Max standing beside the nearest one, waiting for her.

'Have a look,' he said triumphantly as he pushed it open and walked in. 'This is my part of the house.'

She had to move along a short passageway, then down two steps, before walking into the study. A large bay window was on her right where a desk, covered in papers, stood four-square and solid, a large chair behind it. On her left was a heavy cabinet she suspected was a drinks cupboard, and immediately ahead of her were two Italian leather armchairs arranged on either side of the fireplace. An open briefcase lay on the floor beside one of them.

'Sorry about the mess,' Max said, glancing round.

Isabel also continued to look. On her left were two doors, both closed, and on her far right, another door, again secured.

'You see, I do most of my work here,' he went on, slamming the briefcase shut and pointing to the vast, empty expanse of panelled wall to the left of the desk. 'I spend so much time in this room I need some inspiration. It's my office, you see, and it matters to me.'

'I like it,' Isabel said truthfully. It was the only part of the house which had any personality, she thought.

'You do?' He seemed surprised. 'Caroline hates the settees.' He nudged the dark leather with the toe of his shoe and smiled absently. 'She likes the English look, whereas I prefer something a little more masculine.'

That makes sense, Isabel thought, having tried in vain to picture him in the delicate drawing room downstairs. The whole scale of his office was more in keeping with him; large, with big pieces of furniture and no frills.

'I want a painting over the fireplace and a few smaller ones on the walls,' Max continued, suddenly comfortable with his own choice. 'Like these,' he said, pushing the papers off the table and opening Isabel's portfolio again. 'Look, this one would go well there.' One large hand pointed to a painting of two men talking. 'I like this, and this one . . . ' he went on eagerly, his energy suddenly apparent. Gone was the uncertainty, this was the Max Henderson everyone expected. 'But I want a big piece for over the fireplace — something to make people think.'

'Oh, I can do that!' Isabel said, laughing.

He laughed back. His mouth was large, and the lines around his eyes were deep. 'I know you can. That's why I want you to have a go.' He slammed the portfolio shut. 'When can you start?'

Isabel shrugged. 'In a couple of weeks?'

'Good,' he said, suddenly the businessman.

456

'I'll write and confirm what we've agreed, and I know your prices.' He moved towards the desk in the window. 'I'm not here much so I won't get under your feet, and my wife spends a lot of her time abroad,' he said, walking back to Isabel and passing her a card. 'This is my private office number if you need me, otherwise Mrs Gunn, our housekeeper, will look after you.'

Isabel took the card from him, their fingers brushed momentarily and Max blinked, then moved to the door. 'Well, I'm glad we've got everything sorted out, Miss Hall,' he said, walking down the stairs with her to the front door. 'I'll tell Mrs Gunn to expect you, and if there's anything you need, just tell her. She sees to the nitty gritty.' He smiled, but the ease had gone. 'You know the kind of thing, dust sheets, et cetera.'

Isabel nodded.

'So, we'll see you in a fortnight then,' he said, hoping that his discomfort was not apparent.

'In a fortnight,' Isabel agreed.

It took her nearly two days to get Max Henderson out of her mind. Finally, in a fit of exasperation, Isabel pulled on her tracksuit and went for a furious run in Kensington Gardens, then pushed herself on into Hyde Park. As she ran she wondered if even this wasn't a ploy to think of him — after all, hadn't they first met jogging? Her eyes scanned the horizon automatically, looking for a big man in a tracksuit, and then she smiled to herself. What would she say if he did suddenly materialise? 'Do you run here often?'

She laughed out loud, and a woman pushing a

pram gave her a suspicious look. The pram brought Isabel up short, and at the thought of Sybella she slowed down, her breaths coming in little puffs. Her daughter seemed to have turned over a new leaf, and having found a few friends at boarding school it would appear that she was finally settling down. In fact, she was even offering to help Isabel with her attempts to raise funds for the Institute.

Breathing hard, Isabel slowed her pace even further — Sunny de Souza and Ivy Messenger had been generous with donations, and Baye had contributed, but there was still such a long way to go. What she needed was one major financial backer. But who? Isabel asked herself. And where would she find him? The dream was going to take a long time to fulfil, she knew, but she had that time, and little else to occupy her.

Except for the exhibition next week, she thought suddenly, stopping dead in her tracks. From the following Monday she was on show, with a selection of other figurative artists, at the Farnese Gallery on the Mall. She smiled slyly to herself as she pushed some damp hair out of her eyes. Oh yes, it was going to be fun next week . . . She had supervised the hanging herself, picking her spots carefully so that her work would be displayed to its full advantage — hanging directly opposite Stanton Feller's.

Kneeling down to tie her shoelace, Isabel noticed her hands shaking and frowned, suddenly anxious. Perhaps it was a risky thing to do; perhaps someone would find out her secret. By examining her work against Stanton's, would some perceptive eye see more than an artistic similarity? Or was that what she really wanted? Isabel straightened up. No, she wanted to be known as David Hall's daughter; not Stanton Feller's.

But how safe was her secret? She chewed her lip thoughtfully. Perhaps she was worrying unnecessarily. After all, Virginia would never betray herself, and Prossie was hardly likely to admit the truth. As for Stanton? Isabel frowned, he might. He might. If he got drunk enough, or mean enough, he just might tell the world that he was Isabel Hall's father.

The thought jolted her. He had to be persuaded to keep quiet — he had to, for everyone's sake. But how could she ensure that? If the news did come out, so would the reason for David's suicide, and that Isabel was determined to avoid. Suddenly alarmed, she began to run back, not to Kensington, but to Holland Park, her feet striking the pavements to the rhythm of her heart.

★ ★ ★

He was sitting on the dais in the studio, drinking a pot of tea, his bare feet stretched out in front of him.

'Christ!' he said, as Isabel's head appeared over the studio steps. 'Nemesis.'

'Oh stop it, Stanton,' she replied, walking into the studio and standing before him.

'Is it raining, or have you just broken out in a sweat?' he asked, leaning back and regarding her damp hair thoughtfully.

459

Isabel ignored the comment. 'I wanted to have a word with you — '

'So get on with it, I've got Geraldine Monty-Flynn coming at ten.'

'I want to ask you for a favour, Stanton,' she said.

'Well, why not? After all, I'm sure I must owe you one, even though your mother's true life confessions meant that Prossie dumped me.' He sighed. 'I've been fucking lonely.'

Struggling to keep her patience, Isabel knelt down on the studio floor in front of him. Stanton looked tired, his sense of mischief gone out, like a night light suddenly extinguished.

'Stanton . . . I don't want anyone to know that you're my father.'

'Why?' he asked mockingly. 'Are you ashamed of your dear old dad?'

She took in her breath, studying him. Stanton seemed older, all passion spent.

'Stanton, it's not that — '

' — oh shit, don't snow me! Of course it is,' he replied, putting down the empty mug and leaning towards her. 'You want everyone to think you're David Hall's little girl.'

'I loved him.'

'Sure, we all did,' Stanton replied drily. 'Your mother was just crazy about him — '

'Shut up!' Isabel snapped violently. 'Please . . .' Her voice dropped again. She was still kneeling on the studio floor. 'David was, to all intents and purposes, my father. It would do no one any good if the truth came out.'

'Oh, I don't know. I might like to brag about

my famous Isabel — and about my conquest of Mount Virginia.'

'Stanton, please . . . ' Isabel said, her voice low. She was startled by his bitterness. 'Please, do this for me. You must feel some guilt — your actions made David take his life — '

'That was his frigging choice!' Stanton said sharply. 'Dear God, if I'd committed suicide every time a woman cheated on me — '

'David wasn't like you,' Isabel said reasonably. 'He cared for my mother in his own way, and he loved us — we were his life — '

' — especially you.'

She nodded. 'Yes, especially me. He thought I was special and he gave me such a wonderful childhood . . . You can't know how much I loved him. He was everything to me.'

Stanton gazed up at the studio ceiling. 'He used to bang on about you too, on and on, like there was no other kid in the world.' He glanced back at Isabel. 'It used to make me feel jealous sometimes.' He paused, then added savagely, 'It seems funny to think that you were my child all the time.'

Isabel winced. 'Stanton, please let this remain a secret between us. Please . . . '

'I might, and then again, I might not.'

Her patience broke. 'Why do you want to tell the truth? What the hell would you gain by it?'

He raised his eyebrows. 'Revenge? I lost Prossie because of you.'

Isabel wasn't sure if he was serious, or not.

'How the hell did I end up being the villain of the piece?' she snarled. 'I have every right to hate

461

you, Stanton, for what you did, both to me and to David. Instead, I've been reasonable — '

'Hah!' Stanton replied, sitting upright and staring directly into her face. 'How would you like it if your child didn't want to know you?'

They both flinched at the words, and then slowly Isabel began to smile. 'Oh dear, that's not a very convincing argument, is it?'

He looked away, suddenly defeated. All his temper and energy folded inward, and he seemed suddenly smaller. In that instant Isabel felt real pity for him.

'I feel bloody old,' he said impatiently. 'I miss that woman. I miss Prossie.' He wiped his hand across his mouth; almost as though he wanted to wipe the words away. 'She was my life damn you! You scared her away from me.' He got to his feet, turning his back on Isabel. 'I love her, and I thought we'd stay together. I love the kids and I miss her.' The studio rocked with his misery. 'Jesus, nothing matters any more. 'I can't be bothered screwing around — I'm too old. I don't want to have to prove myself.' He glanced back at Isabel. 'Don't get me wrong, kid, I'm glad you're mine. You're a great girl, but you're grown up — and you're right, you'll always be David's daughter, not mine.' He hung his head. His face seemed slack with weariness. 'I never gave a stuff for anyone. Not once, in all my life. And now I've got what I deserve.' He smiled wryly. 'I've turned into a parody of myself . . . David would have loved that.'

Isabel got to her feet slowly. 'Stanton, listen, I — '

He cut her off immediately. 'Oh, save it! I hate bleeding sympathy. I'll survive, even if I do end up in a bath chair, farting on the seashore in Brighton.'

She laughed suddenly and took his arm.

Surprised by the tenderness of her action, he glanced down at her right hand and his fingers covered hers. 'How is the hand?'

'Fine.'

'Sure?'

She nodded. 'Yes, sure.'

'I won't tell anyone, Isabel,' he said quietly. 'Your secret is safe with me.'

She stretched up and kissed him lightly on the cheek. His skin was unwashed, stale. 'Thank you.'

'But . . . ' He trailed off.

'Yes?'

Stanton's eyes fixed on his daughter. For an instant he seemed vulnerable, and her heart shifted. 'If you can, Isabel . . . only if you can. Try and get Prossie to come home . . . tell her . . . oh, shit, you know.'

Isabel nodded. 'Yes, I know.'

29

Max Henderson arrived home and slammed the door behind him, wincing as it banged shut. Immediately, Mrs Gunn came into the hall and looked at him questioningly.

'Mr Henderson? Is everything all right?'

'Fine, thank you,' he replied, walking into the drawing room. 'You can have the night off, if you like.'

She hesitated in the doorway. 'Isn't Mrs Henderson coming back for the weekend?'

'No,' he said simply, turning back to the housekeeper. 'She's not feeling too well, so she's staying with her parents for a while.'

Mrs Gunn nodded sympathetically. 'Then I'll make you something — '

'No, don't bother,' he said quietly, 'I'm going to do some work upstairs. I'll probably get myself a bite to eat later.'

She nodded and left.

He waited until he could no longer hear her footsteps and then flopped on to one of the chintz settees, his head leaning back again the cushions. Damn Caroline! he thought, after all the money he had spent on this house, she never wanted to be there. Always with her parents, or ill, or busy with committees — always anywhere but here. He closed his eyes, then, suddenly impatient, got to his feet again and made his way upstairs.

He hadn't seen Isabel Hall for several weeks — avoiding her in reality, just as he tried to avoid thinking of her. He was married, he didn't need complications. I love Caroline, he told himself, and she needs me . . . Flicking on the light, he moved into his office and then stopped dead. In front of him, over the fireplace, was a painting, a letter on the table underneath.

The picture was of four people, two men in deep discussion, a woman watching them and a child gazing out at him. It had an air of unreality, although the people seemed luminously real, and he found it difficult to drag his eyes away long enough to read Isabel's letter.

Dear Mr Henderson,
This is a painting which I had already finished — I was going to keep it, but after our talk the other day it seemed perfect for your room. Please tell me if it's not suitable, and I will, of course, paint you something else.

Max glanced at the painting. The child's eyes fixed on his and he felt suddenly as though it had always been there. Isabel Hall was a clever woman, he realised, the picture was exactly what he had wanted.

I am already working on the designs for the mural for the first floor corridor — I should be ready to start work next week. I'm afraid it will take some time to complete — a couple of months, at least, during which time I will be working on the other paintings you commissioned.

He felt unreasonably pleased by the thought of her working in his house, even though he would be seldom there — after all, someone should be making use of the property he had worked so hard to afford.

Mrs Gunn has been very helpful so, unless I hear otherwise, I will begin work next week. Kindest regards,

Isabel Hall

He folded the letter and put it in his desk, then looked out on to the garden. He tried to imagine Caroline walking across the lawn, her fair skin shielded with a hat, her arms freckling with the sun, her movements unhurried. That was what had first attracted him to her; her fragility and her stillness. Having hustled all his life to get to the top in the media, he saw her as a millpond, her calmness steadying him. She had been sweet too, unlike the usual aggressive women he met, and he had loved that, spoiling her and promising her the world. As all lovers do.

But due to some quirk in her nature the world turned inwards on Caroline, and after they had been married for four years, she suffered her first nervous breakdown, the second following two years later. Another man would have resented her dependence but Max didn't, and in collaboration with her parents Caroline was lovingly coaxed back to life. When he was away, she went home; and when he was back in England, she left her parents and returned to him. Usually . . . but not always.

Strangely enough, it was the upturn in Max's fortunes which affected Caroline adversely. She felt threatened by his success, by the new home he had created for her, the high-profile life he now led, and stayed with her parents. Without understanding that he was alienating her, Max worked harder to give her more; whilst Caroline pined for the uncomplicated past and dreaded the future he offered. Not that she told him that. So by remaining silent, he thought he was pleasing her; and she was too afraid of losing him to admit the truth. Max's eyes remained fixed on the garden. No birds sang, no dogs ran down the lawns, and no children wandered amongst the expensively tended flower beds. On a whim, Max turned and glanced at the child in the painting and wondered how long it would be before he would have a child of his own; how long before he could watch his own son running through his spectacular house.

⋆　⋆　⋆

'So how did Stanton look?' Prossie asked, lifting You Too off the table in The Ridings kitchen.

'He looked old.'

'Good!' she said peevishly, turning to Bracken as the girl ran in from the garden.

'When are we going home?' she asked, picking the cat up clumsily. It wriggled in her arms.

467

'I don't know, sweetheart,' Prossie responded. 'Hold the cat properly.'

'But I want to go home now . . . ' Bracken moaned, Eloise siding with her sister.

'Now hush!' Prossie replied, surprised. 'You like it here, don't you?'

Isabel glanced at the girls, waiting for their response.

'Yes . . . but it's not like home . . . '

'But you've been so happy here,' Prossie reasoned. 'Why get upset now?'

Isabel turned to Eleanor and raised her eyebrows. 'Can you take the girls shopping? I want to talk to Prossie.'

Both women waited until the kitchen door closed and then Prossie looked at Isabel suspiciously. 'Why the sudden yearning to be gone? They were fine until yesterday.'

'Stanton phoned here last night,' Isabel said.

'What!'

'Hang on, I didn't know about it — but he had a chat with the kids, and so now — '

' — they miss him,' Prossie finished for her. 'How bloody typical of Stanton to try and get to me through the kids.'

'And through me,' Isabel admitted.

'Through YOU?'

She nodded. 'I saw him, as I told you — he wanted me to ask you to go back to him . . . I hadn't got around to mentioning it.'

'You hadn't got around to mentioning it!' Prossie repeated incredulously. 'What the hell is the matter with you — do you want me to go back to him?'

468

'I want you to do what you want — '

' — really?'

'Yes, really,' Isabel replied, ignoring the sarcasm in Prossie's voice. 'He loves you.'

'Hah!'

'And you love him too.'

'I *did* love him,' Prossie said coldly, 'but not now — and how come you're taking his side?' she asked. 'A little while ago you hated the mortal sight of him.'

'I don't like what he did — '

'But you're coming to terms with it?'

Isabel's temper flashed. 'Hey, come on!' she snapped. 'What do you want me to say? I didn't know about him and my mother; it's not my fault what happened.'

Prossie had the grace to look abashed. 'I just can't think of him the same way any more,' she admitted. 'I just keep seeing him with your mother — and then I remember that he's your father.' She rested her head on her arms on the kitchen table. 'It was all so easy before — now it seems so . . . embarrassing.'

'Why?' Isabel asked softly. 'I don't think of him as my father.'

'But I do!' Prossie moaned. 'Trouble is, I still miss him. I thought I wouldn't, but I do.' She turned her head and glanced at Isabel. 'I miss the studio — do you remember that model who took Stanton's money? And Lady Sherwood?' Isabel nodded. 'And the way Stanton made those sandwiches that night? Just before you had Sybella.'

Again Isabel nodded, but her mind went back

to the way the studio had looked the previous day — darker and grimmer. Prossie had been the light for Stanton; just as she had been the light for David Hall. With a shudder of premonition, Isabel realised what Prossie's absence truly meant to Stanton Feller.

'I miss the smell of paint . . . and sleeping next to him,' Prossie went on. 'He use to rub my stomach every night when I was carrying the kids . . . ' Her eyes flickered with sudden anger. 'But I also remember him making love to that flaming Greek whore too . . . oh, yes, I remember all the women . . . '

Isabel stroked her friend's hair gently. 'Do you still love him?'

Prossie closed her eyes. She seemed for an instant to be about to fall asleep, and then she said simply, 'He is my heart.'

★ ★ ★

It took quite a while for the workmen to set up the scaffolding on the first floor of Max Henderson's house. With agonising slowness, they erected the platform upon which Isabel would work, and then asked her to try it. She did so and pronounced it safe, after testing it thoroughly before they left. She then carried her drawings and charcoal up and stood for several minutes, thoughtfully regarding the blank wall. The area had been replastered so that it was prepared for the tempera paint, and it looked inviting as well as daunting. Confidently, Isabel glanced at her drawings.

470

Almost immediately, Mrs Gunn materialised to see how things were progressing. 'Is there anything you want?' she asked, looking at the wall and the scaffolding in amazement.

'No, nothing yet, thanks,' Isabel replied cheerfully.

The woman put her head on one side. 'You see, Mr Henderson said I was to make sure you were well provided for.'

'I am,' Isabel said patiently. 'I'm just about to start. I'll be down later.'

'Well, if you're sure . . . ' Mrs Gunn replied, reluctantly moving off.

Almost as though she was performing a ritual, Isabel paused, closed her eyes, and worked her right hand for nearly a minute — opening and closing the fingers — then she began. Within a couple of hours she had the first outlines marked out in charcoal, the corridor coming to life as a scene began to take shape. Supple and fit, she stretched up to reach the highest areas, then descended the scaffolding to draw in the figures at normal height.

She whistled softly under her breath, always happy as she worked, and was surprised when Mrs Gunn appeared with her lunch on a tray.

'It's one o'clock, dear, time to eat.'

'Already?' Isabel asked, pulling off her headscarf and sitting down on top of the stairs.

'Oh, you are coming on,' the housekeeper said, peering round the corridor. 'You must eat though, to keep up your strength. I'm always saying that to Mr Henderson, but he doesn't listen. A big man like that should eat well. But what can you do?' She smiled, a thin woman in her late fifties. 'He won't be bothering you though — he doesn't spend much time here. And if he does come to his office, he'll use the back stairs.'

'So you don't see much of him?' Isabel asked, curious to know how much time Max Henderson spent at home, especially as she had received no reply to her letter.

'No, not much — he likes to be with his wife as much as possible, and she hasn't settled here yet. She's a very frail woman, you see, and he's devoted to her.' Mrs Gunn looked at Isabel's plate. 'Now come on, eat up. You need to keep well.'

Isabel smiled and dutifully ate her meal, passing the tray back to Mrs Gunn and mounting the scaffolding again, her mind churning over what she had been told. So Caroline Henderson was a frail woman, she thought, and her husband was devoted to her. A quick prickle of jealousy slid over her — how she would have liked a caring husband after the attack.

Angry with herself, she sighed and began to work again, her thoughts soon fading as the figures in the mural crept slowly down the corridor walls. At five she was still working, and by seven she was exhausted. In the silent house she rubbed her neck and shoulders, wandering over to the window and looking out into the darkening garden. The scaffolding rose over her head like the vaulted ceiling of a church, the white dust sheets spread out along the carpet like a wedding train, and as Isabel turned back to look at her work she was suddenly startled by a figure at the end of the hall.

She blinked but the figure had gone, and yet she was certain, quite certain, it had been Max Henderson.

★ ★ ★

Ted Cavendish expressed his outrage loudly to everyone who would listen, knowing full well that he had a captive audience in Sterling Thompson and a variety of other dealers all of whom were obsessed by the same piece of news. Isabel Hall was trying to collect funds to set up an Institute — it was laughable, who the hell did she think she was, some artist trying to make herself immortal?

'Well, I suppose she's just hedging her bets — after all, if she doesn't get the brass ring with her work, she can have another go at it with her blasted school.'

'I don't know why it bothers you so much,' Baye Fortunas replied evenly. 'Perhaps it's simply that she has some very wealthy and influential friends?'

Ted Cavendish gave the Greek a slow look. The art world was in a perilous state, and competition between the dealers was fierce. Only a year before, spectacular sales had made prices rocket, so much so that a hundred thousand pounds for a painting had become the norm — but the recession had set in and people had stopped buying. Now any dealer who sold a painting for ten thousand pounds celebrated. The last thing anyone wanted was for the small amounts of money available to go to other sources — like Isabel Hall's school.

'Baye, you know as well as I do that Isabel will never pull this off in the present climate.'

The Greek sipped his white wine thoughtfully. 'I wouldn't be so sure, Ted. You see, Isabel is a very determined lady, and she sees this school as a monument to her father.'

'She should buy him a bigger headstone and be done with it,' Cavendish replied sourly, then changed his tone when he saw the look on Baye's face. Calm down, he told himself, this man is a buyer. 'I'm sorry, Baye, but things are hard at the moment, and so many galleries are closing.'

'About time,' he replied evenly. 'You had a good run at it for a long while. All the dealers here and in New York were overcharging — '

'We charged what the market would stand.'

'So don't be surprised that the market has now folded,' Baye replied coolly. 'No one could maintain prices like that — you put paintings out of the reach of nearly everyone,' he continued. 'I have no sympathy for you.'

Ted Cavendish took in his breath, but his face was impassive as he asked, 'Have you put any money into Isabel Hall's little scheme?'

The Greek's eyes flickered with irritation. The question was in bad taste. 'That is my business, not yours.'

'She'll never pull it off,' Cavendish persisted meanly.

'She will. She has guts — and a powerful name.'

'Hall?' he queried. 'Oh yes, it's a very good

name, but along with its intellectual kudos goes a certain emotional drawback.' He avoided Baye's eyes, but his malice was such that he was unable to stop himself continuing. 'After all, David Hall killed himself . . . It seems odd to set up a school in the name of a man who committed suicide.'

In disgust, Baye laid down his glass and walked to the door. 'You know, Ted,' he said, pausing and turning to face the dealer, 'Isabel Hall is building that school in the name of her father; out of love for him. In time no one will remember that David Hall killed himself — but they *will* remember the love which made the building possible.' He studied Ted Cavendish's face. 'I'm going to help Isabel all I can, because I want to see her dream made reality — and I know plenty of other people who will agree with me.'

Ivy Messenger was one. She liked Isabel and found her character intriguing — a heady mixture of confidence and pathos. She also knew that Max Henderson was fascinated by her and was mischievously delighted to see her plan being acted out. If she had any guilty feelings they were momentary; Max Henderson and Isabel Hall were two gifted and strong-minded people — it was inevitable they should like each other.

In her wheelchair, Ivy shifted her position and reached out for the glass beside her. Of course she didn't want to break up the Henderson marriage — despite what Sunny de Souza said. No, she just wanted to stir it up a little, get that painfully docile Caroline up and fighting. Ivy sipped her water and grimaced, it was warm, grown musty over the afternoon. Her one good eye glanced out to the Thames — really, some women didn't deserve their men. There was Isabel, a good-looking, brilliant woman, with no one; and there was Caroline, sickly and indulged, with Max Henderson.

Her thoughts shifted suddenly to Isabel's dream, the Institute she spoke about constantly. Horse feathers! Ivy thought and chuckled to herself. It would take years to raise the money, and even if she did, would the place be a success? How many gifted children were there, for God's sake? Didn't they all spend their time these days watching videos and sniffing glue? Oh, Isabel, she thought indulgently, you must be crazy to think you can pull it off.

'You know why she's doing it, don't you?' Sunny asked her the previous evening. 'She wants to be a mother figure, the Earth Goddess, to all these children — just to make up for her lack of success with Sybella.'

'How spiteful of you, Sunny,' Ivy had countered, glancing across the room to where an animated Isabel was talking to Dimitri Michelous and his French wife. It was obvious from her gestures and the expression on her face that she was talking about the school. You should have a man to take you to bed and make you look like that, Ivy thought; dreams make dull lovers.

'How much have you donated?'

Sunny sniffed loudly. 'I'm thinking about it. I have to talk to my business advisers.'

476

'I know you make all the decisions, Sunny, so don't try and fool me.'

Her eyes flicked pure steel and she glanced away. 'Anyway, if Isabel manages to get money from these people she won't need me — if Baye Fortunas and Dmitri Michelous invest in her scheme she'll be well away.'

Ivy could not resist her next few words. 'And of course there's always Gyman.'

Sunny's eyes bulged uncomfortably. 'Gyman! No, you're mistaken, Gyman isn't investing.'

'Oh but he is. He told me so,' Ivy replied, smiling sweetly as Sunny scuttered over to her son.

It was all going very well, she thought to herself. Oh yes, even allowing for the fact that half the people who promised to donate would drop out later. Her glance moved across the room, passing Gyman and his mother in fierce discussion, passing Baye Fortunas, and finally resting on Isabel again. She studied the younger woman's profile as she talked, Isabel's hands moving all the time, trying to sell her dream to Michelous. Her eyes were vivid with enthusiasm, her slim body turned towards his, all the power of her personality forcing the man to listen to her.

God she is like her mother, Ivy thought, and then remembered David Hall, searching his daughter's face for any resemblance to the dead man. But there was none. Despite his daughter's love for him, she had inherited none of his physical characteristics. Ivy frowned and leaned forward in her wheelchair. No, there was no similarity at all, and yet as she watched Isabel talk, Ivy became aware that she reminded her of someone else. She frowned, trying to remember whom, watching Isabel's hands move, watching the tilt of her head. Someone else has that expression, she thought, suddenly intrigued, someone else holds their head at that angle. But who? Who?

Ivy Messenger sighed with exasperation and leaned back in her wheelchair. The moment had gone, now she looked at Isabel and saw no hint of anyone else. Yet the irritating thought kept fluttering through Ivy's head. Who did Isabel remind her of?

★ ★ ★

'How's it going?' Max called out, Isabel turning at the top of the scaffolding to glance down at him.

'OK, but there's a long way to go.'

He nodded and, aware that he wanted to say something else, Isabel climbed down, a brush in her hand.

'I don't peep, you know,' he said. 'I read somewhere that artists hate anyone seeing their work until it's finished.'

Isabel smiled easily. He was a good six inches taller than her and she had to glance up at him. 'Michelangelo started that. He couldn't bear anyone seeing what he was doing in the Sistine Chapel.' She jerked her head towards the ceiling. 'Not that this is quite in his league.'

Max smiled, but was obviously ill at ease. He

had watched her sometimes, when she wasn't aware of it, and after a while he had found himself making excuses to return to the house just to see her. Before long he could hardly tear himself away from the sight of her, concentrating as she stretched up to paint, her T-shirt coming free of her jeans, a few inches of smooth white skin unnerving him. Then sometimes she kicked off her shoes, and would pad about barefoot, her small feet with their varnished nails shuffling along the ladders and scaffolding.

Her body mesmerised him, as did the very scent of her. Indeed all the intimate gestures she performed, not knowing she was observed, became magnetic and he would wait for them. The opening and closing of her right hand, and the way she tied up her hair, her neck damp with perspiration, a few curls sticking to the moist skin. He found himself so attracted to her that he could no longer be near her, afraid he might give himself away. But when he was alone he fantasised about her, feeling an immediate rush of guilt when he remembered Caroline.

He had brought her to the house the previous evening, helping her out of the car and waiting for her reaction to the new decorations. Trying to please him, Caroline had looked around, her small face with its over-large eyes taking in every detail. But although she seemed excited, she felt suffocatingly anxious — a beautiful house would be a showcase; Max would want to bring business people here, and he would want her to entertain them . . .

'Darling?'

She glanced up at her husband. 'Sorry, what did you say?'

'I asked what you thought,' Max said patiently, guiding her into the drawing room.

'It's lovely . . . and this looks wonderful,' Caroline said, touching the back of the suite she had chosen in Harrods.

Max smiled. 'It's been here all week — '

'I couldn't get down before today,' she said, immediately on the defensive.

Max was quick to placate her. 'I wasn't criticising you, darling,' he said simply, 'I was just looking forward to having you here with me. I miss you when you're away.'

Caroline smiled, her relief almost palpable, but as she continued to look round, Max thought about the conversation he had had with her father the previous evening. Apparently Caroline had been unsettled, her nervousness more apparent than usual. Max had listened, always patient, and always attentive to what his father-in-law said — after all he was a doctor, he of all people knew the warning signs.

'So you like the house?' Max asked his wife, his heart aching for approval. 'I don't suppose you ever thought we'd have a home like this when we first met?'

Caroline glanced away. They had been introduced by a mutual friend when Caroline was working as a medical secretary, Max an up-and-coming television producer. Their immediate rapport had come as a surprise to everyone — except them. Having no family, Max was looking for a woman to protect and cherish; and

Caroline was looking for a man to admire and rely upon. They were perfectly matched.

'The house is beautiful,' Caroline said simply, without answering the question.

'I want you to be happy. It's important to me,' Max said softly, taking her hand. 'Come and live here, Caroline. I miss you.'

She smiled but moved away, her eyes flicking to the painting over the fireplace. 'Oh, I like that.'

Max followed her gaze abstractedly. 'Yes, it's good . . . very good.' He felt disappointed and faintly irritated with her. 'And I'd like you to have a portrait done, Caroline, which we can hang in here.'

Blushing, Caroline lowered her head, laughing softly. 'Oh, I couldn't sit for a picture, Max,' she said. 'I'd be embarrassed . . . Besides, who'd want a picture of me?'

He lifted her chin and tilted up her face, forcing her to look at him. 'I want a picture of you, Caroline, because I love you.'

Suddenly her eyes fixed on his and a fierce jolt of anxiety went through him. Ten years of marriage, ten years of Caroline's gentleness and mental uncertainty, filled him with a desperate desire to protect her and he pulled her to him, his arms around his wife, his large body shielding hers.

★ ★ ★

Max loved his wife. She needed him. If he left her, she would die. Because Caroline could never cope. Not like Isabel, who it seemed could cope with anything. Death, violence and a crucifying workload did not faze her — but what did, he wondered, what did? Where was her Achilles heel? There had to be one. No one was that strong, no one, unless they were superficial — and he did not think Isabel Hall was that.

'Is Mrs Gunn looking after you?' he asked her now. A banal question, but what else could he say?

Isabel nodded, a little of her hair fell on to one shoulder. He felt a rush of longing. 'She's marvellous.'

'Good,' he said inanely, 'you see, I'll be away for the rest of the week — '

'I'm sorry,' Isabel said truthfully. 'I would have liked some company.'

He frowned and for an instant wondered if she was poking fun at him. But her expression was genuine.

'D'you get lonely?'

'Not when I'm working,' she admitted, 'but when I've finished for the day, then I get kind of morose.' She pulled a face. 'All artists are headcases.'

Max hesitated for only an instant. 'I was just going to have a drink, do you want to join me?'

The painting over the study fireplace looked down impassively at Isabel as Max fixed the drinks and she stood awkwardly in the centre of the room. He passed her her glass and motioned for her to sit down, then sat himself in a chair opposite to hers.

'I heard something about you wanting to open a school,' he said cautiously.

482

Equally cautious, Isabel responded, 'That's right. For gifted children. You know, the ones who are good at the arts and get picked on at school for being soft. Especially the boys. So many well meaning fathers think that boys should play rugby and cricket and steer well clear from the art room. 'It makes them poofy'!' she concluded, mimicking one of the male teachers she had spoken to.

Max laughed. She loved the sound, loud and confident.

'I'm sorry,' he admitted, 'but I hated art myself, I was one of the kids playing rugby.' He tapped his nose. 'That's how this got broken.'

'It doesn't look broken,' Isabel replied, studying it carefully. 'Did you have it fixed?'

He smiled at the thought. 'Plastic surgery? Are you joking? With this face, a broken nose was an improvement.'

She wanted to say that it was a grand face, but lacked the courage, and instead sipped her drink and glanced up at the picture.

'I'm glad you liked it. I kept expecting a letter to tell me to take it away.'

Max's eyes followed hers. 'It's just what I wanted, but I didn't know how to tell you so. I don't articulate myself very clearly, do I?'

Isabel smiled sympathetically. 'You get by.'

'In business, yes.'

'Just business?'

The air was static.

'Men are usually better at talking about business than feelings,' he said and winced inwardly, aware that his words had a double meaning.

Awkwardly, he glanced at the painting. 'You see, the picture moves me.' As you do, he wanted to add.

Isabel drained her glass. The room was suddenly silent, both of them holding their breath. Get out, she said to herself, the last thing you need is an affair with a married man. You'll only be hurt and hurt others. Get out.

'Thanks for the drink,' she said, getting to her feet and smiling.

He was relieved and agonised at the same time.

'It was a pleasure,' he said, following her to the door. 'I'll see you soon anyway. Incidentally, my wife is coming down again next week with me.'

Isabel nodded, her voice suddenly gone. 'I'm sure she'll be thrilled with your progress. I am.'

* * *

Prossie smacked You Too off the table, and the cat fell four-footed on to the kitchen floor before running out of the back door, Eloise running after her.

'Blasted cat!' she snapped, turning back to Isabel, her eyes wide with temper. 'I've had a letter from Stanton.'

Isabel smiled faintly. 'Oh yes?'

'Don't oh yes me!' Prossie responded sharply. 'He writes a good letter, I'll give him that. All promises and hearts and flowers. I suppose he's run out of washing and the sink's piled high with bloody unwashed china otherwise he wouldn't have written.' She flapped the letter in front of

Isabel. 'The studio's in chaos and he threw a sitter out yesterday — what kind of bloody sense does that make in these times? He needs the money — I need the money for the kids.'

'So talk to him.'

'Talk to him!' Prossie repeated, sitting down at the table. 'I don't want to . . . not really . . . well, maybe I do. You see, the kids miss him, and he can't cope on his own . . . Don't look at me like that!'

Isabel raised her eyebrows. 'Listen, Prossie, you don't owe me anything. If you want to go back to him, go. If you want to stay here, stay. But for God's sake, make up your mind.'

'He's your father.'

'I don't think of him like that,' Isabel countered, 'so why should it matter to you?'

'He betrayed David — '

Isabel nodded. 'I know, you don't have to tell me that. But Stanton was good to me when I needed help, and I can't forget that either. I won't pretend to you that things will be the way they were — I couldn't stay at the studio any more. Not now. But we can still be friends.' Her hand clasped Prossie's. 'If you love him, go back.'

'And what about you?' Prossie asked. 'When are you going to meet someone?'

Isabel's eyes flickered momentarily and Prossie brightened. 'You've met someone! Oh, great — '

'He's married.'

'Oh, shit.'

Isabel laughed shortly. 'Yeah, oh shit. He's

everything I ever wanted in a man. He is successful, charming, smart, and . . . married.'

'Happily?'

Isabel nodded. 'Yes. He is apparently devoted to his wife and she is not very . . . robust.'

Prossie frowned. 'Huh?'

'She's fragile and relies on him a lot.'

'Oh, that kind,' Prossie said enigmatically.

'Don't say things like that!' Isabel countered. 'He's married, end of story.'

Prossie frowned, acutely disappointed. 'You sure?'

'As sure as sure can be,' Isabel replied, jumping with fright as You Too leapt on to the table next to her.

'GET OFF! Blasted flea bag!' Prossie shouted, throwing Stanton's crumpled letter at the defiant cat.

★ ★ ★

Isabel worked on in Max Henderson's house, then found after a week that her imagination faltered on the mural and so she turned to the commissioned works for his study. She went up to the second floor and into Max's private suite when she knew he was away on business. The room smelt of polish due to Mrs Gunn's daily ministrations, and the desk top was cleared of papers, giving the place a curiously empty look. Isabel glanced round at the wall on her left, then noticed the two doors, and after a moment's hesitation, opened the first.

It led into a small kitchen, which surprised

her, as did the fridge stocked with white wine, salad, and cheese. The sink was clear, the oven untouched. But the chopping board showed signs of use, as did the knives and the grill. Frowning, Isabel walked back into the study and opened the second door.

She flicked on the light and a large 1930s-style bathroom faced her, one wall covered with mirrors, a large bath in the centre, the other walls black marble. It was most definitely a man's choice of bathroom; the towels were plain white; the soap unscented; and the few bottles in the cabinet consisted of aftershave and mouthwash. Nothing feminine; no sign of a wife at all. Puzzled, Isabel turned off the light and closed the door.

Her attention then turned to the door on the far right of the study and she began to move towards it, then paused, amazed by her own curiosity. Glancing round guiltily she opened this door too, walking into a darkened room and feeling for the light switch. Finally she found a lamp and turned it on, taking in her breath. She had not expected a bedroom — a storeroom perhaps, but not a bedroom.

The walls were dark wood, panelled like the study walls, the ceiling quite low so that the heavy four-poster bed in the centre looked squat and over-large in the room. A dark red spread was thrown across the bed, matching the curtains and the hangings, but apart from a fireplace on the opposite wall there was no decoration. The room seemed oddly mediaeval, the floor uncarpeted, the boards varnished, a large rug by one side of the bed. On his side, she thought, so that he would step on to it in the morning when he woke. Isabel walked over to it, and unthinkingly, slipped her feet out of her shoes and stepped on to the rug. It felt thin, almost cool to her skin and she suddenly jumped back, wondering what on earth she was doing.

Flustered, Isabel pulled on her shoes and hurried out of the bedroom, the door banging shut behind her. Back in the study she tried to settle herself, taking several deep breaths and glancing round, anxious not to leave any clues of her prying. The painting over the study fireplace watched her, the child gazing impassively out of the frame.

'He's splendid.'

Isabel jumped and spun round quickly.

'I'm sorry,' Max said, 'I seem to make a habit of startling you.'

Isabel coloured. Had he watched her snooping? Her voice was strained when she answered him. 'I was just . . . trying to work out what kind of paintings would look best in here.'

'You'll be hard pressed to do anything as good as this one,' Max said easily, 'it has real quality.' He glanced at the painting again. 'I like the child in particular. You're good at painting children.'

'Thank you,' Isabel said, regaining her composure.

'But that's not surprising, is it? After all, you have a daughter.'

Isabel nodded. 'Sybella.'

He looked back at the child in the painting as he continued. 'I envy you that. I love children.'

He turned as he said it, and their eyes met. Isabel's were fixed, without seeing him, the memory of the attack and the magnolia blossom coming back with terrifying clarity. The attack which had rendered her sterile. No more blossom, only the dead twigs of what might have been.

'Are you all right?' he asked, suddenly alarmed by the look on her face.

She remained mute. Caught somewhere between desire and memory.

'Here, sit down,' he said, leading her to a chair and passing her a brandy. 'You've been working too hard.'

She glanced at him, and he saw that her hazel eyes were flecked with green lights. Like flames.

'Go on, drink it,' he ordered, so close that he could smell the scent of her hair, freshly washed. Her hand shook and he held the glass for her. 'Sip it. There, that's right.'

He wants children, she thought, suddenly remembering all her own pain in one instant. A man's longing for his own child made her recall her own longing and her heart was ripped with pain. Isabel closed her eyes. Oh God, I thought I'd got over this.

'Look, you're in no state to go home tonight, you can stay here,' Max said, adding quickly, 'No strings, I'm just offering you somewhere to stay.'

Isabel nodded, in silent agreement.

'Good,' he replied, going out of the room and returning a few minutes later. 'Mrs Gunn has it all arranged. There's a room for you on the first floor. You'll be very comfortable, I'm sure.'

Isabel struggled to her feet and smiled half-heartedly. 'I didn't have much lunch today,' she lied, 'and I was suddenly lightheaded.' She shrugged, full of weary charm. 'Sorry if I made a fool of myself.'

'You didn't,' he said and smiled.

Yet when she walked off he watched her and wondered. Something he had said had triggered a violent response. Isabel Hall's Achilles heel had been revealed, but he could not identify the precise words which had exposed her weakness. His mind ran on frantically, but even when he closed the study door and glanced back at the painting, he was none the wiser.

30

Sybella stared out of the school window, her hands on the radiator, her eyes fixed on the school gate. Beside her lay a letter from Eleanor and a photograph of The Ridings, the figure of Blair tiny in the distance. Sighing, Sybella glanced at it and then glanced away quickly. She had heard the teachers talking about her the previous night, discussing her after lights out, not realising she was listening in the dark corridor by the toilets.

'. . . looking for love, that's what it was. Just a phase,' one said confidently. 'Most girls go through a stage like that, and after all, Sybella's not had a normal upbringing, it was obvious that she would look for affection.'

The second voice was curious. 'Yes, but do you know all the details?'

'Well, not *all* the details,' she admitted reluctantly. 'One hears rumours, that's all.'

The second teacher was unimpressed, and her tone implied it. 'Oh,' she said simply.

'Sybella Gray is *promiscuous*,' the first woman said, emphasising the word, obviously anxious to revive some interest in the topic, 'but that's all I know for sure. You know what I mean though — she's boy crazy.'

In the dark corridor, Sybella closed her eyes disbelievingly. Boy crazy. Blair a boy? Well, maybe more so than others . . . but they were wrong to make it sound so dirty . . . so wrong. Her heart thumped uncomfortably in her chest. Blair had been kind to her, so she had been kind to him — in her own way. She had the right to find affection where she could, hadn't she? After all, until recently her mother had shown little interest in her. But now things were changing . . . a rush of warmth flooded over Sybella. Yes, lately her mother had included her in her plans for the Institute and had started to make her feel as if she was proud of her — instead of ashamed. Sybella shook her head. Oh yes, she knew now that she had been wrong to behave like that with Blair — but that was in the past, it was the present that mattered.

'It's in the blood, that kind of behaviour,' one of the teachers said suddenly, interrupting Sybella's thoughts and pulling her attention back with a jolt. 'I suppose she did it to make herself feel important. It's a shame, but you see, I doubt if she has either her mother or her grandmother's strength of character.'

At that moment Sybella walked out of her hiding place and defiantly looked the teacher square in the face. The woman faltered, hugely embarrassed as she watched the girl walk off, straight-backed. In that instant, Sybella Gray came into her own.

★ ★ ★

The Ridings was quiet under an autumn sun, the light glinting on the windows, the first leaf falls mottling the lawn. Far away, a few cars drove towards Skipton or South Stainley, the sounds of their engines coming only faintly down the drive to the quiet house. Sybella was home, spending half term with Eleanor, Prossie having finally decided to visit Stanton. She insisted it was only a chance for them to talk, and left her three daughters behind as collateral — or so Eleanor teased her. The girls were easy to cope with, happy in each other's company, as temperamentally stable as Sybella was highly strung.

Yet she had begun to quieten down, apparently finding at last some middle ground where she and her mother could communicate. Gradually she began to accompany Isabel to various functions, always holding back a little, but at times employing her formidable charm to interest people in the scheme. And thankfully her sexuality seemed to be held in check at last — indeed, she even seemed ashamed of her previous actions.

When Sybella returned home to The Ridings for the first time after being sent away to school, Eleanor had been rigid with apprehension as she got out of the taxi, her overnight bag flung over her shoulder. She expected the girl to be embarrassed at least, but she had underestimated Sybella's character. Blair watched her avidly, greedily, and then approached her, Sybella turning and smiling with complete innocence, as though there had never been anything between them but friendship. Eleanor saw Blair falter and then shuffle away, confused, his memories already questioned.

Sybella's homecomings were easier now that she seemed so much more settled. Confidently she would tell Eleanor about the school, even bragging a little about her intelligence, because now that she had been forced to work, her true potential was finally coming out. Her appearance had altered little, although her slight boldness was toned down, and she got on well with Prossie's children. The change in her should have heartened Eleanor, but it intrigued her instead, and she found that though she loved Sybella she felt with her the same unease that she felt with Virginia.

'D'you think Prossie will go back to Stanton?' Sybella asked Eleanor, watching as she dead-headed some late roses in the garden.

'I don't know,' she replied, rubbing her back as she got to her feet.

'I can't imagine him as my grandfather,' Sybella said simply.

Eleanor gave her a sidelong look. 'I find it a little difficult myself,' she replied, thinking immediately of David and glancing over to the window of his study. 'Stanton Feller was never someone I liked.'

'But Isabel worked with him, didn't she? She seemed very keen on him once.'

Eleanor didn't like the tone in the girl's voice and was about to confront her when Sybella deftly changed the subject. She had a habit of doing that. 'Where's Blair? I've hardly seen him.'

'Neither have I, come to think about it,' Eleanor replied, looking round the garden hurriedly. 'He's kept to himself since you came home.' She cursed herself for the words and glanced over to Sybella, but the girl seemed totally unconcerned.

'Does he ever go out alone? I mean, away from the house?'

Eleanor shook her head. 'Only very occasionally. Sometimes he drifts down to the shops, but he's never really had enough confidence to go further.' She paused, thinking. 'Funnily enough though, he has been wandering a little more lately.' She glanced round again and automatically called out for Blair. But there was no reply and she shrugged. 'He'll be back. He just likes his privacy, that's all.'

Blair was, at that moment, walking away from The Ridings towards South Stainley, his big feet pounding the earth as he crossed several fields. He knew where he was going, but not why. He just wanted to get away from the house, and think. Clumsily he rummaged for his cigarettes and lit one, blowing the smoke into the autumnal air, his eyes screwed up against the late sun. He knew the truth, he knew he had made love with Sybella — he blushed fiercely — yet she acted as though nothing had ever happened. Blair ground the newly lighted cigarette under his foot. He couldn't understand it! He wouldn't understand it! It was all wrong, all horrible . . . He had thought she loved him, and yet she seemed hardly to like him any more. Why? Why? he asked himself over and over again.

The answer roared in his ears. Isabel. Isabel had told her daughter to ignore him. She had frightened Sybella away from him. Stolen her away. Isabel Hall was hateful and she was ruining his life! Blair gasped, the pain in his heart as savage as his anger. It was all her fault, he realised, turning his eyes back to the house. It was tiny on the horizon. A child's house, full of childish dreams. It was all Isabel's fault, Blair repeated to himself, and he would make her pay for it! He would take what she loved away from her, he thought, lifting his fist and bringing it down suddenly, in his mind crushing the little house on the skyline.

★ ★ ★

Isabel worked well into the night at the Henderson house. Knowing that he was away, she had slept over the last few days, so that she did not waste time commuting backwards and forwards. The mural took shape, in fact it became more complete and perfect by the day, easily her best work. The reason was obvious, she wanted to please Max Henderson, and so, like a child, she showed off. Look at this, she was saying, haven't I done well? Approve of me . . . And he did, and because she was easy to talk to he began to open up to her, coming in and sitting on the ladder whilst she worked, chatting easily, and gradually putting his own hopes forward for her opinion.

'. . . and so he thinks it'll be a good deal.'

'It sounds like it.' Isabel bent down and stirred her brush in some paint, glancing over to Max. He had loosened his tie, and was sitting, leaning forward with his large hands resting on his knees.

He glanced at her, but Isabel had already looked away, her attention directed towards the painting. And when she didn't look at him, he

496

found it easy to confide.

'I'm going to make an offer for it.'

'Good!' she said simply. 'Now move — I want to paint that bit of wall.'

She would not think of him as anything other than an employer, a friend. She could not afford to; Max was married, and he wanted children. Full stop. Isabel faced up to the facts, she did not like them, but as ever she confronted them. And in confronting them she decided that she wanted to make her mark professionally, to dent his life with her work. When she was no longer there her paintings would remain as her ambassadors; in the drawing room, in the hallway, and in the private suite of rooms in which he worked.

Two months passed and Max spent more and more time at the house, and more time with Isabel. He found that having begun to confide, he could not stop; and she encouraged him to talk. It became apparent quite early on that he was lonely, and that his loneliness was due to his wife. The marriage baffled Isabel, but on the few occasions Max offered any insights, it was clear that he loved his wife. And he had no reason not to love her. Gentle, docile, and in need of protection, Caroline was sweet-tempered and demanded little; the perfect wife for a busy man — or so he had thought. Now he wasn't so sure, a docile wife was easy to live with, but hard to include in his world.

The comparison between Caroline and Isabel was stark. Two totally dissimilar women; one gentle; the other strong. One afraid of the world; the other determined to take it on head first.

Caroline is a shadow woman, Max realised suddenly, looking at Isabel as she blocked in an area of colour on the white wall; Caroline is as insubstantial as this woman is whole, and very much alive. There was no hint of sickness around Isabel, no threat of the need which bound him to his wife. And God how he wanted her.

One night Isabel was sketching late in the study when she was disturbed by a sound downstairs. Startled, Isabel went to the door and listened, knowing that Mrs Gunn had retired for the evening. Cautiously she moved out on to the landing. A floorboard creaked below and she flinched, her heart banging. She waited, holding her breath. Several moments passed, but there were no other sounds, she finally relaxed, turning back into the study — to find Max Henderson standing in the middle of the room.

He seemed about to say something and then shrugged, glancing away.

His head seemed about to explode, his heart thumping, roaring in his ears. Torn between duty and desire, he had tried to resist returning to the house, but had found himself parked out in the drive, then climbing the back stairs to his study, knowing that Isabel was working at the top of the house. He paused, hearing her moving about, and held his breath, one part of him not wanting her to hear him, or to come downstairs. But then something inside him forced him up the stairs, towards her, taking the back steps to his study, where he paused, watching her as she stood, unknowing, on the landing outside.

Go, he willed himself, go, before something

happens. But he couldn't move, all his desire locked inside him and focused on this one woman. Not dependent, not timorous like Caroline, no, living flesh with the scent of hair and skin and sex which tore into his guts like glass slivers.

Then he said her name. 'Isabel.'

She turned, not yet knowing why he was there.

'Are you all right?' Isabel asked, moving away from the door and facing him.

'I just came back for some papers . . . ' He glanced round. He could smell her perfume faintly, and smiled when he saw her bare feet. 'You'll catch a cold.'

Isabel looked down and grinned. 'It's a habit. My teacher used to work in bare feet too. Funnily enough, it makes you feel more comfortable.'

He caught hold of her quickly, before she had time to move and kissed her, his mouth pressed against hers so hard that her top lip ground against her teeth. Isabel struggled, but he kept hold of her, putting his large hands on either side of her face.

'I want you.'

'Max, don't,' she said, trying to push him away. 'Don't.'

He didn't seem to hear her and instead lifted her up in his arms and carried her into the bedroom, kicking the door open with his foot and laying her on the bed. Isabel struck out at him, suddenly angered, the memory of her attack coming back.

'Lie still,' he said.

Lie still, let them do want they want.

'Stop it!' Isabel repeated, as his hands gripped

her arms and he moved on top of her.

His tongue prised her lips open as his hands began to pull at her clothes, his weight so heavy that she could hardly move under him. His face was altered beyond recognition, he seemed to hear or see nothing.

'You bastard!' Isabel screamed, tears pouring down her face and stinging the cut in her lip.

Max flinched as though he had been struck, and moved off her. His reason returned sharply, coldly, along with a numbing sensation of shame. Oh God, he thought, I never meant to hurt you, I just wanted you and I didn't know how to ask, or what to say. I couldn't tell you what I felt. When he turned back to her she was curled against the pillow, weeping bitterly. Instinctively he reached out to hold her, to offer comfort. This time she came willingly into his arms.

'Don't, don't,' he said tenderly, rocking her as though she was a child. 'I'm sorry, I didn't know what I was doing. God, I'm sorry, I just wanted you so much.'

She cried helplessly, weeping for all the pain through the years. She cried for David, for Sybella, for the attack, and for all the children she would never bear. In his arms, Isabel sobbed out two decades of anguish and then clung to him, shaking, as he pulled a blanket round her.

'Darling,' he said simply, kissing her forehead and then kissing the palm of her right hand. 'I never wanted to hurt you.'

'But people do. Always!' Isabel said shrilly. 'They take and hurt and it never stops.'

He held her tightly, trying to comfort her. 'Sssh.'

'It never stops!' she repeated helplessly. 'One day you think it will. But it doesn't . . . everyone wants something from you.'

He felt the rebuke and laid her head against his shoulder, rocking her. 'I don't want anything from you — except what you want to give me.'

She seemed not to hear him, her words running on blindly. 'When I was attacked, I thought I heard my father talking to me — he said, 'Lie still and let them do what they want.' But I didn't want them to touch me. I *didn't* want them to do it!' Her voice rose with pain and when she looked into his eyes his heart moved with pity. 'I don't want anything any more, except to be safe . . . I just want to be safe . . . safe.'

For an instant he couldn't reply and then said quietly, 'You're safe with me.'

Isabel shook her head. 'No, nowhere is safe.'

His voice was hard. 'Not in the past, no. But the past's gone.' He stroked the back of her hand to soothe her. 'All the horrors are over, Isabel. No one will hurt you now. No one will ever hurt you again.' Gone was the confident Isabel Hall, and in her place was someone bewildered and vulnerable, and she moved him unutterably. 'You're safe with me . . . ' he said, touching her cheek gently. 'I'll ask nothing from you, I swear, and I'll give you what I can — and loving you is the best security I can offer.' She glanced at him, and his comfort turned to tenderness as he continued to talk to her. 'I love you, and I will love you. Always.'

Finally peaceful, her body relaxed against his, the memory of magnolia blossom fading, the years of anguish dissolving in the dark well of the room. And because she wanted him, and his comfort, so much, Isabel slid her arms round his neck and kissed him. He responded eagerly, but tenderly, undressing her and then himself, before lying beside her. Curled up in the foetal position, he touched the soles of Isabel's bare feet and then smiled, rubbing warmth back into them with his hands.

'You have such pretty feet,' he said, bending down and kissing them. 'And pretty ankles.' He moved up her legs, tracing the skin with his lips and tongue.

Isabel moaned and arched her back, and Max moved on top of her again. His skin was cool against hers, his hands moving in her hair, lifting the heavy waves to his face and smelling the scent of her, their bodies moving rhythmically, his feet kicking the blankets off the bed as he cried out and climaxed.

She held him for a long moment then he rolled away from her, perspiration shining on his forehead and down the front of his chest as he caught hold of her elbows and lifted her into a kneeling position on the bed. Their eyes met.

'Now I'm going to make you happy,' he said gently, his voice low, his hands roaming. 'Very, very . . . happy.'

★　★　★

Prossie arrived back at The Ridings, sweeping her children into her arms and doling out the dozens of presents Stanton had sent. They talked

502

together excitedly, Bracken taking a Sony Walkman from Eloise, Chloë wandering off with a Joseph jacket. Eleanor watched them, smiling, and then glanced back to Prossie.

'Well, am I to take it that you'll be moving back in with Stanton?'

Prossie kissed her on the cheek and raised her eyebrows. 'Not yet. I thought I'd let the old fool stew in his juices for a while longer.' She sieved through her post and frowned. 'A letter from Isabel?' she queried, glancing at Eleanor. 'Why write me a letter when she'll be home this weekend?'

Eleanor's face was all innocence. 'No, she won't. She's got a man. She won't tell me who, but I know the signs.'

'A man?' Prossie said, archly. 'Ooooh, how lovely.' She glanced at Eleanor and winked. 'I shall let you read this when I've censored it.'

'You think it might be too much for an old lady like me?'

'I'm just worried it might give you ideas,' Prossie replied, going up to her room and closing the door.

The letter had been written by a woman in love, about the man she loved. It was clumsy in parts, not at all like David Hall's letters, and it veered uneasily between euphoria and guilt. Prossie read it and sighed, then read it again, affected by the words, alternately hopeful and poignant.

Dear Prossie,
    I had to put everything down on paper

— as much to let you know what was going on as to try and clarify things in my own mind. Max and I made love — we made love — and for the first time it was complete. Not just something that was expected of me, or to prove something, but tenderly, without any promises that there might be a tomorrow for us.

David would have been able to express this so perfectly. I can't. I don't have his talent, but I love Max. Simple. Only not so simple. We made love greedily, without thinking of the consequences, it was done and now I can only think of the person we cheated — Caroline. You know how much I hated my mother and Stanton for betraying David, and yet now I am doing the same thing. And it doesn't make it right.

But I do love him. He is my breath, my heart, my thoughts and all my waking moments. His voice is the one voice I hear amongst a thousand others; his face the one I see everywhere. Broken nose and all! He wants children, Prossie, I knew that before we made love but only told him afterwards, so that if he wanted to walk away I had something to remember.

It's all timing, isn't it? And that is the one thing I was never good at. I should have met Max instead of Teddy and married him; and he should have been Sybella's father. That was how it could have been — that was how it *should* have been — but the timing got all out of control and now I love a man who is married and not free to marry me, a man who wants children — the one thing I cannot give him.

I hate those men who injured me, Prossie. Now I hate them with all my heart because they have taken away the one thing with which I could have kept Max's love. I wouldn't have asked him to divorce Caroline, but I could have had his child. I could . . . but the timing was wrong. On the wrong street at the wrong moment.

But I love Max, I do love him. He is part of me, and I part of him. The future? Who knows — I only know that Caroline must never find out. It's another secret to keep, Prossie, another secret to tuck amongst the rest.

My love to you, good friend.

Isabel

Prossie weighed the letter in her hand and then folded it, tucking it away at the back of her drawer for safekeeping.

★　★　★

Isabel and Max made love frequently, whenever the house was quiet at night, keeping their affair a secret from the staff, making sure no one could point a finger at them. Except themselves. They longed for each other, and yet every time they parted both of them fell into a gulf of unending guilt. They talked about it and then agreed to end the affair, but the following day Max would arrive and sit at the bottom of the stepladders and talk, and Isabel would respond and climb down and rest her head on his shoulder. She hated what she was doing to Caroline and hated the effect their actions were having on Max, but was in a terrible way pleased to see how the guilt tormented him — if he had been unconcerned she could never have continued to love him, or trust him.

'It puts you in such a terrible position, darling,' he said, 'I don't want to treat you like a mistress.'

'You don't,' she replied, nudging him into a good humour. 'You haven't even bought me any sexy underwear.'

He touched her, big hands around her face. 'I don't think of you like that.'

Her heart shifted, and she glanced away. 'I know . . . I know.'

Yet Caroline remained an enigma. She was so little in the picture that it was possible sometimes to discount her altogether. Who was she? Isabel wondered, who was this frail little creature who needed Max so much? And who kept a place in his heart so firm that he would not consider leaving her? Was it just her fragility, or some other quality she possessed which had made him love her?

Isabel speculated about her often, but never came to any conclusions — until Caroline arrived unexpectedly at the house one morning standing on the step like a stranger as Isabel opened the door. She knew her at once.

'Hello, Miss Hall. I'm Mrs Henderson ...
Caroline.'

'Oh, come in,' Isabel said, flustered, 'how nice
to meet you at last.'

Caroline walked diffidently into the hallway,
almost as though the house was not hers. She
was slightly built, her skin pale and delicately
made up, her red hair tied back with a black
velvet bow to emphasise her large pale eyes.

Isabel studied her, mystified by the woman, so
unlike her husband in every way. Where Max had
energy, she was listless; where he had physical
size, she had the careful fineness of limb which
preceded illness.

'Your work is lovely,' Caroline said. 'I'm only
sorry we haven't met until now.' Her voice was
genuine, but lacked warmth or energy, her eyes
trailing wistfully from the drawing room to the
mural upstairs. 'How are you getting on? Max
has been telling me all about your progress ... '
Her attention wandered suddenly. 'Well, I have
to be going. I just wanted to drop in and
introduce myself. You must have thought me
very rude, not showing an interest.' Suddenly
bewildered, she glanced around her at the
magnificent rooms. 'I never thought Max would
do so well,' she said simply.

The words made Isabel feel awkward and
ashamed. Caroline was no longer a shadow
figure, without substance, she was flesh and
blood — and they were betraying her. In her
house, and under her roof, her husband was
committing adultery. That was the truth of the
matter, and it burned inside Isabel. Struggling to

find something to say, she wondered about Caroline's visit — had she come merely to say hello? Or to confront her rival, knowing that once she met her, Isabel could no longer ignore her existence? From now on, Caroline Henderson was not simply 'the wife' unseen and unknown, she was real, and her reality was frightening.

'Well . . . ' Caroline said finally and abstractedly. 'I have to go now.'

'Must you go so soon?'

'I have to.'

'But what about some tea? Mrs Gunn can get it in a minute.'

Caroline frowned. The skin on her forehead was taut, almost stretched, and she had a sudden air of distraction. 'I have to go!'

'Fine, whatever you want,' Isabel said quietly, soothing her as she rushed to the door. 'Would you like me to call a taxi?'

Caroline wrenched open the door then turned. 'I've got one — he's waiting for me,' she said, glancing over Isabel's shoulder. 'It's a lovely house, isn't it?'

Isabel met her eyes. 'Yes, and it's yours,' she said.

The door closed softly behind Caroline as she left, leaving no trace of perfume or personality behind her. Unutterably depressed, Isabel sat down heavily at the bottom of the stairs. Any other woman she could have fought, anyone tough and clever, but not Caroline. This woman seemed so nervous and frightened. A woman who needed a strong man — a man like Max.

508

So maybe the timing had been right after all, Isabel thought. Caroline needed Max in a way she never would. Oh, she might want him but she did not need him to live. That was the difference, Isabel Hall could survive alone. Life had taught her that; experiences which would have crucified others had only succeeded in making her more resilient. There was nothing she could not face; that was Isabel's strength, and her weakness — because in the end a woman who had only half her character would keep the man she loved.

31

Six months passed and the affair continued. Unable to confide his thoughts and anxieties to Caroline, Max unburdened himself to Isabel; and she told him all the secrets of her life. She trusted him so much that she even confessed to him that Stanton Feller was her father, knowing that he would never betray her. She spoke too of the trauma of the attack, she wept a little, and tried to explain her anguish at being sterile. Not that she could ever truly articulate that sense of loss.

He listened and held her in the dark four-poster bed, down under the blankets when the nights got cold, and he wondered how much he loved Caroline and if he could ever part from Isabel. The thought jolted him, it felt as though someone had thrown him over a cliff and he was falling without hope of being saved. No, he could not imagine life without Isabel.

And then again, how could he live without Caroline? Easily, he thought, with a stab of guilt. But though he might be able to let go of her, she could not let go of him. It was her vulnerability which held him, that and the promise he had made when they married. For better, or for worse. He had believed it and lived by it, until now. He had never been a man to sleep around, he had avoided extra-marital affairs, although there had been temptations. But they had never been tempting enough, until Isabel.

She was, quite simply, his ideal female. She was clever and successful and brave, yet under all that astounding capability there was such a poor child. No amount of bravado ever covered that in his eyes, and when she slept he would hold Isabel's right hand and imagine her lying on the street, broken, with no one to help her.

So he swung between the two women in his life and ached for both of them, and yet knew that Isabel's inability to have a child was the one real reason he did not leave his wife.

'Oh God,' he said one night when he thought Isabel was sleeping beside him. 'If only we had met before.'

She lay silently, but her eyes flickered under the lids and her heart turned.

★　★　★

'It's not your damn money to give away!' Sunny screeched at her son.

'It is!' he replied, squinting at the row of flags on the dining table. 'Why the stars and stripes?'

'We're having the American Ambassador to dinner,' Sunny replied, sniffing. 'And don't change the subject!' she snapped. 'You can't give all that money to Isabel — what will people think?'

'The money is for her school, not for her to buy herself a penthouse apartment — '

'Perhaps it would be better for you if it was,' Sunny replied darkly. 'It would do your reputation a power of good to have a mistress.'

511

'I'm gay, Mother!'

Sunny sneezed and then brushed aside the suggestion. 'Of course you are, darling, but it's something you'll grow out of when you meet the right girl.'

Defeated, Gyman slumped into a chair. 'And Isabel is the right girl for me?'

'Well . . . ' Sunny hesitated, then fiddled with the place settings. Her puffy face was pink. 'She might be . . . although she has a bit of a reputation.'

Gyman narrowed his eyes, ready to defend Isabel. 'How so?'

'People say — only *say*, mind you — that she's having an affair with Max Henderson.' She paused, thinking. 'And it is a little bit mean of her, considering that his wife is on medication.'

'*You're* on medication, Mother.'

'Don't be obtuse!' Sunny snapped. 'I mean medication for the mind . . . ' She tapped her temple. 'Caroline is a little dotty. You know — '

'One jump ahead of the butterfly nets?'

Sunny frowned. 'Whatever does that mean?'

'That she's crazy,' Gyman said, straightening up in his seat. 'Well, she isn't. As usual, you have all your facts wrong, Mother. She's just a weak-minded female who can't face the world.'

'That's what I said,' Sunny said emphatically. 'She's mad.' Her thoughts shifted again. 'Anyway, I don't want to talk about Caroline Henderson, I want to talk about money — the money you're *not* giving to Isabel Hall.'

'It's my money.'

Sunny's smile was like a knife blade. 'Gyman

512

darling, I would suggest that you have a little chat with the solicitor — just to clarify things for you. We wouldn't want you to make any silly little mistakes, would we?'

★ ★ ★

All at once Isabel Hall's life began to flow easily. Exhibiting at the Porchester Gallery, her work was spotted by an Italian diplomat who commissioned Isabel to paint several notable members of the aristocracy. The money was useful, but the publicity was invaluable. Soon Isabel's face was seen in the glossy magazines and occasional quotes cropped up in the papers. Her reputation, so long in the shadow of Stanton Feller's, suddenly matched his, and the word spread. Especially to Holland Park.

'Fucking hell!' Stanton said, dropping the morning paper. 'Isabel's gone and got that commission from Dimitri Michelous. Bloody kid!'

His voice was angry, but underneath there was a real feeling of admiration. You could give me a run for my money any time, he had once said to her, and now she was. Good girl.

Prossie glanced at him, unperturbed. She had returned supposedly for a trial period, but as soon as they got into bed all thought of a trial anything was quickly obliterated.

'I'm glad she's doing well,' Prossie said simply. 'She deserves it.'

'And I don't?' Stanton queried nastily.

'If you got what you deserved, my love,' Prossie countered, 'you would be dead by now.

513

You ought to be on your knees thanking the heavens that you've been spared.'

Stanton scowled. 'I'm atheist — thank God.'

★   ★   ★

The phone at The Ridings kept ringing, the article in the paper having caused a flurry of interest in Isabel Hall's school.

She glowed with achievement as she talked to Eleanor.

'With Gyman de Souza's money, and Baye and Dimitri, and the bank stumping up the rest,' Isabel squealed delightedly, 'I can do it! I can!'

Eleanor looked at her with delight and hugged her. She had never seen Isabel so well, her personal and professional life finally giving her the happiness she deserved.

'Even Stanton said he was going to contribute . . . well, after a bit of persuasion. I told him he owed me one, after all, I persuaded Prossie to go back to him.'

'Oh Isabel, how could you?' Eleanor said, laughing. 'You knew she would go back — '

'Ah, but he didn't,' Isabel answered, changing the subject. 'I knew I could pull this school off! I knew it! All that crap I had to take from Ted Cavendish and Sterling Thompson — all their sneering — they laughed at me, talked about me behind my back. Well now I can return the compliment.' Her euphoria faded suddenly. 'Nothing can go wrong now, can it?'

'No, sweetheart,' Eleanor assured her. 'Nothing can go wrong.'

Isabel looked past the window and she saw the dream school built, fine and clean and ready for children. 'I've seen the land — or rather Baye took me to look at the place yesterday.' She felt her heart race and touched her breast. 'Oh God, I'm so excited.'

'Where's it going to be?' Eleanor asked, glancing down at the sheaf of papers Isabel pushed across the table towards her.

'Only three miles from here. I wanted the school in Yorkshire, near David. Otherwise it wouldn't make sense.' Her hair fell forward as she looked at the plans. 'The Institute won't be that big at first, we'll have to extend as we go along, but I want the architecture to be simple, on classic Greek lines.' She paused, thinking of her mother.

Virginia could have helped her and given her advice, but they hardly ever saw each other any longer. There was the odd letter, and maybe a phone call, but conversation was stilted, Virginia sounding much the same as she had ever done. America seemed to suit her, and although she was getting old she was still working.

'Gyman knows some marvellous builders, and he's going to arrange all that, and Baye said he would look after the finances — '

'Do you trust him?' Eleanor asked suddenly.

Isabel frowned. 'With this, yes. This is David's memorial and Baye loved him, so he won't cheat me.'

'And if you get this land, how long will it take to build the school?'

'Six months,' Isabel said triumphantly.

Eleanor raised her eyebrows. 'I'd say a year to be on the safe side, sweetheart,' she said, smiling and watching Isabel pore over the papers. She seems very young again, Eleanor thought, knowing that the school meant a lot to her and yet suspecting that a man had more to do with her current happiness.

'So, how's your private life?'

Isabel stiffened and glanced up. 'You wouldn't like it if I told you.'

'Try me.'

'I'm happy — but he's married.' Her hand touched Eleanor's shoulder. 'I know what you're thinking — that my mother betrayed your brother — but I didn't plan to fall in love with Max and I wouldn't have had it happen for all the world . . . it just did.'

'Does he love you?'

'Do you mean, will he leave his wife for me?'

'Don't put words into my mouth!' Eleanor retorted.

'I'm sorry,' Isabel said softly. 'Yes, he loves me, but he wants children, and only his wife can give him those . . . so we just enjoy what we've got.' She shrugged. 'It's not ideal, but Eleanor, I would rather be with him ten per cent of my life, than with another man all the time.' She turned back to the papers on the table. 'Besides, I have this to occupy me.'

And it did, and suddenly Isabel's life was filled as she moved from plans for the school, to her work, and to Max. She felt supremely confident, sure of the future, and every day she saw concrete evidence that her dream was coming to fruition. The land was bought and in March the builders began work, laying down the foundations for a school which would outlive Isabel and bear David Hall's name for ever.

That birthday the letter had come from David, as usual. Only this time it was eerily prophetic. Did he see the plans for the school? Isabel wondered. Wherever he was, did he look down and watch the preparations and follow them? It seemed as though he did . . .

Darling Knuckles,

Happy Birthday — well, what are you up to? Something very grand, I think. How far you've come, my love, and how brave you are. Braver than I ever was. You can make your dreams come true, can't you? Just as I knew you would. Which dream is this one, Isabel? The second, or the third? Make it come true, for yourself and for me, make it come true.

Once when I was young I went to London and had my palm read. A gypsy stopped me on the street and I hadn't the heart to shoo her away . . .

Isabel frowned, surprised at the admission.

. . . she told me a great deal about my life and about my future — *none of which came true* . . .

She laughed suddenly.

517

... which only goes to prove that your future is in your own hands. So use it, sweetheart, and mould it and shape it into what you want. It's such a huge dream you're working on, but you'll do it. I know you will. I know you'll do it for both of us.

It begins, Isabel, it begins ...

All my love,

David

As Isabel thought of the letter she felt the sun on her face and watched the first preparations being made.

Baye walked up behind her and touched her shoulder.

'So, it's finally beginning.'

She smiled dreamily, like a child. 'Yes. It's beginning.'

★   ★   ★

The afternoon dragged into evening, Eleanor growing more worried by the minute as she paced the floor. She was alone again. Prossie and her daughters had gone back to Holland Park, Sybella had returned to school, and Isabel was in London, working at the Henderson house. The Ridings was very still, and Eleanor felt suddenly old, past her usefulness, her limbs aching.

It's just reaction, she thought. I've had a lot to occupy me for a while and now everyone's gone the place seems depressing. She glanced round, pulled on her coat and walked out into the garden, calling for Blair. She had been repeating this same ritual since four o'clock, when he hadn't come in for his tea. It had surprised her, and then she began to remember other little quirks in his recent behaviour, which she had been too busy to comment upon. His secrecy, his sullenness, his sudden refusal to help her. All his gentleness gone — as though he was ill. Eleanor frowned, maybe that was it, maybe Blair was sick.

She called out again, but he did not reply and she glanced towards David's window, hoping to see some shadow, some impression to assure her that she was not alone. But no one appeared at the window and no one called out — not David or Blair — and all Eleanor could hear was the wind blowing through the spring trees and the hurried cawing of a flock of crows.

★ ★ ★

Isabel left Max that afternoon because Caroline was coming to stay at the house for a few days. She checked and rechecked everything, making sure she left no imprint of herself anywhere — not in the kitchen, or bathroom or on the sheets. There was to be no perfume to give her away, or hairbrush left to betray her. All that remained of Isabel Hall was the scaffolding on the hallway and the paints and brushes in the outhouse where she cleaned her equipment.

'I don't want you to go,' Max said, hugging her to him as she waited for a taxi.

'I have to.'

'Then let me drive you back to Kensington.'

She shook her head. 'No, you stay here. I want to go alone.' She traced the line of his broken nose with her finger and smiled. 'Love you, darling.'

He frowned, suddenly unable to bear the parting. 'Listen, Isabel, when Caroline goes back, we have to talk.'

'No.'

'We have — '

She covered his mouth with her hand. 'No . . . Be happy with what we have. I am.'

Then she hurried out without another word.

Caroline arrived an hour later, she seemed wan and faintly embarrassed, and responded childishly to Max's greeting, pulling away from him quickly and looking round. She had chosen the décor for the drawing room herself and was happy there, but the other rooms she found too ornate and was uncomfortable in Max's study.

'I can't think why you got that horrible old bed,' she said gently, looking at the four-poster.

Max glanced at it, but could only see Isabel lying there and looked away.

'I like it,' he said simply, 'I sleep here when I'm alone . . . but we'll use the main bedroom while you're here.'

'Oh no,' Caroline said eagerly. 'You can stay here if you want . . . if you like.'

He felt suddenly uncomfortable, too big and too clumsy for her. 'No, we'll sleep downstairs.'

The whole evening was agonised, Caroline ill at ease, Max careful with her, treating her more as a child than a wife. They tiptoed around each other, finally making clumsy love in the dark, the bed previously unused and the sheets smelling of fresh paint, the whole episode somehow chillingly bleak.

'You do love me, don't you?' Caroline asked, aware that they had disappointed each other.

He looked into her face. 'Yes, I love you,' he answered truthfully.

She leaned against his chest. 'I want to make you happy always . . . always,' she said pathetically, her pale eyes huge with sincerity.

The doorbell rang at six-thirty, Caroline stirring and glancing over to Max. He slept on, oblivious, and so she slipped out of bed, hurrying downstairs to find Mrs Gunn in her dressing gown talking to someone at the door.

Her voice was quick with impatience. 'They're asleep, I can't wake them. Can't you give me a message?'

'I WANT TO TALK TO MAX HENDERSON!'

'Keep your voice down!' Mrs Gunn responded, jumping as Caroline came to her side.

She looked at the stranger and smiled gently. 'Can I help? I'm Mrs Henderson.'

The man smiled back at Caroline and passed her a letter. 'It's supposed to be a secret,' he said, 'but you should know.'

Caroline took the paper and swallowed, suddenly frightened. 'Who are you?'

Blair smiled, unshaven and exhausted in the morning light. 'Doesn't matter who I am . . . you read that. You read it, OK? She deserves to be hurt. Isabel does,' he said, backing away. 'She hurt me!'

521

Max continued to sleep, until a scream woke him. It hauled him bodily out of his dreams, it shook all his secrets and rattled them in front of his face and told him that nothing would be the same again.

He took the stairs two at a time, and arrived in the drawing room to find Caroline holding the letter Isabel had written to Prossie all those months before.

32

That early morning was fearful for two households. Up in Yorkshire, Eleanor was phoning the police after a sleepless night to report Blair missing, and in Hampstead Max was facing his wife. Caroline's hands were clapped over her ears to block out his words; her face was blotchy and swollen with crying, and her voice failed her repeatedly. Oblivious to his words, she was hysterical. In a frenzy she ran to him, then ran away, up the stairs to the bedroom, snatching hold of her sleeping tablets and swallowing several before Max caught up with her.

He emptied the bottle down the toilet and shook her violently. 'How many have you taken? How many!'

She was stupid with distress. 'I . . . I . . . '

'HOW MANY!'

His voice shocked her into sense. 'Only a few. You should have let me take all of them — '

'How many is a few?' he asked.

Caroline's face was white, her eyes almost colourless. She looked dead and he shook her again. 'Tell me!'

'I don't know. I don't know.'

Quickly he opened her mouth with his hands and stuck one finger down her throat. She retched violently, throwing up over him and the bathroom floor, then she sank to her knees, sobbing.

Calmly Max got a flannel and wiped her face and the front of her nightdress. He felt nothing, just deadness and pity. For her part, Caroline merely gazed into her husband's eyes, bewildered, and when he carried her back to bed and pulled the blankets round her, she simply whispered, 'I love you.'

The words felt like steel round his heart.

★ ★ ★

Eleanor was meanwhile pacing the floor of the hall at The Ridings. She had explained to the police exactly what had happened — that her cousin, Blair, had wandered off. She hadn't seen him since the previous morning. No, she answered in reply to their questions, he was not normal. So why was he allowed to wander about? they countered. Blair was disabled, not dangerous, Eleanor replied coldly. Please find him, she begged, please find him.

When they left she thought about phoning Isabel, and then decided against it. No, the chances were that Blair would soon be back home, so why worry her? Eleanor frowned, touching her forehead as though the action helped her to think. Where could he have gone? Where would he have wanted to go? Her thoughts rushed on. The only other occasion he had wandered off was in London when Isabel was in hospital. There had been a reason for him to go missing then, but what reason was there now?

Sybella? No, Eleanor thought, immediately

dismissing the idea. Could he really have made his own way to Brighton to see her? But the idea seemed less ludicrous the longer she thought about it, and when she hurried upstairs to her room and found fifty pounds missing, Eleanor was suddenly certain that she knew where Blair had gone.

She phoned through to the police, then replaced the receiver thoughtfully. Brighton was a long way to go, and for what? she wondered, convinced that was where Blair had gone. She imagined him on a train, confused and baffled, trying to make sense of a strange and terrifying world. She imagined his bewilderment and his fear; his childlike confusion; she imagined him on a platform trying to read the timetable, and asking for help. People would laugh at him, or make fun of him, anyone might do anything to him . . .

She worried for him and urged the police to hurry to Brighton — never once thinking that Blair was in London, and that he knew exactly what he was doing.

* * *

When Max was certain that Caroline was asleep, he called Mrs Gunn in to watch over her and drove over to Isabel's studio, ringing the doorbell and petting Sim as he walked in. She knew from the first instant she saw him that something terrible had happened — and for once she tried to avoid the truth and delay the moment.

'Do you want a coffee?'

He shook his head.

'I was just working ... ' she began, then stopped. There was no point trying to avoid the inevitable. 'What happened?'

'Caroline found out about us.'

She sat down heavily, Sim coming to her side and laying his head on her lap. With a trembling hand Isabel stroked his head, her eyes averted from Max.

'How?'

'Some man came with a letter,' he said simply. He didn't sit down. That much she noticed. He wanted to be away.

'Here — look at it.'

The letter was extended towards her and Isabel took it, recognising at once the note she had written to Prossie. Her head buzzed. 'Who brought it?'

'Some man — Caroline said he was tall, good-looking. Seemed a little odd.'

Blair, oh no, not Blair ... Isabel closed her eyes and remembered a younger Blair jumping down from the train that first day he had come to Yorkshire. Grinning, childish. A ten-year-old brain in a man's body. Harmless. Or was he? She remembered how he had tried to destroy her work in the studio at The Ridings. The dark side of the child, thwarted ... and finally she remembered Sybella. He had loved her, wrongly, innocently, foolishly — and he blamed her for parting them. Isabel almost smiled. She had separated the lovers, Harlequin and Columbine were doomed — and Harlequin had, in his turn, doomed her.

'It was Blair,' she said, glancing up at Max. 'How's Caroline?'

'She's settled down.' He paused, loving the woman in front of him, but hopelessly tied to the woman asleep in his bed. 'I think — '

' — we should call it a day.'

He winced. 'Oh, God, Isabel . . . '

'I know . . . I know,' she said, her eyes filling.

He moved towards her, but she put up her hands. Fending him off. Pink palms, closed fingers. Go away. 'Please, Max. Go home. We were wrong.'

'I love you,' he said, looking down at her. 'But . . . there's Caroline — and she needs me.'

'More than I do.'

'I didn't say that.'

She shook her head. 'No, I did.'

'Perhaps when things have settled down, we could talk things over? We could still be together . . . She knows the truth now. If I could just get her used to the idea then maybe, in time, she'll realise what you mean to me. I want you.'

'It's pointless!' Isabel said, getting to her feet and moving across the studio. Putting distance between them. 'If you left her you would regret it.' She glanced at him. 'I know what it is to want a child, Max, to crave for a child . . . I risked my marriage to have Sybella . . . If you married me you might think it wouldn't matter, but one day you would look at me and wonder . . . and think of the children you might have had.' She moved towards him and touched his face. 'We had each other for a little while — such a little while — but you must go back to Caroline. You'll go

527

on and have your children, and I'll have my work.'

He hesitated, held her tightly for a moment, then released her and walked out. Isabel heard the front door bang, and the creak of the gate, then a far-off sound of an engine revving. She counted up to a hundred, giving Max time to leave, to cross the boroughs from Kensington to Hampstead, to move over from the present to the past — and then she began to cry.

* * *

The school grew daily. It progressed steadily, in much the same way that Isabel lived. She found that the grief of losing Max was so intense that all her energy was transferred into the building. Every foot of bricks told her time was passing and she was healing; every problem, every argument with the builders occupied her mind and kept her thoughts away from memories.

Because the memories tormented her. Memories of love-making and tenderness, gone. Lost somewhere in the never-never-land of what should have been. Love had gone, and in its place was hatred, and that hatred was for the person who had broken her heart. Isabel hated Blair with the same passion she had loved Max; she imagined hurting him, hitting him, thinking of how she could punish him as he had so effectively punished her. She plotted revenge — perhaps she would send him to a Home, have him committed somewhere where he could never escape and harm anyone else. For weeks

Isabel plotted her revenge, and when the police finally caught up with Blair, sleeping rough in London, she was the first person at the station to confront him.

Her face was set with anger as she waited for them to bring him to her. A dull headache mumbled inside her brain, her right hand opening and closing. Soon she would confront the person who had stolen her chance of happiness — and she would make him pay . . . Yet she was busy looking in her bag when Blair walked in, and when she did glance up she took in her breath with shock. He was filthy, his clothes torn, his face obliterated by a heavy beard. But the eyes were the same — a child's eyes — and they looked at her desperately.

'I'm sorry . . . '

Isabel remained immobile. I hate you, she thought.

'Sorry . . . '

His nose ran as he cried. She imagined how he had been living rough, and how frightened he must have been. But not as frightened as he was now, facing her and knowing what he had done.

'I didn't mean . . . ' Blair rambled on, incoherently. And still Isabel didn't move. She studied him instead, and wanted to hurt him so badly that her mouth tasted of bile.

'Isabel . . . please . . . ' He moved towards her, the police officer watching him carefully. He was shambling, his arms outstretched, just as they had been that first day when he jumped down from the train. 'Isabel . . . please.'

He repelled her, his smell and his stupid eyes,

and his stupid brain, and his wicked, spiteful, vicious action which had cost her so much. She hated the stench of urine and sweat on him and stood disbelievingly as he continued to move towards her. Then she looked into his eyes, and all the sorrow of the world was in them. A child's eyes, begging for forgiveness.

'Oh, Blair,' she said simply, taking him in her arms.

From then onwards he remained by her side. When Isabel went home to The Ridings, Blair went too, when she was at the studio, he was, and when she visited the building site, he followed behind her with Sim. He was capable of good heavy work, so she let him join the builders and help to create her dream school. Eleanor encouraged him, angered beyond reason at his actions, and determined that he should make amends to Isabel.

'You look after her, do you hear me?' He nodded dumbly. 'You better, or you'll have me to answer to.'

And so he did, out of guilt and fear, and gratitude. He knew that Isabel could have sent him away, away from The Ridings, Eleanor and Sybella; he realised that she had the power to exile him, and knowing he was on permanent probation, he devoted his life to her, and the security she represented.

But while Blair settled down and worked off his guilt, Eleanor remained mystified by his actions and by his resourcefulness. After talking to Prossie she realised that the letter had been written on a piece of Max Henderson's headed notepaper, but how did Blair, the impossibly confused Blair, manage, unaided, to find the house in the middle of London?

A week later, the answer was provided by the postmistress in the village. Unthinkingly proud, she asked if Blair had found his way to visit Isabel in London?

Eleanor looked baffled. 'At the studio?'

'Oh Lord, no. At the new house in . . . ' she paused, trying to recall 'the Bishops Avenue.'

Realisation scuttered down Eleanor's back.

'Such a lovely name for a road, I said so to my husband — '

'Blair asked you how to get there?' Eleanor said, interrupting her and then smiling as though nothing was wrong.

The postmistress was pink with delight. 'He did!' she said happily, pulling down a copy of the *A–Z*. 'He asked if I could show him all the directions so that he could turn up on the doorstep and surprise Isabel. So I wrote them all down for him . . . ' Her voice dropped confidingly. 'He's not that slow, I can tell you. Not when he concentrates. It took us a little time, but he caught on in the end. I wrote down which train he had to catch, the time it left, and the name of the station, and then when he got to London I wrote down all the directions he had to follow there.' She nodded her head, remembering. 'Yes, I wrote everything on a piece of paper for him — in case he got lost, so he could show it to someone and get help. But he seemed determined to master it. Oh, he did so want to surprise her . . . ' she said, smiling

531

indulgently. 'So he got there all right, did he?'

Eleanor's face was stiff. 'Yes, he got there.'

The postmistress beamed with triumph. 'It just goes to show what he can do when he tries. Doesn't it?'

Sybella rallied to her mother's aid as well. She did not fully understand what had happened, for Prossie gave her a sanitised version, telling her that Isabel had lost someone she loved and needed support, but for once Sybella found herself offering sympathy to her mother. She also offered her time in the holidays and asked innumerable questions about the school, defending Isabel against anyone who sneered at her.

'Some bitch at school said her father thought you'd never get the place built,' Sybella said, wrapped up in an anorak and shivering on the building site. 'I told her to dry up — and that you could do anything.'

Isabel smiled, inordinately moved. 'Thanks.'

'No problem,' Sybella replied, looking round. 'My teacher said that you were getting pretty famous.' She linked arms with her mother. The gesture was an unfamiliar one, but affectionate. 'I'm proud of you, Mum.'

Isabel glanced at her daughter and then smiled, squeezing her hand. 'I'm proud of you too.'

But although the family came to her aid, Isabel heard nothing from Max. She waited for a phone call or a letter, but as time passed she was glad that the break had been so brutal and final. It made it easier to come to terms with the loss. Not that she did not miss him. Max Henderson was in her thoughts daily, nothing was done without wondering what he would have said. Would he have approved? Given her advice? As the school took shape, Isabel began to concentrate on her own image, knowing the power of publicity. She gave interviews and appeared on television, constantly drumming up interest for her work and her school. Some donations and commissions duly followed — even though the recession cut deep into people's pockets — and her enthusiasm for the Institute continued to intrigue people, as did her background. Isabel even began to travel, taking the same route as her mother, using the Hall name as an entrée to places and people. And their money.

It was almost enough; and Isabel could have lived quite happily had it not been for a trick nature played on her.

Having been abroad for a week, she returned to London to find an invitation from Ivy Messenger to attend a drinks party. So the following evening she found herself in Cheyne Walk, greeting a vivacious Ivy and many of her old friends. It seemed that everyone was there — Baye, Dimitri Michelous, Portento, and Sunny de Souza, with Gyman in tow.

'Darling!' Sunny said delightedly. 'How good to see you — though you look a little tired.'

Gyman raised his eyebrows. 'Ignore Mother, you look great, Isabel.' Sunny gave him a hard look. 'I . . . wondered . . . if we could have a little chat later.'

Isabel smiled to herself — so Sunny was still trying to prove that her son wasn't gay? 'Fine,

Gyman, we'll talk later,' she said, wandering off.

Baye was in fine form, as was Portento, who came over and kissed Isabel before telling her all about Sterling Thompson getting drunk and driving off the Embankment.

'Is he all right?'

'Oh, fine,' Sunny replied, sniffing, 'except for the fact that he lost that ludicrous little toupé. It's probably well out to sea now, frightening the fishes. Sort of hair today, and gone tomorrow.'

Isabel laughed and continued to enjoy the evening until she overheard a snippet of conversation behind her.

' . . . such a timid little thing, but they say she'll be all right . . . yes, first baby . . . '

Isabel flinched, for no reason.

' . . . dear Caroline, I hear Max is delighted . . . '

Her hand felt suddenly numb and she nearly dropped the glass she was holding. Oh God, she thought, let me get away from here.

Gyman met her by the door as she hurried out. 'Oh, don't go, Isabel. I wanted to have a chat — '

' — not now, please.'

He was firm. 'But, Isabel, I have to.' He followed her out on to Cheyne Walk. The Thames blinked darkly under the Embankment lamps as they walked along. *Caroline is pregnant*, Isabel said to herself repeatedly, *Caroline is pregnant . . .*

' . . . you see, it's not my fault.'

Caroline is pregnant. Max is very pleased about it.

' . . . Isabel, are you listening to me?'

'No! I'm not listening to you! Go away.

Gyman!' she snapped. 'I want to be on my own for a while.'

He blushed, and then said emphatically, 'I can't let you have the money I promised you for the school.'

Caroline is pregnant.

Isabel's thoughts swung back into place. 'What did you say!'

'I can't let you have the money,' Gyman blustered. 'You see, it's Mother, she won't let me — '

Isabel said disbelievingly, 'You promised me that money. If you go back on your word, the school can't be built.'

He cowered in front of her. 'But — '

'No, no buts!' she shouted. 'You've let me down, you cringing little creep. Your mother is right about you, you've no guts. You let me think you were a friend, but you're just like all the rest . . . '

She rushed off across the road, a car blasting its horn as she ran in front of it. Gyman tried to follow but Isabel had already reached her car and was driving off as he stood, waving stupidly, on the pavement.

Isabel drove through the night, arriving in Yorkshire at six. The sun had just risen, the building site still hung with mist, a pile of bricks frosted with dew. A silent concrete mixer stood like a sentinel on guard, the half-completed window frames poking upwards into the ghostly sky, a Portacabin standing square and lonely in the early morning light.

Carefully she walked through the gap in the

bricks where the front door would finally be placed. She stood in what would be the entrance hall and imagined the place filled with children. The empty morning was suddenly ringing with the sounds of running feet, and children laughing, and somewhere at the back of her mind, Isabel heard David Hall's voice.

'It will be built,' she said out loud, raising her voice in the silent air. 'I swear to God this school will be built. I promise you, David . . . ' she paused, 'but I need money.'

She thought of Caroline and winced, shivering in the cold air. 'I need a stroke of luck. I've had it up to here with being brave, David!' Her voice rose with anger. 'I don't want to be strong for ever. I want someone to help me . . . ' She glanced round, the half-finished building looked sad and grand at the same moment. 'I won't give up. I never give up . . . It's been a pig of a night, David,' she said, throwing her head back into the still air. 'Gyman's let me down and Caroline's having a baby.' She laughed, and her breath made little plumes in the cold. 'Oh shit, what a bloody life! Well, I'm not giving up, but if you want this blasted school built in your name, David, you're going to have to help me. Do you hear me!' she called out, glancing round, scuffing her high-heeled shoes on the rubble. 'I need help, David! So help me. Please . . . '

33

Isabel waited patiently for some kind of salvation — which never came. Then she swore violently at David and stared fiercely at his photograph on the piano at The Ridings, surprised that he had let her down.

Yet unbeknown to Isabel, the news that Gyman had redrawn his financial backing soon spread. Ivy Messenger was among the first to hear it and chewed the matter over thoughtfully. She wheeled herself to the table in the centre of her drawing room and glanced at her collection of Russian icons. She could raise the money, after all, she was an old woman, what else did she want to do with her wealth? Her one good eye rested on a very early icon of Christ, His head circled by gold. Even in a recession such valuable pieces commanded good prices at sales. Sothebys or Christies were bound to be interested.

She thought of Isabel and of Caroline. Pregnant Caroline with Max.

'All wrong,' Ivy said out loud. 'Wrong woman with the wrong man.'

And she decided that Isabel needed a stroke of good luck. She deserved it, Ivy thought. So, wincing slightly in her Messenger Corset, Ivy picked up the phone.

* * *

Work was temporarily halted on the building site, Isabel standing with Sybella beside her, watching the abandoned building. Words failed both of them, even though Sybella had tried frequently to offer comfort.

The dream was in abeyance — maybe never to be completed.

'You wanted it so much . . . ' Sybella said, trailing off.

Isabel kept her eyes on the building plot. 'It was my third dream.'

Sybella glanced at her mother. 'But you've got one left.'

Isabel shook her head. The fourth dream would never, could never, be granted. The fourth dream that David had promised her was for the impossible — a child.

'No, sweetheart,' Isabel said, turning away, 'some dreams stay just that — dreams.'

'I hate Gyman! And everyone else. Someone could give you the money. Perhaps you should try praying?'

'I did.'

'No good?' Sybella asked hopefully, adding, 'I don't think God exists, otherwise He would have answered.'

'Oh, God always answers,' Isabel replied, smiling wryly. 'It's just that sometimes He says no.'

'I don't see how you can be so resigned,' Sybella snapped angrily.

'I've learned to be,' Isabel countered, opening and closing her right hand. Her head hummed with the threat of a migraine. She hadn't suffered from them for quite a while — until she lost

Max, and Gyman withdrew the money. Then all the pressure came back with the memory of illness and stress. Isabel sighed and pushed her hands into her pockets.

'I thought I'd give it just a few more days — before I laid off the builders. You know, just in case something turned up.'

'Like Mr Micawber?' Sybella asked, taking her mother's arm.

'Well . . . something like that.'

Three more days passed, in which time Baye phoned Isabel and told her that he couldn't raise any more money. Dimitri Michelous said the same, as did Stanton, and all the numerous other small investors. The rejections hit Isabel hard, and the next morning she rose wearily after a bad night and went into the studio to work. She kicked off her shoes and tried to paint, but she had no heart for it, and found her thoughts wandering.

Caroline was nearly seven months pregnant now, only two months left before Max's child was born. Isabel felt no animosity, only pleasure for him. A child was what he had wanted and a child would make him happy. She thought back to the work she had left uncompleted at the house on the Bishops Avenue. Who had taken down the scaffolding, and moved the dust sheets? Where were they now? Probably in the outhouse, although some unnamed person had kindly sent back her paints and brushes — in a parcel, without a note.

The mural was not complete — just like the school. It would stay that way, Isabel realised, until someone painted over it, and obliterated all trace of her. But they couldn't paint over the pictures, Isabel thought, oh no, Max would see some part of her every day in the drawing room and in his study. He would look at the painting over his fireplace and be forced to think of her. So by proxy Isabel kept some tie to him, as she waited for the news of his child's birth.

Only two months to go. Two months in which the school could have been finished . . . Isabel sighed in irritation. The dealers and critics were having a field day. All the people who said she could never bring it off were being proved right. She felt small suddenly, threatened and tired and bewildered and when the doorbell rang she had to summon up all her energy to answer it.

The cheque came anonymously. No letter, nothing except for a few typed words — *For the school*.

There was nothing to indicate who had sent it. No name, nothing. Just a cheque from the heavens.

★ ★ ★

Up went the bricks again, higher and higher until they reached the height of a house, and then the roof was completed. The windows were put in, glass fitted, doors fixed, every portion of Isabel's dream becoming more real by the moment. She found herself pinching her arm, trying to make sure she was awake and that she wouldn't suddenly open her eyes and find it had all been a dream.

But that was exactly what it was. A dream, Isabel's dream, created for David Hall, in memory of him as a promise for the future ... Invigorated, Isabel came back to life, she felt secure again, useful, as though the pattern of her life was finally set. I can teach here, she thought, I can follow my career and teach as well. Stanton can come, and Portento, and children can learn here — in the same way I learned from David. The potential of the school filled her with a new enthusiasm for life, her world seemed sweet again. Limited, but sweet.

Sybella saw the change in her as did Prossie.

'She looks great.'

'Good,' Stanton said half-heartedly, flinging down his palette. 'I'm glad that bloody school's getting built, I was wondering if my money had just disappeared down the sodding drain ... When's the opening?'

'In a month's time,' Prossie said, remembering the date that Caroline's baby was due, and wondering if that was why Isabel had organised the opening then.

'After all this time,' Stanton said, squinting at his painting. 'Isabel turned out to be quite something.'

Prossie glanced at him thoughtfully. 'Like her father,' she said.

* * *

Exhausted and yet excited, Isabel went for her check-up and was pronounced fit, although the doctor warned her against overwork. She smiled

541

happily and told him to keep his advice, returning to the school and waving to Blair who was busy cutting back the wilderness which was to be the garden. The school was virtually complete, and as Isabel walked in a couple of decorators called out a greeting to her.

The walls were pure white, without a mark, the staircase reaching upwards to the studios above. Slowly Isabel climbed the steps and then pushed open the first door. A large studio opened out before her, a raised dais at one end of the room, the whole area bathed in the cool North light. She felt suddenly faint with pleasure and hugged herself, turning as she heard footsteps behind her.

'It's nearly done,' Eleanor said, slipping her arm around Isabel's shoulder. 'I'm so proud of you.'

'Do you think David would have liked it?'

Eleanor nodded her head. 'He would have loved it — just as he loved you.' She changed the subject gently. 'Well . . . you did what you set out to do. The question is — will it be enough for you?'

Isabel shrugged her shoulders. 'I think so. For a while at least.'

'You'll find the right man in time.'

'No, I don't think so, Eleanor,' Isabel said, moving away and standing in the middle of the studio. The light fell on her hair and over her shoulders and illuminated her so brightly that for an instant she looked unreal. You are special, Eleanor thought. David knew that from the moment of your birth, but it is only now that I really understand what he meant.

'I don't want another man,' Isabel said. 'Max was the man I was supposed to love, and it didn't work out — '

'But you're still so young.'

Isabel nodded. 'Yes, but what's youth? I've experienced more in my short lifetime than most people ever do. I've had a crash course in human behaviour which would take most people eighty years to learn.' Her voice was controlled. 'I've been confused, afraid, and at times very, very happy. I don't expect such intensity to carry on — I'm almost glad it won't.' She glanced up to the windows overhead. 'This school was my dream, Eleanor, and I made it possible. I had four dreams and three came true — that's not bad going for anyone.'

The interior was finished within weeks, and the press were notified of the grand opening which was to fall on 23 April. Invitations went out, and enquiries came in, parents enrolling their children even before the school opened. And Isabel kept working, travelling to ensure that the Institute would be a success and make money — money she needed to repay some of the loans. She never seriously doubted that it would be a success. It was built with a good heart for the right reasons, and that had to count for something. Indeed, she travelled so far afield that, in the end, almost a third of her pupils were to come from abroad. David Hall, Isabel thought, would have liked that.

Daily easels, desks, and equipment arrived, the last coats of paint being applied, the divans being placed, ready and waiting on the daises in the studios. And daily the various interested parties came to see the result of Isabel's labours — and to check where their money had gone. Baye walked around happily, Dimitri Michelous pronouncing himself satisfied, and Ivy Messenger sending a message via Stanton.

'She saw the photographs and liked the place,' he said, going from studio to studio. 'I'll tell you one thing, Isabel, I just hope you can find enough talented kids to fill the place. In my experience, most children are too frigging stupid to take anything in.'

'Except yours?' Isabel countered, suddenly aware of what she had said.

Stanton looked at his daughter for a long moment and then touched her cheek. 'Yeah . . . all my children are special.'

He walked off after that, swearing violently at some decorator who knocked into him. Isabel watched Stanton go and wondered if he was hurt by her actions — knowing that the school was a monument to David Hall, the man she still called her father. The man she regarded as her real father. She also wondered if Stanton would be able to keep the secret, and then decided that he would — Prossie was back with him and he was getting too old for mischief.

The only people who did not seem interested in the school were her mother and Max. The latter Isabel forgave, but she resented Virginia's indifference, and even considered writing to her. But to what end? If she had to contact her and force her to be interested, what was the point?

She had to *want* to know about her daughter's achievement and get in touch herself — and it was patently obvious that she had no wish to do so.

So the days began to rush ahead, press interviews and television taking up a good deal of Isabel's time as she promoted the school all over Europe. And at night, when she got back to her hotel room, she would phone back to Yorkshire and ask Eleanor how things were progressing, Sybella often interrupting the calls.

'The garden was landscaped today! God, you should see it, Mum. It's heavenly.'

'You got all the shrubs? There should be thirty-five — '

' — all of them,' Eleanor answered on the extension. 'Blair's been marvellous, oh, and Ivy Messenger sent a wonderful tree for the front garden. It's a — '

' — Japanese fire tree!' Sybella chimed in. 'It goes bright red in the summer.'

Isabel smiled down the phone. 'Remind me to write and thank her when I get back, will you? Oh, and how many people are coming to the opening?'

'We've got two hundred definites — '

'Hey!'

' — and a dozen or so maybes, and of course, some rejections.'

'Anyone important?'

Eleanor grinned. 'Not really, mostly dealers.'

'Stuff them!' Isabel replied happily, then added, 'Has my mother been in touch?'

'No, sweetheart.'

545

'I just wondered . . . you know . . . '

'Yes,' Eleanor answered, brightening immediately. 'Portento's donated a portrait for the front hall.'

'Good, we should ask Stanton to do the same.'

Sybella laughed as Eleanor replied frostily, 'If we did, he would only give us something crude — like a nude.'

'As long as it's not of him, I don't care!' Isabel answered laughing.

34

The 23rd of April began cold, then sunny, then chilled towards evening. The school was due to be opened at six, many of the guests having already arrived, some with their children. In a large hall there were drinks laid out, staff milling in and out of the guests, a few celebrities mingling with their celebrity children, a small contingent of cameramen up from London to record the event.

There had only been one hiccup, but it had been enough to startle Isabel and nearly panic her. Making one of her very infrequent excursions out of London, Ivy Messenger was driven up to Yorkshire for the opening, arriving in plenty of time. Isabel was delighted to see her and pushed her around the gardens, showing her where they had planted the Japanese fire tree. The old woman was full of gossip and chattered easily, her brain as nimble as ever and when some of the other guests began to arrive, she was happy to be given a glass of champagne and left to watch the proceedings from her wheelchair. It was all very satisfying, she thought, musing how her well-timed phone call to Max had ensured the school's completion. Oh yes, his generous — and anonymous — donation had made Isabel's dream reality.

Her good eye missed nothing, and her tongue was very vocal, especially when she castigated Gyman for his lack of guts. Hugely amused, Ivy then turned her attention to the other notables, nodding towards Stanton and holding a long conversation with Prossie. It was then that she saw Isabel and watched as she greeted Stanton. Prossie talked on as Ivy's glance fixed on the couple across the room. Stanton said something and Isabel put her head on one side . . . and a memory stirred. Ivy sat bolt upright in her wheelchair, smiling slyly.

Minutes later, she beckoned Isabel to her side. 'You've done so well, my dear.'

'You helped enormously, Ivy,' she replied, leaning down to the old lady. 'Thank you for everything.'

She waved her hand as though to brush away the suggestion. 'It's a lovely monument to David Hall,' she said finally.

Isabel smiled, not scenting danger. 'Yes, I loved my father very much.'

Ivy glanced over to Stanton and raised her eyebrows. 'I dare say . . . '

The colour drained from Isabel's face. Ivy saw the effect her words had had and tapped Isabel on the back of her hand. 'I don't blame you in the least, my dear, Stanton is hardly anything to be proud of, is he?' she said softly, adding, 'I shall tell no one the truth . . . ' Her glance moved to Stanton again. 'And do you want to know why? Because David Hall was the right father for you, Isabel. I don't care whose blood runs in your veins, you have his soul.'

Isabel remembered the words as she dressed that evening, choosing a soft peach-coloured dress and leaving her hair loose over her shoulders, her legs fine in high heels. After all the months of frenzied activity she took pains with her appearance and liked the good-looking woman who stood proudly at the top of the stairs, ready to face the crowd.

In the moments she waited, preparing herself, Isabel remembered the last New Year she spent with her father, and the day of his funeral when all eyes were on her. Only then they had expected to see her grief, and now they were expecting to see her triumph. The wheel turns, she thought calmly, walking down the staircase.

A hundred heads glanced up, flash bulbs going off, the sound of clapping loud in her ears. I've made it, Isabel thought, I made it. Her eyes filled momentarily and as she reached the bottom of the stairs, Prossie kissed her on the cheek, Eleanor winking at her from the other side of the room. On a wave of euphoria, she moved into the crowd, thanking people, posing for photo-graphs, talking to children and outlining her plans, and then after another few moments Isabel suddenly clapped her hands and everyone stopped talking.

'Ladies and gentlemen, first of all, thank you for coming tonight. It's a very special time for me, a dream I've carried for a long time has finally come true. But there is one thing I want to make very clear . . . ' She moved towards the door and pointed to a small plaque on the wall. Everyone's eyes fixed upon it.

'This school was built in memory of a man.' Isabel paused, suddenly emotional, and then carried on. 'He was quite extraordinary, and I have the privilege of bearing his name.' She saw Stanton watching her, and paused, but he merely raised his glass in a silent salute. 'This school is David Hall's monument — he made me a happy child and I hope many other happy children will live here under his roof, and under his name.'

The applause was thunderous, and Isabel smiled, moved almost to tears as she turned to step back into the mêlée. Then she saw someone standing watching, alone. An older woman, fierce and dry-eyed. Struggling against the crowd, Isabel hurried towards her and then, without hesitation, she clasped her mother to her heart.

★ ★ ★

The morning dawned to find Isabel at the school. No one else was about, but she had wanted to spend time there alone, thinking. The dream was now tangible, she could feel the walls, and touch the panes of glass. It was accomplished, and with its completion, came a faint sense of anti-climax. The papers would come with her name in them, and the school register would fill, but where Isabel would go from here was another matter. Contented as she was, she knew that soon she would be in pursuit of another dream.

This, it seemed, was to be the pattern of her life. So she accepted it and wandered like a ghost in the empty school, touching the plaque dedicated to David Hall, and thinking of the future, trying to make plans in the early dawn.

She did not hear the car drive up at first, until

it stopped, and then she moved to the front door, jerking it open. Max came towards her, passing the Japanese fire tree, big and powerful in the early light.

'Max?' she said, running out to him.

He stopped in front of her and caught hold of her hands. His eyes were dilated, his face pale, like someone in shock.

'Come with me.'

'What?' she asked, baffled.

'Please, trust me, come with me.'

She resisted. 'Where, Max?'

'Back to London. Please. Please.'

His voice was so strained that she nodded and climbed into the passenger seat, sitting in silence all the long drive back to town. Nothing she said could coax anything out of him, but when he finally drove into the hospital car park she turned and looked at him.

'WHAT IS IT! For God's sake, Max, tell me.'

He still did not reply, merely caught hold of her hand and guided her towards the maternity ward. The sound of crying babies pierced her ears, her longing for a child returning fiercely as she tried to loosen his grip on her hand.

'Max —'

He turned to her suddenly. 'Caroline died in labour last night — '

'Oh God!' Isabel said, her legs giving way as she slumped into a seat in the corridor.

He seemed dull with grief. 'Do you love me?'

She nodded. 'You know I do.'

'Enough to take on someone else's child?'

'My father did,' she said, her voice a whisper.

His face relaxed and he let go of her hand and walked away. For a while she sat alone in the empty corridor and then finally she heard footsteps and saw Max walking towards her, holding his son.

'I need you, Isabel,' he said simply. 'We both need you now.'

And carefully he laid the sleeping child in her arms.

⋆ ⋆ ⋆

One year later.

On Isabel's next birthday a letter arrived. As ever, it was in David Hall's handwriting.

Darling Knuckles,
    This is the last letter I write to you, because by now, my love, I know you will be happy and at peace. I hope you will forgive all these letters from a dead man but you were the best of me, and even though you weren't mine, I could not have loved you more.
    In you I had the world. And what a world it was, all kindness, darling, all kindness.
    Well, I hope you've used your four wishes wisely and now I'll add my own — be happy with your man. Love him, and love your children.
    And remember me.
    Goodbye, darling.

David Hall

We do hope that you have enjoyed reading this large print book.

Did you know that all of our titles are available for purchase?

We publish a wide range of high quality large print books including:
Romances, Mysteries, Classics
General Fiction
Non Fiction and Westerns

Special interest titles available in large print are:
The Little Oxford Dictionary
Music Book
Song Book
Hymn Book
Service Book

Also available from us courtesy of Oxford University Press:
Young Readers' Dictionary
(large print edition)
Young Readers' Thesaurus
(large print edition)

For further information or a free brochure, please contact us at:
Ulverscroft Large Print Books Ltd.,
The Green, Bradgate Road, Anstey,
Leicester, LE7 7FU, England.
Tel: (00 44) 0116 236 4325
Fax: (00 44) 0116 234 0205

PRIVATE VIEW

Alexandra Connor

Behind universally admired works of art — *The Laughing Cavalier* by Hals, *The Birth of Venus* by Botticelli, *The Thinker* by Rodin, and many more — are the artists themselves, whose lesser-known eccentricities are revealed in *Private View*. Here is Fra Filippo Lippi, a friar who had to be locked in a room by the Pope in order to keep him at the easel and away from the bedroom. William Blake, who talked to the dead — and Theodore Gericault, who brought the dead home with him to use as unpaid models. Here is Rembrandt, who not only owned a monkey himself, but once painted a similar creature into a patron's family portrait. And of course the swaggering Michelangelo, who as a child recommended his 'perfect' services 'in all humility' to the Duke of Milan . . .